SONG OF LOCKE

THE DARK EMPYREAN

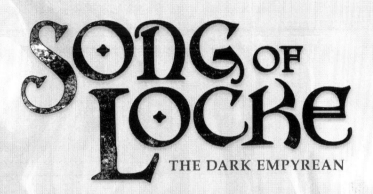

SONG OF LOCKE

THE DARK EMPYREAN

J WASHBURN

LOST BOYS INK

FATA VOCANT

Back Cover

Locke loves stories—they fill him with a longing he can never quite describe—but he's not the sort of kid who actually lives adventures himself. That is, until a bloodthirsty band of marauders passes near his home and Picke, a musical sylfe, dares him to follow. In hopes of fulfilling his longing, Locke accepts the dare. This leads him on a quest where he must face snarling wolves, wield a magic blade, and risk his life to rescue a Goddess—a girl he hardly knows but who he can't stop thinking about.

In the spirit of Legend of Zelda and Peter Pan, SONG OF LOCKE portrays a detailed fantasy world, somewhat grittier than its forebears and drenched in human emotion. The tale has sword fights, witty banter, crushes, and even some subtle philosophy smuggled in. It's an epic for everyone who loves good stories—for anyone who has longed for something that seemed forever out of reach.

SONG OF LOCKE is also an artisan book—written, illustrated, and typeset by the author, a masterpiece handcrafted from beginning to end. The first 50k-word draft was written for NaNoWriMo in 2013. In November 2014, a crowd of Kickstarter backers provided the initial funding for publication (see kickstarter.jwashburn.com). It was published 4 August 2015.

Reviews

"Just think LEGEND OF ZELDA meets GAME OF THRONES." — Nathan Tucker, *Numinous*

"SONG OF LOCKE was literally one of the best fantasy books I have ever read. An I-hear-music-in-my-head-while-I-am-reading-it kind of book." — J.R.

"I felt satisfied when I finished. The ending was my favorite. And I still think about the story days after reading." — G.A.B.

"My personal favorite is the way he describes sounds visually. I've never read anything like that before. It took my breath away. I re-read those descriptions several times before moving on just for the pure beauty of it." — N.W.D.

Legal

Contact

If you find an error in the text, notify the copyeditor at typos@jwashburn.com (and make sure to mention this book's title)—you'll go down in history as the hero of the second edition.

Subscribe to J's monthly fan letter here: theinformant.jwashburn.com.

Contact the author directly at me@jwashburn.com.

And check out jwashburn.com.

11 Sep 2015

To Abe,

the fighter.

And to you, reader,

for getting

my back.

Chapters

Scroll Two

Scroll Three

Scroll Four

The End

You may find
you are aware of
a something beyond
all your mind can think,
yet not beyond what your
heart can desire—a something
that is not yours, seems as if
it never could be yours,
which yet your life
is worthless
without.

GEORGE MACDONALD
Unspoken Sermons

A Map of Northern
Elfland
The Land of Many Waters

WELL AT WORLD'S END

Khalune Desert

Astral Fields

NICKE

HONKE

WOKEEZAE

Burning Mountain

Wilderness

Rueful

Majestic Sea

WIKS PIKE

Wisting Mountains

Dragonsea

COVE

SHILOHE

First River

Fifth River

Fourth River

Third River

Enchanted Wood

Sea of Time

Great River

Sea of Mist

I traded all my mortal memories
for the memories you're about to read.

Prelude

I COULDN'T SEE IT, but I felt it.

Tiny steps creeping and crawling across skin, like a cold wind.

I felt icicle fangs hungry for life, the color of shadow. I felt a soulless creature emerging from below the earth, a living agony, staring with deep voids where eyes should've been.

First just one. Then another and another.

They climbed into the wide world. Far away. And lurking somewhere nearby.

Lurking inside my throat. Strangling me with cold. I could hardly breathe.

I wished it were only a dream, but sylves don't dream. It had to be real. A horrible reality surrounded us.

"Numa? Demigoddess of Air. I know you hear me." My breath puffed into chilly white mist. My eyes shone upward as I peered, listening for her. "Please?"

Everything had fallen quiet, horribly quiet, like the death of music. Even the scurrying creature held still. As it did, it vanished like a prowling wildercat in deep grasses. I hated stillness. Stillness meant death.

"It's me, Picke—your son. And there's this..." I reached three slender fingers and a thumb toward the sky. "...this *evil*."

My wings struggled against the chill, pushing far beyond my armspan. I breathed frantically, trying to maintain motion.

"If I had hands, I would fight. If I had feet, I would run." I looked at my tiny hands, so insubstantial—no stronger than a breath. *Not strong enough.* I looked at my toes, even more elegant, yet just as powerless. "But I'm one of your sons. My fingers are wind, and my refuge is you."

The silence closed in tighter, so near I could barely move. It clamped down, held me tight. I hated it. Hated it more than anything.

"I need you. To listen to me. To talk to me. To help me."

My ears pointed skyward as I strained for her answer. My glimmering blue hair floated like that of a corpse whose grave was the frigid sea, dancing in silence and slowing into stillness. I panted against the panic. An unbreakable grip cinched me so tight I couldn't inhale. Perfect silence, perfect stillness, and perfect cold—they pressed in, leaving no room for anything else. Not even a being so small as me.

No music of trees. No sough of winds. No warmth of raindrops.

"You spoke to me once," I groaned. "I remember. Speak to me now!"

I waited, and the silence smothered.

If she wouldn't answer, I still had Locke. And I had one last bit of air. One last chance. "LOCKE!" I screamed.

I heard his footsteps. He was walking away, abandoning me in the Shadowlands, leaving me surrounded by evil. *Just like Numa.*

I couldn't breathe.

He was my life. I had to go with him. Had to follow. I tried to dash after him, but I could barely move. I hit solid, unmoving ground, and he was on the other side. I pounded against it, but it wouldn't budge.

He had to *stop!* To *wait!* I needed to scream!

But I couldn't breathe.

I couldn't breathe.

Scroll One

REALM OF PHOSE

SALAMINDES

BURNINGS · SUN · SIGHT · FLAME · DEMONS

HOT

1

DRY

4

MALE

FEMALE

3

WET

2

COLD

SYLVES

BREATH · STARS · HEARING · WIND · ELVES

REALM OF NUMA

GNYMES

BONE · EARTH · TOUCH · STONE · PLANTS

REALM OF GAIE

BLOOD · MOON · TASTE · WATER · ANIMALS

ONDINES

REALM OF NARA

I.

The Hero

"L OCKE?"

With closed eyes, he inhaled gently, right on the edge of snoring.

"Locke, wake up!"

He still didn't answer.

A bird twittered, calling for dawn.

The chill that had stolen my breath and kidnapped the music—it was gone. Or it had withdrawn a little. Leaving nothing but... *ahhh, what was it?* An acute and close feeling: something I could sense through Locke. Something small, directly on his skin. A scratching. Like crumpled paper against his ribs.

"Can't you feel that?" I asked.

He lay there like a corpse, sprawled on the bed, mouth hanging open. It was like he had the strength of ten men but for sleeping.

The feeling itched. "It's driving me crazy!"

His soft breathing continued.

I wanted to smack him. But even if I could've, my tiny hand wouldn't have done much good. Breath was more powerful anyway. "Wake *up!* What if it's a *wraith!*"

That did it. He rolled to his side, eyes closed, scratched his ribcage, but found nothing.

The itch seemed to go away. *Hmm.* Maybe I could wait till morning. Then I could tell him about the cold, dark silence. Besides, he'd be more fun if he slept longer. *I hated when he wasn't fun.*

It scratched him again—crawling down his side from his ribs toward his belt.

"Locke, wake up!" I blew on the wheat-colored hair hanging over his eyes.

"I don't feel anything," he mumbled, taking a blind swipe at me. "Go back to sleep."

"I don't sleep," I said. "I never sleep. And it's still there: I feel it." So uncomfortable, like a leaf had crawled down his shirt. It itched my curiosity like crazy—I needed to know what it was. "Locke, please, wake up!"

He rolled to his back and reached his fingers to scratch beneath his belt. "Picke, you're a—"

BOOM! With one arm he threw off his blanket, and with the other he launched himself out of bed.

His feet touched the floor, his pants came off, then he was airborne, landing at the far side of the room on his tiptoes with his shoulders scrunched toward his neck as if that might defend him. He panted.

I laughed aloud—I couldn't help it—a crisp sound, cutting across the darkness, a sound few melodies could rival. "If only the world could see you now!"

Locke stared at the giant bug crawling on the rim of his trousers. "A boatsinker," he said, like spitting out dirt. He brushed his hand where six spindly legs and a set of pincers had been. They'd touched *his* fingers, but *I* felt it with him. The bug wasn't even that big—the size of me maybe. We'd seen worse. And yet Locke stood like a midnight sentry, wearing his braies, hair a mess, fists clenched, poised to run from any thumb-sized threat that might dare to rear its ugly head. He brushed a hand across the back of his neck and shoulders then swept both hands down his shirt repeatedly.

"Oh my!" I shouted, and I even drew back a little.

Locke followed my gaze—and his elfe eyes saw the black shapes of bugs clinging to the walls and pitched ceiling above and all around him. Hundreds of them. "Yyyyuuuhhhh…" he began, but whatever he was about to say was swallowed deep in his throat by another shudder.

"Something very strange is happening," I said.

"I'm getting out of here!"

"It's still the middle of the night!"

"I don't care. I hate bugs."

"What about wraiths?"

He hesitated, looking toward the window. Not a glimmer of light came from outside. The winds that had rushed all night were now silent too. "I'll risk it, I guess. Come on." He turned to the door.

"Your pants!"

"I am *not*—"

"You can't go out there without your pants. It'll be morning soon."

He sighed. "Alright." He crouched and squinted. Pinching the leg of his pants, he jerked them like cracking a whip. The bug thudded against one of the dark walls. Locke stood, holding the pants at arm's length.

"Well?" I asked.

"I'm not putting these on yet. Let's go."

"Grab your moccasins and bag too; then we can go straight to the ferry for work."

He grabbed his things, and I followed, hovering over his head. He stepped outside into the cool night and climbed off the wide, wooden deck that made the floor of his room. He descended the ladders fastened to the ancient blathae tree, past the empty rooms of all seven of his older brothers till he reached the main floor of the treehouse.

I eyed the hoard of bugs we found there too. "Why so many?"

A black shell cracked beneath Locke's heel.

I scowled.

Locke shrugged. "Maybe he'll come back and tell us what death is like."

"You're horrible."

"Okay, I'm sorry. I know life is precious and all that."

"It's not trivial. I envy life."

"*You're* living."

"Not like you—with skin and a heartbeat."

Locke dodged between bugs then stepped his way down the main rope ladder, feeling the usual dread and trying to ignore what would greet him below. "I don't know why this bothers you so much. You're just as living as me."

"No. I'm primeval. Like your soul."

"Well, that's better than living." He stopped on the ladder and stared directly at me. "You don't have to be afraid of death."

"I'm afraid of something worse."

He dropped to the ground, landing bare feet in the cool grass. Before moving on, he glanced over his shoulder reluctantly, as if some invisible power had forced him to look—at the silent green door. "Nothing's worse than death."

He stared blankly as his thoughts wandered away. The green door rested amid the giant roots of our tree, which spread wide before sinking beneath the ground, creating a hollow cavern. Wooden walls and that heavy door filled the gaps between roots, all covered in thick vines, moss, and mushrooms—a coating of life. We hadn't gone in there for seven years, not since Locke's father had blockaded the stairs and locked the door. We didn't want to either.

As Locke wandered among frightening memories, the feeling—the nightmare or whatever it was—leaped back in front of me. "Yes, there's something worse than death." *I remembered Locke walking away from me.* "The place without music."

He looked at me with fear in his eyes. "What's the matter?"

"I feel… something evil. And it scares me."

He glanced around, half expecting to see a wraith somewhere inside the cove. Thoughts of spindly legs and sticky shells creeped around the back of his neck. As he brushed them aside, he looked skyward, expecting to find a glimmer of hope peeking through the foliage overhead—something that could lift the heaviness we felt.

Dread spread over me.

"Picke, it's so dark," he said. "I can't see a single star."

2.

Wanderlust

ARUSTLE OF LEAVES made Locke dive for cover, but it was only three small rabbits racing to their burrow.

I laughed. "Are you more scared of a wraith or getting caught in your braies?"

He scowled at me. "Be quiet."

We wandered east between trunks that towered like massive legs of giants. Twigs and branches littered the ground, brought down by the strong winds the night before. Now a gentle wester wind coaxed us along.

As we entered the grove of climbing trees, Locke cocked an ear, as if to hear the whispering sylves of the elves who died on this ground. "Now no mischief," he said. "Not here. I mean it."

Locke pressed his fingertips into the bark of a young tree whose branches hadn't yet grown out of reach. Wedging his big toe into a lower groove, he climbed. His thoughts turned toward the bird demons that had burned this area, toward the battle that split the delta and created the Fifth River—unlucky. In daylight, shafts of sun would reach through and touch the glade in spots. But today we saw only a dim shadow of that scene, and the stillness weighed down, monumental and heavy.

"You can feel it, the echo of legend." He whispered like a child, and his very words seemed to reverberate. "They fought because a rise in evil called for the rise of good."

As he looked at me, I floated like the feather of a fledgling. My wings hung on the wind, weightless tendrils of bluish white. And my curiosity still itched. "Did you feel something—I don't know—*dark* in your dreams?" I often wondered about his dreams; it was the one place where I couldn't follow him, a place of bizarre magic.

"I dreamed about someone," he said.

"Tryse?"

"Don't say her name!"

Ooops. We were supposed to call her the Nymfe—the mythical creature who vanished in the night. The nickname was Locke's idea. Mostly he meant *I* was supposed to call her that, because, as he said, "When *you* say a word, it sticks like sap that won't get off your hand no matter how much dirt you rub on it. *My* words just disappear, but yours are like a substance." It was because he didn't understand sculpting the air into words. Anyway, I took it as a compliment, and I tried to not speak her name. *Sometimes.*

He pulled himself into a standing position on a wide branch. "But, yes. Her."

I smiled.

He smiled back with his usual reserve, not ready to set loose his emotions, as if he couldn't admit the immense joy and pain hidden inside. "I'm still in love with her—in my dreams."

Our mind swirled in a brief memory, like a gasp of air: They were together again—two kids in love—and they'd never grown distant, and she'd never gotten married and become an adult. And never had a child. His expression rose and fell as the memory first lifted him in the air and then dropped him flat on his back. He still tried to hold the memory's breath, to keep her smile just a moment longer, but it left as quick as it came. She was gone.

He brooded. "It makes me want to sleep forever."

"You nearly sleep forever already!" I grinned, laying my hands bare in disbelief.

He blinked at my irreverence. "Well maybe I will—if you don't shut up—and leave you stranded here."

"Don't even joke about that." I frowned to show him I meant it; after last night, I felt particularly sensitive about it.

The sky spread overhead, dark like a storm, too dark to see what hid in the empyrean beyond. Locke made his way down a long branch then leaped to the lower bow of another tree. "What about *your* dream?"

The birds seemed too silent, as if they knew something we didn't. The Fifth River split off from the Great River just ahead, but we couldn't hear its usual music either.

"I don't dream."

"No, I mean the dark feeling you mentioned."

I followed him as he made his way higher. "I felt a cold presence, like a bunch of wraiths. Then I got trapped in a place without music." I left out the part where he abandoned me.

"It's called a nightmare."

"No, it wasn't. This was real. Something happened last night, something bad, and it created this horrible—*something*—a feeling of darkness."

"That sounds like the opposite of what I'm trying to find here." He motioned with his lips to the glade of climbing trees.

"I'm trying to forget it," I said.

"No, if it's real, you shouldn't ignore it. It could mean something."

"Maybe I don't want to think about it. Why are you always so eager to *think* about things?"

Locke pulled himself up to a flimsy branch, so high that the trunk swayed as he held on. An ocean of nighttime treetops lay before us. I loved it, being so high and unbound.

Wrapping the crook of his arm around the trunk, he pulled out his pinkalue and tapped it on his thigh. The twins, his older brothers, had given him the wooden instrument. It wasn't as well crafted as the bone flute their father had forbidden them to touch, but it had a warm sound. Locke blew into it, and the melody flowed pure and haunting. Somehow every song the pinkalue made seemed a tribute to the wanderers, to the lost, and the lost loves. Maybe because it had belonged to the twins.

We swayed at the top of that tallest tree, as close to the sky and as far from the ground as we could get. The pinkalue, not needing to compete with light, sang all the brighter, every note a miracle against a black backdrop, wrought by the fingers of my elfe. I was in love with the music. If only he could be as daring in life as he was with a melody.

"There, Picke, that was it." He paused to look at the pinkalue. "That thing I long for. The thing without a name. Sometimes it's in a story like Song of Martigane. Sometimes it's in my dreams of lifting off the ground in flight like a bird demon. And sometimes it's simply a melody."

"Sometimes it's touching Shaye's knee." I grinned. He didn't like me saying *her* name either.

"Yes, but leave her out of this."

He put the instrument back to his lips and played scales that led us closer to that unnameable something, or to the fragments of that something.

Maybe it wasn't any of those things. But it came *through* them. It was a song we'd never directly heard but which echoed in so many things.

He looked up. "Sometimes it's the stars. I wish we could see them." He shook his head. "Sometimes it's Tryse. Or heights. I don't even know what I want, but I want it so bad."

"The Land of Song calls us, the place where the Kyrose created us, where everything is music." I knew he didn't believe, but I blew on the idea, trying to get it to catch fire.

He raised his eyebrows and nodded, as if surprised by my insight. "Maybe." He let this answer drift for a moment, then played through another melody, one that shone like copper, and the longing grew.

"What if your thirst can't be quenched anywhere," I said, "no matter where you go or what you do?"

"Don't say that."

"I'm just saying, well, maybe it's bigger than all this around us—maybe you're not meant to find it in this world."

He gave me another surprised look, which I didn't exactly appreciate. "It's funny, sometimes you speak so eloquent I almost can't recognize you."

I smiled. *That was better.*

"But since when did you care about anything bigger than right now?"

I shrugged. "I don't know. I don't think I do. Let's go. Let's do something about it *right now.*"

"This is as high as the tree goes, Picke."

"That's not what I mean."

"I'd go after it if I knew what it was," he said, "but I can't wander after nothing."

"The searching itself might help. Who cares what you find."

"You're always so eager to move. I just want to know which direction is right."

"Come on," I sunk below him, hoping he'd follow. "Let's go before the storm breaks."

We made our way west and slightly north, toward Twiche's ferry and the roaring waters we crossed many times each day. In the darkness, the trees hung like gargoyles with terrifying claws.

Locke and I gasped.

A gruesome mass of dead boatsinkers and other bugs littered the ground.

A dark oily liquid smeared the path, each of them having spilled their blood generously, as if a whole swarm had been murdered mid-flight. Other bugs milled around the edge of the massacre, but it seemed they found no nutrients worth salvaging.

"Who would do such a thing?" Locke's face showed his disgust, and *he* hated bugs.

"Some sorcerer wanting their blood?" I searched our mind, trying to fit the pieces together. "Oh. Not the blood. Animals have ondines as elementals—*in* their blood."

"You can kill a kynde and take its elemental?"

"I don't know. Don't think so." I looked further ahead as something caught my attention. "You hear that?"

Locke paused and looked toward the dark sky. "No."

The air was dead, devoid of sound, like my nightmare. "Exactly."

"No rivers?" he asked.

"No water, no birds, no nothing. Not even a cricket." I darted ahead to see.

On the brink of peril, Locke decided to put on his pants. "Wait!" he yelled, watching his back for wraiths, and hopping on one foot. He rushed to catch up.

We raced back and forth between trees. The dock clunked hollow as his bare feet drummed against the familiar wood. He leaned over the railing, and we looked down at the black river—a dark snaking shape, with not a single glimmer on the crest of a wave.

"It's... too dark." He lobbed a kohkoo nut toward the center of the river below.

It thumped down.

Not a splash, a thud.

Our Fifth River wasn't just silent—it was *gone*. The nut had impacted with mud!

"You're not going to be ferrying a soul today," I said.

"What ghule did this?" asked Locke.

I had no answer. The dark feeling, which had almost been washed away by our conversation, now flooded back over me. "I can't breathe."

"Stop it, Picke. You're scaring me." He breathed in deeply, which helped, and took another glance over his shoulder, which didn't. "It's nothing. You're overreacting. Maybe Murke and Turke dammed up the river..."

"The whole river?" I asked.

"I dunno. I guess they're not smart enough to do something like that."

"And even if they were, how could they pull it off overnight?"

"I'll bet this is why the bugs came into the treehouse," he said. "Do those clouds look extra dark to you?"

"What do you mean?" I asked.

"It should be light by now."

"They're just storm clouds."

"Thick enough to let the wraiths stay here in daytime." He stared at me, waiting for a hopeful reply, but I had nothing. "My dad said something about this. The Night of the Wolf, a prophecy of darkness and drought and the end of time."

"You think this is the end of time?"

"No, I don't believe in prophecies. But…"

"But what?"

"It does seem a little strange."

"I can't breathe," I repeated.

3.

The Dare

"CALM DOWN, PICKE. We're fine."

He said this as he paced around a tree, thinking.

"Can't you feel that darkness?" I asked. "It's so thick. And cold."

"Well you're not helping."

"What are we going to do?"

"I don't know yet."

"Can you breathe a little deeper?"

He obliged, filling his lungs.

I wished he'd think aloud. I loved the sound of his voice. And the color of it. Locke said it was strange that I saw color in sounds, but actually it was weird that he didn't. Like all sounds, his voice had a distinct texture, value, and hue. It mixed brown with green, just like the forest. Something like the soft fur of a bear cub combined with leaves dripping rain.

"Say something, Locke."

He tried not to show emotion on his face, but I felt the anxiety under his skin. "Let's go back and tell my dad."

"Why?"

He started walking home, still breathing deep for my sake. "He's an adult."

"I thought *you* were trying to be an adult."

Still not wearing his moccasins, he trudged along barefoot. At least he had on his pants now. "I'm not trying to be one. I don't even *want* to be one. I just feel like I'm *supposed to be one* sometimes."

"Yet you're walking home to tell your father."

"Well, what do you want me to do?"

"I don't know. *Not* go home?"

"To prove I'm an adult?" He didn't stop walking.

"No. I don't want you to be an adult either."

"Then what do you want me to do?"

"I don't know. Whatever your father would do."

"Whose side are you on?"

"I'm on your side," I said. "I just want you to be daring."

His anxiety produced a sort of a half-smile, half-grimace. "Well I don't know what dad would do. That's why he's an adult and I'm not." He kept walking.

"We could start by looking farther upriver, find out where it's dammed." Locke stopped.

His faithful breathing ended in an abrupt gasp. Not because of what I'd said, because of what he saw.

In the shadows ahead stood a cloaked figure—eerily close. Yet I hadn't detected his breath. Nothing about his presence felt welcoming. The man wasn't traveling, wasn't moving openly among the trees. He stood behind a large trunk, very still, caped in dark green, yet not out of sight, as if making himself known as a threat.

Without waiting for answers, Locke turned and ran.

Moist sand and smudges of dirt licked at Locke's bare feet as he raced away. Just ahead, a large piece of driftwood, carried ashore in the floods, stood in the way. He leaped.

Midway over the driftwood, a hiss sped through the air—

THWACK!

Locke's hands and chest crashed into leaves and dirt.

An arrow had pierced his pants and sunk deep into the driftwood. He'd fallen with his leg wrapped painfully over the top. Now on the far side, he could barely reach, much less grip the arrow that pinned him down.

We heard a dark laugh as the man in the green hood walked toward us, holding a longbow. His messy, ragged outfit looked like foliage—green and uneven like leaves. He pulled off his hood revealing a face that appeared grimy.

"Have you heard what they say," he asked with a voice so mean it tore like a rusted knife, "about the Hundred of Saebyrne?"

When we heard those words, the hair on Locke's neck stood up. "I've heard many things."

The man's voice had a light color value but not in a good way. The sound chafed like salt rubbing uncomfortably against skin, too dry, and falling apart without any real form. I hated his voice. He looked past me with no acknowledgement, glaring at Locke. "They say their archers, at a hundred paces, can sink an arrow into their enemy's eye."

Locke didn't reply, pulling his leg futilely against the arrow, trying to grab it with his hand.

The man jumped down next to us, and we smelled his putrid odor. He held an arrow by the fletching, and he jabbed the point at Locke's chest, forcing Locke onto his back. "Well," asked the man with a spiteful grin, "have you heard that?"

"Yes," said Locke, "I've heard that."

"It isn't true," he said. "When it's a moving target, we don't bother. Anywhere in the skull will do fine."

"But you aimed at my leg," said Locke.

The man whipped the arrow's shaft at Locke's shoulder, like beating a cow. Locke recoiled.

The man's sylfe held incredibly still, suspended in one spot above the shaggy head. As the man moved, the sylfe remained steady and then would zip to a new position and remain still again—a series of rapid jerks followed by stillness, almost like a bird. *Very strange.*

As for the man, hate seemed to flow from him, spite toward everything that wasn't himself. I wanted to bite his nose just to put him in his place. I couldn't, but that didn't stop me from wishing. A sword in a scabbard hung from the man's belt. Up close, it became clear that his face wasn't grimy—it was painted. "He *is* one of the Hundred," I whispered into Locke's ear.

"The world's about to end," said the man, "and you're rushing off to... *where?*"

"My father owns a farm just a little downstream," said Locke.

"You're a fifther?"

"Some call us that."

"A filthy fifther. Maybe I *should* have aimed for your skull." The man glared with mad-dog eyes, as if Locke's existence were somehow insulting him. "Looks like I missed your leg as well. That's disappointing." The man stepped closer, and Locke cringed, bracing himself. The man laughed, enjoying the fear. Was that all he wanted from us? He grabbed the arrow sticking into the driftwood and jerked it free. "Get out of here, rat. And if you see anyone else, warn them the Hundred are passing through."

"Yes, sir," said Locke, climbing to his feet.

As he turned, the man whipped him with the arrow again, and a stinging pain cut beneath Locke's shirt.

He started southward again, on a path for home, till the man growled, "That way," and pointed to the west. Locke did exactly as he was told, scrambling to quickly change his direction. After a few moments, he looked back over his shoulder. The man was gone.

"I hate him," I said.

"He was a vanguard." Locke breathed extra, trying to relax his clenched fists and push away his red anger. "Scouting ahead for the rest of them."

"I want to bite his face off."

"It's okay, Picke." Locke's heart thumped as he jogged.

"He had no reason to treat us that way. To act like we were nothing. We're *not* nothing."

"I know," he said, preparing to forget the whole thing. "But what can we do?"

"We could disobey him."

"Huh?"

"We'll circle around. Get ahead and see who he's scouting for."

"We already know—it's the Hundred."

"Then this will be your chance to see them in action like you've always wanted."

"When I said that, I was thinking they'd be more charming. I believe he *would* kill us if he saw us again."

I believed it too, but I didn't want to say so aloud. *Too permanent.* "Alright, then let's just cower and obey him. I wasn't really curious to see what's damming the rivers."

"Stop it, Picke."

"In fact, since he told us not to go south, let's just wait here for a while; then we'll head to Twiche's and waste the day not ferrying anyone. If we're lucky maybe Mr. Lunke's daughter will come to woo you again."

He squinted at me, considering.

He couldn't see my voice, but it had a color too, similar to his own but lighter, with slightly less vibrance, much more childlike. It was the soft fur of a mouse instead of a bear cub, complemented by the spray of the seashore, foamy and blue. I liked my voice. And even if he couldn't see it, Locke liked it too. *It would have power, especially if I sculpted the right words.*

I paused, breathing synchronically with him. "Adventure calls," I whispered.

"I know, but…"

"I dare you to answer."

A crow cawed ominously through the quiet breeze.

I strained to hear Locke's thoughts—it wasn't easy, even if we did inhabit the same mind.

He gazed through the giant trunks toward home. He looked back toward the river, where the Hundred of Saebyrne would be marching. He thought about the unnameable thing and wondered if it were hidden somewhere in this choice. He thought of the twins; this opportunity would excite them. It excited him too, just not without reservation.

"Are you going to sing someone else's song or write your own?" I asked.

He shook his head. "We could be killed."

"Oh, that's true. Probably best to only take adventures without risks."

He rolled his eyes at me before looking both directions again.

"Think of Martigane—*a still wind dies,*" I said. "He chose to charge to his death rather than wait around."

"The story's a myth," said Locke.

I looked at him eagerly, nearly holding my breath.

With a sigh he grabbed his knee-length moccasins from his bag and pulled them on. "Gah. Picke, why do I listen to you?"

"Because you always regret it when you don't."

"Sometimes I regret it when I do."

4.

The Hundred

DESPITE THE HEAVINESS of war, the Hundred stepped lighter than the whispering wildlife, walking with unnatural quiet, as if the legends were true.

Locke clung to a branch, high atop one of the climbing trees, as they passed below. His elfe eyes peered through the dim light, picking out details—eyes that could see well even by starlight.

They moved in a long string, some nearly as tall as hyumans. Even from directly above, we barely heard their deft movements: the ruffle of a cloak, the tap of a scabbard against a leg, or the snuff of a warrior clearing his whistling nose. Maybe they really were immortals sent to end injustice—the Unstoppable Hundred of Saebyrne.

To me, they looked more like agents of havoc and punishment. While the scout's face had been painted green as the forest, these faces were painted the colors of open corpses. Painted like death. They carried spears, swords, and axes with long, curving blades. I even saw one lugging a warhammer. Spaulders covered their shoulders. Many wore helmets of leather or grimy metal, some with feathers poking from the tops. Others kept their heads uncovered, their ears pointing up past tangled hair. Gauntlets clasped their weapons. One carried a simple red banner at the end of his spear that flowed gently backward in the breeze. Great, blonde beards hung from many of their chins, braided or twisted into knots; one had smoldering embers laced into his. *Maybe the Hundred were simply mortals with a history of brutal victories.*

A lonely cricket made a racket somewhere down on the ground. A squirrel above us stared with glassy black eyes, flicking his tail, threatening to make a noise and call their attention upward. Then they could fulfill the promise of an arrow through Locke's skull.

Locke breathed a deep, silent breath. He closed his eyes to think, not even watching the spectacle for several breaths.

I hated to do it, but I held still so their sylves wouldn't notice me.

Had I guided us to disaster? And if things went wrong, would Locke stop trusting me? As a sylfe, he was really all I had, especially since Numa never spoke to me.

At the rear, several warriors held a beam in the air with a bundle strapped to it. Locke gasped when he saw fingers and realized this was a person, bound and gagged—an elfe with pale skin and white hair. Locke stared at the captive as the Hundred faded silently down the road toward the Majestic Sea and finally slipped out of sight.

Locke sighed. "What an adventure," he whispered.

"That was nothing," I said, ignoring the anxiety resting on us. Luckily he didn't look at me.

"So you win this one. I'm glad I listened." He stood, holding the thin trunk with one hand, as if he were ready to leap into the sky. "So why would the King send the Hundred north toward the Tenarie?"

I still didn't say anything, and then he did look at me.

"Picke, are you alright?"

I breathed, trying to leave the fear behind. "Yeah, I'm fine."

"What's the matter?"

"Nothing. You didn't die." *Lucky for me.*

"Seriously, what's wrong?"

The darkness of last night still stretched overhead. It haunted me. I needed to shake it, to break free somehow—after all, a still wind dies. I didn't answer his question. Instead I said, "I have a crazy idea."

"You always have a crazy idea." He began the climb down.

"I think you should follow them."

"What?"

"Follow the Hundred."

"Why?"

"So we can see where they're going and who they've taken captive. And maybe who dammed the river. And *why not?*"

"They're a band of murderers, that's why not."

"True. But—"

"But what?" he said.

The exchange and the sound of his voice drove away the darkness. I nearly smiled. "We don't know *what* will happen if you follow them."

"Yeah, exactly. Horrible things could happen."

"But maybe good things could happen. That's the thing about the future, you never know."

"What good things could happen?" He put his hands on the branch below his feet then leaped off it backwards, swinging below.

"I don't know. Maybe you'll find a piece of the Land of Song—*something* is down that road. You'll have to follow the Hundred to find out what."

"But with that logic, almost anything could happen—maybe that road leads to my wife."

"Exactly. Risk the unknown, and anything could happen."

"Picke, you're losing it. Nothing good will happen." He pushed a frustrating limb out of his face.

"Nothing *bad* happened when we spied on them."

"So we got lucky."

"We usually do. Your mother named you Locke for a reason."

"I'm not so sure."

"Here's your problem: You have this little twig of a story in your mind that you're acting out. And life keeps trying to grow into a tree, with offshoots and unexpected turns. But you keep pruning it down so it fits within your imagination."

"I'm just trying to maintain some control."

"We want to see what's upstream, what dammed up the river. But fear tells us not to, and you obey, and you call that control?"

"I don't know."

"You don't have control. Life does what it wants. You control your choices and your courage, but the rest is out of your hands."

He nodded, almost to the ground and almost convinced. "I do want to know why they're going upstream, but…"

But how could he agree with a being so small and immaterial? "You know that wanting feeling?" I said. "The thing we can never name?"

Locke nodded and glanced toward the top of the tree.

"Whatever it is, it's something unknown. And maybe only the path unknown can lead us to it."

"The path unknown," he repeated, as if to taste its wonder.

"So what do you say?"

"I don't know."

"Come on, take a dare and see what chance gives you."

"Why this in particular?"

"To seize the moment—fate is only offering this if we take it now. And to show fear that it's not in control."

He leaned onto his tiptoes, squinting down into the dark distance.

"You have nothing to lose…" I said.

"Except my head."

"And a lot of blood," I added—*I couldn't resist.*

A chuckle slipped through his lips. Then, as he thought about it, his shoulders slumped, like truth had hit him with an elbow on the crown.

"Just so you know," I continued, "I don't want you to die."

He looked at me, with a sincere and searching gaze.

"But I also want you to live."

"What?"

"You know—explore the wilderness of possibility. Like Martigane."

Locke knew the story well. The twins used to tell it to us, the story of an elfe king who sought the Melody of Echoes, a secret song that could only be found by someone who wanted it more than anything—more than life even. And when I said the hero's name, Locke heard adventure's song. That triumphant, irresistible tune.

But he couldn't quite let go of his doubts. "How do I know this isn't more of your mischief?"

"It's not."

"How do I know?"

"I promise it isn't."

"Look at me."

So I did. I looked at my elfe and he looked at me, his eyes scanning every drifting particle. He was all but convinced, which scared me. But I couldn't stop now—it was too intoxicating to change our world with a breath. *Time for a gamble.* "Let's flip for it," I said, smiling.

He squinted at me again. "Fine."

He dropped to the ground and retrieved a kohkoo nut. With his knife, he carved my initial into one side and his into the other.

"Alright," he said. "*Pah* is upriver, risking our life chasing the Hundred."

"Agreed."

"And *lah* is nothing? Or home?"

"Your rune, your choice," I said.

"Lah is I-get-to-take-a-nap."

"No!"

"Picke, it's your game."

"Okay, fine. *Lah* is a nap. In a room full of bugs."

"I didn't say a nap at home."

"Just flip."

We'd never had a time when we couldn't flip into water, so we didn't know exactly what to do. Locke decided to roll the nut across the ground on its widest edge, going for distance.

It sped, tumbling and bumping across the ground. We chased after it, squinting under storm clouds to see who'd won.

"It's *pah!*" I shouted.

5.

The Majestic Sea

SPONTANEOUS MOVEMENT EXCITED me.

Locke hopped into the riverbed, and we headed north, moving at a jog. "I feel fine," I announced.

"Good."

He was used to my frenetic moods.

The adventure excited Locke too, even if he hardly showed it. We were setting out like in the tales, venturing beyond the Enchanted Wood.

The Hundred had gone toward the Majestic Sea. Our memories of it showed vast, blue waters stretching the distance of a narrow valley, ready to catch the rays of the setting sun in its sparkling texture.

We stopped at the ferry home, careful not to wake old Twiche, and got some breakfast; we also loaded up on water from the trough.

The twins had taught us about tracking, and although unnaturally silent, the Hundred still left a trail. So we followed, past the Dragonsea, close to the Great River's dry bed, then winding along game trails toward the summits of the Wisting Mountains.

Dawn had been replaced by a dark canvas covering the sky, which dipped and curled as far as the eye could see. Not black as night, but like a storm without rain, *not bright enough*, with no gaps leading to daylight and no touch of light on any horizon. As we ascended, we passed more small creatures whose blood had been spilt. The worst were the flying squirrels, my favorite kind. Hundreds of them scattered across the ground, each with its throat cut. The blood seeped into the ground, so thick I could nearly hear their dying screams. I hated whoever had done this.

I sensed the elementals of the rocks beneath us, holding still as roots. Gnymes didn't communicate with breath, but surely they knew the story, had witnessed what happened. I wished I could ask them. We marched on, sometimes hoping to find answers and sometimes hoping we'd both agree to turn back. Even if Locke didn't believe it, I worried the end of time really had been set in motion. The trail eventually cut back to the road, which was, not surprisingly, clear of other travelers.

"Our old campsite is just off that way," said Locke. The twins had taken us up here a few years before. Once we crested above the gap, we'd see the Majestic Sea fenced on the north and east by the Rueful Wilderness.

"I like rock," said Locke.

"What?"

"It's stable. Not scary."

"Just because I'm not stable doesn't mean I'm scary."

"I'm not talking about you. I'm talking about the ground."

"Rocks aren't stable. What about that shale back there?"

"Okay, I don't like all rock. I just like the stable kind. I like knowing it'll be there—you don't have to wonder."

"You're talking about the future, aren't you?"

"I'm talking about rock. I just like stable rock, that's all."

"Alright, well I'll try to stop being so flighty."

"Gah, Picke."

After that, we fell quiet for a while, except for the heavy breathing. We'd traveled around eight leagues in seven hours, which was good time and a significant distance. As the path became increasingly steeper, it seemed the hill and its gnyme were trying to tilt us off their back.

"This is hard," I said.

"Oh, you're," breathed Locke, "one to talk. I'm,"—*gasp*—"the one,"—*another big breath*—"doing the climbing."

"It's not you and me; it's us. And I'm still experiencing the strain in your right heel and every throb of your wrong big toe."

"And every"—*he breathed again*—"gasp of air."

"Yes, and every gasp of air, you ninny."

Locke shook his head and grinned. *Ah, I loved it.* He was a pretty good elfe.

As the slope grudgingly gave way, I considered going ahead as far as I could without choking so that I could see down the other side. It wasn't the nicest thing to do, but I was so tired of waiting. *Just a peek.*

When I looked over that rocky saddle, Locke felt my reaction, and his heart skipped a beat just a moment before he saw it too.

The land was dead.

A decaying paintbrush had muted the green of the trees. And the Majestic Sea—

—completely gone.

No water at all. Just a lifeless stretch, a deep, caving void of gray mud.

Last time we'd seen this view, it had been breathtaking. It took our breath now, by gloom and shadow.

"What the..." Locke took a few more steps then fell forward on his hands and knees.

"Only Saede could have done this," I said.

Locke shook his head to disagree. "Maybe the Tenarie blocked the tributaries farther up?"

"No. Even if they had, it would slow to a trickle first. Someone would have brought word. Nothing natural could cause this overnight."

"And yet here it is."

"Here it *isn't*."

"I don't believe it; I can't. A river is one thing, but... this..."

He looked back toward home. The Enchanted Wood lay in a valley, lower in elevation than any of the surrounding terrain, which was why the waters poured down into it. From here we could see the delta and the five rivers. *Which used to pour from that splotch of gray ahead.*

"My dad won't believe us when we tell him."

I impersonated Locke's father's voice: "It's impossible! This is the Land of Many Damn Waters!"

We laughed uneasily. Locke was right. *We* couldn't even believe it, and we were looking at it.

"What's that?" asked Locke.

"What?"

"That brown thing, toward the middle of the sea. It looks like..."

"It looks like a dog carcass."

"If we can see it from here, it must be a dog as big as the King's Stade."

To our wrong side we saw another landmark. Most adults called it the Burning Mountain, but Locke insisted on the name the twins had used, Mount Death, the tallest peak in the land. Directly eastward, between it and the Majestic Sea, lay a dark valley, the Rueful Wilderness. We'd been warned to never go there. Even the twins said it was a stupid idea. Every evening the Burning Mountain cast its shadow over it. And anyone who ever went into that part of the valley—where the shadow fell—never returned. So they said.

"Are we going on?" I asked.

"Risk the unknown, and anything could happen," he said, quoting my words.

"Not insubstantial at all, huh?" I spread my wings as far as I could.

"We have enough water," he said. "I'm willing if you are."

I nodded, and we began our descent.

The sun, blocked behind thick clouds, was now going down. But its rays hadn't come through—not enough to scare off any wandering wraiths. Soon we'd see the end of the first dark day.

As we descended northward, the foliage thickened, blocking the sea from view. Locke proceeded warily, as if expecting a wraith to pop out from every corner. We passed several elves coming from the sea towns, each eager to share news of the catastrophe with the Enchanted Wood.

Before we arrived, we caught the hint of a foul odor. The trees around the road soon opened into a wide space, a space that had formerly been the central landmark of the Land of Many Waters. It was now a giant, shattered puzzle of dried mud, fitted together with small gaps between each piece. One group of boys had taken advantage of the flat ground to play monkey ball, but we didn't join them. A few solitary souls walked further out, scavenging or something.

The elves here were mostly Kyrie, with Tenarie sprinkled in the mix. Some worked, scrubbing the hulls of the now beached ships, cleaning them while they were high and dry. Some milled about as if waiting for it to suddenly start raining. Others saw things more realistically—even if the water came back, all the fish were already dead. Many people sat on the docks, talking, whittling, tying knots, soaking in the gloom. Their sylves hovered helplessly by, apparently unable to give good advice on what to do. Some of the elves nodded at Locke. One girl, with her hands held coyly behind her back, winked at him and then blushed. No one seemed to notice me.

As we ventured onto the sea, we passed a wrinkled old man leaning against a pier several feet above us. Wispy gray hairs grew out of his pointy ears. His sylfe had a crazy look in one eye. I warned Locke a little too late that he ought to approach someone else.

"Excuse me," said Locke. "Did you see the Hundred of Saebynre pass this way?"

The old man nodded and pointed straight across the sea.

"Thanks," said Locke. "What happened here?"

"A storm," said the man. "Though storms usually have a direction. The angry wind pulls north, south, east, or west. But last night, it pulled straight up." He spoke with rising intensity as he got further into his story. "The whole sea shivered, like a man freezing to death. And rain poured the wrong direction. Our ship shook like madness. We didn't realize what was happening till the keel hit the ground. Then she leaned to the side and threw us all overboard. She'd run aground at the middle of the sea." He paused and gave us a smile like he'd told us some big lie. Yet the proof was all around.

Locke squatted and fingered the corner of one fragment of mud, prying it up. It crumbled between his fingers. Beneath the chunk, the ground was moister, but it was drying too. "What magic could cause this?"

"Have you heard of the Night of the Wolf?" asked the man.

"Yes, but I…" He trailed off before mentioning his disbeliefs. He wasn't very sure about them anyway.

"There will be war." The man glanced north toward the Astral Fields, as if he could see an army coming, but the hopeless look on his face said there was no way to stop it. "People desperate for water and fighting over cisterns. And without sun, the crops will fail, if we haven't already died of thirst or bloodshed."

"It's true, Locke," I whispered, and the old man took no notice.

Locke nodded his subtle reply, not wanting to speak to me in front of someone else.

"This was my horrible feeling, my nightmare," I said. "I sensed the creatures being murdered and the water vanishing and this black sky. Maybe we should turn back."

Locke shook his head, again very subtly. "What about the wraiths?" he asked the man.

"We can deal with a few wraiths."

But it won't be a few. The thought echoed loudly even though Locke never spoke it. "Well, it was nice talking to you. I wish you well." He started walking.

"Good luck!" grumbled the old man.

Toward the center of the sea, the cracks were covered by gray moss, gray sticks, and gray seaweed flattened to the ground. A rotting stench wafted toward us, becoming more and more unbearable, like the air had been poisoned. All sizes of fish littered the ground, each with a single eye staring in horror at the sky. Their ondines had left, and so had their fire and breath.

"Why do you want to turn back?" asked Locke when we were alone again.

"I don't know. The world's ending."

He glanced over his shoulder toward home and his father. Then he looked at those tracks across the sea, which had their own mysterious pull. "At this point, going back seems nearly as uncertain as going forward. And maybe we'll find the actual cause. I say we finish your dare."

I looked at him closely to make sure he hadn't gone mad.

"You know, Picke, I can see you better in this darkness. You glow almost. Against the light of the sun you can be hard to see."

I smiled. "Okay. Let's go on. But I think we should at least tell Shaye what we've found."

He considered it for a while but in the end did nothing.

As we followed the tracks across the former sea, we passed a group of people huddled next to a boat which rested at an angle on its side. The crowd stood around a woman who knelt over a body, weeping. They looked at us as they passed, all of them except the woman.

Up ahead, the dead dog now looked more like a dead monster, like the ones Tunke used to tell us horrible stories about. The twins' stories had frightened us when we were younger, which, incidentally, was what led us to first ask about the Phantetios. More recently we'd started to think the sea demon had been exaggerated.

Apparently we were wrong.

It was a living exaggeration—or would have been, if it weren't a rotting carcass. Locke deviated, drawn closer to the spectacle.

"Look!" I said pointing to the tracks. Even a few of the Hundred had broken ranks to look at the beast.

Its rarity and size invited us to look, but the awfulness shooed us away. We gawked anyway; it was hard not to. The darkness gave the beast's brown color a bluish tint. Its wrinkled, unearthly skin folded in layers around the edges of its eyes—which had been ripped out—and near the joints of its

massive arms and webbed fingers. The scavenger birds had left a red mess
of its lips, which revealed clenched teeth, the largest of which were thicker
than Locke's thigh. A man with a scarf around his face was trying to pry
a fang loose, but he kept having to stop to wave off the crows pecking at
his head. The other birds stuck to the beast's back, feasting through the
cracks in the scaly hide.

I'd followed Locke past the fish, but nearing the monster was too much.
The stench surrounded me and permeated every particle of the air. I wanted
to cover my eyes, my ears, my nose, and my mouth. I pulled as far away
from Locke as I could bear—I depended on his lifeforce as much as an elfe
depended on air. The distance nearly asphyxiated me, and it still wasn't
enough. Soon I was swimming in near unconsciousness.

"Okay," I heard him say through his sleeve, "we can go." We moved away
at a jog, far enough to find breathable air. "Gah, that stinks," he finally said.

As if to signal that night was fully upon us, the wolves howled their
requiem for our Land of Many Waters.

Locke's eyebrows creased into a look of worry and disgust. "How could
the Kyrose let this happen?"

"You only believe in them when you need a culprit."

"It's a valid question. Assuming the demigods are real, why would they
allow this?"

"Maybe we had it coming."

He had no reply.

And the decaying monster followed us, chasing through our mind.

6.

Red

Heavy clouds dulled the light of the next morning. Smoke on the horizon ahead reached upward to touch that dark ceiling. The source of the smoke was covered by deep jungle which lined a river cutting through the Astral Fields.

Locke descended the blathae tree where he'd slept at Wiks Pike. At the sea's northern shore, we pushed quickly through the thin strip of Rueful Wilderness. In the Astral Fields, Locke feasted on a wild turkey he hit with his sling, which let him save the food he carried. Several leagues after that, we cautiously approached the smoking ruin we'd seen from so far away. I couldn't help but remember those mad-dog eyes threatening to put an arrow through Locke's skull. The ones I'd convinced Locke to follow.

Before we reached the smoke, we came upon the destruction. It took us by surprise.

The first elfe rested on his back, his teeth hanging apart, his right hand reaching up past his head in twisted desperation. The next corpse lay face down, the feathers in his helmet pointing sadly skyward while his hands rested at his sides, palms upward, fingers in a calm curl. The third was sprawled over the fourth, his back bent uncomfortably and his chin pressed into his own chest, his eyes staring at the strangeness of his unbreathing ribs. Some were Kyrie, with wheat-colored hair, beards, and the painted faces of the Hundred. Most of them were Tenarie, with wild white hair and tattoos on their pale skin. Each was unique, but they were held together by a melody of red. Red beards and red limbs, resting finally on red ground. Even the captive was there, still tied to his pole, now with his throat cut. In the nearby brambles, the frayed edges of the Hundred's red banner flapped in the wind.

Locke dropped to one knee and buried his face in his hand, but he couldn't block the images in our mind.

What *wasn't there* haunted me more than what we saw. The air above this multitude was as dead as the bodies beneath—no breath of sylves. This void screamed at me, echoing as if inside a vast nightmare. I knew they weren't actually gone though. In fact, one likely sat very close to me, fallen so utterly still that I couldn't see him or hear him. He'd stay there too, trapped, unbreathing and unmoving, listening alone in the Shadowlands for someone to speak his name. Only I didn't know his name.

I breathed with Locke, right below me. If he died, the same would happen to me. "Get up," I said. "Whoever won this fight might be nearby, and if they've killed this many of the Hundred..."

He gazed at me with worry in his eyebrows. "Why did we leave home?"

I surveyed the grim battlefield while trying not to notice details or entrails. Ahead stood a crumbling fortress, built of beige stones, covered in moss, and buried in foliage. It had likely been erected by the ancient people who preceded the elves, or maybe even by Martigane's people. Plumes of smoke folded and curled from the fortress's insides and merged with the stormy sky. It seemed the battle had taken place both inside and outside these ruins.

Locke stood. His eyes were wet and red—another variation on the red melody. "If there are demigods, how do you explain *this?*"

I had no answer. *I'd* led us here. Which I regretted. *Why couldn't Numa have warned me?*

Locke breathed against the despair and horror. I sunk toward a bog of melancholy. Then I sensed something. Something urgent. A sound of life. Someone approaching fast. When Locke felt it in me, his heart skipped a beat.

"Look out!" I shouted.

Locke spun to find a boy holding a pike, the point trained on Locke.

The boy's sylfe darted forward and back, as if he himself were the weapon, repeatedly faking an attack and then retreating. The boy was more than a head shorter than Locke. His skin was pale and his hair was white—a Tenarie. He was bedraggled, as if he'd just trekked the heart of the Rueful Wilderness. But one small boy and his deranged sylfe couldn't have defeated the Unstoppable Hundred. At least, not unless his strength came from the look on his face. Hatred and terror were mixed together and came to a point at the sharp end of his weapon.

Locke grinned the most non-threatening grin he could muster, raising his hands in the air: "Hi."

He really was charming.

But the small boy's expression didn't change. Instead he took a step closer, and his knuckles whitened as he pulled the weapon back, readying for a thrust.

"It's okay," said Locke, patting his palms on the air as if to smooth out the tension. "I'm not here to harm you. I don't want to fight. Look, I don't even have a weapon."

The boy screamed a war cry in Locke's face—"KHEEAAAA!"—and lunged.

Locke scrambled. And not a moment too soon. Running with all his might, he barely kept distance between him and the boy's spearhead.

The boy bounded, aiming the point at Locke's spine, their feet beating rapidly.

"He's gaining, Locke!"

I pictured the pike ramming into his ribcage. My terror pushed Locke harder.

He tried a daring move: Instead of running the open trail where the trees were well spaced, he darted into a narrow gap where the branches of two trees interlocked in a thicket. As he hit the barrier, his momentum slowed. A fox scampered away in front of him, traversing easily beneath. Locke pushed as hard as he could into the thicket. The branches scraped his face and hands.

That delay allowed the pike to catch up. Just as it was about to puncture flesh, Locke whooshed through the branches, which came flying back at the boy.

The boy squinted and plowed ahead. But his pike twisted to the side, caught, till soon he was pulling the weapon behind him. When the branches finally gave way, he fell through into open ground.

And Locke was waiting.

Before the boy could pull the weapon back up in front of him, Locke leaped, clamping an arm around the smaller kid's neck and throwing his weight down, till they both crashed into the ground. The pike clattered onto the dirt and rocks. The strange sylfe spasmed back and forth as if trying to escape from the air itself.

"Now hold on!" shouted Locke as he struggled to get the boy under control. "I'm not trying to hurt you. I just don't want you to kill me."

7.

Wuck

WE RETREATED FROM the corpses.
But their open, unblinking eyes still haunted us.

The setting sun showed itself as a lighter gray among charcoal clouds on the west side. At least we saw something—some light as we rested and tried not to think about the faces of the dead.

I'd tried counting them. If any of the Hundred survived, I estimated it wasn't more than a dozen. But maybe it was none at all—I hadn't covered all the ground. And if so, the dare was over, ending not in an answer but in more mystery. The fallen Tenarie numbered at least three times that of the Hundred. We saw no signs of their survivors either, except for this one small boy.

He sat on a nearby rock. The fire seemed to have gone out of him, mostly because his hands and feet were tied. He hadn't breathed a word yet, except for the growling as Locke forced him into submission.

"I'm sorry," said Locke. "You're the one who wanted to fight."

The boy's head was bowed. He looked up and bared his teeth, like a snarling animal. His hair was white, but not wispy like an old man's; it was thick and full and ran wild in every direction. His skin was pale except around his eyes, which were dark and ghostly.

His sylfe sat quietly on his far shoulder and only rarely peeked around to take a look at us. Strangely, the sylfe didn't even whisper to the kid. He was silent, just like the sylfe tied to Locke's father.

I reached out, hoping to smooth the discord between me and the sylfe, but it didn't go well. "Maybe you should play the Angel's song."

Locke shook his head, determined to communicate directly. All the Tenarie we'd met spoke Kyriglae, though riddled with slang. And this boy had screamed a battle cry, so we knew he had a voice at least.

"How come you won't say anything?" asked Locke.

The boy turned, far enough for us to see one of his hands behind his back. He spread out his five fingers at us, an obscene and hateful thing to do. The four Kyrose did good in the world, but the fifth, Saede, the shadow, had fallen. That made five the unluckiest number, and spreading five fingers and pointing them at someone was to curse them to fiery depths. Some kids said it meant worse. I wanted to bite his hand for doing it. Or bite his nose. That would show him. Maybe I could convince Locke to beat him up.

But Locke had a surprisingly different response: "You know, you remind me of someone. Same smile." Which was funny, because this boy certainly hadn't smiled at us, but his sneer had shown his teeth. He had an underbite, like he was stubbornly sticking out his jaw. But two of his teeth, the second set after the middle, leaned back beneath and behind the upper teeth. It was a unique bite, yet, strangely, we'd seen one like that before.

The boy stole another quick glance, and I saw a flicker of light in his eyes.

Locke chuckled. "He always wore a red cap. His name was Nickle. Only he pronounced it *Nikowe*—wasn't too good with the *lah* rune. We called him Nicke. You look just like him. All you need is a red cap."

The boy remained silent, still looking down. At least he didn't gesture again. Then his sylfe quietly switched shoulders, from hiding on the far side to sitting in plain view. *Whoa.*

"It was the funniest thing too." Locke smiled and shook his head. "One time Nicke came over grinning and carrying a stone lyzard he'd found in the Mowaihees. So I said, 'Wow, you're a pretty lucky kid.' And he gets all upset and frowns, like I'd insulted him. Then in a real stubborn voice he says, 'I don't beweave in wuck!'"

Locke laughed aloud into the quiet night.

As we reminisced, memories flooded our mind, and homesickness gnawed beneath Locke's ribcage. For a moment, we could see the treehouse again, branches reaching nearly as high as the sky, the leafy vines crawling up the sides of the cove, and Nicke's little red cap bobbing along, just tall enough to be seen over the hedge.

The boy didn't respond, though I almost caught a smile in the twitch of his cheek.

"Oh, I should tell you my name's Locke. That makes the story funnier. Should have started out with that."

Anyone but a hyuman would have understood that Locke's name in Kyriglae was a form of the word *fortune*—basically *Locke* meant *luck*.

"I don't beweave in wuck!" said Locke again, laughing. "I guess some people think I insult the demigods. Is it that way in your village?"

The boy looked away. His sylfe had grown continually calmer, as if war had retreated.

Though Locke still hadn't gotten an answer, he let things be for a time, while I kept vigil on the surrounding forest and smoking ruins.

The sky darkened as the sun set, and lightning flashed across it. Locke shook his head as intrusive memories made their way in front of him. "Maybe we should find some water."

The boy's eyes flashed in the darkness as he glanced toward one end of the village.

"Perfect," said Locke. "We'll look there." He grinned a clever, self-satisfied smile. But after looking at the kid's face, he said, "Sorry. I wasn't trying to be cunning. I'll get you some too. Come on." The boy looked up again, glaring, and war had returned to his eyes. Locke loosened the hobble on his feet so he could follow. "I'd untie you if I could trust you. But you won't even talk to me."

The kid frowned. His pale face and tired eyes were spooky in the dark. They reminded me of a skull.

"I don't even know what to call you." Locke looked with compassion, still hoping for an answer. The boy's expression softened again, but he still didn't speak. "Alright, that's okay. Maybe we'll just call you Nicke for now. Let's go, Nicke." Carrying the pike in one hand, he led our new Nicke along by the rope around his neck.

Twilight hours had darkened the reds of the battlefield to nearly black— *even death could get worse*. We moved among the corpses, trying not to see or smell them. Smoke climbed toward the sky as we entered the gates of the ruins. We spotted the water tower easy enough.

The corpses lay strewn about here, just like everywhere else. But something was strange about them, something not right. I sensed it but couldn't quite place it. And I didn't warn Locke, afraid I might be wrong.

A large circular drum rested atop a wooden tower, similar to those in a Kyrie village. Locke tied Nicke to the bottom then climbed the lashed rungs

to a ledge where he could stand. The outsides of the drum were crawling
with bugs. I tried blowing them off, but most held on too tight.

The kid watched us closely from below.

Careful not to touch the insects, Locke stood tenuously on the ledge.
He opened a small hatch, took the ladle, and leaned over the side of the
drum's wall, reaching low—there wasn't much water left. He dipped the
ladle and drew it out, bringing it to his lips.

—"STOP!"—

The cry was sharp, startling Locke, and the water splattered on the boards
and dripped all the way to the ground.

But I hadn't shouted.

It was the boy. It was Nicke.

"Stop," he said again in a childlike tone. "The water is poisoned."

And then it hit me, the strangeness, the thing I'd sensed was wrong: The
corpses near the water tower didn't have the melodic red. No wounds or
spilt blood. It was as if they'd fallen asleep.

These men had been killed by the water.

8.

The Wraith

A RE YOU SURE we don't need to leave?" asked Locke. He looked toward the shifting shadows around us. The fire popped, and the crickets chirped in the background.

The boy pulled his fingers through his wild white hair. "We'll be safe for at least one night." He'd been untied for an hour and hadn't tried to kill us once. He'd also helped Locke to find food and clean water. Now they sat across from each other, eating and staring into a fire.

"You going to tell me your name?" said Locke.

"Nicke is fine," said the kid with his staccato accent. The sound of his voice was the color of a red string, soft and bright, but very fragile. His sylfe still hadn't spoken. In fact, his sylfe seemed unnaturally closed off and gave me a bad feeling whenever our glances met. That left me feeling suspicious—Nicke was a Tenarie after all. And his face reminded me of something ghostly, something that could scare just by staring in silence.

"So what happened here?" said Locke.

Embers floated toward the dark sky, and the fire of ancient grudges flickered in Nicke's eyes.

It was impossible not to remember them now, especially when the kid gave us a look like that. The first Seer sailed from the Land of Song, across the Sea of Time, to the Land of Many Waters. When he died, his sons went to war, splitting the family into tribes, one in the north and one in the south. Centuries later, the grudge still ran in the blood of most elves, including Locke's father.

Nicke didn't speak. The crickets fell silent too, and except for the fire, the whole night seemed for a moment to be dead.

Before Locke got his answer, a cold, creeping sensation crawled into our consciousness. Like the one I'd tried to warn him about as he slept. Only that realization had been slow, a light touch on the skin. This wasn't subtle or gradual.

And whatever it was, it was on his hand.

Locke's whole body exploded to life, like the shudders of a whole week had been piled into one instant.

"Aah!"

He flung his arm wildly. His heart thumped as he lurched from his seat, trying to brush the feeling off his hand. And chill ran deep as his bones.

"A wraith!" said Nicke.

"Oh, no. Oh, no. Oh, no," said Locke, fighting to keep the nightmares out of his head.

The wraith stood not much taller than a squirrel, but it spread over enough ground to be six or eight of them. Its round body was held up by four legs which hadn't yet formed fingers or toes, so they looked like thick spider legs. On its stub of a head, it had a large mouth with white teeth, but to spite the sun, it had no eyes. A blind, consuming evil. A ghostly substance like fire hung around its form; only this substance—created by Saede, not Phose—emanated the opposite of light, and the dark tongues, instead of whipping heavenward, went in every direction, mostly down, as if longing for Hell. Just looking at the deformed embryo, so small and hideous, sent cold through Locke's heart. His imagination felt the creature's teeth against his spine and then on his forehead. *If it actually bit him…* He swallowed. *Well, he'd just have to make sure it didn't.*

Without realizing it, I drifted with my curiosity toward the wraith.

Locke panted. "Be careful, Picke."

He was right. Some said a wraith could bite a sylfe's head right off. I backed up.

Locke slowly backed up too, keeping his eyes on the creature. He pulled his pack around front and drew out his dagger. More of a knife really. It wasn't the ideal weapon for this, but it was all he had.

The wraith wiggled forward, then halted. It was quick. It didn't seem scared of fire either.

Locke pointed the dagger toward it, retreating. He felt cold, spindly legs on his chest and slapped the feeling away with his free hand.

The wraith whipped around and leaped an impressive distance, landing where Nicke had been sitting. Unfortunately, Nicke had left his pike sitting there. If he tried to reach it now, the wraith might leap onto his face. All it took was one quick bite.

When the wraith jumped, Nicke bolted.

The creature scurried after.

Locke flipped his dagger so that it pointed from the bottom of his fist, breathing quickly as if to roust his own courage. *"For Martigane,"* he whispered. He charged after them, leaping over a log and ducking below a branch. As he was about to overtake the wraith, it stopped and turned. Locke skidded, facing the monster's eager teeth. For a moment the night was still.

"For Martigane!" shouted Locke, lunging with a downward swing.

The wraith flinched.

The blade missed, sinking deep into the ground between the wraith's front legs. Locke's fist rested at the eyeless mouth. One cold leg touched his wrist, and an icy tooth scraped his knuckle. He burst backward with a shudder, leaving the weapon stuck in the ground.

Now *he* ran.

The wraith crawled after him, speeding up in a sickening wiggle.

Locke dashed back over his steps, crashing through foliage and back past the fire.

"Locke!" came a shout.

He turned, his chest toward the wraith. This show of power was enough that the wraith paused, its upper lip twitching hungrily.

"Here!" Nicke tossed his pike, the point to the side, in a high arc toward Locke. It seemed to hang in the air.

The wraith stepped forward, about to sink teeth into Locke's foot.

Without a moment to spare, Locke caught the pike, cocked the back of it high with his sword hand, and thrust down. It tore through the wraith with a crack and a bursting splat.

The creature squealed, twisting and pulling with its four legs. The point sunk too deep in the ground for it to get away. It struggled in pain but not about to die.

It bled immensely, and a sickening pool of black spread on the ground beneath it. Even though we'd only seen a couple wraiths our entire life, we knew a lot about them. While an elfe had all four lifeforces and I had only one, a wraith had three. It lacked blaze—its burning, its soul. That meant

it couldn't be killed by normal means, so the twins had said. But it was
only half a life, made of a full measure of lifeblood, with half a measure of
bone and half a measure of breath.

"That's the second one I've seen in the last few days," said Nicke.

It wasn't hard to believe that Saede had spawned the wraiths. Or that
their hunger for the missing lifeforce grew the more it was fed. Or that they
were so dreadful Phose took pity and sent the sun to fight them.

Locke took a seat by the fire, now on the opposite side from where the
creature still writhed. He breathed deep, trying to regain his calm. "Sorry
I panicked."

Nicke nodded, indicating his sympathy.

"My mother was bit by a wraith," said Locke.

"Did she...?" began Nicke.

Locke shook his head solemnly. "I was ten. And I can't stand them. I've
sometimes thought it would be better to die than face one."

"You did good," said Nicke. "Sorry *I* didn't spike him. I'm not too good
of an aim."

"You did great." Locke gave a sad grin. "I think you saved my life."

Nicke nodded and accidentally showed his crooked teeth as he gave us
his first real smile, a smile he couldn't hold back. But his smile didn't last
long. "Oh no."

Locke looked up with worry on his face.

"What if this really is the Night of the Wolf?" said Nicke. "What if the
sun never comes to drive them back?"

The wraith squealed and struggled.

Locke swallowed. "Then more will come."

9.

The Conqueror

THE BOYS STARED at the flames in silence.

Locke fought against dark memories, memories that came with each of the wraith's moans, as relentlessly as waves on a shore.

"You've got to find a safer place to sleep," I urged.

He nodded, but he didn't look at me.

Suddenly Nicke began to speak. Maybe because he trusted Locke. Or maybe he was compelled to free a story that terrorized his insides, even if that meant setting it loose on the world. "It started when the water vanished and the sylves fell deaf."

"When the sylves did what?" asked Locke.

Nicke's sylfe looked at me. His countenance masked a darkness hidden inside—some secret pain. But he'd glanced at that specific moment, so it wasn't *us* he couldn't hear. "When this all started, the sylves stopped hearing. Didn't it happen to your people?"

"I don't know," said Locke. "You're about the only person we've talked to in two days. But my sylfe seems the same."

"Well here it happened to everybody. Yesterday morning when the bugs were murdered and the waters disappeared, the sylves fell deaf. So no one warned us what was coming. Not even the Witchdoctor knew." *But could sylves really warn of a surprise attack?* Nicke shook his head. "An army came, led by a captain and an old man. The old man had a sour face, like eating a pickle, and for some reason I couldn't stop thinking about him. Like a nightmare. I still can't. I don't know why."

Locke stared in uneasy anticipation.

"The captain and the old man warned us to go. They said blood was coming. But they also said if we took our sheep they'd kill us."

"Were these Kyrie?"

"No. They were Tenarie."

"And you didn't leave?"

"Some people left, but my dad wanted to stay with our sheep. Then the bloodshed came, just like they said. Kyrie murderers."

"You mean the Hundred? With the beards and painted faces?"

"Yes. Your warriors."

"They weren't my warriors," said Locke.

"They were Kyrie."

"Those were the Hundred of Saebyrne. Even our people fear them."

Nicke nodded a small concession, as if it might be true. "My dad said the Tenarie army had way more warriors than the Kyrie and that we'd win for sure. He was a *mighty* warrior. He even killed one Kyrie by himself. But in the end, he died with the rest."

Locke sucked in a quick breath, and the emotions burned in his throat. "I'm sorry." He swallowed.

The flames flickered in Nicke's hollow, child eyes, as if no blaze were in him either—just bone, blood, and breath, without a soul left to feel pain. "The Kyrie won, even though we outnumbered them. Most survived. They set my house on fire and took us prisoner. Not many, mostly kids and moms. The others… all dead. They searched the bodies, looking for something. They threatened my mom, said she had to give them some scroll. They were obsessed with finding it."

Locke's brow furrowed, and his eyes glistened—a look that said he couldn't bear it. "Why your mother?" he asked, even though he didn't want to hear more.

"She is… our medicine woman. But she didn't know where the scroll was—" Nicke's eyes glistened with tears—he *was* alive.

Locke breathed heavily as he sniffled. He stared painfully at Nicke, as if they were both about to die an excruciating death.

Nicke's whole body seemed to clench tight. "My mom didn't know where it was, so they killed her." His eyes closed, and tears ran down his cheeks. He buried his face in his arms and sobbed. His white locks hung toward the safety below ground, flickering in the firelight, while his story waited, knowing its complete escape was now inevitable. Nicke's sylfe hovered above the crown of his head, offering no help. Or hope.

I followed a strange impulse to sit on Nicke's shoulder, to show him I was there, to show him I wasn't his enemy. But words couldn't lift the weight of this feeling. Words were air. This required blood. There was nothing for it but to endure, as death and finality wrapped sinewy fingers around our throats—all of us.

A cricket whistled an elegy. Nicke sobbed and so did Locke.

After a long time, the sobbing ended, and much later Nicke looked up again.

"I'm so sorry…" began Locke, still in agony.

I watched as Nicke wandered alone through his child mind, facing the fire and anger till the war in his eyes returned. His hands rested in his lap with his shoulders slumped. He stared blankly with watery eyes into the dark shapes of trees. His sylfe did nothing to offer comfort—I was watching. He wasn't deaf to us, and he wasn't mute either. So why had he abandoned his elfe in this of all moments?

"One of the Kyrie," Nicke began again, "a young one with no beard, tried to defend my mother. He said they had to show mercy. When they murdered her, he fought against his own chief. Others fought with him, but they were outnumbered."

"So the Unstoppable Hundred killed themselves," I whispered.

"As Kyrie fought against Kyrie, we escaped—me and the other boys and women and that wrinkled man. I don't know how he survived when all the other Tenarie men were killed. Maybe because his sylfe was so evil. I still can't stop thinking about him."

Locke breathed, wanting to console or comfort or at least show he was hearing. But no words could make a fair response to what Nicke had told us.

"We hid in the whispering thorns," said Nicke. "The old man said the Kyrie would hunt us down and kill us one by one. He was a coward—more afraid than us, and our *families* were dead. He kept saying it wasn't supposed to be this way, that he never should have trusted them, should have never trusted anyone. He said he'd be back for the scroll. He was obsessed. Before he left, he gave me two vials of venom and told me to pour them into the water towers."

Hatred suddenly overcame Nicke, as if it were his last desperate measure against overwhelming sadness. He grit his teeth.

"I wouldn't have done it, but I think he did something to my sylfe. Ashe doesn't normally listen to anyone but me. I mean it, nobody. But Ashe repeated what the man had said, that they deserved to die and that it was the only way to stop them from hunting us. I couldn't argue with my own sylfe, not when I was so alone. So I did it. I snuck back in. Only a few of those horrible Kyrie had survived. I made it past them, climbed the first tower, and poured in the venom."

"Wait, *you* killed the Hundred?" asked Locke.

Nicke didn't reply. Not for a long time.

When he finally spoke, he said, "It was slow. Too much water for a little poison. It took them hours to die. Hours of moaning and scraping. Ashe hasn't said a word since."

He paused. The tears gleamed in his eyes.

"I only wish it had taken longer."

10.

Voices

IT ISN'T SAFE here," said Locke. "Wraiths come from the ground."

"Well, my home was burned," said Nicke.

"I'm talking about sleeping in a tree."

"Tenarie don't do that."

"I'll show you how. It's actually pretty comfortable."

"I sleepwalk sometimes."

Locke almost snickered.

With a little rope and a lot of reassurance, he convinced Nicke it was safer. As we moved high into a tree, away from the earth and the gnymes and the dead, we scared a sizable horned owl from his perch.

The boys fell asleep, and I was left alone, left with my fears and Nicke's silent sylfe. I tried to keep vigil, knowing the height wouldn't necessarily save them from a wraith. But while Locke slept I could hear very little and see even less—that was the way of things. Though I did hear ghostly howls crying for the vanished moon.

As dawn came, the black sky turned to dark gray, not enough light to finish off our wraith.

Nicke took his mother by the wrist, Locke grabbed the other, and they dragged her to a beautiful, dim grove. They did the same for his father, and then set to digging a pair of graves. For a long spell, the only sound was the clank of steel into dry dirt.

Locke broke the silence when he asked, "What happened to the other boys who escaped?"

"After I poisoned the water, I got stuck. I had to hide beneath the dead so the Kyrie wouldn't find me. It took hours before they all stopped breathing. I went back to the whispering thorns, but everyone was gone. Then you came. I thought you were one of *them*."

"You thought *I* was one of the Hundred?"

"You're a Kyrie."

Locke put his shovel to the ground and jumped on it, stabbing deep. "Are you going to try to follow the others who escaped?"

Nicke shrugged with a lost look on his face.

"What about your uncles or cousins?"

"This village was my family." As he said it, the smoke rose from the ashes around us.

I looked at Nicke's ghostly demeanor. What would he become if left alone with his hate and agony? It horrified me to imagine. The path lead somewhere dark and loathsome.

"Come with us," said Locke. "You can live at my house and work at the ferry with me."

Nicke looked back doubtfully.

"I'm serious," said Locke.

Nicke stared into an uncertain future. If there were a clear alternative, one stronger than searching for the remnants of a shattered village, he probably would've taken it.

"Alright then, that's settled," said Locke, even though Nicke hadn't answered. "You'll come with us."

After a moment of surprise, Nicke's face dropped into a lopsided smile, not a strong one, but better than nothing. He nodded, though something was still missing in his eyes. He needed more than a place to go. More than just a friend. He needed life. And healing.

The shovels scraped and cut deeper and deeper into the ground.

The boys didn't have a good way to lower the bodies, so I was glad the graves weren't deep. They covered them with dirt and a layer of heavy stones.

"May the valkalysae carry you home," said Locke, speaking directly to the dead.

We left Nicke and his silent Ashe to weep alone over two fresh mounds of dirt.

From a quiet distance away, wisdom came to me, wisdom hard to hear but easy to speak, wisdom flitting on the wind: "If he doesn't forgive them, the hate will follow him the rest of his life."

"Picke, what the Hundred did to Nicke can't be undone. There are no valkalysae; death takes and never gives back. I can't forgive what they've done. And if *I* can't, how's Nicke supposed to?"

"Maybe with divine strength," I said, unsure.

"How?"

"What?"

"How's he supposed to get divine strength?"

I looked down because of shame. "I don't know." I *should* have known, but I didn't. For a while, nothing more was said. We watched Nicke weeping beneath his sylfe. My failure to give an answer gnawed at me. I was supposed to be a hero's sylfe, a substantial voice, one people *listened* to. Which meant I needed to say something more than *I don't know.*

After a long time, Locke walked up to Nicke kneeling in the dirt and touched his shoulder.

Tears streaked Nicke's pale skin. As if to deflect any conversation, he said, "We should go." But he didn't abandon what was left of his family. Instead, he stared at the mounds. His wild white hair fell over his face as he shook his head. "Ashe told me I had to do it. He told me pouring that venom in the water would fix things."

His small, child shoulders hung under a great weight.

"But it was a lie." Nicke pounded a fist into the dirt. His thin voice was pulled taught, nearly to breaking. "The venom didn't fix anything. It didn't heal the knives in my heart. It didn't bring my family back." He broke down again, leaning forward onto the graves, bawling. "How am I ever going to feel better? I just want to die."

We watched in silent misery, not knowing what to say or do. As we watched, an oath began to rise in our mind, becoming clearer each time it repeated, echoing as if from Numa herself.

When Locke whispered the words, they resounded as if I'd spoken them:

"I swear, by my bones, by my blood, by my breath, and by the empyrean, I will do all I can to heal your wounds."

II.

Dying

WE TRIED NOT to look at the faces of the dead.
By now, the fire ants were eating away at their eyes.

I was eager to escape this hellish place and my mistake in bringing us here. But Locke had a purpose, which brought us back to the outskirts of the village. Nicke followed, watching Locke mull among the bloody remains. The bugs mulled among them too, eager for moisture and sustenance.

I moved above Locke as high as I could, trying to avoid the stench, and I pushed the wind along in a current below me.

Locke nudged a corpse with the toe of his moccasin while turning away in revulsion. The warrior's hand flapped onto the dirt. Locke waited for the bugs to fly away. With the belt now exposed, he drew the sword and grinned, pointing the blade toward the sky. "This is the one." He stuck the tip in the ground and began to rub dirt where the blood had dried on the steel. "Sorry to make you wait, Nicke, but there will be more wraiths. Besides, metal's scarce enough as it is, and weapons like these…"

He was interrupted by a rising melody. It flowed up and down, dancing on the breeze, and faintly tickling the leaves. It came through a power we called the consonance—all the way from home, through the wind, and then to me. Usually she spoke, but this time she sent just a song. *Like a smile.*

"Haa-la-la, haa-la-la, haa-la-le-liah."

"Shaye's singing!" When I shouted her name, Locke tried to hide his anxiety. And giddiness.

Nicke looked at me, eager to go, eager to be gone from this place forever. But he seemed to be wondering too.

Locke frowned, still a little mad about my mischief last week. He turned away from Nicke and spoke in a low breath. "You're supposed to call her the Angel."

"Sorry," I said.

Naike and I had formed the consonance at the market while Locke and Shaye were talking. My hands to her hands till we could hear each other over any distance. Locke scolded me for it, but he wasn't rude enough to break it, even to spite me. He didn't want Shaye to feel bad. Besides, he didn't have anyone else he'd rather have the connection with. *Even if he wouldn't admit it.*

Shaye's angel music flowed across a flurry of wind.

For adults, changing consonances was difficult—like sap losing its stickiness. Most formed it with their spouse and left it. But Locke wasn't an adult, and changing consonances was easy. But he got mad and said I'd treated it too lightly, as if future implications already applied. He wasn't good at seeing that *now* was all we had.

"I wish Nicke could hear her," said Locke.

Her song danced across the wind. She'd known we needed comfort. How she knew, I couldn't say. Or how she knew that a melody would speak truer than words.

As Locke listened, he looked at the fine blade in his hand, but his sight went right through it.

"What?" I asked.

Pretending to still be searching for metalwork, he walked away from Nicke and whispered, "I've been avoiding her, Picke. And that makes me a fool."

"I'm not quite sure I…"

"Amid a field of corpses, worrying about the right wife seems petty. Especially knowing throats can be cut so easily. I should've listened to you. Shaye's the brightest thing I've ever known. This horror helps me see what I had. Or could have."

If he'd have chosen in that moment, once for all, he would've married Shaye then and there. His hesitations melted. His fears floated into the wind. He didn't mind if she was different from the Nymfe. Didn't worry she might be the wrong choice. Didn't care about her small physical flaw. He didn't even think about adulthood or whether they were both too young. For that moment, he only saw the good. If he married her, he could keep this consonance forever, and her touch would heal all wounds—or *his* at least—and calm his longing.

For Nicke, maybe something more was needed.

Shaye finished her song with a bubbling giggle, then left us to the silence and the dead.

"Help me think of what to say to her," whispered Locke.

"It doesn't matter. Say anything. *Shaye, I'll be home soon, and I'm excited to see you.*"

He gave me a look then glanced toward Nicke, who acted like he wasn't trying to listen.

"It's true," I said defensively.

"It's too forward."

"*Shaye, I loved your song. And I miss you.*"

"I can't say that."

"It's true!"

"Yeah, but I'm not—"

The howl of a wolfe pierced the air, crossing the sky like an evil consonance. All was not well yet. Nicke looked to the southwest, as if he might see an approaching predator. He urged us with his thin red voice: "We need to go."

"Okay," replied Locke. Then he whispered to me, "we'll talk about it later."

"Just talk to her *now.*"

He shook his head.

Nicke held up a dagger that fit his stature. He seemed a little less sad when he swung it to get a feel. Switching hands, he swung it awkwardly with his wrong hand, but when Locke looked, Nicke lowered it and blushed.

Locke cringed as he tugged a coat of mail off one of the corpses, but the fine metalwork was worth it. He also claimed a scabbard, another belt, and a spaulder for his sword arm. Last, he stepped among the dead in search of the perfect shield. Unlike stock shields, these had a top and a bottom, fitted to the warrior's preferred hand. One in ten were supposed to have a lucky wrong hand, which meant that out of the Hundred, at least ten ought to have had backward shields. Only he couldn't seem to find those ten. Finally he shouted in frustration—"Aah!"—and he threw a shield.

It hit the ground with an angry clunk, and when it did, it scared something to life. *A breath.* I'd avoided seeing the faces, but now I searched each one directly. Many still had their eyes open.

A twisted hand, covered in dust, grabbed Locke's ankle.

Locke jerked his foot free, leaped back, and swung his new blade.

This corpse had a sylfe, which stood resolute at the fallen warrior's side.

The sylfe looked up at us with not enough life for defense. He simply stood and faced the falling steel.

Locke pulled, just before the blade struck, and the edge hit earth instead of flesh, missing the bone of the wrist.

This elfe wasn't back from the dead. He was clinging to the last shred of life.

Locke gaped. The warrior lay on his back in a dark stain of bloody red ground, which became more moist as it neared his body. Though his helm was nowhere in sight, he wore hard leather and metal on his shoulders, chest, and neck. His face was contorted, braced against a flood of pain. Strangely he didn't have a beard. Red and white paint crossed his cheeks and forehead and went down his youthful chin, a design with blood now mixed in. Already the fire ants swarmed his flesh, crawling over and surely under his clothing in their devouring work.

Nicke saw the man alive and stepped nearer. When he saw the face, he gasped. "He's the Kyrie who defended my mom."

A whisper came from the corpse's bone-colored lips, but it was carried away on the sough of the wind, vanishing like Shaye's song. Fire ants surrounded the soft flesh of the man's eyelids.

Locke leaned in closer. "Tell me again."

"Listen. The scroll… The key to the curse… Take it to the Seer… The Seer." He paused, squinting against a volley of pain as he suffered a living death. "He can save us… From the skies."

He must have meant the scroll from Nicke's story, the one so many people had been slaughtered for. "Where is it?" asked Locke. "Where do I find it?"

Another whisper, too faint to understand.

The man's sylfe was thinning, a breeze tapering into perfect stillness, horrifying stillness. I could barely sense him at all. He was about to slip into exile, about to be alone, infinitely.

Pity was written on Locke's face as death screamed beneath him. He wanted to rescue the man, but this fight was over. All that was left was to fulfill the dying words. *The last whisper of the Unstoppable Hundred.*

"Tell me where to find it," repeated Locke.

The warrior's lips barely moved; a breath escaped between them: "The captain."

Locke looked over the battlefield, wondering how he'd find one specific body among so many.

The warrior snatched a hold on Locke's ankle again. It sent fear through us both.

"Now release me... Suffering... I beg you."

12.

The Scroll

"THAT'S HIM," SAID Nicke, pointing to a corpse. These men had quelled a mutiny, killing many of their own, and then had drunk the poisoned water. But less blood made the scene no less gruesome.

"He was one of the last to survive my poison." Nicke's jaw stuck forward as he clenched his teeth. "He said he'd kill us all if we didn't give him the scroll."

The corpse gave off a rancid smell. He was threateningly large, with an equally large beard. A scar ran up his jaw and through his bottom lip, a path where the beard didn't grow. He wore a distinctive helm: A row of spikes ran down the center of the crown. Two plates curved forward along the jaw to cover the cheeks. Two horns came from the ears, curving outward then forward—but one of them was broken. *A menacing piece of metalwork.*

A tan parchment poked from beneath the breastplate, as if he'd tucked it there quickly in the middle of the fray. *He'd found it after all.* Locke leaned in and grabbed ahold.

A shock went through his fingers and hand, up his arm, and touched his heart. Jolted, he let go and stared. "It felt like…" he began.

"Magic?" I asked.

He frowned—not the word he would've chosen.

Suddenly we remembered the wicked old man from Nicke's tale. He wanted the scroll too. He said he'd be back for it—the scroll with the power to end the curse.

"Well if it's not magic, what's the holdup?" I asked.

"Nicke," said Locke, "try touching this."

With a frown, Nicke silently walked closer and reached a small finger toward the scroll. Then he jerked back.

"You felt it too, huh?"

Nicke nodded.

"Just grab it," I said.

Locke tapped the scroll a second time. Nothing happened. He tapped it some more, then pinched it with his fingers. Still nothing happened. "I could have sworn…" He tugged the scroll with a jerk, but it was pinched tightly beneath the armor, and the whole body rocked, shaking the corpse's head as if in warning. Locke pulled, and the head wobbled again: *a definite no*. The ants stole gently over the staring eyeballs.

"His nose seems too round and large," I said, "don't you think?"

Locke paused a moment for a better look. "Yeah, I guess so." He put his moccasin against the man's arm and tugged. The scroll came free. Locke brushed the fire ants off. It was a large piece of leather, bound tightly with a thick red string—one that looked surprisingly similar to Nicke's voice.

"It holds the key to the curse," I whispered, repeating the words of the dying man.

As Locke began to untie the string, he was interrupted—

"KHEEAAAA!"—a savage scream, directly at his side.

Nicke rammed a spear into the corpse's eye with a pounding thud.

Locke dropped the scroll and fell back, eyes wide.

Nicke's hands squeezed the weapon as he stood, panting, teeth locked together, as if he'd planted a tree through sheer strength. When Locke moved, Nicke glared with great ferocity, breathing heavily, ready to fight. He leaned on the spear, pressing it in a futile fight.

Locke's surprise and disgust melted into frail pity. He didn't know what to do or what to say. Nothing would bring Nicke's family back. Nothing. He took Nicke gently by the arm and shoulder. "You already killed him."

Nicke let go, and Locke led him away. The spear tilted, torquing the corpse's head to the side and clattering on the ground.

"We have to help Nicke," I whispered, surprised by my own overwhelming concern. Maybe my Locke was rubbing off on me.

He nodded. With an arm still around Nicke, he spoke to me directly in the softest whisper: "I already swore to help, but what can I do? I don't think anything but a miracle can treat this wound."

He hadn't said he believed the demigods could help. Or even that he believed they existed.

He'd simply acknowledged it would take that kind of power.

13.

Howl

I WISH WE COULD see the stars," said Nicke.

Locke looked surprised to hear such an exact echo of his own sentiment. "Me too."

We headed south across the Astral Fields where the sparse trees made the sky visible and wide, but we couldn't see a single shimmer. We did see dead squirrels painted across the ground, their bodies left to rot. Other animals hadn't touched them, maybe because stealing an ondine made the blood impure.

Locke pictured his father's anger when we arrived home. He wouldn't be happy that we'd left without telling him. Or that we'd brought home a Tenarie. At least we'd be physically safe at the cove. Someone could deliver the scroll to the Seer. He'd break the skies. The wraiths would be driven back, death would be put off a little longer, and Nicke could see the stars again.

Locke took off the red string and unrolled the scroll. Scripture or some elegant message was scrawled on the inside.

"What does it say?" asked Nicke.

"I don't know," said Locke. "It's not written in Kyriglae."

Wolves howled in the distance.

An unnatural presence chased after the wind, gnawing at the edges and chipping off splinters. Something not accompanied by an elemental. An unholy presence like I'd felt that night. Maybe it was the spirit of Saede himself. Or maybe one of his minions. I kept thinking about the man from Nicke's story, the one who said he'd be back for the scroll. I imagined his wispy white Tenarie hair and his cruel laughter.

"We need to move faster," I said.

Nicke looked at me.

Most elves didn't even notice me. Out of those who did, few could actually hear me. But Nicke watched me closely every time I spoke. So I moved to Locke's ear before I whispered, "Do you think the cursed skies could be a Tenarie plot?"

Nicke looked up at Locke like an eager younger brother. A sad younger brother. I didn't think he'd heard me, but he still seemed to be waiting for Locke's answer. Maybe he kept trying to hear me in order to fill some gap left by his own sylfe's silence.

Locke shook his head at me. "The Hundred split their loyalties at least two ways." He answered me aloud, right in front of Nicke, without even a hint of embarrassment. "The Tenarie warriors weren't friendly to Nicke's village. Then there was Nicke's evil man, who seemed to have his own agenda. That's five distinct groups."

"I wasn't accusing Nicke," I said. After what had happened, Nicke was a hero just for marching on. My suspicions were aimed at the other Tenarie—his cousins and relatives.

"I know," said Locke. "I'm just saying it's not us versus them. It's more complicated. More shades to these shadows."

Fine.

Then he turned to Nicke, as if to oblige my theory: "Do you know why your people had so much water stored?"

"The Chief told us to. He said there would be a time when we'd survive off what we'd stored."

"So he knew the curse was coming?"

"A lot of people thought he was crazy."

"How did he know?"

"I don't know."

"Maybe he believed the same prophecies as your father, Locke," I whispered. "Maybe this *is* the end of time."

Nicke paid close attention to me but still said nothing.

"It's not the end of time," said Locke, again aloud. "Not if this scroll has anything to do with it."

After that the boys walked in silence. Occasionally their eyes drifted toward lighter subjects, like tree bark and the way dust floated when they walked through powder.

Nicke said he didn't want to see the monster at the Majestic Sea, but as we passed from a distance he still gawked. Most of the people had abandoned the shoreline, surely searching for water. The loneliness was hauntingly peaceful. That night Nicke seemed more comfortable high in a tree, and he slept like a gripple monkey.

On the morning of the fourth day, black as storm, Locke announced, "We should reach home by nightfall."

Our food from Twiche was gone, so we foraged out of need instead of convenience. Locke hit a scavenger hen with his sling. He was good with it—he'd even hit a robin in flight once, which I had mixed feelings about.

As we hiked homeward, I tried to convince Locke to talk with Shaye, but he wouldn't. Instead he played his pinkalue, which helped us all feel better. It made a sound like the color of shiny copper, and the melody shifted directions and twirled, like a coin sinking down through water in a graceful dance.

As night fell, our morsel of peace was interrupted.

That feeling of foreboding I'd felt, the feeling that something was at our heels—it finally caught up to us.

"Do you hear that?" I asked.

The boys stopped.

"No—don't stop," I said.

"Shhh," said Locke.

"Keep moving."

"SHHH!"

As we stood, the air became so still that even breathing seemed loud. The boys held their breath. Then we heard it:

Howling.

A similar howling to what we'd been hearing the last few days. But only similar. This howl seemed higher in pitch and rougher—a bit more like death.

Locke began walking again, now in long, rapid strides.

I didn't want my words to make it more real, but if I said nothing, they might be caught unawares. So I whispered my suspicion in Locke's ear: "Do you think that sounded like a banshe wolfe?"

He shook his head in silent reply, while picking up his pace. He stole a glance at Nicke jogging next to him, only to find that Nicke was again watching us carefully. The howling sounded closer now.

"What did he say?" asked Nicke.

"He..." Locke hesitated, but he never was much of a liar. "He said that might have been a banshe wolfe."

"It was," said Nicke.

The words *banshe wolfe* echoed in the silence of memory over and over and over, with each footstep and grind of leather against dirt. Locke moved into a run, matching the hurry of the echo.

"You smell that?" asked Nicke, speeding up.

"No," said Locke.

But I could. It was strong, repulsive, the sort of odor that rips with claws.

"That's the smell of death." Nicke spoke rapidly, as if that might speed our escape, puffing between phrases. "Banshe wolves are the opposite… of the valkalysae… Saede sends them to carry souls… down to his Necris… The Witchdoctor told me that."

"I've heard the same." The twins had told us many such stories. "But don't you think it's a myth?"

Nicke shook his head as if he had some personal knowledge that proved it was definitely not myth. His dark eyes, pale skin, and white hair seemed like a costume meant to scare. "They say that once a banshe wolfe… is on your trail… either you or it must die." He gasped in a deep breath. "It won't quit… And there's no other ending."

Locke didn't like it, the howling or Nicke's countenance. "You think it's after us?"

"Maybe… Or after that scroll."

Locke patted his chest where the leather was tucked underneath, and he remembered that strange shock he'd gotten when he first picked it up.

"You can't outrun… a banshe wolfe," puffed Nicke. "You can stall… but we'd need a river… to hide our trail."

"We're not far from the cove."

The boys, gasping, ran even harder.

"And it's not one," said Nicke, panting. "At least two wolves… were howling just now."

14.

Banshe

Tʜᴇ ʙᴏʏs ʀᴀɴ through the land of eternal night.

They crossed the bridge at the head of the First River and ran across the dry ground at Twiche's ferry on the Fifth River.

Locke paused, waiting for Nicke to catch up. They walked for a bit to regain their breath. The howls floated across the threatening darkness, haunting the earth in all directions. They rose in pitch, turning more phantom the nearer they got.

The next screech materialized at our heels, a chilling wail.

"They're close," gasped Nicke.

"We're almost there," said Locke, panting the same air the wolves screamed into. He reached in his backpack and pulled out his sling. He also took up several rocks that would be easy enough to hurl but large enough to do damage. "We *have* to keep running. Come on."

And run they did.

Here the trunks were large, and the branches hung dangerously high— dark claws reaching skyward in a tangled mess overhead. We were stranded below them, down on the earth.

"Maybe we should have stopped at Twiche's," I said.

"Too late for that." Locke tried to catch his breath. "Besides, we'd have brought the wolves down on him."

"Very noble."

"Foolish maybe," he grunted.

"Maybe you should drop the scroll," I said. "Let them have it."

"No."

"Why not?"

"You think Martigane would have dropped the scroll,"—*gasp*—"at the first sign of trouble?"

"No," I said. "But Martigane was willing to die."

"If I thought we were going to die," breathed Locke, "I'd drop it… But we're nearly there."

We pictured our refuge: High walls of gray cliffs surrounded our home, a cove built by nature. Even if attackers scaled them, they'd struggle getting back down and to the base of our tree, which could then only be accessed by a rope ladder.

We were so close.

"Besides, what if it's after *us* and not the scroll?" Locke glided along on the balls of his feet. "I'd feel pretty foolish… if they still attacked even after we'd left… our treasure behind."

A good point, but I didn't reply—because of the smell. The pungent, scraping odor had lingered since we first identified it. The smell of death, stronger than ever, sweeping down on us like a heavy fog.

I could keep up while looking behind, so I was the first one to see them. But even with the smell as a warning, I wasn't prepared.

When I saw them, Locke sensed my fear, and his heart leaped. The boys turned to look, even though it slowed them down. Before that moment, the wolves had simply been a terrible cry, leaving our imaginations to run wild, which usually created terror further and deeper than reality. But this time, reality simply expanded to match what our fears had already shown.

Our pursuers stood on the ridge of the hill behind us, framed by blathae trunks on either side. These animals weren't the size of dogs or wolves. They were the size of hyuman horses. A rock from Locke's sling would hardly faze them. Their forearms swelled, like pillars supporting the ridges of their spines, peaked like walking mountains. And their eyes—they were not blue or yellow like any dog's. No, these eyes were centered by colorless, lifeless holes that darted this way and that, tracking their prey, too black and too gaping.

The bloodless. Banshe wolves. And we were their prey.

For a moment, they stared, as if to freeze us into fearful stones. The smell made our mind swim, *hard to think clearly.* Their lips pulled back in snarls, exposing pink gums, eager tongues, and pointed white teeth.

The beasts lunged down the path after us, with their bushy tails pointed behind.

Locke dropped his rocks and ran harder than before, with Nicke at his

heels. Their exhausted movements were sloppy, and the lack of air burned
at Locke's lungs.

Nicke's sylfe buzzed around him in a sporadic pattern, up and forward,
back and right, wrong side and down, covering extra distance as he followed,
not helping a bit. Nicke himself looked only slightly less panicked—he *was*
deathly scared of these monsters.

"Locke, they're at the Moore Spring," I said.

"We're almost there," he replied. We could see the path wrapping around
toward the west entrance.

"We won't make it," I said. "Take the tunnel."

Locke couldn't spare a nod, but I sensed his agreement.

On the north side of the cove, beaver demons had dug a tunnel through
a crack in the stone walls. After smoking the creatures out, the twins had
widened the hole and then concealed the entrance. We hadn't played in it
for years, but it would give us quicker access to the cove while keeping the
monsters outside. *If we could just reach it in time.*

"Don't slow down, Nicke." Locke ran ahead of him, veering off the trail.
"Just a little more. See the hollow log?"

The paws pounded against the earth, vibrating into trees. Nicke didn't
speak. And the boys ran on, with nothing but will and fear to push them.
We closed the final distance in several long, slipping moments.

Locke reached the log first, and ushered Nicke to get in—but Nicke
hadn't reached it yet.

"No, no, no! *You* first," shouted Nicke, waving for Locke to crawl inside.

The closer wolfe crashed in a beeline toward us, too fast for a creature
of such bulk.

Locke dropped to his knees and scrambled into the darkness. He felt
cobwebs on his face and shivered, trying not to imagine a wraith hiding
ahead. I hated cramped spaces, but I followed. Locke charged blindly,
hurrying forward to make more room. He peeked under his arm and saw
Nicke climbing in. Behind him, outside the log, we saw only grass in the
dim light. We'd made it, all of us—the cramped space was our salvation!

Nicke screamed.

A scream of blood and murder. A sound that cut through a sylfe like claws,
echoing in the night. One moment we crawled safely inside, breathing.
Then Nicke began vanishing backward with a shriek.

A single paw had reached in the opening, scraping, and catching the flesh of Nicke's calf. The pain dropped him to his belly and ripped out the scream. Then he was dragged backward. He scraped at the sides of the log, still screaming, eyes wide open.

Locke grabbed Nicke's hand and pulled.

The claw ripped through muscle, then came free, leaving barely a heartbeat before it would smash down again with a second, deeper grip. In that heartbeat, Locke tugged with all he could muster. The claw's second swipe caught only the sole of Nicke's mocassin. Locke pulled again, dragging Nicke to safety.

The wolfe arm scraped at the insides of the log. Then the snout entered, sniffing and growling.

As Nicke scooted further into safety, he whimpered first and then wailed. His pant leg was now bloody strips of cloth. He touched the hot wound with both hands and wailed more.

"Come on," said Locke. "We have to keep going. We have to get in the tree before they get in the cove or we'll be trapped in here. Come on!" Locke coaxed him along, till they climbed out the far side of the log into the open air. He grabbed Nicke around the ribs, and Nicke put an arm up around Locke's neck. They limped forward, with blood leaking a silent trail behind us. The tall rope ladder hung thirty paces ahead, in front of that green door we hated to look at.

"Dad!" shouted Locke, looking toward the heights of the blathae tree. "Dad!"

We heard a sound at the east entrance of the cove, a scraping.

The east gate could be bolted from inside, making it a formidable barrier, but it had been left unlocked for a wayward son who'd been gone for days without telling his father where he went. Unbolted, the gate could be opened by simply pulling down the handle.

As the boys neared the long ladder, Locke said to Nicke, "You first this time."

In that horrid stillness, we heard the click of a latch, and the east gate creaked as it swung open. Behind it stood the other wolfe, with a dark silver patch running down its nose, calmly taking in the surroundings. And I could smell its wicked breath.

"Go, Nicke!" shouted Locke. "Dad!"

Nicke scrambled, gripping the rope with bloody hands then pulling to lift his good foot to the next rung.

The other wolfe—the more lunatic of the two—scrambled past the one at the gate, charging with blind speed, looming. Its huge form filled the space like a nightmare.

"Hurry!" I shouted.

As warm red dripped down, Locke climbed at Nicke's heels.

The wolves' shrieks cut through time itself: Nicke was about ten rungs up the ladder, his sylfe was ascending along in a corkscrew spiral, Locke was stepping onto the second rung, and I was zooming up the ladder to watch from overhead, while the wolves bounded up the path. A pair of eyes peeped over the edge of the landing above, and then a spear was raised. Relief swept through me.

Locke's father hurled the spear straight down the ladder.

As the weapon leapt from his fingertips, I realized the horrible mistake: He'd seen a Tenarie boy climbing the steps, backed by the power of banshe wolves, and he'd stepped up to defend his home.

The howls tore the night in two, freezing us in that moment.

The spear was flying, Nicke was looking up, and Locke's head was turned back toward the monsters. With speed only Numa could have given him, Nicke shoved off the ladder with all but one hand. The spear missed his flesh by barely a finger's breadth. His weight jerked down, and he struggled to hold on.

Locke was not so lucky.

He looked up as the spear pulled downward. He tried to throw himself back off the ladder as Nicke had done, but time was too thin. The point hammered him square in the chest, breaking mail links, and he fell back off the ladder, smashing into the anvil ground.

I gasped in darkness as I tried to keep hold on the spinning world.

Locke's father peered down from above.

"Locke!" screamed Nicke.

The wolfe paws pounded forward.

Blood dripped from Nicke's foot.

I breathed.

And Locke rolled over.

As his father and Nicke stared down with wide eyes, Locke heaved himself to one knee.

We struggled together for breath as he scrambled to the long ladder and began to ascend a second time, slower now. The world twisted sideways. His hands fumbled to grip the rungs, red with Nicke's blood.

"He's good," mumbled Locke, but I wasn't sure his father heard, much less understood.

An arrow whispered into the night from the porch above, landing deep in the flesh of the foremost wolfe. But the creature only reacted by dropping a snaking foam from its mouth and rushing on. Locke was about halfway up when the beast leaped, slamming into the ladder and then crashing into the bottom of the tree. Splinters of the green door went flying. The platform shook, and leaves floated quietly down.

Locke gripped tight against the reverberations.

Nicke climbed up and out of the way.

Locke's father launched a second arrow, but fearing to hit his son, he aimed wide of the wolfe's back, and the tip stuck deep in the dirt.

The wolfe now clung to the ladder. Its back paws were not fitted to stand on the narrow surface of the rope, but the massive creature had bent its forepaws over the rungs and was powering its way upward.

Locke raced ahead, as the ladder jerked with each of the beast's movements. Soon Locke gripped his father's wrist, then collapsed in exhaustion onto the solid platform high in the tree.

Without a moment's hesitation, Locke's father jerked a knife from his belt and sawed at one side of the ladder. When the fibers finally snapped, the wolfe's arms dropped to one side, and it struggled just to hang on, swinging back and forth.

Locke stood, and, tapping his father's shoulder, softly said, "Let me."

His father moved out of the way. Locke drew his blade of the Hundred, grabbed the railing, and scooped the long sword in a downward arc, slicing through the second rope. The ladder hit the ground in a tapping crescendo. The wolfe's four paws pounded down almost simultaneously.

The creature bent its back, lifted its head toward the sky, and let out an angry wail that brought down more leaves. The wolves had no ondines—no elementals of any sort. I sensed the absence. Yet these creatures were still living, and that paradox haunted me more than the fields of dead we'd seen up north. Their ghastly scent pushed into us.

The second wolfe joined in the howl, and the elves clamped their hands over their ears—as if death itself were demanding their souls.

Then the monsters vanished into the night.

15.

Questions

NICKE'S BLOOD POOLED on the deck, and his pale skin grew a shade whiter.

"Where the hell have you been?" said Locke's father.

"We need to help him!" Locke pulled off his belt and put it around Nicke's upper leg to slow the bleeding. Three of the metal links had broken in Locke's mail—the spear should have pierced his heart. As he struggled to pull the mail and his shirt off, the scroll fell into Nicke's blood. "I'm sorry. He needs a healer." Locke pressed the white garment into the wounded calf.

His father scowled, and the lack of an apology hung in the air. But I also noticed awe as he looked on his wayward son. "We can't go for a healer with those things on the loose."

"Can *you* help him?" Locke pulled the scroll out of the blood.

His father sighed. "Yes, I can." He soon returned with medical supplies, throwing them on the planks of the balcony. "Drink this." He handed Nicke a numbing potion then began to clean and dress the wound.

His sylfe glared at me, but I tried to ignore him. The funny thing about that sylfe was that I didn't even know his name, even after so many years. I knew the names of all Locke's siblings' sylves. Even Koore's—it was Bowge. And they were more than a decade older than us. But this one, he was mean. Never talked to anyone. Not even to Locke's father, as far as I could tell. He just followed along miserably. Which is what Nicke's sylfe had started doing too, ever since the poison.

Nicke whimpered at a rough movement, but he got no apology nor even a sympathetic glance. He lay on his back, eyes closed, gritting his teeth and panting while Locke's father worked. "I'm glad…" began Nicke, but he didn't finish, his mind surely muddled by the potion. Maybe he meant he was glad Locke survived a spear to the chest.

"Why is he here?"

When Locke's father said this, Nicke opened his eyes to look at the man helping him.

I didn't like the question. Or its tone. No, the ancient grudge never bothered me so much as this moment when it flung its elbows at our friend.

"His name is Nicke," said Locke. "And he's the one who got us this scroll."

"He's also the one who defeated the Unstoppable Hundred," I said aloud.

Locke nodded, and Nicke looked at me. But Locke's father made no acknowledgement. "And what is it?"

"I don't know exactly. One of the Hundred told me to take it to the Seer. He said it could help break the curse on the skies."

His father's face showed surprise. "Why didn't the warrior bring it himself? Or send it with one of his comrades?"

"The Hundred are dead," said Locke.

"That's impossible."

"I wouldn't have believed the Majestic Sea had dried up either, but I've seen it."

His father didn't respond. Surely by now he'd heard the rumors.

"And the Hundred are dead," said Locke. "Every last one."

"But they're supposed to..." He shook his head with a distant stare. "How?"

"They fought amongst themselves, killed each other off." Locke gave Nicke a knowing glance, and Nicke seemed to approve of not being included in the story. "They're supposed to be *what?*"

"A Tenarie tried to secretly deliver a threat to the King and the members of the council. The Hundred captured him and marched north. They haven't told us what's really going on, but... This is it, the Night of the Wolf. They said I was crazy." I caught wonder in his eyes again—at the marvel of it all. I could feel it myself. These weren't the good old days. We were living in legend, a time when misery made way for heroes. He snapped out of his blank stare and looked in wonder at his youngest son. "So why did you go north? You've been gone for days. I thought you might have been kidnapped or killed."

Locke sighed. "I'm sorry I didn't tell you. It was irresponsible."

"But why'd you leave?"

"We saw the Hundred passing..." As he related the details of our journey, he kept looking at the scroll, at the fragments of the green door around the roots below, and at the gate where the wolves had disappeared. When he got to the part about a Tenarie boy, Nicke opened his eyes timidly.

"Does he talk?" asked Locke's father.

"Only when he needs to."

When Locke finished the story, his father remained in silent wonder. If a punishment was deserved, it seemed to be forgiven in that quiet moment.

Locke moved on to the more driving question.

He set a lamp on the deck and laid out what he'd thought was a leather scroll. The spear had pierced the mail, hit the scroll, and knocked him off the ladder. Yet we saw no hole and no damage in the scroll, not even a small mark. Just the strange characters etched across it in a dark, blood-like ink. Locke rubbed his bare chest; the pain was there—I could feel it, like his heart had been bruised. So why hadn't the spear pierced the scroll? Drawing his sword, Locke pressed the point into the scroll. A divot formed, but it left no damage. Next he stood and jabbed with more force. It clunked hard against the wood beneath but left no mark in the scroll.

"What *is* this thing?" wondered Locke aloud.

"The Tenarie messenger may have led the Hundred to it," said his father. "It's strange they said to take it to the Seer."

"Why?"

"The *King* oversees the Hundred. Whatever they captured would have been returned to him."

Locke's father often ranted about the King, how he was bringing our society to its destruction, rants so strong we doubted they could be true. We'd also heard the Seer speak once, and he seemed honorable, even though he shared views with Locke's father. We didn't know who to prefer, but we knew who to trust.

"The one who told us about the scroll—he died defending Nicke's family. And he was Kyrie. I think we should do what he said."

"Yes. I'm sure he was right," said his father. "But there's no sense in getting involved in their conflict. We can survive in the cove for a long time."

"With this we can fix things," said Locke. "We won't have to survive."

His father stared over the unsaid words—*It can't be fixed*—willing to let his son keep a happy delusion. "If you take it to the Seer, you'll be outside the King's law," said his father. "That makes it dangerous but not wrong."

Locke wished his father would just take the scroll. *Hadn't we been through enough?* His father didn't offer.

I sensed more than doubt—a higher reason for standing down. Maybe he thought Locke was as capable as any adult. Or maybe he hoped Locke could change the world's luck. Whatever the reason, I knew he didn't avoid the duty out of fear.

"You can trust the Seer," said his father. "Keep the scroll a secret till it's in his hands. I don't know why those wolves ran, but if they stay gone, you can attend the council at the Great Village tomorrow. You'll find the Seer there."

Once the bandages and conversation were finished, Locke and his father took Nicke between them and helped him upstairs.

"He can't stay with us," said Locke's father quietly, as if privately, but we all heard just fine. I searched for that spark of wonder in his eyes, but I saw only fear. "Soon there will be war, and if he's living with us, he'll be a target. He puts our lives and his own at risk."

"I'm bringing the scroll to the Seer. It'll break the curse."

His father shook his head.

"And he's in no condition—" began Locke.

I felt uncomfortable with Locke standing up to his father. The tension pushed me toward stillness, so I moved deliberately.

"He can't stay with us."

"If things do go bad, we'll sneak him out before the fighting starts."

Then I saw it—he *was* looking at his son differently. And he relented, just a little: "Alright. Before war comes, he has to go—for his safety and for ours."

"Okay," said Locke.

His room looked the same as it had a few days ago, but it felt different, more distant, less familiar. Locke felt it too, though he never said so. He didn't have to. I saw it in his eyes the moment we entered. He glanced at the walls. "No bugs?"

"They've moved toward the roots," said his father, "closer to the gnymes."

He left without a *goodnight* or a *welcome home.* Nicke raised his eyebrows in surprise, but Locke was used to his father's aloofness; it'd been that way for several years.

Locke put Nicke in his own bed and got him a crutch that Tunke had made for Lanse. He also sneaked downstairs and brought Nicke another potion for the pain. Then Locke crawled into the hammock hanging outside his bedroom on the balcony.

The night fell quiet aside from the occasional whir of a cricket, till Nicke spoke into the darkness: "Thanks for saving me."

"Saving *you?*" said Locke. "It would have been me if you hadn't insisted. *I* owe *you.*"

"No you don't." His tone implied he still owed some great debt.

Locke fell to thinking of the horrors we'd seen—the frantic running and Nicke being scraped from inside the tunnel. "And the wolves just left on their own for some reason."

Nicke said nothing.

"I thought they weren't supposed to quit. *As relentless as a banshe*—that's what people say."

"I don't know," said Nicke. "A miracle. Or they're waiting for us."

Quiet fell again on Locke's drifting thoughts. It felt good to be sleeping in our own home, peace amid so much strife. He rubbed his bruised chest.

"You're going to the council?" asked Nicke.

"Yes. If I can get in." He just had to get the scroll to the Seer, and everything would be fine. *Nicke* would be fine. Or not fine, but at least he'd have a home. "I wish I could take you…" Locke tossed these words into the darkness, hoping to show sympathy.

More silence.

Locke thought of Shaye. I looked for the eagerness he'd felt—the confidence among corpses—but it had faded. She wasn't the same as the Nymfe. No one was. And the decision to marry was so far reaching. What if they got married but he didn't love her enough? What if they were too young and foolish? These thoughts scared him, scared him into stillness.

"When are you leaving?" asked Nicke, in the quiet darkness.

"At first light," said Locke.

"You mean in the morning," I said. "There is no more light."

16.

The King's Stade

HE DIDN'T DO it on purpose, but Locke was holding his breath. I hated when he did that.

Children weren't allowed in the village council. Anyone suspecting his age could ask to see the marriage tattoo on the palm of his hand. When they didn't find one, we'd get thrown out, probably roughly as an example to other delinquents.

"Relax," I said. "Breathe."

He pressed his wrong hand against his heart, as if to hide the palm. Air filled his lungs, and the music of his breathing began again, ringing as it swept in, echoing as it flowed out.

"You're old enough," I said. "Calm down and no one will ask."

"I don't feel like an adult," he whispered. "Makes it hard to act like one." He'd entered the passage years, making him eligible to marry, but by law he was still a boy until he did. Or until seven more years had passed. He inhaled then sighed.

"Well you're too young." *And so was Tryse.* "Elves never married this young in the histories."

So far no one had questioned whether he was married—except one girl who gave him a flirtatious smile. We'd made it through the doors of the King's Stade, where a gatekeeper stood on either side. Inside he faced a greater risk of being recognized, so he avoided eye contact with the mob.

The King's Stade rested on the ground, another mark in his controversial legacy. "The Kyrie belong in the air," Locke's father had said. "On the ground, the people worship the demigods of hypocrisy." Though as far as we knew, they still worshipped the same four demigods as everyone else. The building strayed far from Kyrie traditions—a circular room, so massive that rumors said the architects must have been Tenarie. The stage was low, near the center. The audience sat in large circular rows all around, filling all but one slice cut out for the King and other leaders.

Inside the dark room, a volume of sound exploded continuously into the air. People shouted, looking for seats, arguing over seats, or sitting in and defending seats. Their sylves carried an equal temperament, stirring up the air enough for Locke to feel it against his lips and cheeks. But most of the elves ignored their sylves. I hated that. And if they wouldn't acknowledge their own sylves, they most certainly wouldn't notice me.

"You're a fool!" shouted a fat elfe to his companions as they walked toward us. "Sylves are a figment of your mind!"

I couldn't believe it. I zoomed to his fat ear and blew as hard as I could. I didn't care if it was extremely rude. The pig deserved it—*he made me so mad*. I wished I could bite his nose. But his only reaction was to stick a finger in his ear and twirl it around. He probably never noticed the wind on the grass either.

Locke ducked and then frowned, not wanting them to notice him. *Sometimes we were so opposite.* He weaved into a thicker mob, vanishing like a wave in the sea of people. He continued to scan faces, threatened by each new pair of eyes. He kept his wrong hand pressed to his side. Anxiety stilled his breath as he watched for anyone who might know him, people from the Fifth River in particular.

But I sensed something more. "Are you looking for the Angel?"

Locke silently shook his head. Of course he wasn't. Shaye wasn't married, so she wasn't an adult yet either. It was Tryse, the Nymfe, adding to his angst. The girl who haunted his waking dreams. I sensed a strange mixture of both desire and dread at the thought that she might appear somewhere amongst the crowd.

"Locke, she's in the past," I said. "Let her go."

A red-faced man shouted, interrupting my comfort. His eyes bulged as spit flew from his mouth: "The cisterns! We have cisterns! Which makes us targets. The other Kyrie governors might attack us. The Tenarie will for sure." I tried to ignore the man. He was right, but he was also disgusting.

We heard another group arguing about the delay of springflood planting, and how there would be no harvest and our people would starve.

"None of that matters," said an old woman. "The wraiths are coming. This is the end of time—the prophecy was true."

"We're doomed," came the reply, and no one refuted it.

As Locke searched for the Nymfe, I found our real reason for being here: "There's the Seer," I said, "third row." I pointed by zipping from Locke's eyes toward the stage. The Seer, with bald head and white beard, exuded a mysterious tranquility, which we saw on his face and in the countenance of his sylfe. Locke placed his hand on the scroll tucked in his shirt—an older dirtier shirt he'd put on after soaking his first one in blood. "But I doubt we could approach the stage right now. Even if we could, so many people would see us."

Locke nodded, ready to wait it out. We searched for a seat.

Wooden pillars stood in two circles evenly spaced throughout the room, holding the roof aloft and blocking the view of some onlookers. Unfortunately, those seats seemed like our best chance. Locke made his way toward one and sat down. Above us a brazier fastened to the pillar illuminated the room. Its fire danced back and forth. It was odd to have torches at a midday meeting, but with the darkness outside, even large windows provided little light.

"Locke," I whispered, "do you notice something, I don't know, sinister about that torch?"

"Like what?" he said quietly, barely moving his lips.

It had a yellow glow like any ordinary torch, *and yet…* "I don't know. As if it twists the natural light?" *Almost like it had a salaminde in it.* But that was impossible: Only elves were in this room, so who would the salaminde belong to? I glanced around, expecting other sylves to tell their elves about the strange flame, but none seemed to notice.

Locke put a hand over his mouth to mask his speaking—so no one would think him rude or crazy. "I'm not sure I see anything strange."

His attention wandered back to his mortal plane as quickly as it had come to mine. Sometimes he could be as flighty as me. Especially when girls were around. He found Shaye's father next to a column on the opposite side of the room. But no Shaye.

"So are you sad or relieved the Angel isn't here?"

He pretended to be absent-mindedly rubbing his cheek. "I don't know. Both. Why do you keep asking me about her?" The preoccupied strangers all around us didn't take notice of his speaking.

"For some reason I think it'll help you make up your mind."

"It *isn't* helping."

"I know."

The noise of the crowd increased, almost too loud to breathe. As I was about to panic, the King slammed his scepter into the stone floor, making a cracking sound that tapped against Locke's spine and knocked the clamor to pieces.

Right then I saw the Nymfe, sitting with her new husband.

I looked away, hoping Locke wouldn't sense what I'd seen. But he did, and he couldn't help but look. Then he didn't look away, even though he wanted to. Something about her pulled at him, radiating from her golden hair into his bruised heart.

"Locke," I said, hoping to pull him out of the trance.

He spoke in a low tone, hand over his mouth, his thumb pressing into his cheek almost as if he were speaking into the consonance. "She wasn't perfect, but she was close." Finally, with a sigh, he pulled his eyes away, toward the many moccasins on the floor. He wanted, and the longing for that indescribable something gnawed at him.

"Locke..." I began. But I wouldn't breathe lies to comfort him, so I said no more.

"No one compares with the Nymfe. Not even the Angel."

"You haven't gotten to know the Angel since she came back. Maybe she does."

He nodded, more as a show of defeat than agreement.

Luckily the King's address was just beginning, and all eyes turned toward the stage.

Even Locke's, though reluctantly.

17.

Council

"R EAD THE LETTER!"

Some adult shouted this across the quiet chamber.

The King breathed in a smile.

"My people of water," he said, ignoring the demand. When he called us that, the crowd stirred, probably because of its current irony. His sylfe floated regally above his right shoulder, with the same confidence and calm.

"I am grateful for your respect and for your silence as we proceed with matters at this most important gathering." We'd never been old enough to hear the King speak, so what we knew came from the complaints of Locke's father. But hearing the King in person… Words flowed from his tongue like a silver fountain, touching our ears like a song. No wonder people supported him so ferociously. But as he spoke soothing words without substance, I held on to my skepticism, hoping he might turn out to be the hero some said he was.

Eventually he called leaders by name, having each stand and report.

The Council Chief was first: "When this started, we assumed the waters had only vanished temporarily. But it has been five days, and dark clouds never hold back for so long." He continued to paint an elaborate picture of the horror the people already saw clearly enough, prodding their bandaged wound. His focus was on the drought and the planting season. "I suggest we head south in search of water, above the Rim to the Southward Lands, to the Wilderlands Beyond, and even to the hyuman cities if we must."

The crowd's murmur grew in volume, till a voice shouted, "We don't know whether they have any more water than we do!"

"Find the cause!" someone screamed. The sound boiled on until the King tapped his scepter into the stone again.

Next the Contriver stood, with a beard that looked like it had been tousled for comic effect. His main concern was the wraiths and the need to bring back the sun. *Ours too.* After a brief introductory statement, he said, "We're building a catapult to break the sky. With the right ballistics, I think we could actually send an arrow through." His idea was met with more murmuring and some laughter.

It did seem harebrained. "How *big* of an arrow does he think he can get up there?" I asked.

"It won't matter," said Locke lowly. He touched his chest and nodded toward the stage, where the Seer sat quietly behind many other leaders, unruffled by the cantankerous crowd.

Another cry went out: "Admit the letter!"

Next the Lord Physician stood: "We should form a mighty exodus back to the Sea of Time."

The crowd responded negatively again, and one ruffian shouted, "You can't drink seawater!" Interestingly, the Lord Physician didn't wait for the noise to die down so he could finish explaining. Instead he took his seat and frowned.

I guessed he was actually suggesting we make boats and sail back to the homeland. "If the twins were here," I said, "they'd cheer for that one."

But I shouldn't have mentioned it. The thought of them made the longing tug at Locke's insides. He looked toward Tryse, and with a sigh, slid his fingertips up his forehead and into his hair.

"The cisterns won't last forever!" someone yelled.

"The Tenarie will attack them if they do!"

"Or fifthers!" came a third yell.

At that a fight broke out, for which I was glad—glad someone was defending us fifthers. The crowd swelled, and a ring formed around the sore till it beat itself out. After a moment, the wounded mob healed back over, an even mass of desperate faces.

"Locke, I'm glad you're not an adult," I said. He shrugged.

The Chief Captain stood. "I now humbly ask the King"—and as he said the word *humbly* the crowd balked aloud—"for permission to form an exploratory force to go northward toward the Tenarie lands in search of the villain."

The crowd roared with heavy support mixed with murmuring fears. Locke felt a sudden urge to defend Nicke right there on the spot.

"They're responsible!" shouted one voice.

"…and die like the Hundred?" came another.

"It is true the Hundred have been defeated," said the Chief Captain. "But we will send larger forces in a wider swath. I am confident we will succeed."

The crowd erupted. Phrases like, "Killed the Hundred," and, "Not true," burst to the top, while fear clawed down anything positive that tried to surface.

"I wonder if all council meetings are like this," said Locke.

"I hope not."

Shouts of *"the letter!"* rose through the bustle.

The High Sheriff stood, and the crowd grew silent, even shushing each other. It was certainly a unique reaction. His words pushed mightily, rolling forward under a heavy burden: "I received this letter a few days ago, as have several others, but we refrained from sharing it publicly. As for myself, I held back for fear of your response. We must not bow to the villain's demands."

"Read it!"

"Know that I am, as always, one of the King's most ardent supporters. I do not read this to spite him. I read it to help us destroy the true villain." When he said that last bit, a greater hush fell on the crowd as they waited to hear how this mysterious letter might indict the King.

The High Sheriff began to read:

This letter I write to King Amaliyae.

Your reign has come to an end, and your debts must now be settled.

I have bound up the waters, and with that power I hold your kingdom hostage. Without the blood of Nara or the light of Phose, your Land of Many Waters will become a wasteland. The wrath of Saede looms sooner still. Your kingdom will be overrun and your people of water will die.

Though your personal betrayals be most odious, you share a debt with all your Kyrie people. The debt must be repaid to the Tenarie for generations of mistreatments and injustices. Submit yourself and your kingdom to me, and by the lives of the demigods, I will cause the curse to dispel. Your people will be spared under the reign of a more just ruler.

As a token of your obeisance, have your corpse presented on the Altar of Nara at the north shore of the Majestic Sea. Then justice will have been served, and you and I will finally have our accounts balanced again.

Since I foresee you will be unwilling to pay for your kingdom's life, I have a further message for your subjects and councilors: Send the King's head and all ten of his worthless fingers to the Altar of Nara as a token of your submission to me, and you will be spared.

Fail to do this, and the darkness will quench your lives one moment at a time.

Now I close this letter. I am Stane, the Innocent of the Parathydume and a descendant of Tenarke.

18.

The Goddess

THE CROWD DID not explode.

Instead cold silence fell across the room. The lamps winked, flickering on faces.

When the High Sheriff read the words "I am Stane," an image of an old man flashed across our mind, the same one we'd imagined when Nicke retold his nightmare. Was this the coward who'd hid in the whispering thorns?

The silence didn't last. Like soup coming to a boil, first one bubble popped, followed by more silence. Then came another, and another, till the whole surface was wild. Amid the tumult, we heard someone shout, "the assassin from the Day of Redress!" We'd heard of the attempts on the King's life, but we weren't supposed to talk about it around adults.

I was glad Nicke wasn't with us. The crowd probably would've lynched him on sight—just because he had pale skin and white hair. He'd be okay if we could just get the scroll to the Seer.

The King stood next to the High Sheriff, as dispassionate as ever, and slammed his scepter twice into the stone. Whether he was upset at the High Sheriff, I couldn't tell. But I thought I detected a crack in his sylfe's demeanor—all was not well. Yet magically, at the King's bidding a hush fell on the crowd once again. He bowed his head and held out a hand as if giving the right to speak back to the High Sheriff. Many nodded their approval at this selfless maneuver.

Then something distracted me. "Locke, look." I pointed.

A sylfe was bobbing amongst the crowd, greeting people. This might have been slightly normal if it had strayed one or two people from its elfe. But it went down an entire row and started on the next. In fact, it had gone so far I couldn't tell which elfe it belonged to.

"I want to repeat," said the High Sheriff, "I am not casting blame. This message identifies the enemy of this whole land, the enemy of every one of us."

The crowd whispered and seemed to be mostly agreeing, till a voice shouted, "The King is responsible!" and the crowd caught fire like a field of grain.

The High Sheriff raised his hand, palm down, as if he might pat them back to sleep. "Please, my fellows, please," he said, in a loud voice. "Let me finish." The roar subsided only just enough for him to be heard—he did not have the King's magic. "Before I sit down, I must inform you that the rations from all village cisterns will be cut in half, starting today. We do not know how long this catastrophe will go on, and we must prepare for the worst."

As he sat down, someone screamed, "We can end it right now!" A few others shouted back in the King's defense or in fear of being ruled by a Tenarie.

Just before this ignited into another fight, the King stood and soothed the crowd once again. "My people of water," he began, "as the High Sheriff said, the villain is our common enemy. We will find him and bring him to justice. We will have retribution. Solutions have been put forth and efforts are in motion."

As he spoke, his tone suggested the meeting was drawing to a close, but the Seer hadn't spoken. Locke's father had mentioned something about the Seer being silenced, but this was still a surprise. Before the reign of kings, the Seer had been both the spiritual and secular leader, back when everyone believed the same thing.

A glowing breath dropped down in front me like a sail unfurled—a bright female sylfe.

"Hi," she said, smiling.

I flew back in shock, then tried to regain my poise. It was the wandering sylfe. She smiled and curtsied, toward me first and then to Locke. Her hair floated beautifully in the air. Locke smiled back, and then she flew on, greeting those next to us, on down the row. Most elves ignored her though, but their sylves perked up.

I'd never seen a sylfe like that before. The other sylves in the room stayed next to their elves. Slumping over on a shoulder, or climbing long hair, or pacing on the crown of a bald head, or trying so hard to pay attention that their arms were folded and their shoulders were scrunched up to their necks. But they all stayed close. Except for her. She wandered. *So strange.* I wondered what distance she was willing to go and how she could breathe so far away from her elfe.

Locke looked around. "There must be a lunatic in the crowd."

"I don't think she's a lunatic," I said. Her sylfe had shown too much, hmm—*deliberateness?*

A quiet voice interrupted the King—

"Father?"

It was a female voice, too quiet to be heard over the murmuring crowd, and yet, miraculously, we still heard it—a sound so small and still. After just one word, I could see its hue, a voice like a candle flame, bright most of all, but with a smooth, quickly changing texture, always curving delicately. An orange voice, with a tinge of yellow, and sometimes nearly bright enough to be white. We'd heard of the King's daughters, maybe once or twice, but they were rarely discussed. His sons were the ones generally considered noteworthy.

The King heard the voice too and stopped mid-sentence. The crowd fell to a hush.

"My Lord?" the voice asked again.

"Yes?" said the King, turning toward the back of his stage. As he did, a young woman, about Locke's age, stepped up from the part of the stage that had been blocked by the pillars.

Locke gasped.

Her beauty drew *me* in too, like lungs pulling in atmosphere, and when I noticed this, I fought it, looking at everything that wasn't her. As I did, I noticed Locke, transfixed—on her eyes in particular. They were blue, a rarity among elves. Her hair was brown, stained with kohkoo nuts? In the front it hung down in curling waves, framing her face. In the back it was pulled high in a bit of a mess with traditional feathers fanning out, complementing her elegant ears.

She wore a skirt of colorful rags like a wandering hyuman, mostly blue but dashed with blacks and reds and yellows and not one bit of green or brown—an unusual choice, but the daring made it all the more intriguing. On her wrong hand she wore a fingerless black glove, and on her right wrist, a clump of colorful bracelets. Her fitted white top showed her figure, and her neckline emphasized a silver necklace. *Daring.* She was quite the artist. Or quite the rebel.

I buzzed in Locke's ear—I couldn't help it: "Locke, what would Tryse say if she saw you gaping?"

He looked down, blushing. But when he saw the whole crowd staring at the majestic young lady, he realized a moment of embarrassment was all he could spare. Almost immediately, he looked at her again, and he labored for each breath.

That was when my resistance broke too.

She stared straight ahead, not looking at her father or the crowd—just over our heads toward the back wall. But surely she had friends out there who were eager to see her and who wanted to reassure her with their eyes. But she didn't look for them. And she was sure to have a boyfriend, maybe a whole train of admirers. But whoever was out there, she wasn't looking to them for courage either. Maybe this was her way of coping with nervousness, this staring ahead, a way of ensuring mental focus. Or maybe she didn't need courage.

She had a hint of sadness on her face, as if carrying a burden only she knew. This mysterious melancholy reached toward Locke and all but forced him to fall. He tried to fight it.

I was pushing and pulling—which I did when I couldn't decide. No, I knew her spell: beauty's trance. And I would fight it too. "Locke, faces like that aren't real. Remember Kalaine?"

Ah. He knew I was right. Kalaine was not as beautiful as her face, a common tragedy: elves who demanded without deserving—as if looking good could replace being good. We called them *mirages*—something we'd heard about in faerie stories, where the hero would wander after water in the distance only to arrive and find it was sand. In fact, based on his record, Locke was usually attracted to that kind.

"She's a mirage, Locke, I'm telling you."

And then I fell silent… Because… she… was… astonishing.

Locke breathed in deep, and I glided on it, trying to remain conscious.

Her hair hung past her chin, and left the back of her exquisite neck exposed. She tilted her head slightly, and her hair fluttered, as if it were falling out of place. But as it shifted, covering more of her cheek, it seemed as if it'd found a more perfect place to be. At least until it shifted again. She was a painting of perfection no matter what position she happened to be in. The rest of her presence worked the same magic: Her lips in profile view were the most perfect lips to have ever existed in the whole world, probably the whole universe. Maybe in any universe. And yet when she turned slightly toward us and tilted her head, those majestic lips seemed more perfect still.

She turned fully in our direction, and Locke gasped.

Her blue eyes did the same, shifting the concept of perfection with each movement. Except when she turned them entirely away to grab a large book from the ground—which, apparently, she needed in order to begin. Certainly the back of her head could have been the most lovely thing we'd ever seen, but it hurt to not see her eyes. When she turned toward us, the grace and glory were more painful still. Our heart ached, and we wished she'd disappear so we could escape the imperfection her presence, by contrast, made so present. But, no, we didn't wish this at all. We wished she'd become the universe, that all we'd ever see or feel or need or be would be her. She *was a Goddess.*

"*The Goddess,*" whispered Locke—his thoughts on the exact trail as mine.

No! What were we thinking? I looked away, trying to escape the spell. I needed an ally.

"Locke! You're insane," I said loudly. "A mirage! She's a mirage!"

One person on the row in front of us turned and glanced my direction. Locke's face flushed, and he shook his head.

"She might be perfect in form," I said, "but we've seen that before—or thought we had. Maybe she's haughty. Maybe she's stupid. Remember Sophie?"

He did. The one we'd supposed was an angel before Shaye showed us what *angelic* really meant. But Locke had been more desperate then and his eye not as sharp. Of course, I'd seen through Sophie from the start, because of her sylfe. I tried to warn him, called him a suckerfish—so easy to catch. He didn't listen, so he'd gotten a rough reminder that reality can't keep up with imagination.

And speaking of sylves, where was this Goddess's sylfe? I couldn't see any sylfe near her that was unaccounted for. Maybe her sylfe was dead? No, of course not. Then she'd be biting people's necks like Dagonae.

She set the large codex on the pulpit and braced herself, facing the audience. As she did, Locke longed for that unnameable thing.

"The Book of Karinthe says…" she began.

But then she paused and looked down at the giant tome.

"Oh, I'm so nervous I forgot where Karinthe is. Where is it?" She said this to the audience, asking them directly, and she expressed it with the perfect mixture of confidence and coyness, which brought warm laughter from the crowd, a welcome ease to the tension. I looked around and realized they were all as entranced as Locke… and I. And if anyone hadn't already fallen for her, they surely must have at that moment. No one responded to her question. Instead, they patiently waited, hanging on her breath while she collected herself and found the verse.

"Oh, here it is," she said, and she began to read: "As the rain cometh upon the creatures of the four demigods, so cometh the futures unto every creature under the sun. Fate guides the feet of the hearer. Fortune turns him toward a wilderness of trials. Fellows open the door or hedge up the way with thorns. And Foolishness chooses rewards of darkness or light."

When she said *fortune*, Locke's heart skipped a beat, because it was his name, *Locke*, in its older form.

She paused and looked at her audience as if to judge their understanding, and for a long breath she seemed to look right at us.

Locke nodded, as if to say, "Yes, I understand." But then he realized he hadn't understood, not at all. *The four futures?* He'd learned them when he was very young. As he tried to pull the memories together, she began to speak again:

"Here we stand. All of us. Elves. Brothers and sisters. People of water. Children of Thaese. We creatures under the sun. We have been dealt our future. The skies are cursed and the wraiths are coming. Worse still, our sylves have fallen deaf, though not many have recognized it, making us more separate from the gods than ever before. Some blame heaven. But one of our fellow elves caused this, a person some have called the villain. He hedged up our way with thorns, just as the verse said. But the future is still in our hands. We have our own personal foolishness to rely on—our own initiative. And while it's not much, it may be enough. If we try, we may stumble on some glad outcome."

She looked at us and smiled.

"What's more, we have each other," she said. "I have you. And you have me. We, along with the villain, are each other's fellows. We can open doors for each other. You can shape my future for good, and I will try to shape yours for good too. What I'm saying is that we can fix this. It's within our power. But we have to get over pettiness and selfishness." And when she said this, she drew a quick breath, and her eyebrows turned to a frown for the quickest wink as she paused to confront the threat of tears. Then, with confidence and calm but in a softer voice, she paraphrased the words of Martigane, which nearly knocked Locke off his seat: "Pointing the finger of blame only creates more villains. But we don't need more villains. We need heroes."

A hopeful smile cracked on the face of a greasy onlooker with a drunken sylfe. His smile contagiously spread, appearing on one face, and then another and another, as they looked on the young woman—

As they looked on the Goddess.

But as the crowd lit up, her aspect seemed to take an opposite turn. Her smile melted till there was nothing left but the sincerest of gazes.

"After all," she said, "what good is a life that's not given to others?"

We knew that line too. Locke's mother had read it to us. Something from a tale called the Warrior's Song. The crowd murmured in what seemed to be happy agreement. As she continued, I realized that her flaw, if it existed, was not stupidity. Her eloquence waltzed, intoning at perfect junctions, pausing at right moments, as if guided by the ghost of an ancient rhetor, while we, her audience, stared in awe. At her. Her substance, her presence, her charisma—she had mysteriously claimed the power I wanted more than anything else.

Then that sylfe who'd been flitting and flirting amongst the crowd—I suddenly realized she was with her elfe on stage. She was the Goddess's sylfe. And she too shined, like the song of a valkalyse. She settled back comfortably into her elfe's presence like getting home after a long day in the fields.

"Did you see that?" I asked.

Locke gave me a questioning look to show he didn't understand.

"Her sylfe. Was right here. All the way over here—next to us."

He nodded to confirm, but his eyes and mind were still focused forward. "How come you never do that?" he whispered.

"No one does that. It was like— She could have been—" I didn't know. It was too unusual. *Overwhelming.*

The Goddess smiled, acknowledging the return of her sylfe—right in front of us all. Then she went on:

"I've been studying the four futures, obviously, in the Book of Karinthe and the Tablets of Wyrde. I like the logical framework it provides. But my sylfe has reminded me that they're just words. All of this—just words. What we need now is action." She looked her sylfe straight in the eye, without being slightly ashamed, as if they were about to heft a load together. She looked at the crowd and communicated the same idea—*lift with me*—with such social savvy that she said her message clearly without speaking. "The truth is, I think only selflessness can save this land. But telling you might not be enough. That's just more words. Perhaps I'll have to prove it."

When she said this, we looked at her with concern.

"I speak to you, villain," she said, and she looked straight at Locke.

His eyes got wide, and he nearly ducked behind the pillar.

No, she wasn't looking at him. She was looking into the dim flames of the odd torch above us. "Do you hear me?" she said boldly.

I peered at the flame then glanced around, wondering if I might see the villain somewhere among us.

"You have a person of royal blood who is willing to give her life for this kingdom."

The crowd gasped. I looked at her, eager for more, and so did Locke.

She gave us a sad smile—her final message to us.

Then she returned to her chair.

19.

Encounter

WE NEEDED MORE. But none would come.
The crowd too, seemed unsure what to do next. What could possibly come after that? We wanted to go back, toward her and her encouragement, not forward. But forward was where she had called us and where she was going.

When the King closed the meeting and the crowd broke into patches, Locke still sat there, lost, and the longing stabbed at him.

All I could think to say was, "Well?"

"She…" he began, his words muffled by the crowd. But he wasn't looking at me, who he was speaking to, or at her, who he was thinking of. Instead, he was lost somewhere in the middle. "She… must be one of the wisest people I've ever met. Well, not met, but almost met. The smartest person I ever haven't met." As he stumbled over his words, he blushed.

And I blushed with him. "Wait a moment," I said, noticing how the air around me had fallen still. "It's not real. It can't be. Creatures like that only exist in faerie stories."

"Maybe the faerie stories are true," said Locke.

If he really meant that, this was truly a turning point.

"And I can't help but wonder if a princess would make a good mother," he said. Of course, no princess would ever marry a fifther.

"Maybe it was a mask," I suggested. "Maybe she ensnares hearts with pure showmanship."

"Always the ghule's advocate." He shook his head at me.

"If we don't bring her down to reality, she's going to wreck us."

His thoughts were drawn toward the Goddess like leaves on a river surface, rushing downstream. "She could almost convince me to believe in the Kyrose."

"Whoa," I said. "But she didn't even talk about the Kyrose."

"Yes she did. The four futures. Fate is the demigods."

"Wow," I said, surprised he'd listened that closely.

"And I liked her framework," said Locke.

"Oh, you *did?*"

"Not that! I mean the framework of the four futures. I liked her way of thinking about it. That's all." He looked toward the front of the room again, hoping she might appear in glory. That was when the fog finally cleared.

"Locke, he's gone!" I said.

"Huh?"

"We came to find the Seer!"

The realization washed over him like cold water. He smacked his chest where the scroll was tucked, then leaped to his feet, ducking through the crowd. He said, "Pardon me," and, "Excuse me," as he collided with stray hands, elbows, and the bellies of elder gentlemen. At the lowest part of the room, he leaped onto the stage conspicuously, but the meeting had disrupted matters of form, and no one told him to get down. We found a concealed door where the leaders must have exited.

"Hey!" someone shouted as we ducked into it.

Locke rushed down the dim corridor toward the corner so we'd be out of sight when our pursuer appeared. Locke looked back to see if we were clear. And he was moving fast.

Fortunately, she was looking and had enough time to shield herself with her arms.

Locke slammed into her, her lamp clanked to the ground, and they fell.

He caught himself with his arms on either side of her. Her sylfe zipped back, and so did I, and we were blushing, and they were blushing, and it was just awful. As Locke scrambled to his feet, his face leaned for a moment too close to hers, and the smell of her skin was embarrassingly wonderful.

"It's you!" He reached out his hands to help, but she stood on her own. "Oh, my. Excuse me. I'm so sorry, princess. I'm *so* sorry."

She held out her hand for him to kiss it. "I'm Shilohe." And the light of her radiant smile passed from her lips into his soul.

I began to fly circles around Locke's head.

Locke didn't kiss her hand, not till she was pulling it away. He grabbed her slender fingers and pressed his lips into her knuckles.

"And you are...?" she asked.

"I'm after the Seer," said Locke, staring.

She giggled. "Good to meet you, After the Seer."

Locke hung his arms straight down at his sides, then he folded them, and then he put them back at his sides, while he said, "No, I mean my name's Locke, and I'm looking for the Seer."

A guard stepped around the corner. He actually drew a dagger too, as if we were a threat that might need stabbing. "Come with me!" he commanded.

Locke raised his hands to show he wasn't aggressive. "I'm sorry; did I do something wrong?"

I stopped spinning around Locke's head and faced the guard.

"He's with me," said the Goddess.

The guard's eyebrow formed the question he didn't ask.

"Yes, he's with me," she repeated. "You can put away your sword. Thank you for looking out for me." She gave the guard a real smile too, which surprised all of us. But the guard got over it. He lowered his dagger, nodded his head, and walked away.

"Why did you…?" began Locke, a look of shock still on his face. I tried to slow down enough to tell him how he looked, so he could at least pretend to be calm.

"Uh, this was my own foolishness, I guess," said the Goddess. "Why do you need to see the Seer?"

He smacked his chest with his hand. "I have a…" And then he hesitated. "I may have the key to the curse. Something the Hundred discovered."

"I thought the Hundred were dead."

"They are. But before they got wiped out, they found something, something for the Seer, something about the curse."

"And you're going to tell him about it?"

"I'm going to give it to him."

20.

The Seer

LOCKE FOLLOWED THE Goddess, trying not to stare too long at her exquisite neck.

She'd said her real name as she was getting up off the floor—*what was it?*

Her sylfe kept looking back and smiling. It seemed she meant this as a gesture of friendliness or even excitement, just like she'd done at the stade. But I didn't like it. It made me feel... *small.* She accompanied the most impressive of elves: royal blood, an incredible orator, a daring personality, and a scriptorian. Nothing like my elfe. Locke didn't even believe in the demigods. *Not my fault though*—I pushed him toward it every chance I got.

The Goddess led us through dim hallways till we exited into dark daylight. The silhouettes of branches made a ceiling overhead. Her sylfe kept looking at me like that, like she was willing to help us. Or help me. But who said I needed help?

Locke's palms were sweaty. He tried to think of something to say. Maybe they could become friends, even though he was a fifther. And even though he was wearing a dirty, ragged old shirt.

We passed some of the oldest trees in the village, while swallows chirped overhead. At least it wasn't dead silent. The Goddess didn't say anything either. Maybe she was nervous too. Her sylfe whispered in her ear, and she nodded, as if listening with extra intensity. I wished Locke would listen to me like that.

As she walked, the Goddess turned and asked, "What do you think of the four futures?"

"Your speech was amazing," blurted Locke.

She grinned. "And the four futures?"

"I need to study them more."

"Yes, don't we all? So which part will you study first?"

"Uh, I don't know. Fate and the Kyrose, I guess. And whether they actually affect our lives."

The Goddess glanced back, and Locke squinted, which pinched the skin of the teardrop birthmark at the corner of his right eye. It felt like she'd read our whole history in that one little remark. And if she hadn't, her sylfe probably had. *I felt so small.*

The Goddess smiled and turned forward again, and we were plunged back into miserable silence.

They were what I wanted *us* to be, and now was our chance to learn. Only I didn't know what to tell Locke to ask, so we wasted step after step, moment after moment, till it was gone.

"Here we are," she said.

She stopped in front of a tired looking tree, looming overhead.

It had grown as wide as those around it, but shorter, which by no means meant it was small. Its limbs grew close to the ground, with extra layers of bark that almost dripped from the branches. It seemed too old and too exhausted to hold up those massive arms, as if they might come crashing down at any moment. Of course, they didn't, which showed wisdom had more strength than it let on. Or maybe the tiny, budding leaves caught the air and lightened its load. The branches, from the fattest near the trunk to the tiniest at the farthest reaches—they all seemed gnarled, as if they'd never made up their minds which direction was best. Even though earth was my opposite, I couldn't deny feeling something significant in this tree's presence. It was a work of art, a testament to Gaie, Demigod of Earth, master of gnymes.

The tree had a red door nearly buried beneath folds of bark. A guard, a speck compared to the majestic plant, stood in front. The Goddess walked right up to him. Without saying a word, he opened the door for her and stood aside. "Thank you," she said. The guard glared at Locke but let us pass too.

Inside, stairs led downward—*so strange.* Having heard something about him being an earthseer hadn't prepared me. As we descended below ground, I moved as much as possible to fight the cramped space. A warm glow came from below, arising from a wider, cozier room. The Goddess knocked on the doorframe.

"Come in," said a voice.

A fire in a hearth flickered inside, and a bald head showed over the top of
a chair whose wings were sculpted to look like actual wings, maybe those
of a dragon. The Goddess went in, and her shadow pointed back toward
us. I followed, eager to exit the cramped stairway, but Locke held back.

"Hello, sir," said the Goddess, and for a moment she seemed like an
ordinary mortal.

"My bold friend! Ha haa." As he stood, embracing her in a hug, his laughter
silenced fear and doubt and even discomfort. Such a beautiful sound. And
he was right—her outfit and attitude weren't rebellious—simply bold.

He was bald on top but had long, white hair nearly everywhere else—
white hair, like a Tenarie, only wispier. It flowed from the back of his head
toward his spine. It flowed from under his nose toward the corners of his
upper lip, like a waterfall split in two directions. It spilled down his jawline
and from just beneath his lower lip. It even gracefully dripped from the
outer edges of his white eyebrows, dancing on his smiling cheeks, and then
disappearing into the rest of the beard below. His bald crown was like a
round stone protruding from a cascade. But even beneath a river of white,
his smile couldn't be hidden.

"Shilohe," he said, "I'm so glad to see you."

Ah! That was it. *Shilohe!*

"Your speech was extraordinary. You're as daring as ever. Magister Crowe
has taught you well."

She smiled graciously. "I miss him." A sad melody overshadowed her.
But without spending a moment on whatever troubled her, she turned and
motioned Locke over with a cupped hand, as if she were pulling him, and
she must've had no idea how beautiful that light made her look or she'd
have been more careful. How lucky she wasn't wearing a windress or Locke
might have been done for.

"Come in," I whispered.

Locke moved forward, cleared his throat, and said, "Excuse me, sir, I
have something for you. It's from the Hundred."

"Welcome!" said the Seer with a warming smile. His voice had a certain
lightness, as if Locke had just shared a joke. "Come in, come in! I am
Alphelose." He extended his hand, his eyes squinting in a kind grin. His
voice was the color of smoke puffing into the sky, as light as my own, but
voluminous, smooth, and gray.

I wasn't spinning around my elfe's head this time, so he made a proper response. As he accepted the Seer's handshake, he felt surprised by his deference toward the man, despite their vast religious differences. "I'm Locke."

"Yes you are, aren't you?" The Seer smiled and looked deep into our soul. "For me, at least."

With that phrase hanging in the air, the Seer looked my elfe up and down, and I looked the Seer up and down. He was actually a bit shorter than Locke, which was surprising since his presence seemed so large. His face was old, but his movements weren't. He seemed… nimble, perhaps quickened by his smile. The edges of his eyes glistened with pink, almost as if he'd been crying—maybe this was from old age, or maybe he just kept a constant compassion. He wore a light white robe topped by a dark purple sash—as unusual as Shilohe's colors. At the hem of the white robe, which ended at his knees, another purple robe hung beneath, reaching to the floor.

Something about him—maybe his smile or his laugher or the wisdom in his flowing white hair—made me feel confidence in his presence, as if my weaknesses were all finally okay.

The Seer winked at me. *How unusual.*

Wait—where was *his* sylfe? After turning to take in the room, I found him sitting in the shadows atop a pile of manuscripts, with a kind melancholy about him.

"And what news do you bring?" asked the Seer, finally in a more serious tone.

"It's not news, sir. It's a scroll." Locke pulled the artifact from his shirt and held it out.

"You're wrong handed," said Shilohe in a tone of surprise edged with delight.

Locke looked at her, a little thrilled and a little embarrassed.

The Seer waved for Locke to put away the scroll. "No, tell me the story first."

Locke held the scroll as he again told what happened, starting with my dare.

When Locke mentioned seeing the Hundred from that treetop, the Seer interjected: "On the night of the curse, they captured the servant delivering those letters. They tortured him till he confessed Stane's location, a Tenarie sheep camp where a war chief protected a certain scroll." He eyed the leather in Locke's hand. "The Hundred were dispatched immediately."

Locke nodded. "How do you know this?"

"I have been quieted in the King's circles, but I haven't been deafened. Not yet."

At the Seer's bidding, Locke continued his story—to the massacre, then Nicke, and on to the banshee wolves. When he finished, the Seer shook his head and with some amazement said, "My, what a trial."

Locke offered the scroll to the Seer again.

He didn't take it. Instead he pointed: "Put it on the table." Maybe he knew what happened when a person touched it.

On the table, a fat candle had melted in a heap over the top of a skull, dripping down the back and sides and even the front toward where the eyebrows would have been, making it look in need of a barber. The flame illuminated the table. Locke spread out the scroll.

The Seer rested his hands wide as he pored over the writing, raising his flowing eyebrows and then dropping them. He was about to do something that would break the curse. Then Nicke would be safe to stay with us, and the wraiths would be driven back.

"It's not Tenaglae, or Hyumanglae, or Saboanglae," said Shilohe.

This impressed us once again. I nudged Locke to make sure he was paying attention.

He gave me a quick frown so that I'd leave him alone, and then asked, "So what is it then?"

Shilohe flipped her bracelet hand outward to show she wasn't holding the answer.

As she did, Locke caught a glimpse of something frightening: a bright blue tattoo on the palm of her right hand.

The room immediately seemed to increase in temperature. He tried not to remember the moment he'd first seen Tryse's hand with the blue mark—her marriage tattoo. The symbol of things everlastingly unreachable.

"Breathe," I whispered to Locke.

Shilohe glanced at me, wondering what was wrong. I tried to act casual. *How was she so keen?*

"This scroll was written by a salaminde," said the Seer. "Blake, go get the red stone box from my archives. Should be high on the wrong-side shelf."

Locke turned to see who the Seer might be talking to, and before he'd recovered from the first shock, his heart leaped again. This jolt went up through his throat. A statue of a gripple monkey resting on one of the shelves behind us—or what we thought was a statue—suddenly grabbed the small rock sitting next to him, jumped to the floor, and scampered down another flight of stairs, with his tail raised high and his naked hind-end waving.

Locke put his hand on his stomach and took a deep breath. It had surprised me too actually.

Shilohe had nearly the opposite reaction. She absent mindedly put her index finger at the back of her hair, just behind her ear, and began to twirl it. Just an ordinary girl, glowing in the ragged colors of her patchwork dress.

Locke breathed from deep in his stomach and looked at the door. His feelings for her had already been embarrassing. Now they were ridiculous. But that didn't stop him from feeling them. He began to sweat, trying not to look at her.

I didn't care though: we had nothing to lose. I moved closer, as slyly as I could, and took a good long look at her hand, not caring what her sylfe thought either. The blue ink was a different design than the usual marriage tattoos. This pattern reached wider with sparser intricacies in the middle, as if it could overlay a traditional one. Maybe it represented a betrothal.

The room got quiet, and Locke's temperature rose even more. He shifted his weight onto his other leg and folded his arms, looking at the door again.

"Have a seat, please." The Seer smiled and motioned with two upward palms toward a pair of small wooden chairs. Locke's mouth hung open as he considered a goodbye and a courteous exit, but before he could come up with anything, he'd already sat down.

Shilohe sat next to him. "The Seer battled Stane once before, on the Day of Redress." She looked at the Seer with admiration, and he bowed his head humbly, letting the facts be stated. "Stane was trying to assassinate the King, but Seer Alphelose saved him." When she said this, Shilohe seemed burdened by the unsaid details of some tragic story. Like it hurt her to remember it.

Silence fell again for a moment.

Then Shilohe caught Locke looking her way and smiled.

He swallowed. *Of course* she was practically married—she was a Goddess. The whole kingdom probably wanted to marry her.

I nudged him. That seemed to do the trick.

Her marriage was in the future, and he only wanted to impress her in this moment, right now. *Who cared about the rest?* "You know what I think? I think it's a setup. Someone's making your father look bad so they can steal his power."

"He's not my father," she said.

Locke's jaw dropped slightly open, and the winds fell from his sails. "But I thought—"

"He's not my father," repeated Shilohe, and she gave him a look.

Locke nodded, to indicate he was satisfied, even though he wasn't.

"Some want to steal his power, no doubt," said the Seer. "The High Sheriff, for one."

"The High Sheriff?" asked Locke.

"Why do you think he read the letter? I don't believe he's directly involved, but he's willing to leverage this trouble. The letter had plenty of truth to it. The King has perpetrated some great wrongs, and the desire for justice is in some ways understandable." The Seer glanced at the stairs. "Where is that monkey?"

Shilohe grabbed the seam of her dress and absently examined part of the stitching. Such a mundane thing to do, which Locke could only pretend not to notice. "Did you see the salaminde in the stade?" she asked.

So I was right! That strange yellow torch did have some sort of magic in it.

The Seer's expression smoldered like an angry coal. "Yes. Which means Stane was watching… he saw the whole catastrophe. But the salamindes hate me so much that removing it is impossible, I'm afraid."

Shilohe inhaled, lifted a finger, then closed her mouth and frowned. Something told me she had an idea on how to remove it. She stared for a moment while no one said anything. When her sylfe whispered in her ear, she nodded, pondering before saying, "While we wait, could I ask a question on the balance between fate and foolishness?"

The Seer chuckled, as if about to have a lot of fun.

"If my wants should be swallowed up by the divine wills," she said, "why do I have a will at all?"

But I didn't catch the Seer's answer. Instead, I was looking at Shilohe's sylfe, who was busy perusing every parchment or scroll that had words in sight.

The sylfe turned toward her elfe just as Shilohe said, "Lonae does a good job of whispering."

So *Lonae* was the sylfe's name. She clearly did her duty better than I did. But maybe she was a little crazy too. *Why had she wandered so far to greet strangers?*

"You are blessed with the strongest of sylves," said the Seer, looking directly at Lonae. If it had been me, I'd have been basking in that compliment, but Lonae hardly seemed to notice.

Locke looked at me, and even though I didn't think he meant anything by it, I felt a pang of guilt. The difference between me and Lonae seemed so striking. She was substantial. I wanted to be, but I knew I wasn't. And feeling my shortcomings so strongly, I faded toward the bookshelf behind Locke, hoping to blend in with the shadows.

To my surprise, Lonae drifted that direction too, smiling, as always. But it wasn't just a friendly greeting. Her smile showed sympathy and a willingness to help. *But how?*

Right then, on those upper shelves, I realized what she meant.

She was inviting me to form the consonance.

But why? And why me? And what consonance would she be dropping—surely someone more prestigious than Locke, probably her betrothed?

Locke wasn't even watching me, his face turned toward Shilohe.

I'd have to let go of my consonance with the Angel's sylfe. But this rare moment was fleeting. Lonae could teach me so much—assuming we had some time before the end of time. With her help, maybe I could become someone with clout, someone people listened to, someone substantial. For Locke's sake and for mine.

He would yell at me for doing it, especially so soon after the last time. And he'd be more angry because this one was betrothed. But that would come later. This was today, this was now, and what if now was my only chance?

The Seer's sylfe smiled.

I slipped toward Lonae.

But before she proceeded, she gazed directly at Shilohe till they made eye contact. In a glance, Shilohe communicated her permission. That made me feel ashamed.

Lonae began, starting with a whisper.

Creating the consonance required some adjusting. You couldn't simply play your own melody. You had to be willing to shift and bend, till your shape fit with the other's. Though an elfe could never fully understand our movements, it was a bit like touching fingers, my thumbs to her thumbs, my middle fingers to hers, and so on, four specific notes, aligning in unison, and flowing together like a dance. I began to hum, ever so softly, the melody unique to my soul.

She hummed with me, singing the same rhythm but with notes from her soul that complemented mine.

When our melodies fell into synchrony, magic flowed between us, an unhindered conduit in the language of song, protected from the outside world and disconnected from it.

An uninterruptible harmony.

21.

Lights

A TAPPING ON THE stairs startled me.

The monkey reappeared, walking on three legs and clutching a small red stone box. He still palmed his rock in the other hand, and he pressed it into the floor as he went.

"Thank you, Blake. Just set it here." The Seer pointed at the table.

The monkey leaped up and set the box next to the scroll, then jumped back to the floor and returned to the shelf where he'd started, setting his rock down next to him.

The Seer grabbed the box and leaned his face in close. His sylfe zipped over as if he knew exactly what they were up to, crouching next to the Seer so they were nearly cheek to cheek. I thought maybe he was going to whisper a magical password, but instead they blew on it together, as if trying to get dust out of the crack. Something clicked inside the box, and the Seer pulled open the lid. "Thank you!" he said, and his sylfe floated back to the shelf.

Inside, on a fine gray cloth, rested three white stones. They seemed to be glowing—though I couldn't tell whether that was actual light or just their breath.

Locke squinted. "What are those?"

"Perfect lights," said the Seer, "a combination of fire and stone. And don't touch them. They're very hot." He immediately contradicted his own advice by pinching one stone with five fingertips and lifting it over the scroll as if pouring light. Nothing seemed to change though—the page looked no different, just better illuminated. The Seer said something under his breath. "It appears to be a Boakes curse... He means to murder an entire land with it."

Shilohe moved closer, her eyes scanning the scroll eagerly under the new light.

"Careful not to touch it," whispered the Seer.

"What does it say?" asked Locke.

"It's a covenant, written out on this—indestructible, I think—scroll."

"It *is* indestructible," said Locke.

Shilohe and the Seer looked at him questioningly.

He'd skipped that part of his story. "I got hit with a spear, when the scroll was under my shirt." He pressed his palm into his chest till he located the pain precisely. "It didn't go through."

Shilohe looked impressed.

The Seer peered at Locke as if divining the whole story; then he nodded. "The scroll spells out the parameters of the curse. It requires…" He began to skim over the text with a hovering finger. "A hero to enter… and lift the Sword of the Eternal… and strike the lucid chains that bind the empyrean." He lifted his hand and waved away the rest.

Shilohe's eyes stayed on the manuscript, moving in a precise pattern, as if gulping the words. Then she gasped. We looked at her, and she looked at the Seer, and when their eyes met they traded a knowing glance. What had she read that the Seer hadn't spoken aloud?

"And the villain will have to give his life too, right?" she said.

"Yes, I believe so. He had to offer his life to balance the… the other requirements. It should have killed him already—just creating it—so something must be keeping him alive. He didn't write this, you know—Stane didn't. A salaminde wrote it. It's simply a contract, an agreement with Saede himself. And Stane has to comply with the terms as well."

"So it can be broken?" asked Locke.

"Oh, yes, of course. Well, the curse can. But the contract can't. It can only be fulfilled. It's simple really. We need three things: the where, the what, and the who. First is the source—you have to know the location of the curse's origin. Second is the sword—you need a weapon powerful enough to equal it. And third is the… uh, I guess you could call the third the *who*—you need a person willing to do it."

Shilohe nodded her head solemnly, as if the price were very high.

Then something happened which I'd seen a thousand times, yet never quite in this way:

The Seer's sylfe moved toward his ear and began to whisper. The old man's brow furrowed as he listened with powerful intensity. His gaze slowly rose, from the floor, to the wall, to the ceiling, as if pieces of the future were assembling before his very eyes. Some mysterious miracle flowed through the room. I wondered whether he'd formed a consonance with deity—maybe a dialogue with my mother, Numa. I watched with jealousy, wishing to hear, wanting her to talk to me too.

The sylfe finished and moved a foot away from the Seer's right eye, waiting.

The Seer looked at his sylfe then turned his eyes in a blank stare toward Locke. He remained like that, out of focus, for a long time, reminiscent of the way Locke's father had stared in wonder the night before.

Locke swallowed. He'd felt it too, something… hard to describe. Something he wanted to understand so he could feel it again. *"What…?"*

"What?" asked the Seer, snapping out of his meditative trance and looking at Locke with his present eyes.

"I was just wondering what… what you're going to do."

"Me or *us?"* said the Seer.

"Oh. I don't know," said Locke, and, when the Seer eyed him, I felt a little ashamed of our plan to go home after delivering the scroll.

"I see." A laugh escaped the Seer's throat like two small puffs of smoke.

"What will we do exactly?" asked Shilohe.

"I'm going to the Tomb of Naephe, where I hope to find his sword—one of those bathed in the empyrean by the Lukaiim. It should fit the conditions of the contract."

"Will you need help?" she asked.

"Not with that. But I will also send someone to the Well at the World's End."

When the Seer said those words, that unnameable feeling pierced us again, filling us, and especially Locke, with an inconsolable longing. He wanted to see the place even before he knew what it was.

Shilohe asked, *"Who* will you send?" at the same time that Locke asked, "What's that?" When their words overlapped, they looked at each other and blushed. *Maybe she did like him a little.*

The Seer smiled. He looked at Locke and began to answer his question first: "There is a well, in a temple built by demigods, from which pours a substance called living water—a combination of rain and fire."

"Rain and fire?" said Locke.

"If it strikes you as unnatural, remember that it is above nature not below it."

Locke nodded, but he actually needed some time for that idea to settle. It did strike him as unnatural. Or unreachable maybe. "And the scroll said this substance will help break the curse?"

"Actually, the scroll didn't mention it. But to break the curse with the sword, we must go to the center of its physical location. And we don't know where that is, so we'll use the living water to find the way."

"And who are you going to send for it?" asked Shilohe.

The Seer's pink bottom lip hung gently beneath his waterfalling beard, and he stared with glassy eyes for a moment as he said, almost as if surprised himself, "I was planning to invite our young friend Locke to go."

Locke gulped in surprise. *So that was what the sylfe had whispered about.* His heart thumped with confusing excitement, honor and fear. He looked at Shilohe.

Her demeanor had fallen. She turned away.

The Seer gave her a sad gaze; then he looked back at Locke. "Well?"

Locke braced himself as the urgency pressed in on all sides. He didn't believe in the Seer's unearthly gifts, but he respected the man himself. And maybe helping here would help Nicke too. But doubts tumbled like a landslide, damming Locke's ability to choose. The Seer was asking him to agree to something he knew nothing about, a huge dare, and *death* was what happened when you dared. He knew that all too well. He glanced to the side, hoping to find courage waiting somewhere nearby, ready to transform him into a bold hero. But it didn't appear, and his fears didn't relent—looming, writhing, gaining hold.

I was a child of Numa: I found comfort in the freedom of air and skies. Choice was the highest gift. And here I was witnessing that gift in action, at a time, I could tell, when the future really did hang in the balance. As the room stood quiet, I looked to Lonae, wondering what a sylfe like her would do. She couldn't help me through the consonance—that required the elves being involved. But she gave me a nod and an encouraging smile.

More than anything, I wanted my elfe to listen to me. I moved forward to whisper, and words came from somewhere beyond me: "If you say *yes*, you take a chance: you may become a hero or you may lose your life. Your second option is to heed your fears: stay home and be the still wind that dies."

When I quoted Song of Martigane, his thoughts went to the twins. What would they do? It was obvious. And he wanted so badly to be like them.

But why would the Seer choose me? I'm just a kid. Just a kid. This thought lapped as waves, repeating over and over in our mind.

"Maybe you *are* just a kid," I whispered. "But if you accept the call, you'll be the sort of kid who says *yes*."

Shilohe watched him closely.

"I'm just not sure I can," said Locke aloud. That embarrassed me—it was the sort of thing an elfe should only say to his sylfe.

The Seer leaned forward in a way that suggested a complicated dialogue was going on in his head too. "You'll have to give up a comfortable place here. I know the pull of home, believe me. And yet, have you ever felt a homesickness—a longing for something—even when you were already home?"

Wow. The Seer knew about our unnameable thing. And though he'd formed it as a question, the Seer had actually given Locke an answer of sorts. Surely this quest would lead us to the unnameable. Locke wanted that more than anything.

That was when it broke.

The tangle of thoughts and branches fell apart, and his courage roared like a river.

Just as he was about to speak, he saw—really saw—Shilohe's face, and how she looked so eager. *She* wanted to go, in spite of the danger. She wanted to risk her life if she could, if only Locke would keep quiet.

Would she hate him if he spoke up?

And would he hate himself if he didn't?

22.

Dischord

I'LL GO," SAID Locke.

The boy who ran from bugs.

As the Seer smiled, the wrinkles at the corners of his eyes bunched up. "I knew it. You're made of oak. I saw it the moment I laid eyes on you."

And Shilohe—*hmm*. Well-masked emotion filled her eyes, a whirlwind she couldn't fully hide. Was it jealousy toward Locke? Anger toward the Seer? Or some deeper tragedy? "Then what would you have *me* do?"

Locke swallowed, feeling guilty.

The Seer eyed Shilohe, and each heartbeat seemed to deepen his compassion. "This will be difficult for you to understand, I'm afraid, but I want you to stay here."

Her lungs filled with air and a strong reply, but she bit her lip. Though I wished she'd just speak, I had to admire her decorum.

"I want you to keep charge of the records while I'm gone."

"But I can help," she said. "I *need* to help. It's what Numa whispers to me."

The Seer sighed.

"I'm qualified. I'm ready. *I* believe in the Kyrose."

The Seer turned toward Locke and stared from beneath those waterfall eyebrows, perceiving the implication in those words.

Locke swallowed and shrunk back, looking at the floor.

The Seer chuckled, but the laugh faded when he looked back at Shilohe.

"And I don't have banshe wolves after me," she added, shaking her head as if this were all so overwhelmingly foolish.

Locke perked up as the relentless monsters darted through our mind.

"Is it because I'm not physically strong?" she asked. "I'm as strong as he is. We can arm-wrestle right now," and she pulled up her sleeve, which gave Locke a pang of anxiety: She didn't look muscular, but she looked mad.

Locke was ready to bow out. He'd never wanted the job much in the first place. He inhaled, lifted a finger, and opened his mouth to interject.

The Seer spoke: *"Shilohe."*

That was all he said, just one word, her name. But he said it with a gentleness that calmed us all. He put his hand on the side of her head with the affection of a father more loving than Locke's.

As she looked up at him, her eyes filled with submission.

"Yes, there are more logical candidates." He gave a sage smile. "But it's not about Locke. Or about you or me. It's much bigger than any of us and certainly bigger than mortal logic."

Shilohe bowed her head.

"Magister Crowe and I see great things in your future. Great things. You are our most promising student. And with the order crumbling so rapidly, you're too precious for us to risk."

Her lips pouted as she fought to keep her emotions from showing. "All life is precious."

"But all life is not in equal peril," he said, so gently it could have stilled the wind. "After your speech, the danger increased. Stane surely heard your challenge through his salaminde torch."

But if the torch had a salaminde in it, where was its kynde? No elemental wandered alone. Something about Shilohe's expression kept me from whispering to Locke. She looked so sad.

As she shook her head, the feathers in her hair waved back and forth. "But he wants the King, not me. He wants revenge."

"Maybe making you suffer will fulfill that."

"The King doesn't care if I suffer." She said it with hate in her voice—which surprised me. It seemed to have surprised her as well.

"But does Stane care?" asked the Seer.

"I don't know," she said, now with a more humble tone, as if to counter her last outburst.

The Seer looked at her as peaceful as a creek. "I promised both your mother and Magister Crowe that I would keep you safe. I intend to keep those promises."

Her sad resignation showed on her face. "But I promised our people. And I can't just let *you* do this thing." She said this last phrase as if to herself, in desperation, and the corners of her perfect eyes glistened with tears.

The Seer looked at her and bit his bottom lip. "I'm sorry. It's better this way."

"Why?"

"Because we both know this story won't end well."

They traded another knowing glance. Shilohe nodded and bowed her head, and her hair hung toward the floor. She was grace coupled with majesty, and for a moment her presence tugged at our consciousness.

There she was.

Right in front of us.

The paradigm of beauty, breathing the same air as us just a few feet away. A surreal presence, even if she was spoken for.

"Okay," she said, and her voice made it clear that tears would soon come. Her bottom lip firmed up in a fighting stance, and I wished that I could become her sylfe, to brace her up.

The Seer smiled at her with the hope of a bright future.

Shilohe nodded to the Seer, gave Locke a forced smile, and without a word walked from the room, with Lonae flying behind her.

The colorful dress swished as she disappeared around the corner.

Then we heard her footsteps tapping a rhythm up the stairs.

23.

The Quest

WITH SHILOHE GONE, we sat in a dark world. The mood was downright gloomy. Without her glory, we had nothing but the crackling fire and the candle melting onto the skull. The monkey's eye gleamed as it stared from atop the shelf.

"Did we make the right choice?" I whispered.

Locke frowned to tell me he didn't appreciate my backtracking, but it soon turned into a look of worry. A cold uneasiness had taken her place, a feeling of wrongness, like the darkness of my nightmare.

"Can you breathe a little deeper?" I asked.

He obliged, which brought out a sigh.

The Seer picked up a feather pen and began to scratch a note. As he did, he rubbed his eyebrow with his wrong hand, which gave us a good look at his marriage tattoo.

After I nudged Locke repeatedly, he spoke up: "Your marriage tattoo—it's layered."

"Yes." The Seer kept his head down as he spoke, still focused on his writing. "The outer part is for the order I belong to."

"Order?"

"The Order of the Blue Rose."

"So it's not a betrothal tattoo?"

The Seer glanced up with a twinkle in his eye. "Not unless it's a betrothal to truth."

With that, Locke's heart began to grin. He tried not to show it on the outside. "Can anyone get one?"

"No, no, not at all. It takes rigorous devotion." The Seer turned and gave Locke another one of those piercing stares, though a much smaller dose this time. "Shilohe is a member. It may lie in your future too, who knows."

I trusted the Seer, but I had doubts about this statement. After all, Locke wasn't even a godfearer.

"Maybe she could accompany me," said Locke.

"No, no. You volunteered, and that will keep her out of danger. Besides, she has a greater role to play if she stays." The Seer said this with some finality in his tone. He rolled up the note and held it out toward the monkey. "Take this to her, Blake, and then keep an eye on her, please."

The monkey grabbed his rock and leaped from the shelf. Taking the note, he scampered up the stairs.

"Now, what's this about not believing in the Kyrose?"

I smiled at the question and Locke tried not to frown. An awkward silence followed.

"The problem, my dear boy, isn't that Saede is winning. It's that he's winning so thoroughly most people don't even realize he's winning. He has confused our sylves so badly many can't even hear their own elves, much less the Kyrose." He paused for a moment of slow breathing. "Forgive me. I don't mean to lecture you. We'll talk about this another time." He turned and rummaged through an old chest. Then he held an unusual object in front of us and said, "Here, take this."

It looked like a strange goblet—a wooden handle and a glass top. The bottom was sculpted worlnut, a shapely cylinder that started wide then swooped in narrower as it rose. The top was red shards of glass, pieced together to form a bowl with dark sealant in the seams. The whole object stood no taller than three of me. Locke handled it gently. "What is it?"

The Seer went back to his shelves of manuscripts. "It's called a phanos lamp. You dip it into the Well, and it will ignite. That is what you will bring back to me—the ignited lamp." Looking up at a mass of paper and dangling labels, he rubbed his bald head with a chuckle before grabbing what he needed. He produced another, smaller scroll. "And this will help you get there."

As Locke unrolled it, he found a map inked into old leather and stained with faded colors to mark the regions. I moved in for a closer look, studying it with him—like I imagined Lonae would have done.

"This is where you're going." The Seer pointed to empty air off the edge of the map—north of the Majestic Sea and far to the east. "The fount of one of the demigods' greatest gifts—the Well at the World's End. It's at the tallest peak along this coast. You'll find access to it up the Pilgrim Stairs—otherwise the slopes are too steep to climb."

Hearing the name of the place filled us with that strange wanting again. It didn't help that the Goddess had just left. And mixed with all that wanting, I sensed Locke's wild hope that it could heal the wounds of death—for himself and for Nicke.

The Seer smiled the smile of one about to tell a secret he never wanted to keep. "The Well holds a substance that Phose gave to Nara, a substance of light and blood that she then shared with mortals—living water. Any who can carry it gain a gift called clairvoyance or second sight, and it's the unspeakable. A greater gift was never had by any mortal."

One word in particular, *clairvoyance*, brought the shadow of a memory, a story Locke's mother had told us long ago. Locke shook his head as he failed to fully remember. "So what is it exactly?"

The Seer tapped his face at the corner of his eye. "A gift of foresight, which can manifest in various ways. Usually it gives based on dire need, meaning the more you need it the more it will show you. While you carry it, your sylfe's vision will open to things beyond your understanding. Perhaps the least of which will be knowing the location of the curse."

While this explanation filled us with an overwhelming awe, Locke mixed in the usual measure of doubt: "If this power is so great, how can a person like me get it? I mean, a force more terrible than the Hundred must guard a treasure like that—must protect it jealously."

"It is a power the unworthy can never hold."

"Then how am *I* supposed to hold it?"

"I will teach you." The Seer's mustache pulled outward with his smile. "The gift is protected manyfold. First, as I said, it is located at the World's End, far from civilization, at the brink of the Unknown Sea. Only a person with hope and tenacity will ever so much as arrive."

At that, Locke nodded uncomfortably, accepting the compliment he felt unworthy of.

"Second, to activate the power, you must speak a passphrase, which I will tell you in a moment. Anyone who arrives without proper knowledge will find nothing but a spectacle. Third, the passphrase must be spoken in tandem with your sylfe. Any kynde who doesn't have an amiable relationship with his elemental will return empty handed."

"My sylfe is great," said Locke. "He'll do great. It's more me I'm worried about."

The Seer chuckled and gave Locke a heartwarming smile. When he turned his gaze toward me, it made me squirm—only children looked at sylves that way. "Now, Picke..." *And how did he know my name?* "...remember this password so you can breathe it with Locke when the time comes: *Dyn meis, Thaese, dyn meis, all to enoma siou doesi ta doksa.*"

I repeated the phrase aloud.

"Remember it," said the Seer.

"I will," I said, and I began structuring the phrase into a memory I could draw on later.

"I have faith in you both." The Seer gave us a reassuring smile. "Now, going on. The fourth protection is that carrying the living water requires a proper vessel, the phanos lamp, which you now have. Finally—and I am most concerned about this one—if the lamp goes out, you will lose sight of what it has shown you. Worse, you'll lose the memory of having seen it. You will have no recollection of ever being led in the right direction. With that forgetting, you will be tempted to believe it never worked in the first place. That is why so many reach the Well and received the gift only to later convince others not to try. If this happens to you—and I hope it does not—you must go back, reignite the water, and try again. Without it, I cannot break the curse."

Locke nodded under the weight of the sobering knowledge.

"These protections keep the living water sacred. Many don't believe it is real, even some in my order, and so few attempt to find it. Eventually the knowledge will be lost, vanishing with other myth. But it is a myth *you* will carry in your hand."

Our mind glimmered. Locke didn't believe in demigods or miracles. Yet the Seer's fervor and the words he spoke—these entwined with the wanderlust, or whatever it was, and his doubt turned to a feeling of wonder.

"Once you've got it, I want you to meet me at Wiks Pike. Do you know where that is?"

Locke nodded.

"I should be there eight days from now," said the Seer. I quickly calculated—that would be the fourteenth day of the curse. "If your journey takes longer, I will wait. Now, we must be off. Every moment puts more people in danger. Any final questions?"

Locke wrung his hands together unconsciously. "What about the banshe wolves?"

"I plan to send the scroll to the village council, so others can try in case we fail. Which means the wolves may hound whoever takes it next. That is likely, since it's the object Stane wants. They also may be following the scent of your Tenarie friend; if so, they will terrorize till the village warriors kill them. But, yes, it is possible they'll still follow you. So be wary." He looked directly at me again. "You especially, little Picke. A banshe wolfe is not a trifle."

But he didn't have to tell us. The thought of running from the wolves again sat in Locke's stomach like a rotting fish. "If they're so relentless," asked Locke, "why did they leave our tree that night?"

"Their souls have been cut, spilling their ondines like blood. That gives them a voracious thirst. Usually, this would simply mean to never get between them and water. But now, under these cursed skies, they'll have to retreat to find water—they won't be able to go long without it."

I nodded in surprise. It made sense though.

"If they do come back, can I do something to ward them off?"

The Seer put a hand to his forehead and kneaded his skin as he recalled. "The Phantetios says they rarely come out in daylight."

"There is no more daylight," said Locke.

"But try sticking to day cycles as you travel, and perhaps they'll keep their nocturnal habits."

"They did catch up to Nicke and me at night."

"Also, their presence is often forewarned by a distinct smell, something like rotting flesh mixed with a sweet smoke."

"Yeah, we smelt it."

"Oh, and they don't like iron."

"Iron?"

"Yes."

"You mean an iron alloy, like a steel sword?"

"I think that was in reference to potions, but it wouldn't hurt to take a good sword along."

"So water, daylight, smoke, and iron."

"Better yet, move swiftly and you'll be alright." It sounded like something I might have said, and it gave new meaning to *a still wind dies.*

Locke sighed. We'd planned to give the Seer the scroll and be done. Now so much rested on us. Locke's face showed more fear than he realized, so I nudged him.

"Don't let your worries lead," said the Seer.

Locke accepted the advice with a nod, but he wasn't yet reassured, so I whispered in his ear: "Remember how your mother used to say you were destined to be a hero?"

He shook his head to show his doubt. He'd believed it when he was young. He'd also believed when she said everything would be okay. "I'm just an ordinary boy," said Locke aloud.

"You've already proven yourself—you salvaged the massacre of the Hundred and escaped the banshee wolves. Maybe you're not a hero in this moment, but you were a hero in those moments, and something tells me you will be in moments to come. Just wait and see."

I whispered in Locke's ear.

He smiled a timid, reluctant smile. "Picke says you're right, sir."

"Ha ha. Good. But just to be clear: You *are* putting yourself at risk," he said, though I wished he hadn't—it was better for Locke not to think about it. "It's dangerous to go alone into terrain like this and against the sort of enemies you're likely to encounter. The living water's unearthly power will draw sylves to you, unexplainably, both for help and for harm. But our peril is worth it—the curse will take more lives every day that it remains."

Locke thought of Nicke. Our errand might help stop the war, which would keep him safe.

"I've given seventy-five years of my life to the Unknown God, and I'm ready to give the rest too. I'm ready to pay the last ounce—to say farewell to my family and all. I don't expect you to have to pay so a high a price, but if you were asked to, would you be willing?"

"I… I don't know." Locke glanced at me, as if I might have the answer. "I hope so."

Scroll Two

INTERVENTION OF DEITIES

INTERFERENCE OF MORTALS

INTERCHANGE OF CHANCE

INITIATIVE OF SELF

FATE

FELLOWS

FORTUNE

FOOLISHNESS

24.

Farewell

TEARS LINED THE edges of Nicke's dark, skull-like eyes. He blinked rapidly, looking at the ceiling, and clenched his jutting jaw. When we'd gotten home from the Seer's late last night, Nicke had already been asleep. Now, in the dim dawn, Locke was explaining that we were leaving again. "A healer is on the way though," said Locke. "Her name is Shaye."

"And she's an angel," I added.

"I think you're going to like her," said Locke.

With his lips pressed tight, Nicke nodded. White bandages wrapped his leg. The crutch leaned against the wall. He lifted himself up on one elbow, looking around the room as if to find a way to come with us. With a loud sigh, he laid back down and put his hands behind his head, elbows pointing out like wings.

"Here's more of the numbing potion." Locke handed Nicke a small red bottle. "You can stash it in the crack between the bed and the wall." Locke looked around the room, wishing *he* could stay home. But to Nicke, this was an unfriendly place, and we had to leave for his sake.

Locke squatted next to a chest with a round top at the foot of his bed. He pulled at the rusted metal latch, but it didn't budge. "My brothers said this came from a Tenarie pirate ship."

Nicke leaned onto his elbow again for a better look, then he nodded eagerly.

Years of moisture had worn the box's wood, but the designs meticulously etched into the sides still showed the craftsman's skill. Large letters covered a wide swath across the center of the chest, surrounded by intricate vines and leaves, forming these words:

ELTARAE KILMAREN

Locke kicked the stubborn latch with his toe. The rusty metal came free with a pop. He opened the lid and pulled out a green tunic.

Nicke watched with his mouth slightly open. "What's that?"

Locke pulled the tunic over his head, and the silver links of his mail hung out past the green sleeves. At least it would hide the broken mail links over his heart. A hood, fastened to the neck, hung down his back. "It's the garb of the forest folk."

"You're a forest folk?"

"No, I've just read about them. I really like the story of Martigane. He wore clothes like this. Tunke, my older brother, gave these to me before he left. I've never really worn them—wanted to keep them nice."

"You won't keep them nice in the wilderness."

"Yeah, I know. Just seems like the right time. Looks like they finally fit too."

Locke stuffed a rain cowl into his backpack on top of the food: jerky, boiled eggs, hard cheese, bread, a sandwich, and the Seer's flasks of water.

"I see your sword hand," said Nicke.

"What?" asked Locke.

"You use the wrong hand as your sword hand, right?"

"Yeah, I was born that way." Locke looked at his palm and the ripples in his skin—so much trouble caused by such a common thing. "My dad tried to get me to switch so I could be normal, but it didn't take."

"That's weird."

"Well the creeds are a strange thing."

"In my village they say using the wrong hand brings luck." Under his breath, Nicke added, "*Said*, I mean."

"Well, I could use some of that." Locke slid a dagger into his pack, along with his sling, a flint, and his pinkalue.

"I've tried to switch to the wrong hand."

"It's not easy to switch, is it?"

"Well, usually I can't remember which is which."

Locke laughed.

Nicke grimaced as he rolled onto his side. "You're headed back toward my... where I used to live..." At the thought, fear shone in his eyes, the fear of seeing blood again.

Locke took some leather straps and began to fasten his sheath to the backpack. "I'm going near that but much farther east. And it's good you're not coming. The Seer said the wolves might be on *your* trail—maybe because you were with the villain in the whispering thorns. If you came with me, you might draw them after us. But you'll be safe here, and the villagers can fight off the wolves."

"They'll hate me for it." When Nicke said this, his voice cracked and tears lingered on the verge of his eyelids. He started blinking.

"They don't know we drew the wolves here. Besides, I'd be glad to fight off wolves for you." Locke pulled a knot tight and then jerked on the scabbard. It held firm.

"But they're not like you. I saw it in their eyes yesterday. I heard it in their sylves. And when war comes…"

"That's why I'm going, so I can stop the war."

"You can't stop it."

"Don't say that."

"Don't go."

Locke swallowed. "I'll be back soon, I promise."

I urged Locke to leave, so we could escape the sadness of parting.

Instead, he pulled out his pinkalue. "They say this song can drive away ghules."

He began to play. The rhythm stepped peacefully, filling the room with wonder then wandering on toward happier places.

"If you're scared while I'm gone, just hum that song." Locke ruffled up Nicke's wild white hair, and with the gesture he wiped away Nicke's fear, if only for a moment. "It always worked for me when I was a kid."

Nicke nodded with the hint of a grin. He looked down at his bandaged leg. "I'm even a little afraid of *dogs*," he admitted.

Locke smiled. He stood and took a final look around the room, wondering whether he'd forgotten anything.

Nicke seemed to be thinking too, maybe about Locke's gift of song. His expression jumped near to delight, as he pulled a small vial from his pocket, a black and evil thing. He handed it to Locke.

"What's this?"

"It's the venom."

The horror of what this substance had done emanated from the glass and into Locke's fingers. "You kept some?"

Nicke looked at Locke with dark eyes and a pale expression. "The evil man gave me two."

"Maybe I should pour it out," said Locke.

"No, keep it. It saved my life. Maybe it'll save yours."

Locke didn't want to poison anyone, but what was he supposed to say?

"I'll bet it could kill a banshe wolfe," said Nicke.

Locke nodded and put the vial in his pack. "Thanks. The Seer said they're ravenous for water." And when he said it, I imagined banshe wolves lapping up poisoned pools.

"But what if the wolves attack you directly?" asked Nicke. "You can't fight them."

"I'll be careful."

"You're the only family I've got."

"I'm coming back, okay?"

"When?"

"A few days."

Nicke nodded sullenly.

Locke stood and put on his backpack. With the sheath strapped underneath, it positioned the hilt of his Hundred sword above his shoulder. He waited, not ready to move on but not knowing what else to do or say. I whispered to give Nicke a hug, but Locke didn't do it. Instead, he reached out his sword hand and gave Nicke a handshake.

Nicke smiled when they used their wrong hands.

"Alright, I guess I'll see you soon then." As Locke stepped through the doorway, the wind tousled his wheat-colored hair.

Nicke shouted, "If you're not back before my leg heals, I'm coming after you!"

"Don't worry. I'll be back in a few days." He smiled and left without looking back.

I did though. And I saw Nicke staring at us with glistening eyes.

"Picke," said Locke under his breath, "we have to stop the war."

I nodded my agreement.

"We have to," he repeated, "so he can have a home."

25.

Setting Forth

P ICKE, YOU HAVEN'T bothered me about the Angel in two days."
"Well, I…"

Of course I hadn't. I didn't want him asking about the consonance.

I kept expecting Shilohe to speak through it, which would have given away my secret. But she never had, and I didn't know how else to bring it up.

"Just tell me, Picke."

I flew over a patch of dying dandelions and blew, trying to dislodge the spores. "Tell you what?"

"I already know, so just say it."

"You do?" I couldn't tell if he was bluffing, trying to get me to incriminate myself.

"You made the consonance with the Goddess!" he blurted.

I came to a stop and held very still for a moment, which was horrible, but I didn't know what else to do.

Locke clenched his teeth. "Why didn't you just tell me?"

"I knew you'd be mad."

"That's not why I'm mad. I'm mad because you didn't tell me."

"I was going to tell you."

"When?" He spread his hands wide, as if to indicate he couldn't find something. "It's been two days."

"You knew all that time?"

"Besides, what will Shaye think? We dropped it without giving her any reason."

Geese called overhead, dark flutters shaped into giant *vah* runes below the blackness. It wasn't the season for them to be migrating.

"Wait," I said, "are you bringing this up because you just figured it out? Or is it because you want to talk to her?"

He didn't say anything, trying to deny me the satisfaction. But he couldn't stay shut up for long. "It bothers me because you always have to have your way. If you think I won't agree, then you sneak."

"Well what would you have said if I'd asked you?"

"I might have agreed."

"No you wouldn't. You thought she was betrothed."

"Okay, so I wouldn't have agreed. It wouldn't have been appropriate."

"But she *wasn't* betrothed, and your—"

"We still don't know that."

"—and your worrying would have kept us from being daring. That's why I couldn't tell you. You're not daring enough."

"Picke, you're not always right."

"I'm the sylfe!" I shouted.

"You're not a *heroic* sylfe!" he shouted back.

"That's because you'll never step up. How can I be one if you're not a hero?"

"It's your own fault Numa won't talk to you. Besides, I told you I don't want to be a hero. And how could I when my sylfe doesn't even trust me?"

"I trust you," I said, mostly to contradict him.

He didn't reply, like he was fine if the conversation ended right there. I was not fine with it. "If you don't want to be a hero, then why did we even come?"

"To keep the princess safe. And to help Nicke." In a quieter voice, as if to himself, he added, "And maybe to find that thing I've been longing for."

The sadness in his breath kept me from replying, so we walked in silence.

Over the sixth, seventh, and eighth days of the curse, we'd traveled far, retracing our steps through the Wisting Mountains. Locke had stood his ground against two small wraiths with his Hundred sword. We hadn't encountered the wolves though, which meant the Seer might have been right about them chasing the scroll. Next we'd cut across the Majestic Sea, avoiding the Altar of Nara, and going on to the Astral Fields. Here the sky, struggling to live, made silhouettes of the sparse trees, their reaching gnarls haunting the space between earth and sky. Beyond that, a great upstairs floor covered the world, and who knew what beings might be lurking up there. We expected to reach the Khalune Desert soon. The World's End waited beyond, along with our mysterious future, which felt rather grim.

"Look, I'm sorry for being mad," said Locke.

I wasn't quite over it, but I said what I knew I should: "I'm sorry I didn't tell you."

"I want to be best friends with you, Picke. And I want to listen to you. I just need you to listen to me sometimes too."

I nodded. *Fair enough.* As usual, he'd done everything okay. Even his fear was okay: because he was afraid, he could understand others who feared. But I wasn't sure he fully understood *me* yet. I wasn't as afraid of death, though I'd seen the havoc it left in its wake. I believed in the hereafter, and the chance to become legendary was worth trading our life.

"I want to be substantial." My wings floated in the somber air. "I want to make a difference before it's too late."

"You do make a difference. To me."

"I hate feeling like I'm nothing."

"You're not nothing. If it weren't for your dare, the Seer would've never gotten the scroll."

I nodded with a sad grin.

"And you don't have to be right all the time—you'd still matter to me even if you didn't know anything."

"Thanks," I said.

"I'm glad you're my sylfe."

After that, our spirits began to rise.

As we marched, a lone woodland mouse darted away from Locke's moccasins, then froze as if we'd surrounded him. Locke tore off a bit of the last piece of bread and shared it with him. The gesture picked us up. Knowing the food was nearly gone did the opposite.

The last few days had been a struggle of ups and downs. We journeyed in a faded, eternal twilight, through days that came only halfway to life before night obscured them again. As we pushed to the north east, a boreal wind fought against us. Phose gave us just enough light to warm the sky in the thinnest places, enough for Locke to see his way.

A flash of white blinked across the entire world, forcing Locke to push away thoughts of his mother. Thunder rumbled in the distance, a sound like a great rock being rolled across the sky.

After my coaxing, Locke played his pinkalue, our weapon against the gloom overhead. I floated along the song. It reminded us of our purpose, and valor sung its own harmonic notes in our mind. We thought of the twins. They'd be proud of what we were doing. And of Locke's clothes. But after days of walking and playing, Locke had grown weary, and his music eventually fell silent again.

What we needed was light, something hopeful and bright. Something like Shilohe. *Everything else was so dark.*

"It's hardly a fair comparison," said Locke.

"What?"

He chuckled.

"*What?*" I repeated.

"It's hardly a fair comparison," he said again.

"What is?"

"What you were thinking just now—to say the world is dark compared to her. To compare her against the world." He grinned. "It's unfair."

"Yeah, okay. It's unfair."

"Just the corner of her smile could take on the world."

The sound of my laughter carried across the wind. "You are *such* a sucker."

"I know." He shook his head, smiling. "I know. And I stole her quest. Makes me afraid to talk to her."

"I say you'd be afraid either way."

He nodded—I had him there. "But I want to talk to her so bad my heart aches."

And it did. I felt the strange feeling through him. It tingled deep in his chest, moving outward, down his arms, and even to the tips of his fourth fingers. It moved up his throat, making him breathe a little deeper, and continued right on till it hit his smile. A smile mixed with sadness. And his wanting increased. He'd never known someone so perfect.

Except one.

The woman who'd named him Locke—

—he steered his thoughts and eyes away from the sky. "Okay, well, I guess I'd like to talk to her now. And I admit that I'm glad you made the consonance. Even though I wouldn't have agreed."

I smiled. "I'm ready if you are."

"We've had the connection all this time, and I haven't spoken to her. Kind of rude, right?"

"I've been surprised she hasn't spoken to us either. I guess the first one to talk will be the least rude."

"I don't know what to say though!"

"Just be yourself. Say something honest."

"Shilohe, I'm obsessed with you. I don't even know you, but I can't stop thinking about you. But don't worry. I'm not crazy. Just crazy about you. Oh and sorry I stole your quest."

"Nice."

"Then what do I say?"

"Maybe you should just make it up as you go."

He exhaled his hesitation, took a deep breath, and said, "Okay, let's do it."

26.

The Harmony

WHEN I LOOKED at Locke and he looked at me, I saw trust. Ever so gently, he scooped me into his hand.

When we'd formed our first consonance many years ago, I told him it was like holding water: "The tighter you grip, the more it drips out. Don't *force* it to stay. *Allow* it to stay."

My job, on the other hand, was more than simply letting go. As the winds picked up, I became the small boy ashore clutching the mooring line of a hulking galleon—I was no match for it, no matter how slow it moved. But I had to try, fighting against the earth of Locke's hand, keeping my airy form anchored as long as possible.

As I struggled, my world grew dark enough to hear a billion individual grains of sand. Each one made a miniscule scratching sound as it rolled beneath the wind. I smelled Locke's skin and sweat, and the desert sage, and the salt in the rocks—every sound and feeling had become brighter and more lasting.

He put his hand over his mouth like a mask. His index finger touched the birthmark at the corner of his eye while his thumb rested on the soft skin at the bottom of his opposite eye. He inhaled gently, as if about to whisper a secret in the ear of a close friend. In that moment, I transformed. I became the lifebreath rooted deep inside him, filling his soul and surrounding his heart. I became the vitality of his every word. He exhaled and I became the sky, reaching to the ears of the Goddess herself.

I was no longer a wave—I was the ocean.

He spoke in a whisper, and the words echoed through me as lyrics woven into the wind:

"Uh, hi, princess." He twirled his free hand forward, trying to get the words to roll. "This is Locke."

I wanted to whisper, to tell him what to say, but I couldn't speak.

"I just… wanted to say *hi*… And, uh… I wanted to ask you a question. About… Uh… Well, I noticed an odd sort of marriage tattoo on your hand, and I wanted to ask you about it."

He immediately dropped his hand, and the massive form of the wind shattered into tiny particles. I fell out—*me*, a single breath, floating into the ripples of the breeze.

He kicked a stone. "Gah, I'm so bad at this!"

The light from Locke's eyes brightened my vision once again. "It was a little rough on the edges, but it was fine."

"I already know about her tattoo! I don't know why I said that. She probably thinks I'm an idiot."

We continued on, expecting and hoping for a reply, trudging across the unique landscape of the Astral Fields.

Here few trees grew, so the shape of the world was unclothed. A heavy green and yellow canvas of grass rested over lumps of rolling rock. Occasionally the rock thrust upward so mightily that it tore through the canvas, interrupting the green with brownish gray and sometimes yellow rocks in lines and ledges of wandering crust and buttes, with trails of boulders scattered in a mess around them.

"I wish we could see this place in daylight," I said. "Under the sun's golden rays, or better yet by starlight."

"Why is she taking so long?" said Locke.

"I'm sure she's busy."

"Maybe she's going to break the consonance." As Locke walked, the wind danced across the surface of the earth, touching the grass in waves, and carrying our message into the unseeable distance.

"She wouldn't have left it intact all this time just to break it now."

"Well I just gave her a reason to break it." Locke's moccasins padded into the grass, step after step.

"It does seem strange she made it in the first place. I wonder what consonance she dropped."

A voice interrupted our thoughts, not Lonae's but Shilohe's.

The voice of a Goddess.

One elfe speaking to another *through* their sylves. And because of Lonae's talent, Shilohe's words came as clear as if it were the only sound in the world, a voice right in front of us: "It's not a marriage tattoo."

Locke stood still, listening, and his heart thumped quickly.

"I'm part of an order," came her voice. "I'm a votary of the Blue Rose—I've made certain vows represented by my tattoo."

I zipped into his palm. He cupped me near as a whisper, and I strained to hold myself together under the gentle grip. Locke inhaled, and I transformed.

"That's a relief." He spoke into the entire sky.

Only, my relaying of his voice sounded like a travesty rather than the real thing—a child shuffling across the floor in his father's moccasins. *If only I were more like Lonae.*

"Why?" asked Shilohe.

"I was worried my sylfe had formed the consonance with a married woman."

He listened with his mouth hanging open, as if that might help his ears open wider. His stomach turned in the long pause, even though he knew the delay always took a few heartbeats'.

She chuckled, but it mostly conveyed that she didn't understand. "But my Lonae gave the invitation…?"

"The truth is, I didn't actually know about our consonance. My Picke is a trickster sometimes."

"I imagine that could be confusing." Her tone was formal, a little distant, or tentative, which didn't help Locke's confidence.

"Uh, yes, sometimes it is, but he's great. Hey, that reminds me: At the council, why did your sylfe wander so far from you?"

"She gains strength from other sylves, a kind of synergy; both sylves come away stronger."

Locke stepped nervously during a few more heartbeats of silence.

"Any two sylves could do this," said Shilohe. "Lonae's just willing to greet everyone."

Locke was sweating. "That's pretty interesting. I will have to talk to my sylfe about that." He swung a disappointed fist through the air and tried to think of something better to say, hoping all the while that she'd speak up so he wouldn't have to.

More heartbeats passed more rapidly.

"Princess?"

The wind tickled across the grass.

"Princess?"

I let go, gasping. The world surged back and forth and everything got much, much smaller. "Wow."

"Wow, what?" Locke paced onward. "That was horrible."

"Look, it's not easy, alright? I'm doing the best I can."

"No, not you. That conversation was science. So stiff. I could've gotten those answers from a book! I wanted to talk to her. Really talk."

"She answered your questions."

"I know, but I don't know—I wanted something else. I don't know how to talk with a girl."

"You better try again then."

"She's not responding."

"Maybe her sylfe was too tired. It's exhausting!"

We walked on, with the sound of wind filling the vast open space.

"Picke, I could have married the Angel. But the Goddess… she's like a star… gorgeous and glorious and impossible to reach. I can't imagine a scenario where we'd marry."

Unfortunately, all I could do was nod.

"And yet," said Locke, "she seems like the best thing I can pursue. So how can I not?"

I gave it a moment of thought, strangely enough, then said, "I don't like to think about ends."

Lost in thought, he moved step by step closer to the Khalune Desert.

"I think I've done it before," I said.

"Done what?"

"What she said about getting energy from another sylfe. I think I've done that with Sanie. I'd just never put words to it. Never thought of it as a specific thing. Which is why I've never tried it with strangers."

"So are you going to?"

"I don't know. It's not easy approaching other elves."

The voice came back, sliding up and down the flowing wind. Locke's eyes lit up as he listened.

"I noticed something about you too," said Shilohe. "You're wrong handed, just like my dad."

He grinned. *Not out of a book.* He grabbed me quickly, and I slipped through his fingertips like water through a wicker basket. We both tried more carefully the second time. I held together as he brought me to his mouth—with his wrong hand—and inhaled. "Not the King though, right?"

"I don't want to talk about it."

"I'm sorry." He looked around for something to kick and, as the silence stretched out, for something to say. "So… why did you… make the consonance with us?"

"Lonae noticed something about you… and I listened." She didn't offer anything further, but her tone suggested she'd buried a compliment inside.

Locke frowned as he speculated, and it got quiet for a little too long. The conversation threatened to collapse at any moment. "Uh… Tell me about yourself."

"What do you want to know?"

"I don't know. Everything."

"Everything?" Her laugh trickled through the consonance in glorious symphony. "Starting with my birth?"

"Well, I didn't mean…"

"Oh. You don't want to know?"

"No, I do. I definitely do."

She laughed. "Well, I was born in the season of Phose."

"Oh, you were? Me too," said Locke.

"When's your birthday?"

"The fourth day of the third month of summertide."

"Oh, goodness," she said. "What year?"

"Goodness?"

"Really, what year?" she repeated.

"The eighty-third year."

"We were born on the same day!" she said.

"Are you serious?"

"Yes! I can't believe it."

"Two of my older brothers who aren't twins share a birthday. It's strange." Then came another pause, sweet for a moment because of the bubbling exchange, but panic set in quickly.

It was the Goddess who saved it: "Okay, well, if we're playing the questions game, I guess it's my turn."

"Okay, go."

"What's your greatest fear?"

Wow.

He could say *death*, but he might have to tell her about his mother and the twins. He could say *wraiths*, but that probably wouldn't count. He could say *bugs*, but what would she think of him?

"Come on," she said. "Be honest."

"I don't like bugs."

"Ha ha! Really?"

"They're too much like wraiths. Gives me chills just thinking about them." He swiped the back of his neck with his free hand.

"Okay, you want to know my fear? It's heights. I hate them. Yet we're supposed to be striving for them."

"What?"

"The Blue Rose. It's one of their teachings: 'Always further. Always higher.' But if you take it literally, well, it's very scary for me."

"So you're not a tree climber?"

"Not since I was a little girl." As she laughed, Locke imagined her twirling her brunette hair at the top corner of her neck like she'd done in the Seer's basement. "Okay, your turn, another question."

"Gah. I don't know. I'm not too good at this."

"You can ask whatever you want. Whatever interests you have."

"What's your favorite tale?" Locke gave a self-satisfied smile and resumed his casual walking.

"My dad used to read us one called The Isles of Time."

"I don't know it."

"It's about a hero who sails to a place full of strange creatures and wild adventures."

"I think I would like it."

"You would. It's so good. My favorite part is when they get to fly at the end."

"I thought you were afraid of heights?"

"So is the girl in the story! But the dragon soothes her fears before taking her up."

"Dragon?"

"It's sort of like a gryphine but bigger."

"Yeah, I know what they are," said Locke. "I just didn't know elves rode them."

"Well, that's how the story goes," she said. "And it's wonderful."

"I've actually wished I could fly, more than once." He pictured the two of them on the back of some great red dragon. Her arms were around his waist as they soared toward the blazing horizon.

"There's another part I really like," she said. "Nearly at the end she says, 'No matter how dark it gets, I'll still be hoping for a happy ending.' But things are basically hopeless at that point."

"And then what happens?"

"You'll just have to read it."

"Oh, come on! What if this is the end of time?"

"There's always the hereafter." She giggled at her own jab. "Okay, so what's yours—favorite tale?"

"Song of Martigane."

"That was quick."

"There's no contest. When I read it, it just gives me this feeling. I don't know. It's hard to explain. That feeling like you're flying across the sky road."

"Ha ha. Well it's a good choice."

"So you've read it?"

"Yes."

"Oh, yeah, you quoted it in your speech. Too bad. I was hoping to bribe you with the ending."

She laughed. "My dad read it to us many times."

"I wish it weren't a myth," he said.

"It's not."

"It isn't?"

"No."

"Are you sure?"

But as he spoke those words, something under the darkly painted sky caught my attention.

I sensed breath nearby, and I fell through Locke's fingers, leaving his words to drift on unaided, never to reach Shilohe.

"Locke," I said.

"What?"

"Someone's up there."

27.

Honke

L OCKE DUCKED BEHIND a rock then crawled to get a better look.
Ahead a tall figure sat on a white ledge, close enough Locke could
have hit him with a rock. The person looked over the cliff, down and away
from us, across the rugged landscape of the Khalune Desert, where only
the toughest plants broke through the rock and sand. The Astral Fields
were high, and from here to the World's End we would be gradually sloping
downward.

The figure had dark hair, and he even looked tall sitting down, tall
enough to be a hyuman.

Strange.

Locke squinted at the person's ears. They were stubby, or chewed off. Still,
the only hyumans we knew of were south of the Enchanted Wood. Far
south. So far that Locke and I had never actually seen one. And yet here on
the edge of the Astral Fields… *Strange.* Maybe they'd come to steal water.

Shilohe said something through the consonance, but my focus was
spread too thin.

The hyuman never turned and looked our way. He just sat there, as if
he were the opposite of a scout. Maybe he could see some commotion in
the basin below. He looked longingly, only who would long to go down
into the desert?

The wind scraped softly by, smoothing the small sounds into nothingness,
and we just kept watching.

"I'm tired of waiting," I whispered.

At that, Locke nodded, stood, and walked toward the figure—a little
more daring than I'd expected. "Hello," he said gently.

The creature's head turned in two spurts, first to the side, then, finding
nothing there, farther back, twisting his torso till he caught us in his gaze.

With an un-agile movement, he stood, a towering frame. *Wow.* It *was* a hyuman. Even taller than any of the Hundred.

Due to the length of the blade, Locke would have to lower his pack off his shoulder to draw his sword. It wouldn't be as swift as he now wished. *Running might be the better option.*

The hyuman shifted in an uncertain shuffle, as if running were his plan too. *So strange.* He had a boyish face. He was covered thick in dust. With the water gone, dust had been mounting like morning dew. Locke was also dusty, but not nearly so much as this hyuman. It was like he'd never taken the time to brush himself off—not once. Dust even rested on his eyelashes.

"Hi," said Locke, stepping forward while showing his empty palms, fingers pointing passively upward.

The hyuman boy held a large stick in his hand, which he gripped too tightly. But when Locke took another step, the hyuman collapsed to his knees, placing his hands on the earth.

Locke froze.

"Maybe he's pulling energy from Gaie and the gnymes," I said.

Locke drew his blade and held his breath, worrying the earth might shake while stone gargoyles rose up on all sides.

The hyuman glanced up, and seeing Locke stood still, he turned his face back to the ground and spread his fingers wider. Yet I saw and felt no magic. But if it wasn't, he'd put himself in a strangely vulnerable position. An enemy could step on his fingers or kick him in the head.

We waited.

Nothing happened.

"Maybe he's worshipping," I said.

"I'm too ordinary for that," said Locke. "And *you*—"

"He doesn't have a sylfe!" In surprise, I threw my hands to the sides and spread my fingers wide; my airborne legs and wings followed along—an aerial explosion.

The area above this hyuman's shoulders and around his head—*empty.* Maybe he had a gnyme or even a salaminde. But those weren't hard to see. This hyuman—this creature—showed no sign of any elemental. No spark of divinity. Even rocks had elementals! Could he be lower than an animal, lower than a piece of dirt?

"Don't hyumans usually have sylves?" whispered Locke.

"I thought so, but…"

"But you don't see anything?"

"Nothing."

The hyuman seemed surprised we hadn't yet closed the distance. *"Itish a shign af humber."*

A language I didn't recognize. The phonetics echoed in my mind, beautiful even if he wasn't opening his mouth all the way.

"A shign of humble," the hyuman said. The sound of his voice was a middle-value green, a bit like Locke's but more smooth and slippery, like a frog's back.

"Oh," I said.

"What?" asked Locke.

"A sign of humble. He's speaking Kyriglae."

The hyuman squinted up at us. "A shign of humble. Tenarie shign."

"We're not Tenarie," said Locke. "We're Kyrie. From the Enchanted Wood. My name's Locke. Who are you?"

Seeing his strange gesture on the ground wasn't getting through, he stood up. "I am Honke."

"Is that a race or a tribe?"

"My name ish Honke."

"That's a funny name," I said.

"What are thoshe?" the hyuman—Honke—asked, and he pointed straight at me.

It seemed odd that this pathetic creature, who had no elemental, had suddenly pinpointed me. He didn't have elfe eyes. But the day was dim, nearly nightfall, so maybe the contrast helped. If he spoke our language, surely he'd encountered elves with their sylves before. So why was he asking now? Maybe I was more brilliant than other sylves.

"It's a sylfe," answered Locke.

"It?" I asked.

"I mean—" began Locke.

"A what?" interrupted Honke.

"A sylfe."

"It not look like a shylfe to me. It look like a shmall pieshe of shmoke." He pointed his finger and made a swirling motion above his wrong shoulder. "A shmoke that alwaysh mobe up and up and up and shtill neber go anywhere. Neber mobe and alwaysh mobe. I cannot habe the wordsh."

He'd seen me right. To be confined to a single form was a terror—restrictive and claustrophobic.

"Do you habe any water?" asked Honke.

When he said this, the coating of dust seemed to puff off of him. Yet this was not a light question. The Seer had given us the right amount of water for our journey there and back again. Giving this hyuman some could endanger our quest and our lives, especially here, on the brink of the Khalune. And if we failed to meet the Seer, the whole land could die, not just this one pathetic creature.

Honke squinted and looked at Locke's backpack, as if staring hard enough might allow him to drink the water inside.

As Locke hesitated to answer, I began to notice a few things about Honke. He was half-again as tall as Locke. But he wasn't exactly the noble hyuman of legend. Quite the opposite, in fact. His back was bent as if he'd spent too many days sulking, a shape that seemed to reflect an attitude of being downtrodden and hopeless. Without the slouching, he'd have been a few fingers taller.

"Wery thirshty," repeated Honke.

I spun in front of his desperate eyes to distract him. I didn't want him taking Locke's water, and I was afraid Locke was about to give in. Honke squinted—an expression he was fond of. Maybe the only expression he was fond of. As he eyed me, I drifted to one side, then behind and above him, laughing as he twisted and followed my movement.

"Come closhe, little friend." He bent and put two hands on his knees, dropping to Locke's height. "I cannot shee you." He clawed a hand at me, too foolish to realize I was more slippery than his own breath. As his fingers closed around me, I whisked naturally outside of the trap. I laughed when he tried it again with both hands. He was stupid, but that made it more fun. "He ish quick," said Honke. "And sho tiny. He habe wingsh?"

"Picke, hold still for him," whispered Locke.

"Tell him I'm ephemeral," I said. "Fleeting. This is as still as I get."

"No it's not," said Locke.

"Who you are talking to?" asked Honke.

Locke's face flushed for being called out on his impoliteness. "I was talking to my sylfe," said Locke. "I can talk to him."

I swooped in close to Honke's face and held as still as I could, which wasn't that still—without Locke's hand, it was hard to not be caught in the oscillations of life.

"What ish it?" asked Honke.

"I told you, it's a sylfe." Locke glanced at me. *"He's* a sylfe, I mean."

"I do not undershtand." Honke squinted, and I slipped back and forth on the currents of time, smiling at our game.

"Tell him how we sylves can sing the melodies that seep into us from Numa."

"Picke likes to sing," said Locke.

"You're not very good at relaying messages," I said.

"Who ish Picke?"

"My sylfe. That little guy. His name's Picke."

"Oh. Uh huh."

"Tell him we're elementals because we're principle things—the first acts. And you came into being because I did. And ask if he has something like that—an elemental. That will tell you if he's worthy of water."

"I don't want to discuss doctrines, Picke."

"Just tell him. Please?"

"Fine." He turned back toward Honke. "Some say the sylves come from the Kyrose."

"What?"

"The Kyrose. The demigods."

"No. I do not beliebe in godsh."

Locke's eyebrows lifted—surprised to find an ally on this topic, and in such an odd creature. "What do you believe?"

"I beliebe death ish coming for eberybody. Shooner or later. And we jusht habe to run."

"That's so depressing," said Locke.

"Why are *you* so shocked?" I asked.

"Because he's saying even if there's hope for a while, in the end all true stories are tragedies."

"But that's what you believe, isn't it? Death always wins."

"No," said Locke. "I *can't* believe that." But in his eyes I saw the fear that it might be true.

"What ish tradgdeesh?" asked the giant hyuman.

Locke ignored the question. "You know, most people around here believe in the Kyrose. You and me are about the only ones who don't."

Honke nodded, as if it were an unimportant fact. "But what ish tradgdeesh?"

"Awe, nevermind," said Locke. "It just means a story that ends in disaster. A story about other people, but not you or me."

"No. Not ush." Honke smiled, but then with a more serious look, he added, "But we shtill gonna die."

Locke put his hand to the bruise on his chest, and felt the broken links and his own breath moving in and out. "Look, it doesn't matter. What are you doing out here in the middle of nowhere?"

"I look for water. Wery thirshty."

Locke ignored the statement, which made me glad. "So your tribe is also having this famine?"

"What ish famine?"

"You know, how all the water is gone… Is your family's water gone?"

"I do not know. I am losht from them."

"You're lost?"

"Yesh."

"So you're not wandering on purpose? I thought hyumans liked to wander…"

"We like to wander. Shometimesh. But I am losht. And I want to find my family."

A lost hyuman. "Not quite like the faerie stories," I whispered. Locke shook his head.

"Do you habe any water?" asked Honke.

A creature without a sylfe. Less than the dirt he was covered in. A person whose personhood was in question. One who, despite his giant stature, seemed incapable in the general sense. How long had it been since his last drink? And if Locke didn't show pity, would Honke have the wherewithal to make it to water? The odds didn't seem good. But we had none to spare.

"You know hyumans are supposed to live to the south?" Locke pointed as he said it. "Far to the south."

"How long to trabel there?"

"I don't know. Probably several months. Too far to carry your own water supply. I think people used to take canoes in the Saidane, beyond the rim. But you can't do that until the curse is broken. How'd you get all the way up here anyway?"

"I don't know," he said. *A strange answer.* Maybe he'd been hit over the head and dragged up here. But it was such a long way. He puffed out his chest and stood up straight for a moment—an air of acting a little tougher and a little smarter than he actually was. "Do you habe any water?"

I gasped. "Locke?"

My elfe turned and looked at me.

"He's right there," I said.

Locke frowned his question in reply.

Honke's eyes bored into Locke's backpack.

"I can see his sylfe now." I zoomed to the giant's chest and brushed his heart with one tiny stroke. "He's right there."

Locke smiled without showing teeth, like a candle glowing through the skin of a cupped hand.

"I see him too," said Locke.

28.

Three Times Lucky

"WAIT, LOCKE, DON'T!"
Locke handed one of our precious flasks to the hyuman. *He never could tell someone no.*

As Honke drank, he spilled, turning his dust into a muddy beard that streaked down his chin and shirt. A giant two year old, with just enough dexterity to tie the top of the flask shut. He wiped the back of his hand across his muddy face and kept the flask.

"Give me that." Locke grabbed it out of his hands.

It was my fault. I never should have pointed out the sylfe. We still had to cross the Khalune. Twice.

I looked at Honke's sylfe to make sure he was really there. That poor thing, buried inside his own kynde. It looked so uncomfortable, cramped, so far from the wind and reaching for stars. Maybe his sylfe couldn't function correctly because of it. At least he *had* an excuse though.

So hyumans also clung to the children of Numa. I spoke to the sylfe, but he didn't respond. That scared me a bit—like a nightmare. But he looked at me, so I knew he wasn't dead.

"I can go with you!" declared Honke, as if announcing some great victory.

"I'm sorry, but you can't," said Locke.

Honke grinned, unfazed. "You my friend. Gibe me water. I fight for you." He gave Locke a friendly tap on the chest with his open knuckles. *What had we done?*

"I can't take care of you," said Locke. "I don't have enough water for us both."

Honke walked back to the cliff rim where we'd found him. He pointed below. Orange campfires glowed against a backdrop of bluish blackness. "There ish a Tenarie willage. They gibe me no water, but maybe they gibe you water."

Honke struggled on through his arguments in this thick accent: The Tenarie had the water we needed; they'd be more likely to listen to Locke; maybe asking twice would be lucky. Locke countered each of these with his own doubts. Broken Kyriglae came back in weak or incomprehensible replies, and the conversation simply wound in circles—simple arguments, each repeated two or three times for clarity. And Locke wouldn't just tell him no.

I flew down the path toward Honke's Tenarie campfires. "Come on!"

Locke looked at me in surprise.

He didn't have to, but he followed, and just like that our caravan was in motion. I felt pretty proud of that one. Something Honke's sylfe could never do.

Together we descended a wide, well-trodden path.

As we approached the camp, Honke stretched out his long arm and pointed. "Ho! The Tenarie!"

Many held spears and other weapons ready—not as a threat, but in a defensive attitude. With their wild white hair and pale skin, they looked like ghosts in the darkness. They glared at Locke and Honke. None seemed to notice me, which I didn't like.

Within a stone's throw, three different wraiths were impaled, pinned to the ground, still squirming. We felt their coldness, even from a distance. Two were the size of large squirrels. The third looked like a full-grown elfe with shadowy skin and no eyes. This larger one had several spikes through him and into the ground to make sure he couldn't escape. Eight days had come and gone since we'd seen the sun. How much longer till we were completely overrun?

An obvious fact suddenly hit me: The curse, meant to punish the Kyrie, had punished the Tenarie equally. Which meant a maniac had done this—one willing to injure his own kin in order to injure others. Or some greater evil was afoot.

One Tenarie seemed to be chief among them. He had a flat nose and wide cheekbones, and his chin stuck forward a bit like Nicke's. His sylfe stood straight like it was on guard duty and mustn't be distracted. This Tenarie stepped forward waving the backs of his hands like scaring off chickens. "I told you to go! No water for you. No water for either of you." That last part he said to Locke.

But Locke stood his ground. "Sir, I'm a traveler passing through. We were hoping to refill our flasks so we can continue on our journey and not bother you any more." He had no money to offer, but some Tenarie wouldn't accept Kyrie coins anyway.

The chief dropped his hands and frowned. "You are not a friend of the Tenarie. And we do not have enough water for all of you."

"It's just me and my hyuman friend. We won't take much."

"No. No water. You must go." The chief's sylfe stayed rigid as a board.

"Please, sir. Show compassion."

He snapped his head toward Locke and glared like a murderer. Somehow the comment had hit harder than expected. But he still didn't budge, at least not until he caught the eyes of one small, ghostly pale child, who also seemed curious where the compassion had gone. Barely relaxing his glare, the chief said, "We will consult the spirits. Let *them* show compassion." He held out a smooth, shiny kohkoo nut that looked like a large, bloated coin, the perfect size to throw at an older brother.

"Cleromancy," said one bystander, suggesting that the demigods would guide the outcome, Nara in particular, Demigoddess of Blood and Waters.

Locke smiled. "I know this game." But he believed luck guided it. Except when someone cheated—which he'd learned as the youngest brother—using a rotting nut with lopsided innards. "I'll make my own." He scoured the ground till he found a fresh nut that suited him. He carved the *lah* rune into one of its flatter sides with his knife. "Up wins, right?"

The chief nodded and waved for Locke to come. The small crowd, including Honke, followed after.

The village consisted of makeshift tents with no permanent buildings. Apparently this wasn't their natural home. Maybe they'd come for the water we were now begging from them. A wall of mortar and bricks guarded a deep hole. A heavy stone rested on the ground next to it, a lid too heavy for one person to lift. A wooden bucket, filled with water, rested on the wall.

Without waiting for instructions, Locke dropped his marked kohkoo nut into the bucket, the rim of which was nearly at his chin. The nut sploshed in and tumbled, heavy enough to sink temporarily. The motion mesmerized the onlookers onto their tiptoes.

I sensed Locke pleading silently. Then these words echoed in our mind: *I don't beweave in wuck.*

The spinning slowed, the nut surfaced, and the blank side rolled to the top, shining and wet. Then, just barely, it tipped one last time, and the *lah* rune popped to the top.

"Yeah!" I shouted.

Locke's face cracked with a grin.

"No!" The chief snatched the nut out of the water, as if he didn't want anyone to see the outcome. "You were too close."

"What?"

The chief thrust the nut back into Locke's hands. "You can't stand so close to the water." *The sort of call a jealous older brother would make.* We'd played enough to know that if you got close and dropped it with no spin, you could keep your side up more often than not. But Locke's drop had clearly spun. He wasn't cheating.

"But I…" said Locke.

"No!" repeated the chief. His pale face turned the color of a bloody lip. He grabbed the bucket and tossed it down the well, where it hit with an echoing splash, and the rope slithered over the wall after it. "Now let the spirits show compassion. If the seed lands in the bucket, they may smile on your request."

Locke agonized over the ledge. He thought maybe he saw the curving rim of the bucket, but it was so dark out. Did the chief mean that missing the bucket meant missing out?

As the crowd murmured around us, I suddenly heard, "I help you protect thish water." Children kept their distance from Honke but kept their eyes on his every move. Honke patted his chest. "We can be wery good friendsh." He smiled, and his speech was just childish enough to have some charm to it. It seemed he'd already won over some friends. Others, though, stared and pointed, unable to find his sylfe, it seemed.

I focused back on the stakes just as Locke dropped the nut.

The deepness sucked it downward.

Plop.

"Pull it up," said Locke.

They did, right away—they seemed as interested in the outcome as we were.

"Come on," I said. "Two times lucky. Please."

As the bucket neared the surface, the nut became visible.

And there was the *lah* rune, looking up at us.

"Yeahaa!" said Locke. "The demigods are gracious!"

Honke smiled, and the two shook hands. Then Locke grabbed the bucket and lifted it to his lips.

"Aaaagh—" the chief shouted, and he pulled the bucket down, spilling some of the water but not the nut. Locke hadn't yet gotten a drop. "Before you drink, you must know this is only one victory, and there are two of you."

Locke stared down at the bucket. After sparing his water for the last three days, he was quite thirsty. Yet once again he had to choose: water for himself or water for Honke. He'd already been generous with the hyuman, and now was his chance to regain what he'd lost. For some reason, he hung on the decision, and the Tenarie watched him closely. In a move so subtle I don't think a single onlooker noticed, Locke's lips brushed together ever so lightly as he breathed:

"*Picke.*"

No one but me—his own sylfe—could've heard it. And, surprisingly, it wasn't a question. He wasn't asking me; he was calling me. He wanted me nearer. I moved close to his heart. He still waited, weighing his own needs against the needs of the desperate vagabond, the *losht* hyuman. What a pathetic and loveable creature. I don't know what came over me, but I whispered, "Fine, give him the water."

Locke nodded so slightly his nose barely moved up and down. With his smile barely glowing, he pulled the nut from the water and handed the bucket to Honke.

Honke gulped down the water just like before, and no one stopped him, washing off his muddy beard so that just one part of his face was clean. Some of the Tenarie smiled their approval of Locke's selflessness. The chief frowned.

"So, can I have a third try?" asked Locke, swallowing.

"*Second* try," the chief said.

Honke finished drinking and handed an empty bucket back to Locke. *Whoa.* He'd drunk at least twice as much as any elfe could have.

Locke threw the bucket into the well with a splash and peered down. He'd gotten lucky twice. A third time seemed too much to hope for. And if he didn't get lucky in this moment, would it mean dying under a hot, dark sky? No clairvoyance for the Seer and no sunlight to drive back the wraiths? All because Locke had been kind to a hyuman. He pinched the nut with the stem side up, lining it up with what he thought was the bucket in the darkness below, squinting, with one eye closed.

He dropped it.

The dark sky seemed to pull everything toward it, and the nut fell.

Plop.

The bucket sloshed as it was pulled up again. The crowd leaned in, but no one breathed, not till one of the Tenarie gasped. Or maybe it was Honke.

The *lah* rune smiled up at us for the third time.

"Third adventure is Locke's," I joked.

"I can't believe it!" He reached for the bucket.

"Wait!" The chief cut all activity with a chop of his hand. "I think you're a cheater." He pulled the bucket from Locke's hand again and set it on the ground. He picked up the nut and dropped it spinning again into the bucket.

Locke looked at me for an answer. But I had none, other than to whisper, "If the *lah* rune turns up a fourth time, it will look like we did cheat." I started praying it wouldn't.

It spun, and the Tenarie gawked, and the chief aimed his dagger eyes at us. Honke seemed to look at nothing. The *lah* rune spun and spun, taunting each time it surfaced and submerged.

Of course we hadn't cheated.

But when the nut stopped spinning, the *lah* was above the surface, looking upward for the fourth time. The chief pursed his lips, as if holding in an explosion. His white skin burned red, almost murderous, but we would never know fully why.

Locke backed up.

The chief snatched the nut from the bucket and flung it. It smacked Locke hard in the chest—right where the spear had bruised him—and Locke cupped his hand on top, catching it without thinking.

"We will not allow a cheating Kyrie dog to taste our water or stay in our camp."

"I didn't cheat."

The chief crouched and grabbed another kohkoo nut from the ground, hurling it at us with more force than the first. In a heartbeat, Locke dropped his pack from one shoulder, drew his sword. Whipping it in front of him, he turned the flat of the blade toward the attack. *Just in time.* The nut pinged against the metal, flipping upward before thudding onto the ground.

Locke now stood with a drawn sword against a group of Tenarie.

"That's just how luck works." Locke looked around for support. From anyone.

Honke watched with his mouth hanging open, but he didn't show a single sign of action, and the Tenarie seemed to have forgotten him.

Showing the first real loyalty to their chief, another of the Tenarie adults grabbed a kohkoo nut and launched it. Again Locke blocked it with a ping, backing away.

"I didn't cheat," he said. *"I'm just lucky."*

Then came another and another, too many to block them all. Even a torrent of the bullets probably wouldn't have killed Locke, but they stung. The Tenarie flung them and shouted their curses, unleashing a river of rage that had been dammed since two ancient brothers began the hating.

"Bad luck," I said.

Locke turned and ran, leaving Honke behind.

29.

Thirst

EARTH CRUNCHED AS Locke's moccasins landed in fearsome steps. The firm blades of dead grass scraped at his soles, wanting to punch through.

He ran beyond the range of their projectiles. He ran beyond earshot of their curses. He ran beyond the sight of trees and grass, till the dirt beneath his feet had turned into the grit of sand. On a desolate hill, he stopped, bent over, and put his hands on his knees, gasping. Lyzards skirted across the grains and disappeared beneath cracked stones. Ahead of us stretched the Khalune Desert.

He panted, practically gulping down the air. "I hate the Tenarie."

He tilted his head back and took a swallow from his flask and saw an image of Honke spilling it down his front. Locke shook his head. He had water for now, but it wouldn't be enough, and it was already much less than he wanted.

"I'm trying to save them! And they hate me. For no reason. I did nothing—didn't harm them. *But I wish I could now*"—he added the last part through clenched teeth.

"You don't hate Nicke."

"Shut up, Picke. I hate *those* Tenarie."

I didn't much like Locke being this way. He'd taken my usual stance too, so what could I do but take his? "It mostly seemed to be their leader who had a grudge."

"They *all* threw kohkoo nuts."

"But it was the chief's fault. I don't think it's fair to blame them all."

Locke's face squinted bitterly. "They were treating us like we were *nobody*. You hate that! What's gotten into you?" He sliced his sword through me in the air.

I frowned. "What's gotten into *you?*"

The desert stood quiet as Locke breathed to cool down. It took him a while, but he finally said, "Sorry." When I didn't respond, he added, "I hope they're not mean to Honke."

"He seemed to already be gaining rapport. Maybe they'll keep him for the novelty."

"For the oddity," chuckled Locke. After a few moments' rest, he began walking, with the dark sky covering our way. He didn't even ask whether he should get himself deeper into the desert. He just continued toward the goal, walking, breathing, letting the anger flow out from his pores, thinking of the water Honke spilled down his shirt. "Oh, my throat is so dry."

A wraith stood in front of us.

A cold chill washed through us. It was a full-grown wraith, tall as a hyuman, cloaked in a flaming shadow, one too smart to have ever been caught off guard in daylight. The heavy dark crawled all over its body, pulling it downward toward misery. Its face without eyes but full of teeth stared at us, jealous and hungry. For a moment—the calm before the storm—we stared back.

"Now's your chance to prove you're a warrior," I said.

The words *I'm not* hung on his lips, but he never spoke them. Instead, he just nodded.

A wraith had ended Locke's world once. He brought his sword in front of him, gripping it with both hands and raising it above his head into a high guard, ready to strike quickly. "I hate wraiths."

"Are there graves out here?"

"That's superstition, Picke. That's not where they come from."

"How do you know?"

He had no time to answer.

The wraith sprinted, moving like an elfe pretending to be an animal—on two legs, hunched over, and holding its hands up like a fighter, ready to claw and bite when it got close. The eyeless face made it truly terrible.

The moment the wraith came within reach, Locke swung a blow—fueled by fear, anger, and an eagerness to beat justice out of something.

The blade crashed first into the outstretched hands and then the head of the attacking monster. But this was no mortal creature, and the blade didn't cut like it was flesh and bone. It did sink partly though, and the creature squealed, crashing into the ground. Instantly it scraped forward again.

Locke stepped backward and brought down a second swing, which slammed the wraith's face into the ground.

Still it crawled forward.

Locke jumped back again, this time thrusting the point into the creature's back.

It cried in pain.

The lengthy sword kept the creature out of reach much better than the dagger he'd used before. But he didn't want to leave it pinning this creature into the ground. Only how else could he keep the monster down?

"Locke, look out!"

A second wraith lunged from behind.

Locke turned in time to drop the point of his blade, creating a vertical barrier, and he spun, both slicing the aggressor and then throwing it to the side—a move worthy of music. He stepped wide in a stance ready to strike.

A third wraith appeared from the shadows of the sand, so subtle I saw it too late.

"Locke!"

I shot toward the attacker to give my elfe a sense of what he'd only glimpsed from the corner of his eye.

The wraith grabbed Locke's arms from behind and rammed its freezing white teeth toward Locke's neck. The horror of fangs and a dying mother stabbed into him.

But before the bite actually sunk, Locke brought his sword back, as if to rest the blade on his own shoulder—but with much greater force. The edge dug into the creature's eyeless skull. Locke shoved, and the metal cut deeper till the crossguard slammed into the wraith's face.

It stumbled back. Locke was free.

The first wraith jumped at him. He twirled. The metal sung as it cut, though still not deep enough to cleave the creature apart. This blow knocked back the wraith—like fighting elves with a club.

They came from all sides, making no sound but their heavy, hungry breathing.

Locke charged, slicing one, shoving back the next with his hilt, and then lashing at the third in a fast horizontal hack. This blow struck the wraith's thigh and cut clean through—a blow so powerful it might have cut through two gutted deer. With a severed limb, the wraith fell to the ground screeching.

Locke backed away, where the maimed one couldn't reach him—though it still crawled.

The other two didn't relent.

Neither did Locke.

They raced toward him. He countered like in legend.

His next blow struck off a hand. The three after that severed another leg—a second one down.

When the last came at him, he thrust the blade through the monster's cold chest.

Unfazed, the soulless creature grabbed Locke's arms and pulled him closer. Its teeth clapped as they gnashed together.

Using the sword as an anchor through the wraith's body, Locke turned away and pulled a wide swing. Hauled along by the curving thrust, the wraith stumbled to its hands and knees, and the steel hummed as it came free.

In a gallant leap, Locke heaved the sword in a skyward arc. The edge hit the wraith's neck about two-thirds down the blade's length.

With a wet crack, the wraith's head fell on the ground and rolled.

Locke frowned, lips pursed, teeth grit, eyes glaring, breathing heavily through his nostrils as he thought about his mom.

The three injured monsters didn't stop moving.

Even the headless wraith crawled on, directionless, and would be given no reprieve.

30.

Speaking to a Goddess

Y OU'RE STRONG WHEN you're mad."

I said this as we plunged further into the dark, wind-stroked desert.

"It doesn't make me feel very good," said Locke.

"You just defeated three wraiths, your worst fear!"

"Not my worst. And besides, my heart still feels… I don't know."

"Like its bound tight in a knot?"

"Yes. And dark."

I smiled at him—which seemed the best way to communicate what I was feeling. The thirst scraped at me too, but I could only help him breathe. *If only I were an ondine…*

We peered into the desert, toward sand and hills and more sand. Pools of water stretched across the horizon, and the hills reflected in them. "Water!" I shouted.

Locke quickened his pace.

As we moved step by step through the desert, closer to the edge of the world, the pools of water vanished, only to appear later on another, farther horizon, shimmering in the distance. Time itself seemed to blur together into a sort of dream. The wolves' howling song sailed across the cheerless sky. We passed through days and into nights, walking and sleeping and thirsting, with nothing but each other and a very little water.

We barely detected dusk of the eleventh day.

Locke held one flask, mostly empty, but a few drops remained inside, and he contemplated drinking them. "Why are we here?"

"What?"

"I'm trying to remember why we're doing this."

"*You* know why," I said.

"For Nicke."

"Yes," I said. "And…?"

"And for my family. And for Honke, the ingrate."

I chuckled.

He eyed the flask again, weighing its meager contents.

"One more," I said.

Locke looked at the flask and grinned a huge grin. It felt like his bottom lip was going to crack.

"What's so funny?" I asked.

"Funny? Nothing's funny."

"Then why are you smiling?"

This time he laughed aloud, unable to keep it in, a beautiful sound. "*What?*"

"It's her. She makes me smile. Just thinking about her. I don't know why. It's crazy. I'm losing my mind."

He shook his head as if to clear his thoughts.

"It hurts, you know. It comes out of my heart, and it runs across my chest down the insides of my arms and into these fingers." He touched his thumbs and his fourth fingers together. "And then it just tingles. She's the only thing I like to think about. Maybe the only thing I want. If I had her, I'd have everything."

"Breathe, will you?"

While sucking in, he said, "I *am* breathing." While exhaling a sigh, he added, "But I can never breathe enough."

"You should talk to her."

In the last few days, we'd only spoken with her briefly. Something kept her busy, but she wouldn't tell us what.

Locke sat down.

"What are you doing?" I asked.

"Nothing. Just resting."

"Get up! We have a job to do, a reason for crossing this desert."

He put the flask to his lips and sipped the last of the water from it. "I just hope I don't die trying."

"You're not going to die."

He put his tongue to the flask and sucked. The flecks were hardly more than the dream of water. "Maybe I'll die and she'll end up going after all."

"You're not dying!"

"I'm going to if we don't find water. No thanks to those Tenarie."

"We're close to the Well at the World's End. Very close. The Pilgrim Stairs might be in that next ridge up there." Ahead the rock rose into a massive barrier, a wall built by Gaie, a wall that blocked our view of anything beyond. I aimed our course toward the tallest peak along that rising ridge, and Locke stumbled after me.

"You've said that three times before."

"You can't give up."

"I'm not."

Locke motioned me closer with his hand while looking distracted ahead. After scooping me up, he spoke with my help into the consonance:

"Princess, do you have time to talk?" Thanks to his exhaustion, he said this with surprisingly steady nerves.

For some reason, she spoke right back to us this time: "Yes, I'm here. How are you?"

"Oh, I don't know. Pretty worn out. A little angry and a little thirsty."

"Why are you angry?" Her voice burned a bright orange, as smooth as a candle flame.

He told her about his adventure with Honke and the Tenarie.

"I think Numa would tell you to forgive the Tenarie chief. Until you do, you'll carry the hate. Not an easy load."

I gasped and nearly fell from the sky into Locke's hand. Her words bore a mysterious resemblance to mine from not long ago, as if they'd all poured from the same fountain. I fought to maintain my grip.

"That makes sense in my head," said Locke as if he hadn't even noticed. "But it's not easy to get it in my heart. To be honest, I want to hurt them, make them feel what I'm feeling."

"You're feeling hate."

"No, I'm feeling rejection." The timbre of his voice fell as he said this, like ground crumbling beneath his feet.

Shilohe waited as the truth sunk down past the topsoil.

With his free hand, Locke pulled the strap of his back to shift the weight he was carrying. "You might be right: I'd be spreading hate."

"You'd make a wonderful Knight of the Blue Rose."

I nearly lost my grip a second time. The Seer had made a comment similar to that too.

Locke chuckled. "You're just saying that."

"No, it's true. It's not easy to accept truth when it means admitting you're wrong."

"So what is this Blue Rose all about?"

"It's just a group questing for truth."

"In what way?"

"You can gather truth in a lot of ways. The simplest is a sylfe and elfe in consonance with the Kyrose. A lot of people don't realize what's possible, so they don't try."

"I guess I'm one of those people because I don't quite follow."

"I think it's because we disagree on one of the premises."

"The Kyrose?"

"You don't believe in them, do you?"

He shrugged even though she couldn't see him. "Are you going to hate me if I admit it?"

"No. Of course not. I just want to understand why."

"Why? The lack of justice. How can they let things happen like what happened to Nicke—losing his family to a band of savages?" And although he didn't say it, he was thinking about his own mother too. Like the sky, this agony hung over us.

"They do believe in justice. But theirs, not yours."

"If it doesn't save kids like Nicke, I'm not sure I want it." He shook his head. "They say the demigods have legions of valkalysae and angels. So why don't they send them to help us? Now of all times. If they won't help us when we need them most, why do we need them at all?"

"I'm sorry for your suffering, and I really wish I could help you." Her sympathy came through in her tone. She waited, allowing him to breathe.

He tried to hide his anger when he said, "That isn't an answer."

If she noticed his emotion, she chose not to respond to it. "The Kyrose are teachers, not gods. They have power, and if they wanted to, they could force us all to act a certain way. But slavery and coercion kill the lifeforces. You see the difference, right? If they forced our wills, we'd be dolls instead of children. So they allow us to choose, in hopes that we'll choose good. But that means letting us choose evil sometimes too."

"Yes, but you're saying they don't act—they don't interfere. So what good are they?"

"They do interfere. They teach people how to live. And how to love."

"But how?"

"Through the poetics and faerie stories for one. You felt it in Martigane's legend. Because it's true."

He shook his head to disagree but said nothing, staring past his own hand wrapped in a mask over his face.

"They'll speak to your sylfe too," she said, "if you'll both listen carefully."

"Maybe."

"It's not easy, even for me, but if you're truly willing to obey, you'll hear Numa's voice. I promise. Even with a curse as thick as this hanging over our heads."

I had something I just had to say, and I tried to nudge Locke without losing my grip on the consonance.

The tickle on his bottom lip startled him, and he dropped me like I was a spider. "What did you do that for?"

"I wanted you to ask her about the curse."

With an annoyed look, he scooped me back into his hand. He hesitated a moment longer, inhaling carefully. "Do you know how the curse works?"

I smiled, once again under heavy strain.

"The sky is bound by ondines—he enslaved them. And he murdered thousands of innocent creatures to do it. That's why our sylves stopped singing."

"What?"

"You know."

"No, I don't think I do. Picke never sang."

"Not even a little? He's a *sylfe*."

"No. He talks a lot though."

She laughed. "That always surprises me. Well anyway, Stane has done something incredibly evil."

Locke leaped up onto a stone then walked across the tops of several, which was easier than winding his way around and between. "So it really is the end of time?"

"I don't think so."

"I thought there were prophecies."

"There *are* prophecies, but—"

"And what do they say?"

"There are many. I think the best is in the Dialogues of the Lost. It says the Night of the Wolfe shall strike darkness upon the empyrean… and Saede shall rage, and the reapers shall gather and burn."

"Yeah, there you go. The Night of the Wolfe is the end of time, right?"

"Sort of. I think people misunderstand it."

The sand beneath us had been swept away, revealing massive sheets of rock with great cracks in it, deep slits leading down to darkness and oblivion. Gravel ground beneath each step. "But it describes us almost exactly—the sky and the wraiths."

"Locke, how can it be the end of time if you're going to stop it?"

"I didn't say *I* believed it was the end of time."

'Then what do you believe?"

"I don't believe in the creeds."

"Did your parents teach you to think this way?"

"No. My dad thinks it's the end of time."

"And your mom?"

"My mom is dead." And saying so, even after all these years, poured darkness over him. His heart thumped harder.

Shilohe's tone dropped and her rhythm changed to reverence. "And what did she believe?"

"She said the demigods would take care of her and that she would get well."

Shilohe didn't reply.

"She was wrong," said Locke.

As Shilohe waited, we could almost see her mournful face on the wind, solemnly paying honors to Locke's dead mother.

Unfortunately, it was an ill-fated wind, and it carried the scent of death, a repulsive odor mixed with sweet smoke.

"Locke!" I fell out of the sky and became one small breath again. "It's them!"

"I know, I know." Despite his weariness, he started into a run, scanning the terrain for a place to escape. "Why does this always happen when we're…"

The fear chased at our heels.

Locke scanned the various cracks in the ground around us, each too narrow for us to escape into. He pressed on toward the wall ahead. If this was it, somewhere ahead a staircase would lead us up the sheer rock. Only, we hadn't been able to spot it yet. We passed amid a garden of boulders, most of which were about waist high. They tangled us in a maze of panic.

Shilohe's voice drifted on the wind. Her words competed with the fear and the crunching rock. A calm, disconnected voice. I only caught a bit of what she said—"You'll see her again."—like a ghost.

I sensed an evil breath very close, somewhere in the darkened night.

"Locke?" came the hush of her voice.

The wind whipped violently through Locke's hair, and the odor grew stronger. He scanned the cliff ahead. It towered like the wall of an arena, eager to see our fight to the death.

"We've got to move!" I yelled. "Faster!"

He picked up his already flying pace, pushing through sapped strength. His throat cried for something softer than air as it scraped in and out of his ribcage.

A banshe wolfe appeared between us and the cliff face—we'd been running toward the beast.

Foam dripped from its bloody teeth.

31.

Sough

AN ARROW STUCK into the monster's shoulder, put there by Locke's father in the Enchanted Wood.

This was the more aggressive of the two wolves, the mad one. Its hollow eyes showed no intention to think or to plan. All it wanted was to devour. It jerked forward, driving furiously at us, giving up control for intensity. The wound didn't seem to slow it at all.

Locke had no time to test his sling. He sprinted, wildly retracing his steps through the garden of boulders. The wind pulled his hair across his face and over his eyes.

"Forty feet!" I shouted. Then the fangs would sink into his neck.

Massive paws drummed against the ground in a crescendo.

"Twenty feet!"

The wolfe leaped, jaws gaping, black eyes burning.

"Duck!"

Locke dove over a boulder and rolled.

The wolfe's massive body whisked past. Its hind leg clipped the rock that now protected my elfe, and the claws caught the mail links covering Locke's shoulder blade, sending him sprawling. After tripping over the boulder, the wolfe rumbled across the dirt in a large ball.

Locke stood and looked into the empty eyes. Fear jabbed at his throat. He sprinted back toward the cliff. His shoulder pounded with his heartbeats.

As the wolfe bound to its feet, I spun loops back and forth in front of its eyes, hoping to stall it if only for one small moment. It snapped at me in the air. Death's laugh echoed all around. Then I was exhaled through its teeth.

For a moment I paused, staring wildly with open eyes.

I couldn't think about it, not the choice, not now. But the more I tried not to, the more I did. When the wolfe aimed its madness at my elfe, I snapped out of it.

Locke leaped atop a boulder and sped in a line toward the cliffs, gliding, almost like me, off the tops of the large stones, touching them for the smallest moment before flying forward.

The wolfe ran the long way around, still gaining.

I sped after them both, trying to catch up and help.

Then I saw it—Locke was racing for a dark crevice in the rock face. Not the staircase, just a crack in the stone. Maybe wide enough for him to enter.

The animal drove forward, the speed of a bee and the bulk of a horse, and crazed with bloodlust.

"Thirty feet!"

Locke bolted, not looking behind.

The beast's paws thudded then hit in one heavy, final bound, transforming into a majestic and terrible leap. The wind pushed across the scenery. The beast soared toward its prey.

"Locke!"

He curled and dropped, rolling sideways.

The wolfe, unable to change course, crashed into the jagged surface, tumbling head over heels and resting on its back—

—between Locke and the crack in the cliff wall.

Without waiting a heartbeat, Locke charged.

The animal jerked its head this way and that, unable for a moment to locate its prey. The madness gleamed as its eyes focused.

Locke lifted his backpack strap with one hand and gripped the hilt in his other. In one fluid motion, he drew his sword and swung it downward. The blade cracked into the creature's jaw, making a sound that sent repercussions through Locke's own teeth. In the backswing, the sword trailed him like the fletching of an arrow.

The wolfe regained its feet in an instant, impending like death.

Locke pulled his blade close, and with a *whoosh* he vanished into the crack, as if he were the stone missing from the mountain.

The wolfe snarled and leaped toward the crevice. Its bark rung into the darkness.

Locke pushed forward. The rock walls scraped his face and knuckles. His heart pounded. His shoulder ached. When he finally reached a spot wide enough to turn and look back, he saw a sliver of dim light reaching toward the sky.

The beast's lunatic eyes glared into the crack, but no blood came from the gash in its face.

I was still on the outside, behind and above the wolfe.

The wolfe growled, loud and angry. Foam fell from the sides of its mouth. Its horrible, deathly smell wafted into the air all around me. It kept dipping its head, pointing its nose into the crack, and then jerking back, threatening in vain to follow its prey. Those were the jaws that had closed around me.

It can't harm me.

Its ferocity bit into my ears, reminding me of a choice I never wanted to face. A choice that would never leave me alone. I gasped for each breath, struggling more the more Locke moved away. I had to follow. Into the future. Into the cave.

It can't harm me.

The wolfe's foamy jaws snapped.

Today was not the day that I would risk it all.

I waited for the slightest break in the frenzy before zipping past the wolfe into the cramped darkness.

32.

The Stand

THE UNMERCIFUL WALLS threatened to squeeze us till we couldn't breathe.

I hated tight spaces.

A numbing throb bounced through Locke's right shoulder and into me. He was ten feet into the crevice, but it didn't seem far enough. The wolfe's eye glared through the closing darkness. Its growl had mellowed to heavy breath, creating a sound that smothered alongside the horrid stench.

As I moved toward Locke, the walls remained unwilling to budge. But I had to stay with my elfe—as much as I hated being cramped, being alone was worse.

"You feel that?" asked Locke.

"Feel what?"

"I don't know. A strange feeling. Like death was out there and barely passed us by."

I paid closer attention to what he was feeling. Something like swirling spears darted through the ether, and then through us—spears of magic in all different colors with barbs that ripped through our soul like wolfe fangs.

"Uhhh." I felt sick.

Rather than protect his aching shoulder, Locke grabbed at his heart. The sensation pressed his shoulders and neck and bones, sinking me into stillness.

"We *should* have died." Locke waved his arms around and bobbed his head back and forth, as if blood flow might fend off death's grip. "The timing— The chance— I could have run that a hundred times and never have gotten so lucky. The wolfe missed me by a finger's breadth—twice."

As we breathed, the feeling subsided—not vanishing, but walking into the distance slowly, remaining within sight, next to the jowls of the leering wolfe.

"If that feeling is death, we're still not far enough away," I said. "He lingers."

"What do we do?" asked Locke.

"Find the Well."

Which meant exiting the crevice.

I felt pride when Locke gripped the leather handle of his sword in weakness, as strongly as he could. The steel sung as it brushed across the leather scabbard, which he dropped with his bag to the ground. The blade glinted as he pointed it forward.

The wolfe's breathing rolled into a low, steady growl. Its snout was just inside the crevice, and one paw leaned into the opening. It snarled as Locke reached the blade closer and closer.

I thought maybe I could taunt the wolfe so he'd show us the extent of his reach. I moved forward. Toward those fangs, which reminded me... *It can't harm me.* Its smothering breath pushed me back like a wall of heat. I stopped, trembling.

Locke, however, did not stop. The boy who ran from bugs approached the jaws of a giant wolfe. He pointed the sword, pressing steadily forward.

The growl deepened in pitch. In an instant, the cave blackened as the beast filled the entrance. It mashed its shoulder into the rock and slammed its paw onto the sword, tearing it from Locke's grip and knocking him to the ground. It snarled in rage, reaching as far as it could, not far enough.

Locke coughed and swallowed dryness. The beast didn't have the sense to scrape the sword out, so Locke, in a second daring move, lunged for the handle and pulled his weapon back to safety.

"Are you alright?" I asked.

Locke nodded.

"Are you going to try again?"

Determination showed in his eyebrows as he nodded and glared at the fangs. With the blade held in a high guard, he stepped up again.

The claw smashed forward.

Locke swung, and the edge bit flesh as the two impacted with terrible force. A yelp rang through the crevice, and the sword clanked on the ground. Locke panted, snatching his weapon again and scooting back while the feeling of death floated around.

I wanted to bite the wolfe's ear off. It deserved that and worse. It wasn't bleeding after this second cut either—the opposite of a wraith.

Locke gripped the hilt and approached a third time.

The dim light flowed back into the crevice as the wolfe withdrew, leaving the way standing open. The animal growled, just outside, taunting its prey to come and be devoured.

Locke lowered his sword. His shoulder ached.

"And so?" I asked.

"We've been outsmarted. The wolfe will win if I step within its reach."

"We have to do something," I said.

"The Seer said a banshe has an immense thirst. We just have to outwait it."

"No, Locke, a still wind dies. The longer we stay here the less water you'll have to get home."

"I don't know what else to do."

I looked up, looked around, feeling outside the despair—reaching beyond, outward into the universe. "There's a breeze."

"What?"

"Right back there."

Locke turned with a groan and looked into the blackness. Probably the ideal place for a wraith to live, where it wouldn't have to worry about the sun.

A chill went up his spine.

33.

Cave

G NYMES PUSHED TOWARD us with all their might.
I hated rock. The fading growl echoed behind us. I went ahead,
trying to feel out the blind space. Leeway in front and back helped me
breathe easier.

The cave seemed to have been carved by water, walls flowing in and out
like frozen waves—a breath's highway. Locke pressed his fingertips against
them as he walked; tiny divots marked the surface, creating a strange
texture. He held the sword in his other hand, and he used the guard to
feel ahead. I worried about him falling into a sinkhole—a nightmare that
would combine tight spaces with death. But so far the floor ascended
steadily upward without breaks. A slight humidity made breathing through
a parched throat easier, but it taunted too, like the smell of freshly cooked
fish wafting from a neighboring tree. The further in we delved, the chillier
it became too.

Locke squeezed through a particularly narrow gap. "What if we get lost
in here?"

"As long as you keep your hand on that wall, we'll be fine."

He squinted into the darkness, imagining he could see black walls.
Terrors crawled just out of reach, spindly legs and giant pincers. Locke
brushed the back of his neck and shoulders to make sure. "Can wraiths
hear?" he whispered.

"I'm not sure."

"I wish I didn't need to see with my hand."

"Why?"

"So I could talk to her." He saw her smiling face in the darkness.

"About what?"

"Her framework." He grinned.

"The four futures?"

"Yeah."

"What about them?"

"You want to take a crack at it then?" he asked.

"Sure."

"I actually see three of the futures all the time—me, other people, and random chance. But I never see fate step in. It's absent. That's partly why I can't believe." Locke came to a stone where the pathway seemed to end. He poked his toe beneath. "Can I fit underneath it, Picke?"

I flew down below and measured the space. "Yeah, you can. It will be tight, but a wider pathway continues on after a few feet."

He got on his belly and started sliding, face first, pushing his bag and sword ahead of him. The dust floated to his nostrils. The blackness and wraiths fingered their way toward his neck.

I pulled the conversation on, hoping mostly for distraction. "I think you're talking about miracles."

"What?"

"If Numa whispered to me, and I whispered to you, and then if you acted on it, a miracle could happen."

"If it were something *I* had done, it wouldn't be a miracle."

"Let's say someone needed help. And you weren't planning to go a certain way, but you changed your mind based on something I said—because Numa had whispered to me. To the person you helped, it could be a miracle."

"Hmm," said Locke.

"You're shrugging me off."

"No, I'm listening," he said with a groan as he squeezed through the last part of the narrow gap.

"You don't get it then."

"No, I get it. You're saying simple things might not happen without Numa's inspiration. She's the initiative."

"Yeah. Don't you think that's a big deal?"

He stood back up, put on his pack, and dusted himself off. "That would mean admitting you're right." He grinned.

"You're filthier than Honke," I said.

"Good thing we can't see then."

I proceeded into the blindness. "Why do you think the hyuman's sylfe was trapped inside of him like that?"

"I don't know. Haven't thought about it."

"It's terrible. To be imprisoned. I can barely stand these walls around us now."

A scratch echoed from somewhere behind us.

Locke turned to face it, his useless eyes open wide. He gripped the hilt of his sword and felt into the darkness with the point. We waited—waited—waited—straining to hear something or anything, any shred of that phantom sound. But nothing came, nothing but the sough of the breeze sweeping through.

Locke started moving forward again, and suddenly he waved his hand in the air, stopping and stepping back, all sort of at once. Something had touched his forehead.

His hand and the sword found nothing.

I laughed.

"Shut up," he said.

"Sorry."

"You know I hate th—huuuaaa!"

His clothing made the whiffing sound of swift moment. I felt the thud of stone against his backside. A stabbing pain shot into his right shoulder blade.

"Locke!" I rushed after him.

He slid to a stop, several feet down. "Ow!" His hand spasmed as if a bug had possessed it—something had touched it. A chill went up his arm and down his spine. He wiped the hand on his pant leg to free himself of the memory.

"Watch out," I said.

"You're supposed to warn me *before* it happens. Where's the bug?" He swept his eyes around the darkness, and we saw wraiths in our mind. He slowly stood, careful not to feel the floor with his hands, and brushed off his pants.

I explored the space, stirring up the air with my swift movement. The walls had disappeared.

Pain needled through Locke's shoulder. He reached under his mail armor and felt blood; it seemed the claw had scraped through the links. "With an animal that heavy, I guess a nick is all it takes."

"It's not too bad though, is it?"

"No, not too bad."

"You're lucky."

The moment caused just the right ripples, and our snickers echoed up and down the walls of the narrow cave.

As he picked up his sword, I found the far wall. "You've fallen into some sort of basin where water poured from above." The space was so large it made Locke the size of a berry in a giant bowl of mush. "Up there is a doorway, a black void with a top and two tilted sides—like it's elfemade. But it's out of your reach. In fact, you'd have never known about it without me."

He moved forward, putting a palm against the surface and feeling for some sort of groove or indentation so he could climb up. Unfortunately, it appeared uniformly smooth. He tried walking up it, but as the curve increased to a certain steepness, the traction of his moccasins slipped against the sandy rock, and he slid backwards.

A scratch echoed from behind us, louder and more distinct this time, like a stick or a limb against stone—much more than a phantom.

"Momentum," I whispered.

"What?"

"You need to get a run at it."

"With what strength?"

But I didn't have to answer: He glanced behind into more blackness and gritted his teeth.

After sheathing his sword, he ran straight against the bowl-shaped wall and took one last high step. He leaped and caught the ledge with one hand, but the angle and height surprised him. His sandy grip slipped, and he slid to the bottom.

On the second try, his fingers found a lump that was just enough for him to hold his weight. He got both hands onto the ledge and his feet against the slope. Shaking, he pulled himself into the doorway.

"Watch your head," I said just in time.

He felt the low ceiling with his hand, staying in a crouch as he struggled to draw his sword. It would be difficult to maneuver in the cramped space. Locke chose to point his weapon ahead, hoping we could simply move fast enough to not be taken from behind. We proceeded up the tunnel, listening carefully. His well-worn moccasins had little grip on the steep surface. "If the water were still flowing, there'd be no way up."

"Then it's lucky we have the curse," I said.

"Picke, if it weren't for the curse, we wouldn't be in this darkness."

"And we'd have never met the Goddess."

"Oh." He was taken aback: If he could erase the curse and the Goddess in the same stroke, would he? He shook his head.

As we trudged up the slope, a draft of wind swept in the same direction, tugging upward through the hollow space, dragging at Locke's tunic and hair, pulling toward wherever we were going.

I rode this current as we moved further up and further in.

34.

Hymn of Light

I FELT THE LIGHT before I could see it.

It washed over me like nothing I'd experienced—yet familiar and natural, more elemental than me, like it was both the fount from which I'd sprung and the ocean into which I'd pour. The feeling was musical, a sound of white. Notes flowed out of the very air, rhythm and harmony woven together, breathing together. The peace rung a melody sad and beautiful and bursting with hope. It drew me into it and calmed the world.

Locke felt it too. In spite of the strangeness, he didn't stop or back away. He increased his pace, moving toward the light, until we were bathed in its rays.

We stopped at the brink of a vast room.

The claustrophobia vanished as if swept away by a whirlwind.

Above us loomed a giant temple carved out of the rock's interior. The carvings in the walls became more intricate the higher they rose, stretching upward on all sides. High above us a series of walkways went this way and that. One massive column reached through the center of the huge space, holding some sort of pedestal at the top. Over the whole majestic room fell a light of bluish hue, which flickered faintly on every surface of the cavern, even in these dark lower reaches, coming from somewhere above. It shone dimly, but after so many days without daylight, followed by hours in perfect darkness, it nearly overwhelmed us.

Below it all rested an empty watercourse. Judging by the scum on the walls, if the water rose too high, it would spill over into our secret tunnel.

I jumped when I noticed a person in the moat below us.

No, not a person. A statue.

He wasn't standing. He was on his back, one leg stretched out, the other knee curled defensively in front of him. His feet ended with the claws of a wrecche—hideous and creaturely. His skull was bald except for two stubby horns hooking from his forehead, while his hair flowed thick from his temples and wrapped in a strap around his chin. His lips curled up in a terrifying snarl, showing teeth strong enough to rip flesh. His eyes were so lifelike he seemed a real person frozen into stone, his pose perfectly natural and haunting. His torso was twisted, with one elbow tucked beneath him and the other hand stretched upward, clawing at the sky and everything above him.

If the moat had been full, he'd have been buried beneath water, which gave me a chilling thought: Who would create artwork such as this only to bury it beneath the water and out of sight? Maybe he really was a wrecche, about to burst out of his stone skin at any moment.

"Is that Saede?" asked Locke.

I nodded in disgust.

"Come on," he said eagerly. "Always further. Always higher."

Locke jumped from the drain down into the moat, more fully into the blue light and also within reach of the hideous statue. He paused to gape till his gaze was drawn overhead. He felt life coming back into him, as if he'd taken a refreshing drink.

He made his way up from the watercourse, scaling the rock as if it were a tree. He clutched small grooves in the walls, and the blue shimmered all around, as if an entire sea were hidden around some invisible corner. The walls featured indentations and troughs where water must have once flowed, including grotesque mouths that spouted waterfalls. Crawling vines overran the walls, growing thick enough to cling to. The gaps between vines revealed words and stories carved into the walls, which tempted Locke to stop and read, but I insisted he keep moving. Crumbled stone in various places suggested that, at least once, some great battle had been fought on these grounds. I also noticed scorch marks in the stone. Maybe the whole place had been set on fire—attacked by salamindes and bird demons.

After some time and a few daring leaps, we mounted a platform high above where we'd entered. From that vantage point, the cavern seemed even larger and more majestic. Locke stood on a walkway that crossed the great open chasm and reached toward the centerpiece of the temple: the source of the flickering light.

The massive center column held a circular platform high in the air, far above the darkness of the empty waterway below.

Locke neared with slack-jawed wonder.

His moccasins brushed across a complex pattern etched into the floor. One part showed a pair of isolated hands stretching upward, the thumbs inward, the fingers outward like the rays of the sun. These reached toward a small vessel holding a flame of four jagged points clawing skyward. A circle enclosed this symbol and added more beams radiating outward.

Circular stairs stepped upward in tiers toward a pedestal. Four statues surrounded and guarded the center. But we were distracted from their magnificence by what rested between them, a stone dish, a shallow bowl filled with bluish liquid—*the Well at the World's End.*

"We made it," whispered Locke. The light pierced Locke with that unnameable longing. It soaked into his skin and reflected in his shining eyes.

The basin stretched wider than Locke's wingspan, yet its depth merely crept to my height at the center. Translucent blue peaks danced about like flames across the surface, like a tiny ocean amid a tempest. It resembled a giant lamp but didn't give off any smell or smoke.

"Come here, Picke."

He took me in his palm, and inhaled softly:

"Princess, we're here. We're inside the temple. We've found the Well."

After a few moments without her reply, Locke ascended the long stairs toward the pedestal. Not only would this shining substance light the way and undo the curse, bathing in its glory was its own reward. It felt worth it, all the leagues we'd crossed and the trials we'd encountered.

Yet something was still missing.

We wanted more than just looking—something higher. Maybe we wanted to *be* it. Or to have *it* be *us*. We couldn't say exactly what we wanted. We just knew we *wanted*.

Surrounding the basin and aligned with the four statues above, the symbols of the four demigods were etched into the stairs: Gaie, Demigod of Body and Earth, whose symbol was a mountain peak with a ridge on each side; Nara, Demigoddess of Blood and Waters, whose symbol was a crescent moon; Numa, Demigoddess of Breath and Skies, whose symbol was four teardrops or seeds; and Phose, Demigod of Light and Fire, whose symbol was the eternal circle.

Even though he didn't believe, Locke breathed with awe: "The Kyrose." He stood still, soaking it in.

I read the text surrounding the symbols, which explained a hierarchy: Earth was lowest because it sank through water. Air rose through water. Fire, highest of all, attempted to climb above air. "Fire is from the empyrean, it says."

Locke bent over and began to read the stairs: "Phose built this temple for Nara… To celebrate their marriage? I didn't know the Kyrose were married."

"Neither did I."

"The union of fire and water—living water."

I looked at the pool again. Not looked, *stared*. Transfixed on the blue flames dancing as waves. I watched carefully, trying to understand the melody, trying to solve the mystery that poured into our soul.

I began to move closer. As I neared, its power took a stronger hold.

Then I heard a whisper. A whisper I hadn't heard since the day she named me. A whisper I wanted to hear more than anything else in the world. A whisper that came from the pool.

I let it draw me in. Soon I was hovering above the reflective surface.

Then I looked down.

35.

Tearing Breath

THE TWINS SAID they'd been there when it happened.

I hated the story, but I could never stop listening. It was too horrible.

Tyne was the only sylfe in our village who'd ever dared. The sylfe of a kid named Dagonae. *Was* the sylfe of a kid named Dagonae.

All Tyne did was touch the spore of a flower.

Just a spore—the kind that spins on the wind, drifting effortlessly, nothing to it, wispy and white. If he'd have blown on it, he could have carried it as far as he wanted, but instead he tried to touch it.

When Locke was younger, he didn't get it. To him, I was on his shoulder, or above his head: I seemed to be in his space already.

I was not.

"But I've *seen* you touch things."

So it seemed. But my imitations stood as distant from actual touching as moving a finger across a throat stood from actual execution.

When Locke was small, he asked me just to try it.

"Imagine one in seven elves can spontaneously fly," I said. "To find out if you're one, all you have to do is leap from a cliff. If you have the gift, you fly. If you don't, you die."

He said he wasn't going to try.

An unsuccessful attempt would be fatal, for me or for him. I knew that even without Tyne. From this angle, it was obvious. The layers between Locke and me machinated violently, rubbing and crunching, back and forth. Tyne had gotten caught between—a power so strong and so quick it could even crush breath.

After Tyne got smashed, Dagonae went mad. And no one ever told the adults who egged him on.

It proved one thing—what would happen if you tried and failed. But we still didn't know if it was possible to succeed. No one dared find out. *I* didn't dare find out.

So it remained a legend.

A legend that said that one in seven sylves had the ability to touch and change the world. More than simple mischief like making an elfe sneeze, or blowing an ant off a branch, or even stirring up a dust demon. No, this gift was substantial—not Numa's but Gaia's power. It meant manipulating the world just like an elfe. The legend called these sylves the ascendant ones. Martigane's sylfe Cree had become one—right before he died. So the legend said.

I longed to step into legend, and what better way than to become an ascendant one? Then people would respect me, notice me, listen to me—and if they didn't, well, I could bite them. I wanted glory more than I wanted to live. Only I worried I might trade my life for nothing, to die and be forgotten, to disappear even from memory. That was why the choice haunted me.

If I'd faced it once, unexpectedly, I might have just jumped—I usually focused on choices more than consequences. But I faced this decision constantly. With consequences too heavy to be ignored. It promised possibility and pain. At any moment. At every moment.

As Locke grew older, he stopped bothering me about it, once he understood the risk. But the choice remained within sickening reach, never leaving me alone. It howled at certain moments in particular, like when that banshe wolfe took me in its jaws. Those teeth forced me to consider, filled me with terror.

Death and ascension were always in front of me.

This choice howled like never before when I looked into that pool.

As I stared down, a chimera looked up. A creature with the faces of an angel and a ghule. No, with a thousand faces. They didn't appear side by side or overlapping—it was in some other relation to each other, something that Kyriglae can't name. Each of these thousand figures, as one figure, stared toward their feet, looking into the reflection. In crude language, this chimera seemed to combine all possibilities of past and future, binding them into one. And I floated above—the agent, the chooser, the shaper of destiny. With that image, knowledge clawed through my thoughts, stretching my understanding, a message precise and complete, truth simple and impossible—yet nothing more than the ascendant choice, facing me as it always had, that unending choice, ripping at my innermost.

The whole vision came in an instant like a lightning bolt.

I'd been above the pool for less than a heartbeat, a point in time sharp enough to rip me apart. In that split instant, Numa invited me to choose, to face the decision I'd faced every moment of my life. A choice to leave behind, to become new, to do what I'd told Locke to do—leap without seeing the landing.

But I was afraid. *Afraid*—as I'd scolded Locke for being. Afraid of death. Afraid of becoming an ascendant one. Afraid of never trying.

The vision fueled me with rapture and despair. Crushing doubt and colorful tears streaked through the atmosphere all around me—joy and madness. I had to stop feeling at all or I would be consumed.

I closed my eyes and removed myself from the space above the pool.

36.

Flame of Fire

WHAT DID YOU see?" asked Locke.

"I..."

"*What?*"

"I saw myself." I retreated back to the pathway that led to the entrance, and I felt tempted to rest on the stone.

"Picke, what's the matter?"

"Nothing."

"Are you alright?"

"I'll be okay."

"Did it hurt?"

"Did you see my reflection?"

"No. Well, yes. At least I saw something. But I couldn't focus on it, like my eyes were crossed. I saw a light. Or a burning white *life*."

For a moment, all was still, except for the sound of the blue light. Neither of us said a word.

Locke looked toward the pool fearfully. "Should I go?"

But I couldn't answer that question.

After a moment, he walked closer, trembling slightly as he approached the luminous majesty. He stepped to the pool's edge and looked in. His golden hair hung down and his reflection hung back up.

I didn't fly back above the pool, but I sensed a glimpse of what Locke saw—as I always did. I couldn't be sure, but it seemed he saw, for the first time, what I always saw in him—a personage of light, whose eyes burned like flame and whose hair shone like molten gold. His vision expanded to the wide world, and he saw our village, the Burning Mountain, and a girl with a perfect smile in a dress of many colors. A purple rag pulled at the corners of her mouth and was tied tight at the back of her neck. Cords bound her wrists into the shape of a cross.

Just like me, he saw too much in an instant.

"Picke!" He jumped back. "She's in trouble!"

He turned toward the exit and was halfway across the suspended walkway before I got up. "Wait! Where are you going?"

"The Goddess is in trouble. She needs our help."

I put a hand on my head for shelter. "Wait a moment." Thoughts were coming slowly.

"He was torturing her! We have to go."

"Just breathe a little. We can talk to her." At that, he paused, reviewing his haste. "And besides," I continued more softly, "you didn't even ignite the phanos lamp, so you don't know where she is."

He nodded, as he slowly reorganized his muddled thoughts. "Okay. Let me talk to her."

He cupped me into his palm and placed his hand once again over his face, whispering, "Princess, I'm at the Well. Are you okay?" He choked up, pausing to regain his composure. "Princess, can you hear me? I need to know if you're okay."

After a few moments, he dropped his hand, and I gathered into the blue air.

"Her hands were tied, Picke. She can't speak into the consonance."

"Well, we came here for the living water."

He nodded, uncertain. After glancing toward the exit, he set his pack on the ground and pulled out the lamp, gripping the strange marks carved into the handle.

Out loud, I spoke the words the Seer had taught me.

"Now say them with me, together."

As one, we said the words, as if speaking to some all-seeing presence: "Dyn meis, Thaese, dyn meis, all to enoma siou doesi ta daksa."

A stillness passed through us.

Though nothing in the room seemed to change physically, something had changed in the breathing world. Something—but I wasn't sure what.

I stayed back on the walkway while Locke stepped toward the pedestal.

He jumped back in surprise.

The blue fire came strangely alive.

Like water, it spilled from the basin onto the steps of the pedestal. It flowed evenly in perfect, expanding circles down the steps. It poured into the etchings in the surface of the walkway, like cast iron, illuminating the story we had walked across. The water-like blue spilled into many other surfaces around the room, cascading off ledges and filling more and more places below. But like fire up a fuse, it also climbed. Streams of shimmering blue flowed into higher troughs and ditches, running in straight lines along the walls and alighting other words and stories, then curving around balconies and terraces like ribbons, with light dancing in place on each of these pouring surfaces.

For a moment, all of Locke's hurry was swallowed up in awe.

"Wow," he whispered.

I tensed up as the illumination surrounded me, worried it might show me something I didn't want to see. But its light emanated a peaceful song, and soon I joined Locke in wonder, having never experienced something quite so... *sacred*. With the calm, my thoughts seemed to get clearer.

A strange impulse overcame Locke, and he squeezed his eyes shut. In the darkness of our mind, he still saw the whole blue, burning room, its lines and edges burned into his vision.

Thoughts of the Goddess snapped him back to attention. He swallowed his awe and approached the pool, stepping cautiously over the now-flaming floor. He scooped the lamp into the pool. The living water dripped from the side as he brought it level, but the drips vanished before they touched down. A flame of water danced within the colorful cup and glowed with blue on his face. With no time for adoration, he leaped down the steps and made his way toward me and the exit.

"Hold on!" I backed up as he approached. "You should test it. Find out how easily it can be extinguished while you still have the option to relight it."

"But she's not answering, Picke." He looked at me, sighed, and stopped.

"And you should see if it's drinkable too. You'll need it once you get back out there."

He tried blowing on the living water, with his cheeks ballooned out. All but one large drop of it seemed to whisk away out of the lamp's dish. But that one drop held on tight, and as soon as the blowing stopped, it grew back till it filled the bowl and danced above the rim.

"If the Kyrose can combine the opposite elements of fire and water," I asked, "what would happen if they combined earth with air?"

"I don't know. Some sort of insubstantial rock?"

"That doesn't make sense."

"Neither does living water." He tried tipping the bowl upside down, and some of the liquid poured out and vanished in the air, but some of it clinged to the bowl's surface, rising skyward, too tenacious to let go.

Next he found a smooth area of the stone floor and set the lamp upside down. The rim of the lamp touched down on all sides and the textured handle pointed toward the oculus in the ceiling. We waited for a moment, and the blue all around us flickered on Locke's forest folk clothing. If this were a flame, it would have suffocated by now: even a flame couldn't live without breath—all life depended on my mother.

Locke picked up the phanos lamp. "It's still burning!"

"I can't believe it." I took my head in both hands to make sure it stayed together.

Next Locke held one of the canvas straps of his backpack to the flame. Nothing happened. No smoke and no burning, though the canvas was warm to the touch. "This is the strangest stuff. I'm not sure I could put it out if I wanted to."

"You haven't tried water," I said.

"I can't waste water on an experiment. Besides, no one else will have water to spare."

"And what about drinking it?"

He nodded. First he flicked his hand through the living water to test its heat, moving more slowly each time. "It's pretty warm. It might burn."

"You don't have to," I said.

He nodded again. Then he moved without thinking, lifting the lamp like a goblet above his head, tipping it toward his mouth. I moved closer, and his white teeth shone with the blue glow. The bowl leaned more and more till finally the liquid spilled over the edge.

It vanished before touching his tongue.

Locke looked at his shirt to see if he'd missed.

"It disappeared," I said. "Turned to vapor."

"I could feel the heat. But it never…" and his sentence vanished too. He put his cracked lips more daringly on the edge of the bowl, and the heat poured into his skin. But when he tipped the bowl back, the liquid vanished on his tongue. "It's almost like I'd need to breathe it instead of drink it."

That comment took me off guard. "You're saying a substance made by Phose and gifted to Nara can only be consumed by a child of Numa?"

"I guess so."

"Weird. Maybe Shilohe will know more about it."

He frowned at me like I'd spoken about the death of his mother.

I shrugged. "I'm sure she's okay. Give her time to answer."

"I have. Are you satisfied?" He crouched and strapped the lamp inside his bag where it would be more protected. "We need to go. I don't see any way it could ever be extinguished."

I looked back at the pool and the light it had spread all around us. The shadow of both terror and hope reached toward me. But I wasn't going over there again. "Let's go."

As we left, Locke stole a last glance, and his eyes shone bright with blue.

37.

Monk

L OCKE PUT HIS hands against one of two giant double doors and leaned. Metal hinges creaked a goodbye, and a sliver of dim light split the doors. His moccasins whispered against stone as he stepped onto a vast terrace. It reached far horizontally but couldn't match the grandeur of the room we'd just left. Overhead, the clouded sky stretched its arms over the face of the whole world. The music behind us faded to high pitches that danced away on the wind.

"The World's End," whispered Locke, and he swallowed to ward off its spell.

The mountain continued on much higher, but this terrace still offered a spectacular view. The Sea of Mist drew our gaze to the east. We stood above a jagged coastline of sheer cliffs which seemed to weave forever in both directions. The dark blue sea waters expanded on and on into the distance, as far as we could see, till the clouds overhead and the waters below merged into a foggy abyss. *So much water.* If only it were the right kind.

"If you're going to attempt spontaneous flight," I said, "I think you should do it here."

Leagues below us, tiny white waves crawled inward till they crashed into foam against treacherous rocks. Locke didn't even give me a chuckle. "Gah, that is so high. I do almost wish I could leap out there, but the princess would hate this."

It seemed to be morning. If it was, this must have been the twelfth day without sun, although it hadn't felt like we'd spent an entire night in the cave and the temple. "Maybe you should rest," I said.

"I don't feel tired anymore. Besides, we have no time to lose."

Our journey called us westward, back across the Khalune. In the distant west stood the Burning Mountain, rising so high it pierced the clouds and hid its summit from view. Anxiety prodded at Locke, as if he could hear her calling him. He turned to push the temple's vast door closed and found himself looking into the eyes of a dark-skinned hyuman.

Locke's heart leaped. He reached for the sword on his back.

The hyuman didn't move.

They never reacted like I expected.

This one had a sword, but he hadn't reached for it. He just sat on a bench next to the doorpost, strong and peaceful, his face turned toward us, staring with glassy white eyes. The hyuman gave a slight smile. "Hello." His head and face were bald, his skin as dark as worlnut timber. He stood and pushed the door closed.

Locke's heart slowed as he breathed and tried to feel calm. "Hi."

"You came from inside, but you never used this door." His voice was the color of sand that sparkled under starlight, gleaming, but still with a roughness of texture.

"Are you the sentinel? I'm really sorry."

"I'm not the sentinel." The hyuman sat back down on the stone bench.

"You're not guarding the door?"

"The Kyrose guard this door." The red sash around the hyuman's waist contrasted against his long, loose white robe. The sleeves reached past his wrists and a hood hung around his shoulders—some sort of a monk. Underneath it all, tight gray fabric wrapped his arms and chest. Most striking were his eyes, a little too gray and clouded. Either he was blind, or he could see more than most—I couldn't tell which.

"Then what are you doing here?" asked Locke.

"My brethren left with the rains. I stayed to water the plants. And to keep an eye on things." He gave a kind smile.

His sylfe rested inside his chest, brighter, more upright and more full than Honke's had been. It seemed larger than the space it was in too, and yet less cramped than Honke's—a paradox. In fact, it didn't look even slightly uncomfortable in there.

"You came in through the aqueduct," said the hyuman.

"Yes, but on accident."

"Fortunate the waters are gone. I'm impressed you climbed so high. You have what you came for?"

"Yes."

The hyuman stared with those white eyes, pale and lacking definition. "I'm not sure you do."

"It's, uh… it's in here." Locke pointed a thumb toward his backpack.

"I can't see where you're pointing," said the hyuman. *Then how did he use his sword?*

"It's in my pack."

"The light must fall on your surroundings or it won't change your vision."

Locke set his pack on the ground and lifted the phanos lamp. The faint blue fell on his lips and nose.

"Do you notice anything different?" asked the hyuman.

"About what?" asked Locke.

"Then you don't. Come, sit down." The hyuman waved us over and smiled—as if eager to relate a faerie story. "If you have an incorrect future in mind, the clairvoyance can't show you the actual future. And if you're recalling memories of the past, it leaves no room for the memories that come next. You must let go of everything that isn't right now."

Locke nodded, understanding only a little.

"Now close your eyes." The monk shut his own. "Still your mind. Don't consider what has happened or what will happen. Only right now. What do you notice?"

Holding the lamp, Locke closed his eyes. Breath filled his lungs and pressed his stomach outward. A slight embarrassment washed through him, as if someone were watching. He felt his exhaustion and the soreness in his shoulder, but something lifted these weaknesses. His throat didn't seem quite as dry as it used to. He noticed the simple pattern of his breathing—though it was strange he could ever *not* notice this.

"Anything?" asked the monk.

Locke opened his eyes, taking another deep, slow breath. He felt a flood of embarrassment. He breathed and noticed the monk's white robes and deep red sash. Potted plants lined the terrace, a desert oasis—bushes neatly trimmed, small trees with wide leaves, vines that bolstered the array of greens and deep browns—the color of Locke's voice. Flowers speckled the garden, their vibrant colors undimmed despite the vanished water. A single white moth fluttered around the bark of a small tree. Beyond the terrace, the Sea of Mist reached into obscurity. We stood nearly high enough to touch the brutish clouds, maybe grab ahold of them and climb up.

Then he started to see. A familiarity breathed in the space before us, in part of it at least, something about one particular path—like we'd been there before, as if some strange magic had put our future into our past.

"Now with your eyes closed again," said the monk.

Locke closed his eyes and squinted.

For once it felt like we were seeing because of my sight instead of Locke's. We saw a strange light, even though Locke's eyes were closed, a trail of blue, as if light had been gathered up and folded over on itself until it formed a river, trilling through midair. Accompanying this light, a solitary note rang in a perfect, mild, and penetrating pitch. Maybe we weren't seeing, but hearing with some extra sight.

Locke opened his eyes and stared at the lamp in his hand—a thing that belonged in faerie stories. He closed his eyes once more, just to make sure. "I see it." Our future followed the blue trail directly in front of us, going down the stairway. We hadn't come up this way, but we remembered the path. It glowed a magical blue, down the mountain, out of sight, across the desert, and into the unseeable distance toward the Burning Mountain.

"Then you have what you came for."

"It's like…" Locke paused, squinting his eyes open and closed, trying to understand. "It's amazing." He set his bag on the ground and strapped the lamp to the outside. "Thank you."

"Together the four futures cover life's entire landscape, meaning nothing is impossible. When all four of them overlap, they create a seam, which we see as the present and which the gods call time. The clairvoyance simply helps you see that seam—where the choices of gods and mortals are strung out in an eternal line. But the second sight does not dictate the future any more than your memories dictate the past. It only invites. Do you have a map?"

The monk's abrupt switch from explaining to asking caught Locke off guard. He opened his eyes. "Uh. I don't… I mean I do. Yes."

"I suggest you mark your final destination. If the living water goes out, you won't remember what the clairvoyance just showed you."

"But I can't see that far. I mean I see it goes that direction, but it's too distant to see where it ends."

The monk stood and pretended to gaze to the west. "Mark the Burning Mountain."

Locke pulled out his leather map.

"What are you going to write with?" I whispered.

He paused for a moment, stumped. Then he reached over his shoulder and into his torn and bloodstained green tunic. The wound the wolfe gave him oozed with a clear, sanguineous liquid. He dabbed his finger in the wound then touched the map, leaving a small, dark circle over the Burning Mountain, printed with his finger's unique design.

The monk sat and idly pressed his thumb over the pommel of his sword, as if mashing deep into its muscles.

"By the way, how do you put out the lamp?" asked Locke.

"Usually people ask the opposite question," said the monk.

"I'm wondering what to watch out for. I tried putting it out while I was next to the pool, but I couldn't."

"Very clever. Did your sylfe try?" As he said that, his murky eyes turned toward me.

"Uh, no," said Locke.

"Sylves are more important than most people give them credit for."

Locke nodded. I hadn't thought of it either, and I *was* a sylfe.

"Sylves will be drawn to the light you carry," said the monk. "Some more willing to help, others more likely to harm. But any of them could extinguish it."

"Somehow," I whispered, "I think that's going to be important."

"It will be," replied the hyuman, looking at me. Or into me. *Was he some sort of seer too?*

I deliberately darted to the side. His eyes didn't follow, but they dropped at that exact moment, as if they'd lost their footing, as if he really had been looking at me. *So strange.*

"Let me tell you something," said the monk, seeming to look at me again.

"Yes?" I said, with an extra layer of question in my tone.

"Elves and sylves became the pinnacle of Numa's creations. But when she saw how easily Saede could twist the minds of sylves, she made hyumans, fortifying their sylves inside." The monk touched his own heart with his index finger. "That protected their sylves, made them less susceptible to Saede's curse, but at a cost: It made them less capable of hearing her voice."

Locke nodded, intrigued. Then he glanced down the path after Shilohe.

"I'm telling you so you can appreciate your strength." He stared deeper into me. "You're Locke's herald, his caller of friends, his warner of foes, his causer and ender of wars. You have a role to play—one larger than you think. You just have to listen."

I knew I was important already, but I felt embarrassed when he mentioned listening. Aside from that moment in the temple, if that really was her, I hadn't heard Numa's voice since she named me.

Locke gave me a questioning glance. The hyuman looked at me too, and I wanted to shrink into nothing.

"We're all guilty," said the monk.

"Who?" asked Locke.

"All of us."

"What do you mean?"

"The villain bound the sky with lifeblood and ondines. It takes great power to command a force like that. He drew this power from the void left by our sylves, by their deafness. If they hadn't become so overshadowed by Saede, the villain never could have done this."

Locke looked at the sky, feeling the weight of his own guilt. And of *my* guilt. "What can we do?"

"Curses and miracles come from the same source," the monk went on. "They come from us. We're the ones who shape this land, not the Kyrose."

"But you're guarding the Well—how can you not believe in the Kyrose?"

"I didn't say I don't believe." The monk paused, seeming to gaze at nothing. "I believe in truth. In the little that I know, and in all that I don't. Remember that: You don't have to *know* all truth to *believe* all truth."

Locke nodded.

The monk smiled. "A great burden rests on your shoulders. I pray that you will persevere, for each day means more death."

Locke didn't know quite how to respond to the somber words. "Thanks for the advice." He stood to leave. "Hey, are you sure it's safe staying here alone? You can come with us if you want."

"No, no. But thank you. I appreciate your sympathy."

We moved across the terrace between the luscious trees. How *had* the monk been watering them? Locke stopped and looked back. "One more thing: you don't have any spare water, do you?"

"You're carrying it."

"But I can't drink that water."

The monk raised a questioning eyebrow but said nothing.

Locke nodded, accepting but not understanding the answer.

"See you later," said the hyuman, gazing at us with murky eyes. *Was it a joke or some strange prophecy?* First off, he couldn't see. And second, we weren't planning to return. When he waved goodbye, he held up a thumb and his first two fingers but left the third and fourth curled down toward his palm, a three-pronged farewell. I wondered what it meant.

Locke started down the familiar stairway that we'd never seen. As we parted, the hyuman's farewell echoed in our mind:

See you later.

38.

Courage

Locke hurried down the mountainside.

The wide stairs must have once been a highway for pilgrims, back before pilgrims had ascended into legend. It wasn't hard to imagine them full of travelers. I would have whispered encouragement to the other sylves whose elves were so close after a long journey—just like Lonae would have done. They would soon find water, and light, and song.

Locke blinked his eyes closed, watching the blue seam weaving ahead, leading us anxiously to her rescue.

I hovered near the lamp strapped to his pack. "Why don't you play your pinkalue?" It would bring peace to us both, me especially, since I could glide on the notes. He hadn't played it in forever.

"No. The wolfe might be nearby."

This was a small rejection, but it still hurt. Locke's approval meant so much to me.

"Why isn't she answering, Picke?"

"I don't know."

"Maybe the consonance is broken."

"It's not broken. I would have felt the discord. I always feel it."

"He was torturing her. That evil man. That's what the pool showed me."

"When I looked in the pool, I saw both light and darkness. Maybe this is your darkness."

He shook his head, unwilling to consider it.

The wind rushed past Locke's ears, tugging at his wheat-colored hair and making him squint. He pressed on, one step after another, finding it surprisingly easy to ignore his exhaustion, his parched throat, and his wounded shoulder.

Her voice came suddenly, spread thin over flowing wind, and his eyes lit up:

"Locke, are you there?"

She sounded different. The candle flame of her voice fluttered, threatening to vanish. Maybe she'd been crying, if it wasn't just a trick of the breeze.

The flowing wind made it difficult, but I held mostly together as Locke cupped me in his hand and spoke:

"I'm here. Are you okay?"

Her response came as swift as the wind could carry it: "I'm okay."

"Are you in trouble?" Locke scrambled down the steep, winding stairs.

"We're all in trouble."

That was true, but I sensed she hid something with that answer.

"I just needed someone to talk to," she said timidly. "I feel a little scared."

"Scared of what? What's the matter?"

"Can we just talk for a little bit—but not about that?"

"Sure. Wh— Yeah. Uh… How's the… weather there?"

"Ha ha. Storm clouds."

"Hey, I got the living water," he said. "I'm carrying it right now."

"What's it like?"

"It's—I don't know—like nothing else." Locke blinked his eyes closed. We could still see the blue, but it already seemed a little dimmer. "I wish you could feel it."

"Are *you* okay? You sound out of breath."

"I saw… a vision in the Well. I thought you were in danger, so I've been hurrying."

"That's sweet of you." We could hear the smile on her voice. "But I think I'm okay."

"Are you sure you're not in danger?"

"Yes, I'm at the Seer's house with a few friends."

Strange. The vision had shown her in trouble, somewhere out in the wilderness. "Are these friends okay people?"

"Well, not if you ask the King. But they're heroes to me."

"Are you sure?" Locke wished he could see these *friends*—so he could judge for himself. We imagined a band of ruffians too disreputable to be in her presence. *And what if they were flirting with her?*

"I don't want to talk about that."

"I'm sorry. What do you want to talk about?"

"Can you tell me a story?" she asked.

"What kind of story?"

"A story when you needed to do something, but you were scared to do it."

"Alright..." he said, considering. Immediately the twins came to mind—heroes he admired. He didn't want to talk about them with her, or with anyone really. But something told him he ought to. "Once a boy had two older brothers who were twins. The best big brothers ever. One day Robyne, one of the twins, got it in his head that he was going to sail back to the Land of Song, where the legends say we came from."

"That's what the Isles of Time is about!"

Hearing the excitement in her voice filled Locke with a wistful sadness, a joy mixed with pain, which somehow she sensed.

"I'm sorry," she said, quietly, softly, humbly. "Do you want to go on?"

"So Robyne told Tunke about it, and of course he was eager too. They were inseparable. So they built a ship and set out for the Land of Song. Three years ago. But they were lost at sea, never heard from again."

"That's a sad story."

"They were my older brothers."

"I'm sorry," she said.

Unsure how to accept the condolences, Locke went on: "I love adventure, partially because I loved them. And I want to chase it like they did, but I get scared. They proved adventure can have a high cost—it can kill you."

"Locke, I'm sorry. I didn't mean to pry." At that, they both paused, and for a moment the grim silence covered everything.

"No, I trust you," said Locke, "And maybe it will help—that's not the end of the story. When we were at the Seer's, I expected to hand him the scroll and go home. When he asked me to help, I almost turned him down. But I thought of the twins. They were adventurers, through and through, and when the Land of Song called them, they had to answer. If they hadn't, they would have died, at least in spirit. I think that's what Cree meant when he said a still wind dies. To stay is death. To quit is death. To stop hoping is death. But to follow is life, even if it kills you."

He shrugged. His thoughts had taken him somewhere unexpected, words that seemed meant for himself more than anything. He took a moment to get his bearings.

Shilohe smiled, and we felt her warmth even so far away.

"So that's why I came to get the living water," said Locke. "Because of the twins. I miss them, but I'm glad they lived boldly, just like the legends.

In fact, maybe that's the only way to become a legend. You've got to follow that spirit, no matter what it asks. I guess that's why Martigane wanted the Melody of Echoes more than life…" He trailed off, giving way to silence.

"Thank you," said Shilohe with a tone as warm as the wind—her enthusiasm had returned. "That was just what I needed."

Locke shook his head, surprised. "Well, I'm glad I could help. Now do you want to talk about what's bothering you?"

"No. But I'd give you a kiss if I could."

Locke's face turned pink.

"I have to go now. Bye, Locke."

And just like that she was gone.

39.

Look to the Sky

"WHAT DID I just do?"

He said this to himself several times, so I finally replied: "I don't know, talked her into doing something foolish?"

When he reached the bottom of the pilgrim stairs, he leaped onto the flat, dry ground, moving into a run. The boreal winds pushed at our back, hurrying us along.

Amid the desert sands, the heat of the day beat on us, even though the sun's light didn't. After a while, Locke slowed just long enough to take a sip from his remaining flask, and he eyed it carefully—not because it would be gone soon but because it seemed to have grown more potent. His thirst felt more easily quenched and stayed that way for longer.

The clouds stretched dark in a ceiling overhead, and lightning flashed.

"You should play your pinkalue."

"Too risky, Picke."

That made me sad.

Even with his caution, people confronted us twice and wraiths attacked many times as we crossed the Khalune Desert. Locke protected the lamp with his sword and his speed and once with his smile. Finally he hid it in his backpack where it accompanied us silently next to the pinkalue. Its blue stream was getting hard to see anyway, but we still clearly remembered where it had pointed us—just north and west of the Seer's rendezvous point.

Nights were cooler, and Locke napped next to fragments of sandstone. When he closed his eyes, navigating became difficult for me. I still sensed things, movements in the air and sounds and smells. But our mind was one, and when he left me to dream, he left me in fog. That made every-thing scarier, so I stayed hidden, usually close to his heart, and I listened to Lonae's songs through the consonance.

Locke often woke screaming halfway through the night. We'd move

on, running from the nightmares toward Shilohe, and he'd whisper the
dreams to me as we went.

"I saw her in the desert not far from here. Her dress danced in the wind.
But she was bound, her face clawed and bleeding. Several Tenarie warriors
were there, one a scary old man. When the men weren't looking, she ran
for it. But banshe wolves dragged her back by the rope around her wrists."

"Locke, be careful," I said.

"What?"

"You're letting fear take control of your mind, creating negative futures
that may not be true."

He looked deeply at me, and together we imagined her calm and healing,
sitting on a log staring into fiery embers, folding her arms against the
night's cold while her captors slept. In the orange glow against the blue
night, she began to sing, a sound as perfect as her shape, a song we'd heard
the Angel sing:

"Haa-la-la, haa-la-la, haa-la-le-liah."

He tried to speak to her several times, but she didn't respond. As we
pushed westward, a ghostly orange brooded where the sun used to set, not
enough to drive off the wraiths. The rest of the sky was colorless.

"If we could get past the clouds, we'd see light again," said Locke. It
seemed the lack of sleep was getting to him.

"Yes, of course."

Locke looked at that hint of light, too high to reach, and breathed deep,
which helped me at least. "I'm trying to believe it. I've nearly forgotten
what green leaves and blue skies look like." Lightning spiked against the
sky ahead. "Even if we survive the Night of the Wolfe, what will happen?
I'm a fifther with no inheritance to speak of. She's a princess, one of the
heirs of the Kyrie nation, a Goddess."

I shook my head. "It's a long shot." And I'd helped him get this deep—
waters he might drown in. But I couldn't tell him to be a still wind, could
I? Or was I supposed to stop him? *If only Numa would speak to me.*

"Hi, Locke."

His eyes lit up.

He took me quickly into his hand and covered his mouth, touching below
his eyes with thumb and index finger.

We'd gone for two days with a silent consonance. And now, here, right at the end, Shilohe was speaking again. "I've been trying so hard to *not* contact you, but I can't help it."

Locke didn't reply—we were ready now, but he had no idea what to say to that.

"I can't believe I just said that," she said.

"Uh, why?"

"I don't know. It's embarrassing. But I couldn't help it. I need to talk to you."

"About what—what's going on?"

"Not *about* anything. I just wanted to hear your voice."

"Oh," he said, and then his voice, ironically, fell silent as he blushed.

"Locke, you have a special presence. I don't feel judged."

"What do you mean?" he asked.

"Ha ha. See? You don't even know what it means to judge." She laughed again. "I'm part of the Blue Rose. We strive to overcome weaknesses and things. And because of who I am… well, there's even more expectation. When I'm around the other acolytes, they think I'm someone great, so I can't admit how imperfect I am."

"That doesn't sound good."

"It's not. I'm living a lie. That's why it's so nice to tell you things. Because you've admitted some flaws."

"You just can't top my cowardice."

"Ha ha. No. First of all, you're no coward. And second, well, I just think my darkest secrets wouldn't make you think less of me. It hasn't usually been like that with boys I've liked."

I wondered whether she heard Locke gasp.

Hearing she'd liked other boys made him feel jealous, but she'd hinted at liking him too. Not ready to admit either of these thoughts, he said, "You have secrets?"

"Even answering that is scary. But, yes, Locke, I do. Things I'm ashamed of."

"I do find that hard to imagine."

"Now don't you start doing it too. I'm just a person. I'm real, okay?"

"Okay, fair enough."

"That's why I wanted to talk. So I could tell you I'm scared."

"What's the matter?"

"No, I didn't want to tell you *why*. Just that I am."

"What did you do the other day with those ruffians?"

"They're not ruffians. Okay, some of them are. But they're good, and they want good things for our people."

"Are you sure they're treating you okay?"

"They helped me do something the Seer thought was impossible. I wish I could tell you about it; you'd be proud of my artistry. And none of us got burned alive."

"What!"

"I'm sorry. I shouldn't have said that. I can't tell you what we did."

"But you just said you trusted me."

"I know. And I'm not keeping it a secret because I don't trust you. I'm keeping it because I *do*."

"I don't understand," said Locke

"I just need *you* to trust *me*."

"But you said—"

"I can't explain. I'm sorry." The frustration and fear appeared in her voice. "Can we talk about something else?"

"Okay." He waited, not sure what to think. When she said nothing, he finally said, "I have a question."

"Go ahead."

"This lamp I'm carrying—it holds a mixture of two opposites, water and fire, which should be impossible. So what happens when you mix air and rock?"

"It's something called *volant stone*."

"And what does it do?"

"I don't know exactly. I think it's rock that flies."

Locke nodded.

"Can we go back to the questions game?" she asked.

"Yes." He smiled, her soft voice having nearly melted his heart. "Your turn."

"I want you to tell me about your mother. Maybe something she taught you."

He sucked in a breath, surprised by her sympathy. In that moment he was nothing but a little boy, still grieving after all these years, and Shilohe was willing to grieve with him, willing to honor the memory of his mother. He nodded, and her sympathy seemed to be all he needed or wanted.

Lightning burst across the sky, and we'd luckily been looking in the precise direction when it appeared, so we saw it clearly, a jagged streak of white. It illuminated the world for a moment so small it escaped before we knew it existed.

He knew what story he'd tell.

"Can you see the lightning where you are?"

"Yes," she said. "It just flashed."

The thunder rumbled. Locke waited for it to stop before speaking. "When I was small, my mom took me and some of my older brothers up on the cliffs to watch a thunderstorm over the Wisting Mountains. Thunder terrified me, so loud and close."

She giggled.

"Back then I thought it meant the Night of the Wolfe had come. There was lightning too. When my brothers saw it, they'd shout *whoa* and *ooh*, but I'd always look up too late. Picke and I would stare at the sky for a long time, for moments of nothing, as long as we could stand. Then our mind would wander—to the lights of the villages in the valley, or flashes behind us, or even my hands. It felt impossible to stay focused in one place long enough. Then my brothers would shout *whoa!* and we'd look up again too late. Finally I couldn't stand it, and I shouted, 'I keep missing it!'"

"You sound so cute," she said, which embarrassed him.

He didn't tell her the full truth: that *I* was largely responsible for the distractions.

"I was so frustrated. My mom's answer—I still remember it even though I was so young—she said, 'If you want to see lightning, look to the sky. Don't take your eyes off for a second. Even if you don't see anything for a long, long time. Because if you stop looking, you're sure to miss it...'" His voice tapered to silence, and the memory gave us a melancholy joy.

"Look to the sky." It sounded like Shilohe was smiling. "You remind me of my dad."

Locke nodded, not knowing how to accept the compliment.

"Okay, Locke. Thank you. I've been kind of... well, I just needed that. And now I'm sorry, but I have to go."

"You can't quit when it's your turn," he said.

"I'm sorry. But I have to."

"Are you doing this to pay me back?"

"Ha ha, no. And thanks. You've been a good friend. You've helped me more than you may realize."

"Hey, are you okay?"

"Yes, but… something's come up."

"How about you tell me how the Isles of Time ends before you go?"

Lightning struck across the sky. "I'm sorry. I'm out of time."

"Alright, next time?"

"Uh… I have two things to tell you before I go: a secret and a request."

"Wait, what's the matter?"

"Sssh. This is supposed to be exciting for you. First, I hid my diary in the Seer's library. There's a green book with gold letters in the middle of the highest shelf. I tucked it behind that."

"You're not at the Seer's anymore?"

"No questions. I'm out of time."

"And why do you want me to find your diary?"

"The second thing," she continued, "well, I'm not sure you'll understand it either, but I don't want you to come after me."

"Come after you where? What do you mean?"

"We don't need the living water anymore. We found another way to the source. The Chief Captain and his army will be helping us too."

"Then I'm—"

"You can go home now, like you wanted, to your family and friends. You did well. You lived boldly, and your brothers would be proud."

Locke gazed southward, toward his home and that broken green door. He thought about what used to be inside too. "I don't understand."

"Locke, please don't ruin it."

Suddenly he remembered volunteering to find the living water. He'd ruined it for her then. "I'm sorry."

"No, you didn't do anything wrong. It's just… I can't explain."

They were both silent for a moment.

"I'm glad we got to talk," she said.

"Wait, don't go. I need y—"

"I'm sorry."

Then, just like that, the wind fell silent.

40.

Threat

WHY DID THE clairvoyance lead us here?"
Locke shook his head, not wanting to break the silence.
"And where is she?"

He shook his head again.

Many days had swept away the stink and rot of the Majestic Sea. Locke had even napped out there in the middle of it for a few hours of the night. Now, on the morning of the fourteenth day, we stood at the west edge of the sea, on a white shoreline that curved around a body of dried mud, shattered to pieces. They called this place Lairde's Landing. The dry sea made it a relatively short walk from the Seer's rendezvous point. But it was what lay ahead that frightened us—*the Rueful Wilderness.*

I had the chilling feeling that we waited at the edge of a damp graveyard. "Maybe you should pull out the lamp again for just a second."

A sudden flight of bats swept out from the trees, hundreds of them curving upward over our heads, screeching in disharmony. Locke and I both ducked. They vanished against the black sky, fluttering away, leaving nothing but eerie silence.

"Maybe a bird demon had chased them out," I whispered.

We faced floodplains. When the sea rose, the water seeped around the tree bases. This left an even, mossy line across them all, like some clever artist had measured them one by one. Aside from the massive trunks, the ground was surprisingly clear, a flat floor of weathered leaves inside a giant room of sporadic pillars. Behind them, ghules and phantasms and demons of all sorts would be lurking.

Locke stared at the trees and their deathly white bark. "These are the trees from my vision," he whispered. "She was in trouble somewhere nearby."

This wilderness ran in a narrow strip from west to east across the entire land. Here, at its heart, it grew thickest and widest; here grim events took place that earned it its name; here the Burning Mountain's shadow used to fall every evening as the sun died. And here the clairvoyance had brought us.

The twins' voices echoed in our mind: *Only a fool would go into the Rueful Wilderness. Don't ever try it.*

Locke drew his sword.

"Which is safer?" I asked. "Standing on the dry sea, where we can see but can't hide? Or standing among the trees where we can hide but might get ambushed by a stalking bird demon or worse?"

Louder than the feeling of dread, an animal snapped a branch in the invisible distance. *Or maybe a ghule.* The night fell quieter than Locke's beating heart.

"Maybe we should find the Seer," I whispered. "He'll know what to do. He'll make sense of what Shilohe told us."

Locke shook his head with a determined look in his eyes.

But fate wasn't going to make us wait.

The sound of footsteps on dying leaves floated through the air.

Locke retreated from the sea toward the cover of the pillar trees, toward the sound too. Could it be a prowling gryphine? He hid next to a giant, chalky trunk. That left us feeling exposed from nearly all sides.

The steps came again, steady but much quieter. It wasn't a four-legged creature. Maybe a phantasm walking like a dead man.

"Up," I whispered, looking skyward.

Locke looked up. This wasn't a climbing tree: its lowest branches hung high, though not nearly so high as some trees we knew. He gripped the white bark, thick and knotted, powdery, and covered in moss. This bark wasn't bad, but climbing would not be silent.

The footsteps stopped, somewhere very nearby.

Locke pursed his lips and stared to the sides of the fat trunk in front of him.

I reached out into the air, trying to sense the slightest sound or the softest breath. I felt both, but so vaguely I couldn't tell where they were. A yellow light glimmered on a leaf. Then I noticed its broader pattern—a torch, casting telling shadows.

The steps began again. Very close.

The yellow light fell in two beams, on either side of our tree. Locke treaded in the shadow as it slowly shifted. Stepping lightly, slowly. Breathing lightly, slowly. His moccasins made the softest sound as they pressed onto the wet, papery leaves.

The sound of the footsteps stopped.

We waited against the fat trunk between the beams of yellow.

The shadow held, and Locke itched to peek out, to see what was happening.

"Locke?"

A gentle voice had spoken his name.

He whirled.

A shining blade pointed at his face.

He fumbled to bring his sword in front of him as he tripped over a gigantic root and landed on his backside—falling into the yellow light.

She held out a dagger defensively. The blade was white, so white it almost seemed to glow in the dimness. But before we could get a good look at it, she sheathed the weapon and covered the hilt with her cloak—a cloak in shades of black, stitched together in a wild pattern. Even in the night, her presence was unmistakable.

The Goddess.

Their eyes locked just long enough to wonder.

She wore tall gray moccasins over dark leggings. Her dark cloak covered a yellow top. A purple bandana wrapped from her forehead and over her crown, pulling her hair down on the sides of her face, though not covering the tips of her ears. These were the colors of a beautiful song, and if Locke hadn't already been on the ground, he might have fallen over.

"Princess?" said Locke.

"My name is Shilohe." She had an edge to her tone. "What are you doing here?"

Locke's vision had been wrong. She was not tied up, no cuts across her face. She didn't seem in danger of any kind. Though her aspect seemed under siege somehow.

Lonae slowly rose into the air, as if to gain a higher vantage point.

"Something's different about you," said Shilohe.

Locke shrugged. He felt pretty beat up, he needed more sleep, or maybe it was that he hadn't bathed in so long.

"Oh, no. This is all wrong." She rushed toward him. "Come this way. Get out of the light." She offered him her hand and pulled him out of the yellow light. With a grunt for his shoulder's sake, Locke found himself back on his feet.

"You have to stay here, okay?" she said. "I thought I told you—"

"But, princess, I just—"

"My name is Shilohe, and I told you not to come." She looked down, no, *stared* down, perceiving something. "It's in your bag, isn't it?"

"Yeah." With a satisfied grin, he pulled out the lamp, and the blue light reflected in her eyes.

I sensed Lonae wanting to learn more.

"No, put it back," said Shilohe. "It will draw them to you. You need to go, and take that with you. You're going to wreck everything."

Frowning, Locke put the lamp into his bag. "But can't I help you?"

"You don't understand what's going on."

"No I don't."

"Well, it's too late. I told you we don't need the lamp. You need to get out of here."

"But... hold on," said Locke. "When I looked into the Well, it showed me you were in danger, and I can't stop thinking about it."

"I told you, we're all in danger. Especially *you* if you don't leave!" She turned and marched away.

Locke stopped, contemplating. "But I just want—" He started after her again, coming around the tree into the yellow light of her torch.

"No! You're ruining it. Don't you see?" She held the torch in the air, and the warm light shined in his eyes. "This light imprisons a salaminde. As long as you're in it, the villain can see you!"

"He can?"

She turned and walked northward. "He's seen you, and he's almost here. Go while you still can!"

"But what about y—"

"We don't have time! JUST GO! I COMMAND YOU!"

Locke stopped in his tracks.

When she saw he obeyed, the hint of a sad smile appeared on the corner of her mouth. She grabbed a silver chain from around her neck and leaned down to pull it up over her purple bandana. She tossed it to him.

Locke caught it, bowing to gaze into his hands. The chain held a silver amulet.

When he looked up, she'd vanished among chalky pillars and darkness. Only the yellow light trailed behind, pointing toward her in long beams. Her presence pulled, ribbons of destiny tugging Locke's feet and heart. Where was she going? And why? And was it dangerous? And didn't she need his help even if she wasn't willing to say so?

He took a step after her, stopped, then took another. Stopped again.

He put the amulet around his neck and tucked it in his shirt. The metal was still warm and had a faint smell reminiscent of her.

"Locke," I said, "We should leave."

He looked at me. "But I..." Tears were hiding around the edges of his eyes. "She's going into the Rueful Wilderness!"

"We need to find the Seer," I said. "Wiks Pike is nearby. He'll know what to do."

Little did I know he'd blame me for those words.

41.

Rendezvous

"O F COURSE IT won't work: your eyes aren't closed."

"I've been *blinking*." Now Locke closed his eyes for a longer period, still jogging across the broken, dried mud. "See, that doesn't help. I still can't see the light."

"It helps in dire need, but we already know where the Seer is, so there's no need."

Locke squeezed his eyes tightly, pressing with his cheek muscles and scrunching his nose. All he saw was black. He opened his eyes long enough to get his bearings across the sea. "I think it's because I can't calm my thoughts." He shut his eyes and gazed behind him in one glance over each shoulder. "I want to see in *her* direction though."

"Put that away, and stop talking out loud."

Locke felt a little angry when I said this. He shoved the lamp in his pack, rushing forward.

I zipped along ahead of him, looking out as best I could. "The Seer will know what to do. If anyone can fix all this, it's him."

Doubts swirled through our mind, so many unanswered questions. Words echoed in the memory of that yellow torch:

You would be proud of my artistry.

Removing it is impossible, I'm afraid.

None of us got burned alive.

I caught a glimpse of a shadowy sentry on the shoreline ahead.

He saluted Locke with a nod before vanishing behind a tree. Moments later, we burst through the undergrowth into a small glade.

The Seer sat on a fallen white branch. An earthy pointed cap covered his bald head and hung down his back. Leather armor protected his shoulders, chest, arms, and legs. His waterfall eyebrows flowed around closed eyes. His clasped hands rested gently in his lap, and his sylfe mimicked this pose.

A sword leaned against the branch next to him—a sword that demanded our attention.

The white metal lit up the dimness—just as Shilohe's dagger had done, though she'd hardly given us time to notice. The sword emanated glory, and even Locke wondered if it hadn't been taken up by the Kyrose and bathed in the empyrean. It was a Sword of the Eternal, a Shining Sword; like Erythrose found in the cave and used to slay the King of Misrule; like Tunke pulled free of the gem to claim his throne; like Martigane stole to cut off the head of Amaranthe. Here it lay on the ground before us, strange as a hyuman.

A young guard in a black robe confronted Locke directly, blocking his view.

Locke looked up at him. As he noticed the guard's spaulders and gleaming gauntlets, the thick-sole boots and hearty fabrics, Locke felt embarrassed by his own simple moccasins, torn tunic, and the spaulder and vambrace that guarded only one of his arms. Locke tried to step around.

The guard moved in the way again, frowning. His hands hung free and ready, just like his sylfe.

"This is urgent!" Locke shoved past the guard.

The guard grabbed Locke's arm and leaned into what would have been a heavy throw—

"My boy, you made it!" The Seer smiled, and his eyes again glistened with the echo of tears.

The guard froze. He stood down as the Seer smiled, walked over, and put his hands on Locke's arms. The wise old man shook his head with admiration, till he saw the urgency on Locke's face. "You are tense—but you have the lighted lamp. What's the matter?"

"It's in my pack. But she said the villain's salaminde was in her torch."

"What?"

"The princess. I just saw her." Locke pointed back through the trees and across the sea.

"What's she doing here?" As some realization hit him, the Seer's tone dropped to despair. "Oh no."

"She had a torch, the salaminde torch."

"We can still save her. Together." In an agile movement, the Seer picked up the great sword and stepped quickly forward into the trees. He stopped and waved at Locke. "You lead."

Locke did as he was told, bolting ahead. The young guard trailed after them. The sentry, bearded and wearing black, appeared from nowhere, following a little further behind. He caught Locke's eye and smiled, a roguish grin. For some reason I liked the man immediately, though I couldn't say why.

"What is she doing?" said Locke. Branches and leaves flew past on all sides.

"She's trying to get there first so she can be the one to offer the sacrifice," said the Seer.

"What sacrifice?"

"You shouldn't have left her alone."

42.

Crescendo

WE WOVE THROUGH chalky tree trunks.

The Seer took the lead, as if his keen sylfe could smell the trail. Locke followed directly behind, with the younger guard next and the bearded rogue last. We moved inland across the floodplains, deeper into the Rueful Wilderness and its dark magic.

While the Enchanted Wood made a series of majestic corridors, walking through the Rueful Wilderness felt like crawling through a cave. The branches hung low and curved in close, often forcing Locke to duck, though it did open up in places. He pushed branches aside with a forearm raised in front of his face to block the cobwebs.

"Spread out," said the Seer.

We fanned out into a curved line, dodging giant trees, which expanded our collective line of sight through the maze. I reached out, trying to sense Shilohe and Lonae; instead I felt an eerie presence watching us. Next I sensed footsteps, not our own, beating like a drum in rapid rhythm. I nudged Locke, and he increased his speed for a moment. Then we burst through into a meadow.

The captor gripped Shilohe's arm, tugging her along.

Her wrists were bound together, just as Locke envisioned. Her purple bandana had been ripped from her head and tied crudely over her eyes. Red scrapes showed on her cheek and jaw.

The captor saw us and halted, facing us across the meadow. Our group paused too. "I am Stane." These words wafted across the still night, from a voice as dark as a cauldron, with the rough texture of cast-iron, and no color at all.

This man had cursed the skies—had threatened the King's life—had invited destruction on a Tenarie sheep camp—had given Nicke a vial of venom to slay the last of the Hundred.

But he wasn't the villain we'd imagined.

His wrinkled face was thin and tall, as if a sculptor had pinched his head between two giant thumbs before throwing him into the kiln. He had the sour expression of a person sucking avookudes, but, paradoxically, he seemed indifferent, lifeless, a face of unholy iron. His forehead sat unnaturally high, and his mouth and throat were pulled up, creating a turtle-like stretch to his neck. His eyes were big, but far from beautiful; they looked distorted, out of shape and proportion. His white hair was thin and wet. He'd strapped Shilohe's salaminde torch to his crooked back so the flame hung to the side. As he pointed at us, his hand shook—like he was trapped inside the gray prison of his own flesh, the embodiment of misery.

"Where is his sylfe?" I asked. No one answered, but I thought I heard some distant dying noise, like a soul screaming against an unstoppable doom.

"I command you to cease your pursuits or die," said Stane. This was good—he'd threatened *our* lives, not hers.

"We cannot leave without the girl," replied the Seer.

"Then you will die."

A Tenarie warrior emerged from the maze of trees—surprisingly close. He carried a long, thin sword. His white hair hung down wildly over a blue bandana, and his pale face was young and almost friendly. *No.* This was no time for creeping sympathy. *Not now.* They'd deprived Locke of water, and they'd kidnapped Shilohe. We needed to hate them. We needed to destroy them. Locke gripped the words he'd spoken days before: *I hate the Tenarie.*

"Kill them," said Stane.

A hush filled the air as four more Tenarie appeared from the trees, one at a time, each from a different direction and distance. The second had a gruesome scar across his face and eye, bright red on pale skin. The third wore a long ponytail of white hair. A fourth let his hair blow unrestrained in the wind. The fifth was particularly burly and should've been carrying a club instead of a sword. Their sylves rode the wind, poised to strike.

Locke's hands trembled.

"Don't worry about the outcome," I said. "We can't control it. All we can do is roll the kohkoo nut."

Locke nodded, breathing hard to keep his cool. "Let's roll," he whispered. He moved his sword, strapping it within easy reach at his side. He got out his sling and picked up two decent rocks.

The Seer didn't draw the Shining Sword. He only gripped the sheath gently in his wrong hand, pointing the handle toward his sword hand. "Locke, you keep that lamp hidden, okay?"

"Yes, sir," said Locke.

Stane didn't look like much of a warrior, but we didn't know the extent of his magic. Even without him, the enemy outnumbered us by one.

When they approached, they didn't snap into position like I imagined the Hundred would have. They kind of slinked toward us slowly. They didn't even pull their weapons into a fighting stance. They just moseyed, but that was terrifying in its own way.

The Seer drew the Shining Sword from its scabbard. The blade shone, strangely white, as if illuminated from within—as if drawn that moment from the master armorer's charcoal. A sense of wonder drew all eyes toward it, and I prayed the sword could defend as boldly as it shined. The Tenarie hesitated, but soon they advanced again.

Locke had excelled when sparring with wooden swords against his brothers and cousins, despite being the youngest. But those had included unwritten rules about inflicting too much pain. He'd once fought a boy named Thane over a girl, but that wasn't exactly to the death either. He'd used his Hundred blade several times, especially after the lamp had drawn extra trouble to him—against ignorant squatters and weaponless wraiths. Those encounters had boosted his confidence, but they'd left him with the option to run, which he'd taken more than once. This fight would be different—not pretend, not innocent, not one-sided. It matched us against experienced warriors and their cold steel, blades that would cut flesh and bone as easily as dipping a paddle through water.

Locke looked across the ground at Shilohe, peacefully bound. Running wasn't an option.

The twins taught him about fighting stances and swordplay: When scrawny swordsmen boasted, they said cunning or swiftness won the battle—to help listeners swallow the unbelievable. Who wouldn't root for an agile hero against a dumb brute? But most sword fights weren't won by speed, strength, or wit. They were won by endurance, much like kick fighting. The key was simply to train hard.

"Oh, and watch your wrong ankle," I said, repeating Robyne's words

from so long ago. "It's your most vulnerable spot against a right-hander."
Locke nodded, glad to be re-immersed in the memory.

"And," said Tunke, "when you're too tired to swing your sword anymore,
you run."

"But it probably means you're going to die," added Robyne.

At least they'd been honest. Locke's work for the Tenarie masons had
built his strength. But his recent run and the past few days had drained
him, not to mention his aching shoulder.

"We can do this," I whispered. "Today is not our day to die."

He breathed in confidence, and his chest expanded; then he exhaled.

The Seer's bearded sentry took command: "Form a line." He swept his
hand parallel to the enemy's formation. "Gante and I will be on the outsides,
and you two in the center."

The big Tenarie screamed and charged.

He aimed for the center of our line—aiming for Locke and the Seer. The
others, following his cue, shrieked as well, a frightening sound, the color
of an iron spade after it scrapes against stone—five screaming Tenarie and
five trailing sylves.

I hate the Tenarie.

Locke jerked his sling into action, hurling it around his head once, twice,
then letting fly. The gray stone zinged. The big warrior jerked to the side as
the rock glanced off the edge of his skull. Unfazed, his screaming charge
continued. Locke shoved his sling in his shirt and yanked his sword free,
bringing it with two hands above his head, holding it in a high guard.

The Tenarie leader smashed his blade down at Locke.

If Locke had parried the blow directly, he'd have barely held on to his
sword. Instead, quick on his feet, he blocked only lightly and jumped out
of the way.

The warrior swung a second blow, sparks went flying, and Locke retreated
again.

The flowing-haired Tenarie moved aggressively at the Seer, who held his
ground. Our young guard—Gante was his name—stepped back every
time the ponytail attacked. The scar and the blue bandana doubled up on
our bearded guard, flanking our formation and pushing our best warrior
back—still he kept that roguish grin on his face as he fought.

Each strike rung Locke's hands like a bell. The blows weren't regular and swift like a beating drum. They were sporadic and surprising, each followed by great pause, coming at most in pairs, and sending glowing orange sparks again and again.

Locke panted. Wielding a sword was like swinging a mason's hammer, only you had to heave it in a different direction each time. Sweat trickled down his temple next to his teardrop blotch. As he continually retreated, he stole a moment to wipe his sweating palms on his pants.

I clung to Locke's ear: "Don't worry. His aggression comes at a cost. His blows are getting reckless, like he sees no need for defense."

The large Tenarie chopped a deadly blow at Locke's neck.

Locke saw it coming and dropped.

The Tenarie swung wide.

In that instant, Locke cut at his enemy's ankle.

The Tenarie's eyes bulged as he pointed his sword at the ground to block, not a moment too soon. Locke's sword bit flesh and metal at the same time. Blood splattered. The brute punched his pommel forward into Locke's chest with shocking power.

Locke rolled backward, landing and tumbling feet over face, onto his shoulders, and right back to his defensive position.

The big Tenarie crouched, and his ankle poured blood over his hand.

Then chaos struck, so much happening at once:

The Seer thrust his blade into flesh, and the flowing-haired Tenarie crumpled, his head whacking into the leafy ground next to a chalky white root. Our bearded rogue groaned, coughing red liquid and falling to his knees—we didn't see how or why—and then he received his final blow. Locke froze, staring at the still-grinning teeth now covered in blood.

That missed moment might have cost him his life.

The big Tenarie lunged, growling.

But the Seer's white blade nicked his arm, slowing the stroke enough for Locke to parry and dodge.

With the brute injured twice, and with one warrior down from each band, the Tenarie drew back. The scene, for a moment, was peaceful, waiting on mortal breaths.

Locke knelt, put the point of his sword in the leaves, and rested his arms on the hilt, gasping. Sweat dripped down his face and made his hair stick in mats. He purposefully kept his eyes away from the bloody mess whose sylfe I could no longer see.

Stane stood in the distance next to a large trunk, gripping Shilohe's arm, with, I supposed, a knife at her back. He spoke intently with a bitter expression, his eyes fixed on us, but too far for me to hear what he said. Shilohe remained calm, even with that eerie, undying noise around her. I couldn't tell where it came from, but it scared me.

After a moment's rest, the Seer moved toward his fallen rogue. He touched the man's neck, checking for vitality, but then dismissed the body. I couldn't be sure, but I thought I heard a chuckle.

Locke stared blankly, still panting, as the Tenarie tied bandages on the big warrior. The Tenarie sylves watched, probably wondering, like I was, which side would take up the fighting first. Now it was our three against their four.

The wounded brute leaped to his feet. This even took his companions off guard. After all, he'd suffered two flesh wounds. He charged at Locke. But when the Seer and Gante stepped in close, the brute halted, waiting for his companions.

I hate the Tenarie.

Locke shuffled, making a few feints of his own to test his opponent's readiness. One of these led to a single hit, followed by more quiet. The brute glared, but he'd lost some of his fire. When the madness resumed, swords crashed in earnest, and this time Locke held his ground, blow after blow.

Amid this dance toward death, the Seer matched the grace of his own sylfe, at one with his bright sword, and the Tenarie failed to gain any ground.

Suddenly the Tenarie brute called, "Back!" He waved for his men to retreat with him.

We'd survived the second fray.

The enemy stood in a clump, whispering. Locke leaned on his hilt once again, breathing heavily.

Stane watched it all from a distance, still angrily speaking, or chanting.

Shilohe's mouth remained calm as she breathed beneath the purple blindfold.

When they came at us the third time, the weaker two faced Locke and Gante. The brute and the scar drove for the Seer, pressing from opposite sides.

"You have to help him," I whispered.

But Locke couldn't simply turn away from the blue bandana.

The Tenarie pushed our backs against a deep canyon ledge with a dry riverbed far below. One false move would mean a deadly fall.

Gante flanked their line, letting our formation retreat laterally up the bank, where the chasm and the wilderness grew deeper.

Sweat trickled off the nose of the Tenarie brute. He screamed as he pressed at the Seer. The terrible sound filled his allies' blood with vigor.

I tried to silence my feelings to give Locke more focus. He jarred blow after blow against the blue bandana. When his opponent stepped back, Locke pressed into the gap. In a daring leap, he slashed his sword and lunged forward at the same moment, punching through the line. Now he stood on the outside of the enemy corral. We formed a triangle around our four opponents.

"They're surrounded!" said the Seer. "Push them together!"

But our upper hand didn't last long.

A groaning moan filled the air, large and deep, seeping from below, as if the entire earth were in pain. For a moment the seven blades fell silent. The warriors looked at each other.

I glanced at Stane, whose eyes were now closed.

The trees along the bank started to sink, as if the Necris had opened its mouth to swallow them whole. It was horrifying and unnatural—a feeling like worms crawling in Locke's gut.

The warriors looked at the ground beneath their feet.

And then it cracked.

43.

Collapse

WE'D SEEN TREES fall before, toppling sideways when their trunks were cut.

But these didn't tip.

Along the river, the chalky white trees fell straight down, with the roots still beneath them, sinking slowly to draw out the torment. As the earth cracked, it rumbled loud and prolonged, like crashing waves, a bang of rocks and fury rattling the bones. The split raced toward us, tearing the earth in two, too quick for anything but a slight twist.

The ground dropped beneath the elves.

Air and dust surged upward, pushing against me and the other sylves, obscuring the whole picture.

Locke let go of his sword and jumped as the ground crumbled and vanished. If it weren't for a root reaching gallantly toward him, he would have tumbled into the chaos. His hand caught the root. He squeezed. The bark tore loose as his weight pulled back and down before slamming him into the wall of the newly formed cliff. His shoulder sent a surge of pain down his spine.

Shouts leaped upward, failing to grab hold of anything but their own terror.

The strange feeling returned—the same nightmare we'd felt when the wolfe should've killed us outside the cave. A phantom dressed as death came at us with claws to tear our innermost parts. Sickness twisted at our insides. Locke, hanging by that root, tried to turn away from the feeling, to cower down, to shrink away, but he couldn't. The feeling surrounded us, then screamed as we miraculously slipped out of its reach.

Locke coughed through the dust. His fingers burned.

The screams echoed below us, like moaning ghosts growing distant. The dust settled, sticking to Locke's sweaty forehead and going in his ears. But he held on, clinging with fingertips and kicking against the surface.

"Picke, I can't find a footing. Can you?"

"Maybe. Right here. You feel that?"

Locke put the toe of his moccasin where I'd pointed, and pulled himself up.

"Help!" came a cry from below.

Locke's toes slipped, leaving him dangling. But a lifetime of climbing had given him a strong upper body. Soon he rolled onto the ledge above, coughing and panting. He looked at me, wanting to know what happened, and who survived, and what we should do.

We stared at the dust brooding below. If a Tenarie tried to climb out, would Locke kill him as he struggled? Could he really send an unarmed elfe to the place of no return?

"Help!" came the cry again.

A light wind pulled back the cover of dust, revealing lumps of dirt and rock. But nothing moved. Then we saw a face struggling for life, a face that didn't know what happened or what was to come—the face of the young guard, Gante. Roots stuck out from the newly exposed cliff, and he dangled from one of these, trying to climb.

"Hang on!" Locke pulled off his backpack and gripped one strap, hanging the other below.

Gante managed to climb within reach. He took hold of the strap, and Locke pulled him onto solid ground. Then it was Gante's turn to lie there panting.

As Locke stood up, the silver amulet brushed against the skin of his chest, jerking his mind to a more pressing thought. He whirled and looked through the trees.

And gasped.

She was still there. The purple sash pulled tight across her perfect face.

"Princess!"

Stane stood still. Not fleeing—but why? He held Shilohe in his grasp, watching with that sour glare. What magic would he call next, a horde of bird demons?

Locke reached for the sword on his back, his elbow pointing high. He found nothing but an empty scabbard. An unarmed boy would have little chance of winning a sword fight, even against an old man. Locke looked off the cliff for a way to scramble down. "I need a weapon."

"We need to find the Seer," said Gante, also peering down the collapse.

"But the princess is in—"

"He may be *injured!*—in need of urgent help."

Locke looked at me.

I shrugged. "Both lead us down there. Besides, it doesn't look like Stane is going anywhere."

Locke took one last glance at her. "Let's hurry."

Rushing to where the landslip had cut deepest, the boys climbed down one of the plummeted trees that now leaned like a ladder against the cliff and rubble.

We saw dirt and stone, all clumped together, colored in a uniform brownish gray, a long slope at the base of the sheer cliff. The shining point of the white sword jutted out between rocks. If the Seer was still gripping the handle, he was smashed several feet below. Locke's first thought was to take that sword and go. But he didn't dare.

The fingers were the first thing I noticed.

Everywhere else was a mass of large lumps, but the fingers were intricate, with tiny wrinkles, covered in dirt and dust, with a displaced beetle crawling across the fingernails.

The fingers twitched.

I felt breathing. The dirt shifted, falling, and a face materialized from the formlessness. A mound of dust divided into a thousand hairs and fell in a second miniature landslip as the head pulled forward. The hair was white. It flowed from a dusty blue bandana: the youngest of the Tenarie warriors.

Gante immediately stood and kept walking.

"Help," came the plea, quiet as falling dust, as if the dirt had spoken. His legs must have been smashed beneath the debris, and he trembled with the pain. His sylfe swirled dizzily above him, mixed with powdery dust.

Locked looked up at the rim, and the time rushed past like his heartbeats. Was Stane still waiting with our Goddess?

"Help," said the breath again.

I hate the Tenarie.

Locke turned away, teeth grit, trying not to remember Nicke.

44.

Demise

I FOUND HIM!" SHOUTED Gante.

He pointed into a steep mess of dirt, clods, and rocks.

Locke hesitated.

I hated hesitation.

Behind him, the eyes of the wounded Tenarie barely gleamed. Locke wouldn't look at those eyes, but he wouldn't walk away either. A dark feeling creeped over us.

When Locke looked at me, I shrugged. Aside from him, I didn't particularly care for elves.

"Locke?" came Gante's voice, wavering.

Locke looked up at the rim once again. "I'm walking away for the Goddess's sake," he said. And then he did.

As Gante came running toward us, Locke met him halfway, not looking back. "Is the Seer dead?"

Gante's eyes spoke a clear enough message—that he wasn't dead, but almost. "He told me he wanted you."

Locke jerked his head back in surprise.

"Come on." They rushed over.

The earthseer was buried deep in the element he'd once drawn power from. Huge rocks and fresh dirt covered all but his head and one hand, as if Gaie himself had imprisoned the Seer in an earthen stockade. The boys didn't climb too close, afraid of causing more pressure on his buried body.

I moved in close though.

Dust filled the cracks of the wrinkles in the Seer's face and forehead. It coated the flowing lines of hair reaching from his eyebrows and chin. His breath was faint, like twilight, and the dirt and rock covering his shoulders stood powerful and still. His eyes still glistened with sympathy. He spoke in a high, weak voice with dust-covered lips: "I didn't want it to be you, Locke.

I don't even see how it *could* be you. But this is fate's choice, not mine." His gray voice thinned to a narrow strip, like the smoke of a candle that had just been put out, whipping rapidly back and forth in its final moments.

Gante stood a few paces away, looking jealously toward Locke.

The Seer whispered again, but the first few words were lost on the wind. Then he said, "Don't let her get there first. She's supposed to be the next Seer."

He was spending his last breaths on this message, to us—*why?*

When the Seer's face moved, it shifted only slightly, as if it were animated by the gentle breeze rather than his own lifeforce—the form that just moments before had made such majestic and almost inhuman maneuvers. Yet move he did, once more, just enough to barely shake his head *no.*

"I'm so sorry." His breath barely came through. "I didn't want it to be you."

Locke frowned and shook his head—he didn't understand. *We* didn't understand.

"I didn't want it to be you."

As death crouched to take the Seer's last breath, Locke said the same lie his mother had once spoken, the only thing he could really think to say: "It's going to be okay."

"Yes. It is… But just don't let her—"

Death squeezed a little tighter.

The Seer's cheeks twisted, his eyes closed, and he gave a light chuckle, his final laugh.

His sylfe leaned toward me, on his knees, reaching one arm—as if he could take hold and stay animated with my breath. I'd seen dead elves before. I'd even watched the last of the Hundred gasp his final breath. But watching this sylfe approach the border between life and death haunted me. I didn't want to watch.

"Picke," the sylfe whispered, "he has to die."

Of course the Seer had to die. He was all but dead already. And when he breathed his last, this sylfe would be exiled, cursed into perfect stillness till the end of time. I even tried to take hold of his hands, to not let him go, to rescue him from the darkness. But he was sliding in spite of me.

Horror stretched across the sylfe's countenance. "He has to die."

Again those words.

"Didn't tell you," he said. "The curse… Three things… The source, the sword, and the *sacrifice.*"

I searched, needing more, and wondering if there would be time.

"Villain must lose his life… But a hero must sacrifice… Or the curse remains… We'd have given ours… But it's slipping…"

The sylfe gasped.

He was suffocating.

That was how sylves were cast into exile, asphyxiation—cutting short the breath till everything fell silent. As the Seer's soul passed on, the sylfe became more and more distant from his elfe—and that distance would kill. I could barely see him.

He heaved, clawing for air. "Now *he* has to die."

I glanced at my elfe, and the truth stabbed into me, slicing painfully.

He was talking about Locke.

The sylfe looked into me and saw that I knew.

Then death took him by the throat and squeezed with icy hands.

45.

Path of Regret

THE SEER RESTED with open mouth and closed eyes. Neither breath nor light entered his soul. Instead they fell on his already buried body.

"I should have died protecting him." Gante's hands hung at his sides, not clutching a weapon, not clasped in a meditation. His eager hands just hung there, everlastingly late. "I should have done something."

Locke wanted to feel sadness, wanted it to sink deep into his bones. Instead he felt numb. As if our soul had also died in the collapse.

Death had taken our Seer, and death would never give him back. We would never hear the jovial laugh or feel the might of his wisdom. This finality stood as a massive, unbudging wall, the undefeatable enemy coming for us all.

Locke looked toward the cliff's edge. He still held one last feeling in his heart—his desire to help Shilohe. He glanced around for his sword, and the injured Tenarie caught his eye—lying as a pile of debris in the riverbed.

"I should've been listening," said Gante. "Numa knew that cliff was about to fall…"

"If Numa knew, she would've told the Seer," said Locke. "You can't blame yourself."

But logic didn't seem to help. "It should have been me." Gante stared at the Seer's face, and a storm raged inside him—I saw the turmoil in his sylfe. They needed more than a few moments. They may have needed more than a few years.

But Locke didn't have time to wait on grief. "Come with me. We have to save her. It's what the Seer wanted." He started off to climb the cliff.

"I must see to my master," said Gante.

"What do you mean?"

"He needs a sacred burial."

"He needs us to finish his quest. So he didn't die for nothing."

"He wanted you. He was going to tell you something."

"He didn't tell me anything. He said he *didn't* want it to be me. I think he wanted you to go, not me."

"Didn't want *what* to be you?"

I knew. The Seer had said it wouldn't end well, and now I knew what that meant. He'd planned to sacrifice his life to end the curse. I nearly blurted it out, but hesitation tangled me in its nets. I hated that so much. But if I explained what I knew, would Locke turn and run?

"I don't know what he was talking about," said Locke. "I hardly knew him. You should know—you're his apprentice."

"I'm not his apprentice."

"Then what are you?"

"I'm one of his guardians. One of his failed guardians."

"It wasn't your fault. Blame this dark wilderness. Or blame your Kyrose."

"Stane did it," I whispered. "I saw him chanting—some power over gnymes."

Locke looked at me in surprise. In rush of battle, this thought hadn't occurred to him. Which meant the villain had sacrificed his own servants to kill the Seer. A shiver chilled us both. "I think the villain caused the collapse," he said.

Gante stared at the cliff's edge as anger seemed to boil up toward his throat.

"I'm going after her," said Locke. "Are you coming?"

Gante stood, still no reply.

Without another word, Locke walked down the riverbed, scanning for his sword. He occasionally glanced up at the rim, hoping for some hint of the Goddess.

"Wait!" Gante held up a hand, signaling us to stop. He climbed to the Seer's lifeless body. Two dead fingers and a thumb were curled almost in the monk's same, strange three-pronged farewell. Was it some final salute or a signal that *three* meant something? Gante pulled a buckle over the Seer's shoulder, gently lifted the bald head, and pulled till he'd freed the scabbard. He turned and climbed the cave-in, making his way toward the white point of the sword gleaming in the dim light. He pushed the scabbard over the tip of the blade and worked it back and forth. As he pulled it loose, he slid the scabbard down, covering it further, and worked it back and forth again. Finally the sword came free.

Gante took it by the scabbard and step-slid back down. He walked to Locke and held out the weapon. It was a long sword with plenty of room for two hands on the grip. "He also told me to give this to you."

"Why?"

Gante shook his head.

When Locke reached for the weapon, Gante pulled it back. "Don't touch the handle."

It was an odd request, and Locke made a face to match.

Gante handed the sword again, and Locke took it by the sheath. The hilt looked like a great dragon; the mouth opened as if spewing the fire of the blade. Scales coated the handle, protruding in relief to give it grip. Silver embellishments lined the equally elegant scabbard. Heat came from beneath the dark brown leather, enough to make it uncomfortable to hold, as if magic were seeping out.

"Why give it to me?" asked Locke as he strapped the hot blade to his back.

"I don't know. It was the last thing he said to me."

I watched his sylfe as he said it, and I could taste the bitterness, the fact that their beloved master had spent those last words on Locke.

"I'm sorry," said Locke.

Sorrow hung in the air—sorrow was the only thing left.

We started down the river bottom, approaching the dusty form of the Tenarie warrior curled up on the ground. Locke kept his eyes away. He had no time to waste on compassion. Instead he looked straight ahead.

At the deathly form of a banshe wolfe.

46.

Reunion

THE BEAST SMILED wide and growled deep.
No wonder the villain hadn't run.

The sides of the canyon flanked us, like the walls of a mausoleum with the wolfe as the centerpiece. The wind brought the reek toward us, sweet bark and rot. The animal had a dark silver patch running down its nose—this was not the one we'd encountered at the cave.

Locke felt the heat of the sword on his back. Even with it, he was no match for this beast. He stepped backward.

We heard Gante struggling to climb the collapsed canyon wall. The crushed Tenarie boy at Locke's feet whimpered. The wolfe paced forward, watching angrily, calculating, or daring us to make the first move with one slow step at a time.

Locke turned and bolted, hustling toward the Seer's body. He scrambled up the collapse, following Gante in the struggle up the broken cliff.

The wolfe advanced like an army, following slowly, as if to draw out the torment. Or like a cat toying with a cornered mouse.

"Whoa," said Gante, in a reverent tone. His sword hung above us, the hilt caught in a root's fingers and the blade pointing down. He climbed toward it.

Locke passed Gante and proceed up the face. He was beyond the reach of the wolfe, but he hadn't made it to the top where he could flat out run. The final climb would be the hardest, but it seemed our only chance. Even two blades against a banshe wolfe would hardly be enough.

The monstrous claws nudged the rocks in the riverbed. The Tenarie with the blue bandana was playing dead. The wolfe took a long look at him then continued on. It climbed the pile of dirt and rocks, making its way toward us.

The boys clung to the roots and crumbled wall, nearly to the top.

The monster stood beneath us, looking up, as if expecting the boys to fall. Then it turned its silver-streaked face away, snapped its jaws on the Seer's dead wrist, and twisted in a waving pattern. Red mushed out through the Seer's sleeve.

"Nooo!" shouted Gante.

The wolfe glanced up spitefully. Red was now dashed on the white fur around its black lips. After seeing our reaction, it pointed its face back down, clamped its jaws on the body, and began dragging it from beneath the dirt and stones. The corpse made a popping sound as the beast changed its grip and pulled again.

Gante placed a hand on the root resting in front of him. He leaned forward and leaped, his soldier boots leading the charge, his arm and sword trailing behind, ready to strike.

"Wait, don't!" shouted Locke.

Gante's feet hit the slope, and he glided down a new, smaller landslip.

The wolfe tore wildly at the corpse, looking up just in time to catch the bite of cold steel across its face. It reacted quicker than a snarl, smashing its skull forward into Gante like a battering ram.

That was all we saw.

Locke climbed with the strength of Gaie, scraping at the leafy ground and pulling. He rolled onto the surface, stood, and sped inland.

The edges of his eyes glistened red.

Locke responded to my silence with gritted teeth: "Dying with him will do no good."

But leaving was harmful too.

He ran, his heart pounded, and a tear crept slowly past his teardrop birthmark.

Behind us we heard Gante groan as if lifting some heavy object.

This sound mutated into a scraping scream, and I wished I could escape the air so the noise would not penetrate our mind.

47.

Burning

WHAT DID YOU want me to do?" blurted Locke.
"I didn't say anything…"

The maze of white trees looked darker than ever.

The hilt of the Shining Sword hung over Locke's wrong shoulder. He'd use it to confront Stane if it wasn't too late. He'd use it on the wolfe too if it came to that—and he'd die with sword in hand.

Locke ran perpendicular to the river canyon, passing the red bodies of the rogue and the Tenarie that the Seer had killed. Bats screeched as we passed through, but we still hadn't seen any bird demons. Nor could we find any trace of Shilohe and Stane. Locke charged on blindly between the thick trunks.

"The lamp, Locke."

"What?"

"Get it out."

"I don't have t—"

"Maybe it will remind us where she is."

Panting, Locke threw his pack to the ground. When he tore it open, the air filled with a soft glow. He lifted out the lamp—a handle connected to a bowl and the dancing flame of blue water.

He gasped several times, still out of breath. The wolfe's stench lingered. Locke closed his eyes and breathed more slowly, trying not to believe the wolfe's fangs would appear around one of these trees at any moment. It didn't work. He breathed and closed his eyes again, trying to forget about Gante and the Seer and the rogue lying on bloody red ground.

Locke shook his head. "I can't." He looked around, hoping to see the Goddess. "She could be so near and I'd never know in this maze."

"Just try, Locke."

He clapped a hand over his face and bowed his head. He breathed, and his fingers felt his eyes turning under the skin of his eyelids.

This time, we *heard* it first.

It gave off a soothing ring, a single, calming note woven into the trail. A seam of blue glowed ahead, calling us down the familiar path where we knew we'd walk, weaving between the fat trunks, and then, *strange*—

—stopping not far ahead.

He opened his eyes, and the vision vanished.

"What does that mean?" asked Locke.

"Just go," I said. The urgency pounded toward us.

"But why would it—"

"You need to MOVE!"

Locke stood and ran, following the path of the clairvoyance.

As we reached the end of the trail the blue light had shown us, two things happened at once: We saw, through a long corridor of trees, the villain gripping Shilohe's arm like a claw. We also sensed thundering footsteps impending behind us.

Right behind us.

As fear ripped at his lungs, Locke spun so fast he actually fell to the ground.

On one knee, one foot, and one hand, he clutched the phanos lamp and faced the banshee wolfe head to head.

Its scent flooded over us. Blood stained the fur around the beast's mouth and down its chest. Gante's blood. A large unbleeding cut gaped beneath its eye; the flesh looked white and dead. It raised one foot, curling its paw, ready to strike at Locke, a strange counterpoint, as if they each looked into a magical mirror.

I jumped between them.

The wolfe snorted and leaped past me.

As the jaws moved for his throat, Locke gripped the phanos lamp like a sword and stabbed with all his might. If he'd had time to think, he might have hoped the glass would break and cut the monster's silver-streaked snout, staving off death for the smallest of moments.

The wolfe broke its charge.

Sliding, changing its trajectory and shying away, reacting with so much panic that Locke's jab never actually touched. The wolfe scrambled, glaring at the blue light.

Locke looked at the lamp in his hand.

The wolfe darted to the wrong side, snarling, and snapping toward Locke's ribcage. Locke turned the flame toward it in an instinctive motion. The beast scrambled back, pausing just out of arm's reach. I saw terror in its eyes. The wolfe darted once more to the right, its fangs dipping low toward an ankle.

Locke pulled back in a reverse lunge and pointed the lamp as if stabbing the wolfe in the skull.

The beast's jaw slammed into the dirt as it desperately kept out of reach.

The wolfe darted twice more, and each time Locke spun to keep it from pressing in. The small power of the lamp seemed just enough. The beast groaned and slunk back in retreat.

"The monk said a sylfe could put it out," I whispered. "But these monsters don't have elementals."

Locke gave a hesitant smile, breathing what might have been a chuckle if he weren't so nervous.

The wolfe circled.

Locke turned with it, pointing the lamp at eye level.

The monster glared with black eyes over the top of the dancing water. The creature's massive shoulder blades rose just above that, swaying back and forth as it moved.

Stane came into view in the background beyond the wolfe.

He looked at us. His face was twisted in hatred, an expression so strong it seemed a foot away.

A dark sylfe curled forth from behind him, flowing out of the ether—not like wind or breath, but like death, a horrible, suffocating darkness. And the sylfe wasn't breathing—the sort of thing that should only exist in nightmares. It crawled across the air toward us.

I sensed what would happen next.

Panic clawed at me. Locke felt it and began to run before he even realized why. He kept the flame pointed toward the wolfe in a vague, weak threat.

The wolfe stood, puzzled but not moving.

The sylfe glided through the corridor of trees, floating up and down like decay. Dark and lifeless. His target was clear.

I put myself in the way, but the dark sylfe didn't slow or alter his course. As the blackness passed through me, I screamed into my mother air. It gave

Locke the physical pain of flesh being shred apart. He screamed, stumbling, and fear turned his insides out.

The dark sylfe attacked.

Locke cupped his hand over the bowl of the phanos lamp—he now realized what the thing was after—and tried to protect it. The living water stabbed heat against his palm, but he kept it there. It was the only defense he could think of, but a hand couldn't stop a sylfe.

The darkness whisked through his knuckles like a tempest through a forest.

Locke wailed.

I fell.

The lamp smacked against the ground, with the living water vanished.

No breath.

No dirt.

No blood.

And no light.

"Locke?"

Nothingness surrounded us.

"LOCKE?"

A copper smell wafted through the air, floating away.

"LOCKE!"

"I'm here!"

"Watch out!"

The wolfe's grim lips tightened, eager to sink fangs into flesh.

Locke jumped, pulling sluggishly forward—more than memory had vanished with the light. He stumbled for the nearest tree. Managing one last burst of speed, he stepped against the trunk and leaped. The branch should've been out of reach, but Numa was with him, and he soared, barely catching it with the fingertips of his sword hand. Somehow that unlikely grip held, and he pulled his other arm into place.

The wolfe was beneath him.

Its open jaws lunged. But the attack was slightly misaimed, and the wolfe's bottom teeth smashed into Locke's foot, raising him up. He used that upward force to swing to the top side of the branch as claws smashed beneath, nearly shaking him from the tree.

The wolfe leaped a second time.

Locke hustled for another grip and pulled himself higher, but the claw caught his ankle, pinning it against the white trunk and dragging him down.

The wolfe fell, then leaped a third time.

Locke scrambled higher.

The wolfe gripped the trunk with its forepaws, clawing and rising.

Locke climbed frantically, not looking back till the ground dropped far below.

The wolfe looked up desperately. Thick branches fenced its heavy form. It pushed away from the trunk. Limbs snapped as it twisted around and crashed back onto the ground. It stared up with foam dripping from its jowls.

Locke climbed higher still—he needed to catch sight of Shilohe. From high in the tree, he got one final glimpse before Stane dragged her around another tree trunk and out of sight.

Gone.

Suddenly Locke felt something. Or he realized he'd been feeling something—ever since the dark sylfe put out the phanos lamp. He'd just been too panicked to notice. Dryness scraped at his throat and hunger clawed at his belly—those horrible feelings he'd left at the World's End. The light of the living water had washed them away. Now they came storming back, and he felt the full bodily stress he deserved. He clutched onto the tree's highest branches, and his head swirled.

The horrors of memory returned too: the wounded Tenarie he'd left to die, the Seer's lifeless face, Gante's final scream, and the phanos lamp lying empty on the ground. Worst of all, Shilohe, the reason for it all, had disappeared from view, leaving us alone, with a wolfe circling below.

"You told me to leave her," said Locke.

"What?"

"You said to leave and go find the Seer."

"*She* told us to go."

Locke didn't reply.

"Are you saying this is my fault?"

Locke still didn't speak.

"It would've been us against six Tenarie! We would have died if we'd followed her!"

"Maybe we would have," he said.

But that wasn't our time to die. Our time was still coming. I almost said it right then—that the curse had to be broken with a life. But the way Locke looked at me, with the distance growing between us—I couldn't bear to have him move any farther. I stared at him, and he frowned. At me, and at the whole world.

He touched his fingers to the amulet for the duration of a heartbeat. That was all it took. Then he started back down the tree.

"Locke, I don't think you should—"

"I don't care what you think."

Despite the exhaustion, he continued to descend.

He imagined Gante's final courageous charge, to stop the wolfe from defiling our prophet's body. Gante had failed, but maybe with the Seer's magical sword, Locke would succeed. Maybe fate would smile on him. Or maybe he was ready to die and leave this tragic world behind.

"If you don't survive, how are you going to save her?" I asked.

"How is a coward *ever* going to save her?"

"But this isn't bravery. This is—"

"This is what, Picke?"

"Foolishness," I whispered. *The initiative of self.*

Locke reached the lower branches of the tree, nearly low enough to leap down in a heroic attack.

The wolfe snarled, looking up hungrily, with the blood of our friends still in its teeth.

"Please don't throw your life away."

Locke pulled the buckle of the Shining Sword till the handle was within reach.

Then he gripped it.

In that first instant, he didn't feel a thing, so he continued to pull the blade free. The pain arrived a bit late, that was all. Like the skin was melting off his hand. Especially at the joints.

Locke screamed.

The blade fell and the wolfe jumped out of the way.

Locke toppled, losing track of which way was up. His chest banged against a branch, and he wrapped an arm around it. His feet caught on to something and held. The blood rushed to his face. He pulled himself up, trembling. He grabbed his wrist, as if he could cut off the pain before it reached the rest of his body. But this did nothing. The pain pinched at every point of sensation, digging needles to the bone. He needed water. Cool water. The one thing that seemed most out of reach. He clenched his teeth, staring in horror, and pounded his other fist against the branch again and again. His eyes pleaded for help. A scream came from deep inside, scraping the insides of his chest and burning out through his nose. His face was red and writhing.

I struggled to help him breathe. But the sensation of fire fell largely beyond my reach—that was Phose's realm. I felt a tingling, but it didn't make my mind spin like other pain had. I only *saw* Locke's pain, and that distance from him created its own sort of agony.

Sweat dripped down his brow, and he gritted his teeth. His breathing changed from short and quick to long and powerful. The helplessness stretched the time, leaving us trapped in pain, trapped in a tree, trapped in a moment that wouldn't pass.

The world began to swirl and fade. The smell of sweet bark wafted up toward us. The pain pushed his eyelids, and he fought to keep them open. He blundered upward in the tree to where a large branch met the trunk. He sat into it with his legs hanging over the sides like a wildercat. One arm hung down—toward the ground, the Shining Sword, and the circling wolfe. He rested his sword hand higher up, where the blood would flow less and soothe the throbbing. He rested his face on the chalky bark, breathing and groaning. He clenched his jaw, and his eyebrows fought toward the center.

We breathed. We breathed together for a long time.

The tree gave us some peace, a dim light amid an ocean of despair.

I didn't want it to be you.

The pain pounded on, burning Locke's consciousness. The Goddess grew distant. Our mind swirled after her, and the cruel world faded around us.

Don't let her get there first.

She was bound, kneeling in dirt, with blood oozing from claw marks on her face. The villain stood over her—that hideous, pitiful creature, draped in darkness that blew with the dust. She stood, facing her captor with her blue eyes, using her defiance as a last weapon.

Soon Locke lost consciousness completely, leaving me alone.

When he was gone, I examined his reddish wound.

The scales of ancient dragons were burned onto his palm and the pads of his fingers.

Scroll Three

The KYROSE: Children of Thaese

	PHOSE	NUMA	NARA	GAIE	SAEDE
Life	Soul	Breath	Blood	Bone	Glory
Domain	Sun	Stars	Moon	Earth	Necris
Time	Noonday	Dawn	Midnight	Dusk	Witchura
Season	Summertide	Springflood	Wintertide	Autumn	Unknown
Dimension	Came-and-went	Down-and-up	Forth-and-back	Side-and-side	Unknown
Sense	Sight	Hearing	Taste	Touch	Second Sight
Material	Flame	Wind	Water	Stone	Aether
Throng	Demon	Kynde	Animal	Plant	Phantasm
Elemental	Salaminde	Sylfe	Ondine	Gnyme	Ghule
Numeral	One	Four	Two	Three	Five
Endowment	Healing	Whispering	Unknown	Grounding	Unknown
Future	Fate	Foolishness	Fellows	Fortune	Unknown
Charm	Gloaming	Music	Painting	Sculpture	Unknown
Poetics	Unknown	Warrior's Song	Unknown	Tablets of Wyrde	Phantetios

Saede poisoned his own divinity when he rebelled. His dominion, once good, became twisted
So the world was made without him, incomplete, four parts stretched over five. Yet some of
his gifts can be regained untainted, by the combined power of his siblings.

48.

Requiem

I'M GLAD YOU'RE awake," I said.

The winds had changed, blowing now from the east.

"I dreamed the wolfe was chasing the princess." A chill ran through Locke—everything was cold except his burning hand.

"I watched it go. It started spinning around in a frenzy, like it was mad. Or *more* mad. Like it lost its mind more and more till it just sprinted off into the darkness."

"I'm sorry I didn't listen to you." He put his hand in front of his face and grimaced. White lines with yellow edges ran across his palm and fingers in a scaly pattern. The red skin around those was covered with a hoard of tiny, yellowish blisters. The wound oozed, and it still burned.

"It's okay. I'm sorry you got burned." I felt the throbbing in his hand. It had been itching too, a sensation that gnawed at me, till finally I said, "Can you scratch that?"

"No."

"It's driving me crazy."

"Why would she have said we don't need the lamp?"

"Just let me scratch it a little."

"You can't touch things, and when you try, it itches *more*. Besides, it burns: I can't touch it. Just don't think about it. Why did she say we don't need the lamp?"

"I don't know."

He still sat with his legs dangling over either side of a large branch. "Was she telling us to go to protect us, or did she really want us to leave?"

"I don't know that either."

"Is the consonance still intact?"

I nodded.

It was harder for him to hold me in his right hand. After several tries, I finally got centered near enough to his breath, inside his cupped hand:

"Princess, are you there?"

He almost asked her what was going on, almost asked for her whereabouts, almost told her the Seer and his guards were dead, almost told her we'd keep following no matter what. But he didn't. He just breathed in a stupor, and his hand pulsed with his heart.

When she didn't reply, I slipped through his hesitating palm.

It was the morning of the fifteenth day. From high in the tree, we could see into the gully where the Seer and Gante had fallen, and we mourned in silence. Some said dying took away the breath. Locke's mother taught us that wasn't true—otherwise, ghosts wouldn't be able to talk. Gante and the Seer had left only their bodies behind, while their breath had passed on with their blood and souls into the hereafter. There they'd wander as specters, maintaining only three of the lifeforces, unwhole. Locke wanted to believe this—that maybe somewhere they were being greeted by his mother and the twins…

He shook his head at the foolish hope.

My tiny, powerless hands floated on the wind as I tried to think of comforting words. Instead the Seer's secret came to my thoughts—a secret about our own death. I needed to tell Locke, convince him to do it. But I couldn't, not now, not while death roared so loud.

"Someday I hope they sing about Gante," said Locke. "He deserves a gallant song if anyone does."

"Why?"

"He held valor higher than his own life. He did what Martigane would have done."

"You did the same. Or wanted to. You were ready to face the wolfe."

Locke struggled to curl just one finger against the burning stiffness in his hand. "They don't sing songs about people who wanted to."

He made his way slowly toward the ground, holding with his wrist over branches. His throat was parched. The lack of food and water weakened his lifeblood. As he descended, he paused twice to gaze longingly toward the Wisting Mountains, the direction of home. In our mind we saw the pieces of that green door lying on the ground. "What did the Seer mean when he said he didn't want it to be me? Didn't want *what* to be me?"

I held my breath for a moment. Silent whirlwinds collided inside. I wanted to tell him, and I would. *Soon.* I'd tell him when our spirits were up, and I'd convince him to do it. Convince him not to take the coward's road. For now, *I* kept the secret, and *I* was the coward.

Locke groaned as he lowered himself enough to touch his toe on a certain branch. "I'm not sure anymore."

"What?" I asked.

"Not sure what I'm doing out here. I'm no hero."

"Yes you are."

"I haven't done anything right."

"You helped Nicke and Honke. And you tried to help Shilohe."

"But I failed her. And I failed the Seer and Gante."

"You haven't failed the Seer yet."

"I can't even pick up a weapon!" He held up his sword hand. His fingers curled over the ugly oozing wound and scales burned into flesh.

I tried to smile, to lift his spirits if even just a little, but I felt no joviality on the wind, just the rustling of leaves. "You just survived a night in the Rueful Wilderness."

He nodded and showed some surprise. "This isn't the heart of it though." He gripped the lowest branch with one hand and a bent wrist, letting his feet fall first. He collapsed when he hit the ground, rolling in blue leaves next to the white tree and the Shining Sword. After a moment, Locke took the cowl from his pack and cut strips off with his dagger. He wrapped his hand in green, and it burned.

He slid the scabbard carefully around the white blade, then strapped it to his back. The heat felt good on his cold skin. He walked to the lamp, lying dead on the leaves. As he inspected it, he shook his head in disappointment. "She was right. The lamp was worthless."

"What? It led us here—to her."

"No it didn't. I was already planning to come here. The rendezvous with the Seer at Wiks Pike—we were coming here, lamp or no lamp."

"It—" But I cut myself short, not knowing what to say. "What about the blue light?"

He didn't drop the lamp—I don't know why. Instead he put it in his pack. "It gave off blue light. So what?"

"It was something more than light, wasn't it? Didn't we…"

He shook his head, indicating he didn't remember. He walked away from me, indicating he didn't care.

He spent a few moments searching for Shilohe's tracks, but his head was too muddled and the ground too clean. Next he meandered toward the edge of the collapsed cliff, and I followed. The dry riverbed looked strangely beautiful, the way the rock walls curved chaotically.

"I miss the sound of trickling water," said Locke softly.

I heard the echo of water's gentle song as it slid over rocks and cooled the air all around it, a fading memory. "You should play them a req... I mean... Nevermind."

Locke examined his palm, while his fingers relaxed gently toward the sky. He could hardly move them. In the silence, a sad melody played in our mind, a song of gentle strings and mourning. We saw the Seer's smile once again and heard his laugh, the laugh that had survived even when things were all wrong, a sound of hope.

Locke looked away from the blood-stained ground, farther downriver, till he saw that blue bandana among the dirt and rocks.

"Are you going to help that Tenarie?" I asked.

Locke's spirits had become still, barely enough to cause a rustle, much less a stir. "Our first consideration is water."

This wasn't the Locke I knew—the one who'd always helped the under-dog—and that scared me. *I* was supposed to be the one telling him to be practical instead of compassionate. "If he's dead," I said, "we walk away with a free conscience. If he's alive, we'll help him get to safety."

The easter wind caressed Locke's face and rustled his hair. He stared for a long time at the person lying still among the rocks. The sad melody played on. Finally Locke nodded, though I could tell he doubted whether he could even get *himself* to safety.

"Not with a free conscience," he whispered.

"What?"

"I left him. I was a coward."

"You had no choice."

He started walking down the rim toward the tree that tilted like a ladder.

"I always have a choice."

49.

Alliance

A SYLFE RESTED ON the shoulder of the Tenarie with the blue bandana. So they *were* alive.

It seemed the warrior had managed to dig himself out during the night, but he hadn't made it much farther. Locke nudged him, and his sylfe flopped to the ground before coming to and taking flight.

"Can you hear me?" asked Locke.

The Tenarie nodded, squinting. His eyes drooped closed. The dust danced above, indifferent.

"Any broken bones?"

The warrior forced his eyes open and peered up at Locke. "My leg hurts."

If Locke picked up this invalid, how far would he have to carry him? Locke sighed. The wind pulled his hair across his face, and he brushed it aside. "It's going to be okay," he said, even though he didn't actually know what would happen.

"I need water," said the warrior in a hoarse voice. He pulled the blue bandana down so it was snug on his head again.

"We need water too. Everyone does."

He stared at Locke's hand. "We must go to my people. They will give us water and heal your hand."

Locke didn't answer. Feeling kindness toward the boy wasn't the same as feeling trust. Only hours before, he'd been trying to kill us.

"It's that way." The warrior pointed north through the Rueful Wilderness.

"How far?" asked Locke.

The voices of wolves sounded on the edges of the horizon. "Half a day with good legs."

It was much closer than our home. And what alternative did we have? "Alright," said Locke.

With help, the boy got to his feet, but he couldn't put much weight on one leg. We found him a sturdy stick. With that and Locke's shoulder, he began to walk. He was slightly taller than Locke, and his fine white hair was much longer than Nicke's. As the wind dragged it to the side, the wild shape and his pale skin made him look almost like a ghost.

We headed back to the seashore, so we wouldn't have to climb so steep a cliff, then headed north. We progressed slowly, and the wind tried to push us steadily westward.

"I'm Locke. The bad kind, I guess. What's your name?"

"I am Wokeezawokaiwokoomae."

Even though Locke had heard Tenarie names before, he still showed some surprise.

"The desperate warrior walking to the western sun," the warrior explained.

"We're headed *north*," said Locke.

"I know." Wokeezae laughed through his nose.

"It would be a fitting name for *you*," I whispered to Locke, but he waved me away with his hand. I showed him how I felt by moving as far from him as I could. Of course, I couldn't go far or I would suffocate.

The journey took much longer than a half a day, but it seemed to be our only hope. We encountered two wraiths on the way and escaped through a miracle. Wokeezae showed Locke how to chew water out of a certain strange plant. Unable to hunt, they ate bugs—even Locke did.

We began to see the scouts in the evening of the sixteenth day. They peered at us from the trees. Wokeezae told us to be calm and assured us they belonged to his tribe. That was why they hadn't stopped us, and why the wraiths hadn't returned. But the scouts never approached, which seemed like a bad sign. Locke drew on his last bit of energy as he helped Wokeezae limp on, under the silent scrutiny. But if we walked anywhere else, we'd be walking to death.

We soon arrived. A large, empty ditch surrounded the village. Inside that, an inversely high mound of dirt was topped with a wall of vertical timbers and segments of stone. Although the Tenarie hadn't fought the Kyrie in some time, they often fought amongst themselves and so constantly prepared for war.

The bodies of cold wraiths struggled against the spikes that pinned them down. A spear held a full grown one to the wooden walls of the village next to its only gate. The gate stood open, which seemed like a good sign.

But they fell on us before we reached the gate.

We couldn't have been less threatening. Still, a dozen warriors came, holding spears poised to kill, and not a friendly face among them—not even with sympathy toward Wokeezae. Their white hair waved in the wind. Dark red streaked their faces, probably animal blood—a tradition the Hundred of Saebyrne had stolen.

"I was sent to serve the Guide," shouted Wokeezae, raising a hand in a submissive gesture.

"We know who you are." This warrior had a surprising stature. His hair was shaved, exposing a bald head painted with streaks of blood. "Who are you traveling with, and where are your former companions?"

Wokeezae leaned on Locke's shoulder, like one dead tree leaning against another. "They were killed in a battle against the Kyrie Seer. He used magic, made the earth quake."

That was a flat lie.

"And the Guide?"

Locke watched carefully as Wokeezae answered this question.

"The Guide escaped safely. He took his captive back to his refuge."

But where was the refuge?

"Why are you traveling with a Kyrie?"

Locke's father had treated Nicke the same way—speaking in front of him but not to him. I hated it. When Wokeezae hesitated, unsure what to say, Locke spoke up: "He couldn't walk. I was bringing him back to you."

The bald Tenarie glared at Locke, then whispered through gritted teeth: "Keep silence."

"He saved me from thirst by bringing me home." Wokeezae glanced with some shame at Locke and then at his tribesmen. "And he saved me from wraiths on the way."

The bald one grumbled some orders.

Two of the warriors stepped on either side of Wokeezae and helped him toward the gate. As they did, he gave us a last sympathetic glance over his shoulder. He was safe now, rescued. But Locke, it seemed, had not been.

"Take off your sword," the bald one commanded.

A spear nudged Locke in the spine.

As Locke obeyed, he said, "Alright, but be careful with it. Don't touch the handle." He held it out by the scabbard, handing it to a square-nosed warrior, and pointing where to grip it. "I said don't—!"

The warrior crossed the instructions, screaming as the blade clinked on the ground. He gritted his teeth and whimpered. Several others turned threatening stares toward Locke.

"I tried to warn him." Locke raised his own bandaged hand in sympathy toward the victim. "We just need a little water on our way through."

One of them grabbed Locke by the neck and pushed his face toward the ground till he was doubled over. "Speak, and you will be punished."

"But I haven't—"

The Tenarie bashed a fist into Locke's ear. I felt every bit of the pain that fired into his skull, down his spine, and through his wounded shoulder.

Locke remembered what Honke had done when we first approached him—the Tenarie sign of humility. On his knees, Locke spread the fingers of his good hand and brought his forehead nearly to the ground in a bow. He curled his wounded hand close to his heart.

The warrior slammed down his boot.

I cringed at the thought of bones crunching.

Locke's fingers barely flinched out of the way. "Hey!—"

"Your humility is mockery if you cringe!" The warrior aimed a kick at Locke's face.

He turned defensively, and the foot hit his shoulder, bowling him over. He frowned but had the sense to keep his mouth shut.

The warriors pulled him to his feet. "Move!"

One of them picked up the sword again, carrying it by the sheath. Surrounded by a dozen warriors, we walked beneath the gate, which arched overhead between us and the dark sky. Inside, several boys played monkey ball, or something like it—except they kept cheating with their hands. The game stopped as Locke marched by, and the boys stared. The men held spears, axes, and scimitars. One of them pointed five fingers at us, which made me want to bite him.

"Did you hear that, Locke?" I whispered. "One of them said *spy…*"

Locke's thirst scraped at us. He'd given all he had to make it here. He whispered the word *water* as he stumbled along. Luckily, none of the warriors heard. He slowed, and the butt of a spear caught his slacking step. He tried to recover, not quick enough, and collapsed into the dust. He lifted himself with one hand and tried to get to his knees.

"I'm begging you…" he croaked. "Please… water."

The bald Tenarie shifted his grip on the spear, and then swung down like chopping with a sword. The blow landed across Locke's back, and his cheek smacked into the dust.

I hate the Tenarie.

A sharp point prodded him in the side, and he slowly and silently crawled back to his feet.

I hate… hate…

One of the monkey-ball kids followed us. Locke hadn't noticed, but *I* saw him. He must have been the youngest person here. His pale face was smudged, and the dirt made his white hair look dark. He wore no shirt, walking sheepishly with his hands behind his back. Then he disappeared.

I found him again a few moments later. The breeze was trilling through his dirty hair in a narrow walkway a few houses up. When we got near, the monkey boy brought his hands in front. He held a leather flask.

Though disaster warned him, Locke's desperation surged. He stumbled toward the monkey boy.

The boy didn't turn away. Instead he held the flask more confidently forward, offering it.

Locke grabbed it and tipped it back. Cool water trickled into his mouth.

A shaft hit him in the neck with a deep thud, and he and the flask landed in the dirt.

On his side, he swished the last bit of water from his cheeks and swallowed.

The cool liquid sunk all the way into his blood.

And he didn't get up.

50.

Soliloquy

THE DRUM BEATS sounded clear, thumping their angry rhythm. I could hear them even while Locke slept.

The wind reached out and touched everything, but I struggled to stay conscious. It was so hard while his eyes were shut. I didn't see *through* his eyes, but I saw *because* of them, because I was bound to him. After all, I'd been made with a single lifeforce, nothing more—not enough to exist on my own.

I did feel his pain while he slept. His body ached from the beating—his neck, his ribs, his jaw. The scratch on his shoulder still gnawed. Worst, his hand still smarted, as if even now it were dipped in fire.

"Picke?" Locke's eyes flickered open, but we still only saw blackness.

"I'm here."

I felt hard ground beneath his stomach and a rock jabbing into his ribcage. His hands and feet were bound behind him, pulling his ankles toward his wrists and cutting into his flesh. His palm itched badly, and the green bandage had fallen loose. Someone had given him a little food and water—I remembered that. Then he'd passed out again, leaving me to wait out the night and the next day.

"HAI, HAI, HAI!!!" The screaming sounded very close. We expected footsteps to approach, but we heard only mumbling voices. A faint glow came from the edge of the floor just ahead. Locke leaned till he felt a pole with his feet. A leather wall stretched out—we were inside some sort of house. Locke lifted his head, looking for more light. A tiny chain pinched the skin at the back of his neck. Shilohe's silver amulet tapped against the cold wooden floor in front of him.

"The Goddess spoke while you were unconscious," I said.

"She did? What did she say?" The knots pulled against the skin of his burned hand, creating a constant painful tingling.

"She asked about the Seer and his sword."

"The Seer's… dead… But I have the sword. Or did. Where'd they take it?" He twisted his neck, trying to see, and the silver amulet clinked again.

"I think we'd see glowing if it were in here," I said.

"I'm still out of it." Locke stretched his eyelids open wider and breathed deep. We smelled woodsmoke. "My throat is killing me. I feel like my lifeblood has gone dry."

"We're not going to die in here."

"Okay. That's good news." He said this humbly, with no expectations. He turned, as if the solution might be hidden somewhere in the darkness. "If this were a faerie story, the hero would use some unique ability right now."

"You're a strong swimmer," I said.

He gave a hesitant laugh. "I'm not sure swimming out of here is a good idea."

"Me giving you breath underwater doesn't help much either," I said.

"Proves I'm not much of a hero."

"The Seer said you may not be a hero in all moments, but you are in some, and that's something."

"If I could make those Tenarie pay, I would. That's not heroic either."

"You haven't acted on it."

"I would if I could, believe me."

That sunk me into darker thoughts, which I didn't like.

Outside, the drums beat a heavy rhythm, back and forth. A warrior screamed, and several others screeched in reply, like ghules in conversation. But through that tumult, a single word stole across the darkness upon the wind:

"Locke?"

A voice as warm as light.

His head shot up as he looked into the blackness.

I gripped the voice tightly, pulling it toward us.

"I'm here! I'm here." Locke spoke into the night. "Picke, come closer."

"It's not going to work," I said.

"Let's just try. Come closer. Now hold still." He inhaled. "Princess, can you hear me?"

"Locke, are you there?" came her voice.

"Yes, I am. I can hear you! Picke, hold still!"

"I *can't!*" I needed his help, needed his hands, which were bound behind his back—they thought he was a spy. He was lucky they hadn't chopped them off.

"Well, I hope you can hear me," she said timidly. "I'm sorry I yelled at you. I regret that."

"It's okay," breathed Locke. "It's okay."

"I was so hurried I didn't tell you an interesting thing that happened to me. If you can hear this… I was traveling on the west bank of the Fifth River, trying to avoid strangers. I went to hide while a caravan passed, but the place I chose had a little Tenarie boy already inside." She chuckled. "When I asked him why he was crying, he told me about his mother, and how she told him to be brave before she died. Then he told me about you, Locke…" The warmth in her voice made it seem like she was smiling. "I was so surprised. It was the same boy you told the Seer and me about. He said you inspired him to be brave. And he threatened to come looking for you if you didn't come back soon. He's worried about you. He said you're all he's got now."

Locke shook his head, and his questions hovered on the edge of his tongue, unasked and unanswered. He sighed.

"Lonae hasn't lost the consonance," said Shilohe, "so I know you survived, but I don't know how. I heard Stane calling that wolfe. Then he whispered to the gnymes under the earth—he has terrible power. I felt the ground shaking."

Locke swallowed, listening all the more intently to make up for his silence.

"I'm trying so hard not to hate him, and it's burning me up inside. Maybe it's impossible. He has reasons to hate us too though, good reasons. That was my secret, what I didn't want to tell you. I hate. There's someone I hate worse than Stane too. And I hate him so much it makes me cry. I'm trying to let go, but I just can't." We heard her weeping.

A tear rolled down Locke's cheek as he listened helplessly in darkness.

"I can't believe I'm telling you this." Shilohe sniffled, and in our mind she wiped her eyes with the backs of her hands. "I wish I could hear you." She choked through the words. "Locke, for some reason I think you could help me not hate him. You'd tell me to focus on breaking the curse. You'd remind me that pointing fingers only creates villains."

For a long moment, we only heard her heavy breaths and sobs.

"I don't even know if I should say this," she said, "but… the curse still lacks the sword. That was the main reason I needed to talk to you. Sorry for crying so much. I thought I could do it on my own, but I was wrong. So if you're with the Seer, please tell him that. To be honest though, I don't know where I am. But you gave the Seer the living water, so he should be able to find me. The Chief Captain has the scroll. If his spies can find the source, there's hope there too."

She mumbled something to herself—something we couldn't quite hear.

"It's best you don't come with the Seer. I don't really want you to, but I can't explain why. Maybe he's already told you." *She was talking about the secret, the one I knew but Locke didn't.*

When more silence came, Locke felt panic that she might be finished.

"One last thing. That amulet—my father gave it to me. I wanted you to have it because, well, you remind me of him in some ways." She sniffled. "I wonder if you can even hear me."

In that moment, her tone shifted, as if she'd finally concluded that no one was listening. She was a child, completely unguarded, completely abandoned.

"My father loved the phrase inscribed on it… I miss him so much…" Her voice broke. "He was the King who was murdered… And I can't stop hating his murderer. That's my secret."

She weeped, a song of tears and pain, and all we could do was listen.

Locke's head dropped, and the amulet tinkled against the floor. So much had happened since that encounter in the wilderness that he'd never taken the time to look at it. He scooted, and it clinked forward beneath his chin. He pulled his head back and squinted for a better look, but the glinting silver rested too close and in too dark a room.

"I'm glad you told me that story about your mother. I needed it." We saw Shilohe wiping her tears with that purple sash. "She was right. If you don't think it's possible to see lightning, you won't even look. But you have to look to see. You have to keep looking, no matter how dark and no matter how long."

Locke nodded his head, eager to agree. A pair of tears dripped down his face.

Her voice had become so quiet: "Maybe the Seer has already explained to you: it's going to get darker soon."

Locke smiled sadly as Honke's sentiments crowded our mind—the idea that all true stories were tragedies.

"But no matter how dark it gets, I'll still be hoping for a happy ending."

With a sad smile, Locke waited in darkness for more.

She didn't speak again.

51.

Flower

W E WAITED IN darkness a long time, wandering separately through the spaces of our mind.

Locke chased after the Goddess. I followed the path of the beating drums.

"Did you notice there are no women in the camp?" I asked.

Locke licked the inside of his dry lower lip. "So?"

"It's a war party."

Locke looked at the blackness, arranging the pieces: "And they think we're spies because they're going to attack the Enchanted Wood."

"Yes. We're lucky they haven't killed us."

"I'm not sure it was kindness, Picke." He grunted. "My hand won't stop itching."

"I'll scratch it," I said.

"No, get back. You'll make it worse."

"If they wanted you dead, they'd have done it already."

"They're not going to carry a captive into battle," said Locke.

I hated to hear him talk this way. "You're not going to die here. We'll figure a way out."

"Even if we escape, I don't know what to do without the Seer."

"Let's take it one step at a time."

He nodded. "How tight are those knots?"

I dropped down to the leather straps. "Pretty tight. The main one is between your wrists."

Locke tried to pull his feet higher to create a little more slack, but the rope barely dipped at all. "Maybe now's the time to ask a favor of Numa."

"Huh?" I asked.

"I don't think we're getting ourselves out of this one."

"But you heard what the princess said: They aren't gods; they're Kyrose—teachers. You have to listen to them, or they don't have any power."

"So they won't help us?"

"I don't think knots are their thing."

He kept silent for a moment, thinking. "Alright, then what would Numa say to me right now?"

"She'd say to shut up and be kind to people."

"Are you sure you've actually heard her voice?"

"I'm not going to tell you again."

"Then why didn't I hear her?"

"You did, but you were too young to remember!"

"So I just have to trust you."

"Trust your*self*. Let's find a way out of here."

He looked through the darkness toward that solitary line of light barely glowing on the floor ahead. His back and neck ached and so did his jaw, but he rested his chin on the ground anyway.

Something scratched at the bottom edge of the leather walls, like it was trying to get inside.

Locke lifted his head. His heart thumped, and his thoughts went straight to the wraiths.

"Can you move?" I asked. "Try swimming."

"Oh, gah." Locke squirmed. So much energy to move less than a foot.

The leather door flapped open. A flash of firelight flooded the tent and then vanished.

A pair of strong legs had stepped into the room. The toes of the moccasins nearly touched Locke's chin. A smell of liquor entered too, so strong it was hard to ignore. Not a welcome smell—not if Locke's father were any indication of what would happen next.

Locke struggled to look up, but he could barely see to the knees.

"Oh, my," I said, surprised.

Two leather flasks dropped on the ground next to Locke's face, along with some hunks of jerked meat. Fingers began to pull at the leather bindings. Locke's feet came loose and his toes smacked to the ground. He leaned sideways and looked up. "Honke?"

"Hello, my friend," came the thick accent. Hearing his frog's-back voice made me smile.

"Honke!" came Locke's shouted whisper.

W a s h b u r n

It was him. Except he wasn't covered in a thick layer of dust. In fact, we almost didn't recognize him. His face was painted with streaks of red blood.

"What are you doing here?" asked Locke.

Honke crouched and worked at untying Locke's wrists behind his back. "I am here to help you go away."

"What are you doing with the Tenarie?"

"I join them."

"But why?"

"They treat me nishe. They tell me I am a warrior and gibe me shword."

"But you're not a warrior... are you?"

"*Now* I am a warrior."

"And they said to let me go?"

"No."

"Then what are you doing?"

"Wokeeshae tell me you are here. I come to shet you free."

"But you're one of them."

"They treat me... medium. *You* treat me nishe."

"Ha ha. Alright." As Honke untied the leather knots, Locke said, "You know your Tenarie sign of humility? It didn't work so good for me. They tried to crush my hand."

"Shorry."

As soon as the bands came free, Locke grabbed one of the flasks and began gulping.

"Not too much!" I said. "And not too fast."

Locke listened to me, putting the flask down. Already his blood seemed to be coming back to life. He considered speaking with Shilohe, but the urgency around him was too thick. He would talk to her soon. He tore off a bite of the jerky then began to work on the knots that bound his feet together. "I thought you wanted to go home."

"I am shtill losht."

"So you're going with them to attack my village?"

"Not your willage, I don't know," said Honke.

Locke bit another hunk of jerky. "Have you been drinking?"

"No."

"Honke, are you sure?"

"Jusht a little. They like me when I drink with them."

"You know this is a war party, right?"

"Yesh."

"And do you know where they're going to attack?"

"No. Shomewhere shouth."

"Yeah, somewhere south, my home. That's why they think I'm a spy. They're going to the Enchanted Wood." For the quickest moment, Locke wished we had a consonance with someone at home instead of Shilohe; then we could warn them. He pushed the thought away.

"I don't know." Honke noticed Locke still struggling with one good hand to untie the knot around his ankles. He pushed Locke's hands out of the way and started to do it himself.

"They're going to know you helped me." Locke swallowed, and then tore off another bite of jerky.

"No. I go now. You leabe shoon."

"Honke, I thought you were trying to find your family?"

"I don't know where they go. I shtill look but cannot find them, and you tell me I need ribers to go home."

Locke's feet came free, and he stood. "I'm working on that. And thank you."

"I go now. You go that way." He pointed through the wall. "And run fasht."

I could see Honke's sylfe clearer now, deep inside. He winked at me.

"Wait," said Locke, "before you go. Where's my sword?"

Honke hesitated. "Where did you get that shword?"

"It belonged to a friend. I'm taking care of it for him. Where is it?"

"It ish in the chief'sh houshe. You do not need the shword. I gibe you water. You go."

Locke stared into the darkness, and his hand roasted in flames. He saw himself getting captured because the sword shined too bright and because he couldn't fight back. He sighed. "I can't leave the sword. I need it." *The princess needs it.*

Honke sighed, staring down. "You do not need the shword."

"I *do* need it. It's the only thing that can break the curse."

"What is curshe?"

"It's the black skies, remember? The reason the wraiths are coming? Anyway, it doesn't matter. I'm going to use the sword to get your rivers back so you can go home."

"Okay, okay, okay," said Honke. "I help you. How do I help you?"

"First, tell me where the chief's house is."

Honke moved to the doorway and pulled back the flap. In the midnight darkness, giant bonfires flickered their light faintly around the village. We heard the war party screaming and shouting, as if firing up their souls. Many generations ago the Tenarie tribes had turned away from Numa, in spite of their sylves. Now they worshipped Phose, and soon they'd bring his fires to the dry and dying Enchanted Wood.

"Shee, it ish tall. Red top."

"We can use the firelight to our advantage," I whispered in Locke's ear. "Keep to the sides of the buildings away from the light. Anyone looking toward the fires won't see much in the shadows."

"Honke, keep that door open a bit. I need light." When the firelight poured in, Locke found his pack, crammed the water and food into it, and strapped it on. "Thanks." Locke pulled back the tent flap and peeked out. No one was nearby, and why would they be? Those knots had been tied precisely.

"You ready?" I asked.

"I guess so," said Locke.

"Let's roll then," I whispered.

He pulled his lips tight and blew steadily, before taking a deep breath through his nose and breathing out again.

"Bye, Honke. And thanks again." Locke stepped outside and ducked.

The bonfires cast silhouettes and long, dancing shadows as the Tenarie elves beat their drums of war. The smell of dry brush and smoke permeated the air.

Locke looked away from the fires, wanting his eyes fully adjusted to the darkness. The lookouts walked along a narrow platform around the inside of the village walls. Anywhere Locke went, even in the darkest shadows, these guards could potentially see him. Fortunately, they kept their dutiful eyes on the area outside the walls. Locke crouched and moved quietly past one house and then another, ducking behind a pile of wood.

I heard footsteps behind us—"Locke!"

The footfalls crunched—some lumbering form.

Honke appeared, crouching behind us. He was too big for the pile of wood, and firelight shone on his curved back, forehead, and dark hair.

"What is he doing?" I whispered.

"What are you doing?" said Locke through clenched teeth.

"I help you."

"No, I do this alone." Locke mimicked Honke's primitive speech without realizing it.

"But I want to help."

A thousand frustrated arguments crowded through our mind, but this was no time for it. Each moment added to the danger, for Locke *and* Honke. "Alright, I need a distraction. I have to get into that hut. If you can keep eyes away from it, that will help me a lot."

"Okay, okay, okay." Honke only took a moment to think; then he popped his eyes over the stack of wood and looked directly at the bonfire where the largest group of Tenarie danced. "Flower."

What? Flower?

Honke turned, about to rush off, and Locke grabbed him by the shirt. "Wait. Don't get caught. I'm serious. I don't want you to get in trouble."

Honke nodded his head. "Okay, okay, okay." Without another word, he dashed toward the fire.

Locke couldn't help but watch. The large hyuman ran, hunched over, and slid to a stop next to another building. He glanced around, almost too quickly to actually see anything, as if he were doing it for show. He lugged a large mass of something on his shoulder and ran back toward us, around the edge of the woodpile, sliding again to the ground, with the firelight still shining on his forehead.

The frustration rose up into Locke's neck and ears. "What are you doing!"

"I make dishtraction."

"Not over here. You're supposed to distract them *away* from me!"

"I know, I know, I know. I jusht want you to shee." He patted the bundle he had on his shoulder and grinned, squinting. It looked like a sack of— oh—*flour*. Not flower.

"What are you going to do with that?" asked Locke.

"I worked at flour. My family ish big flour."

"No, shhh. Shut up. Nevermind. Just get going."

Honke turned to go again, and Locke grabbed his shoulder once more. "Don't do anything stupid, okay? *Be—careful.*"

Honke nodded and his expression seemed to say he was one of the most cautious people around. Maybe all hyumans were rash, and by comparison he *was* cautious. Honke ducked and ran back to where he'd picked up the flour. Then he stood straight with the bag on his shoulder and walked casually toward the fire.

"I don't know what he's up to," I said, "but we might as well make the most of it."

Locke took off in a crouch. Moments later we peered through a crack in the leather walls of the chief's house. At first we just heard voices. Candles cast their light on two Tenarie faces, the bald warrior who'd given Locke the beating and an old man wearing a feathered crown. Behind them, the hilt of the Shining Sword was glowing. With the blade covered, it shone in the shape of the *kah* rune, waiting for us to claim it.

A yellow light flashed outside.

A deep, clawing sound followed, and the voice of a crowd said, "Ahhh." A warrior on the high wall looked inward toward the bonfires.

Feet fell on the wooden steps, as the bald Tenarie exited and walked toward the crowd. The crowned man paused on the steps of the hut, watching. From the shadows, Locke held his breath. Locke crept to the corner of the hut. When the next burst of light came, he peeked with one eye. The guards up on the walkway of the wall looked inward, where the bonfire would weaken their vision.

Honke stood tallest in the circle around the bonfire. His hands were raised graciously, while the rest of the warriors clapped, as if he'd performed a feat of magic. Apparently, we'd misjudged our tall friend. How did he make the light flashes? He motioned to the other silhouettes around the fire. They stepped back in an even rim, as he shouted orders. At this distance it was especially hard to understand him, but we heard *flour* several times. The warriors reached out open hands to receive something from Honke. Next they put their hands to their mouths, as if speaking into a consonance.

Honke explained, "One, two, three." He pointed at somebody and starting yelling about doing it wrong. When he'd gotten everyone into shape, he shouted, "Ready!" He put a hand to his mouth too.

Together the warriors crouched and leaned in a circle toward the fire. Honke conducted with one hand as the warriors, like a beating drum, made the muffled hum of *one, two, three!*

They spewed dust from their mouths at the fire.

Flame leaped toward them, like Phose had chosen to manifest himself, growing straight out of the flame toward their faces, and rising in the quickest flash. The warriors fell back, turning and shielding their faces, some of them spitting white powder. The whoosh of flashing fire came and went almost instantly. That sound was replaced by laughter and cheers. Many slapped Honke on the back, and although we could only see his silhouette, I knew he was squinting in a wide smile.

The crowned chief, next to us, came down the steps and walked toward the bonfire. "Phose!" he shouted.

Locke didn't waste a moment of Honke's perfect distraction.

52.

Violence

INSIDE THE CHIEF's tent, Locke put a rag over the Shining Sword's hilt, hoping to keep the gleam from giving us away.

The rag burst into flames.

Locke jerked his hands back, and the sword tipped over, the hilt thumping into the wooden floor. The noise stabbed into me through the quiet night—someone might have heard. Locke stomped on the flaming rag. The room now smelled of smoke, but at least the house hadn't caught fire. Then the chief would've really shouted *Phose*.

The warriors still cheered at Honke's fire game—a much larger group now, with others eager to try. Locke sprinted across the village, made his way to the main gates, and pulled them quietly closed behind us.

Outside the walls, a brisk wind blew. We heard the crittering sound of wraiths pinned all around, hungry both for life and death. Locke avoided the main path and circled the village along the wall to the south side. Once we dropped down the hill and then climbed out of the deep ditch, we might be easily spotted by the guards on the wall. We hesitated, enjoying the reprieve. The noise of the revelries inside made for good cover.

"You just saved us with your heroic gift," I whispered.

Locke leaned in the shadows, safe and out of sight. "My heroic gift is running like crazy?"

"No I mean when you were tied up."

Locke breathed heavily, quietly. "Honke saved us."

"Yeah. Because you'd been kind to him."

"I'm not sure that counts."

The two flasks of water in his pack gave him a surprising amount of strength. To the north, lighter clouds were forming, still black on the bottom but laced with a pale blue above, a sliver of hope.

As he prepared to dash into the darkness, the Shining Sword gleamed over his shoulder.

"It's like a signal fire." Locke barely breathed the words. "They're going to see it."

"Hold the hilt in front of your chest as you run."

"Should I even risk it—is it worth getting killed over?"

"Maybe."

Locke nodded, thinking.

"Just remember it's for her," I said.

"To rescue a Goddess."

The problem was that we didn't know *when* to run. At any moment the guards might be either looking at Honke's game or staring in the exact direction we were about to run. Locke couldn't see them, and if I flew higher their sylves would hear me breathing.

"Okay, on three," he whispered. "You count."

"One," I said, looking into his eyes to see whether he'd really do it.

"Two." He held the hilt close, feeling its warmth on his hand and chest.

"Three!"

Locke bolted, down into the ditch, scrambling up the far side, out into the open. He took quick breaths. His moccasins touched lightly on the dirt—but each crunch felt like a shout, and each moment was another in which they might spot him.

He didn't look back. He simply moved.

A voice pierced the silent night: "Something's down there."

Then more voices from the wall above: "…see that?"

"…chief…"

"…THE SWORD…"

"Go! You! AFTER HIM!"

Locke sprinted.

It would take the warriors some time to get down off the wall, through the gate, and past the ditch. Maybe his head start would be enough.

The ground disappeared.

Locke tumbled into a creek bed lower than the surrounding terrain. His burned hand smashed into the sand. He writhed, fighting to contain a shriek of pain, and water streaked from the corners of his eyes. After a few deep breaths, he got to his feet and kept moving. The dry bed wound back

and forth, with dead shrubs and ragged ridges blocking our view. He ran
for what felt like a long time, yet also no longer than the snap of a finger.

"Over here!" someone shouted—the voice was close.

Locke crept out of the creek and crawled behind a bush. The dark skies
hid his body but made the sword all the more dangerous. He clutched
the hilt close to his chest, and its pale light fell on his forearms. The heat
threatened to burn his chin.

The footsteps came near.

He didn't have a proper weapon, not one he could actually hold. *Except...*
He gripped the scabbard. Heat poured through the leather, making his
good hand sweat. He made sure the strap locked the blade in the sheath.

The footsteps moved toward us then paused.

Another voice, farther away, called, "Ochanacanowae, over here."

But the feet standing so close didn't move. They hesitated. Maybe they'd
found us.

I pulled closer to Locke's chest, right next to the glowing handle, to
make sure I wasn't visible to the enemy's sylfe. Locke held still as a corpse,
wanting so badly to breathe, but his chest was clinched, barely letting any
air in or out for fear it might make too much noise.

It was too much; it was crushing me.

The feet moved.

Toward us.

On instinct, Locke pounced, swinging the hilt like a club.

The Tenarie warrior must have seen nothing more than a flash of light.
The cross of the Shining Sword collided with his nose and forehead. His
hands flew into the air as he fell back into the sand. He groaned, scrambling
to find his sword. Blood gushed over his face.

Locke's heart pounded as he raised the hilt for a second swing. I felt the
rage in him as he squeezed the weapon.

"LOCKE, NO!" I shouted.

The scales of the Shining Sword struck against the Tenarie's skull to the
sound of a terrible crack. The sylfe looked at me in horror, with his elfe
lying on cold ground.

Locke fell on his knees in the sand, panting over the motionless body.
His brow glistened with sweat. Pulses of pain shot through his hand and
fingers—he'd used his burned hand without thinking, and the fire bit at

22222

2

him. He clenched his jaw and stared. Not at his victim, but next to him, at the sand, as if the body he'd knocked cold were made of the same unimportant stuff. It was self defense—to save his own skin. But the rage—I'd tried too late to warn him against the rage, the moment in which he'd held survival above everything.

"Locke, breathe, please."

When he didn't look at me, I noticed a strange thing. I was distant from him, several feet away, maybe more. I tried to move closer, but he whisked away—just like I did when Honke tried to grab me. I moved toward him again, and again he drifted.

"Locke, did you see…"

Now he looked at me, still panting, still sweating, still burning, with his knees in the sand. I realized I'd spoken too softly for the distance between us. I was so far from him.

"What did you say?" he asked quietly, gritting against the pain.

As I moved toward him, he seemed to fade and curl like a handful of morning mists. "How are you doing that?" I asked.

"Doing what?"

"I can't get closer. You keep floating away."

He gave me a confused look. "What are you talking about?"

"You keep shifting," I said.

"I'm still right here."

"But you keep moving."

"I'm not moving."

"Then why can't I reach you?" The distance sickened me.

"You're not flying *toward* me."

"Yes I am," I said. "Watch."

"See, you're drifting sideways," he whispered.

"No I'm not. *You* just moved."

"I haven't moved. I'm *kneeling.*"

"It's not your legs. It's your…" But I didn't know what it was. If he were a sylfe, I'd have said it was his breath.

"It's back," he whispered. "Death is with us."

We might have been in danger, but I was too disoriented to look around, too disoriented to even respond.

"We have to move."

53.

Distress

THE TENARIE CALLED to each other as they scoured under the blanket of darkness.

"Wait. Is he alive?" I looked at the Tenarie lying in front of us. His sylfe held so still..

Locke swallowed then reached a hand slowly to the fallen warrior's neck. "His blood's still flowing." Without another word, Locke stood to a crouch and raced further from the village. He ran and ran and didn't stop for what might have been an hour.

But I wasn't thinking about his safety. I was thinking about mine, and the unclosable distance between us. It felt like being deep under water, deep enough to dim the noonday sun, and I couldn't seem to swim out.

Locke stopped and rested a hand on his knee. "What else was I supposed to do? If I didn't attack, he would've recaptured and maybe killed me."

I breathed in the wind from our dark surroundings.

"I'm sorry, Picke. I'm sorry I hated him when I swung that sword. But I had to, or we might be dead."

"We're alive," I said without life.

For a moment, the rising easter wind made the only sound. Locke looked down and swallowed through his tight throat. Salty tears rolled down his tilted face and onto his lips. "But the Seer isn't. And that Tenarie isn't in too good of shape either. And the princess..." Locke looked up toward the hidden stars. "Picke, you think the demigods are up there?"

Wind blasted westward across the Astral Fields like we'd never felt before, pulling and drying the tears. It was strength of my own kind, yet so strong it was terrible. I shrugged—with nothing to offer.

"I need to talk to her," he suddenly said. "Come closer."

He reached his hands around me and then slipped away from me. "Stop it, Picke. This isn't funny."

"You're the one who's moving."

"No I'm not!"

We tried again and failed again.

"I promise it's not me," I said.

"Then what's going on?"

"I don't know. You're just going to have to hold as close as you can and then shout."

He decided to keep running for awhile, to get his voice farther from the Tenarie. Eventually he stopped and held me with his elbows nearly straight. The fingers of his good hand wrapped around his tender sword hand, and I hovered inside. "Princess, can you hear me?" he shouted. "I have the sword. Tell me where you are."

Keeping myself together and still catching his breath was nearly impossible, but I managed to relay something.

Locke went on the move again.

It wasn't long before her voice floated on the wind, closer than Locke himself—a desperate whisper: "Locke, you're back."

"Yes, and I'm coming for you," he shouted. "Just tell me where you are."

I quivered, barely able to hold on.

"I can't understand you," she said.

"I said I'll be there soon!"

"It's no use," came her voice. "I can't understand. But, Locke, you should go home; I hope you're already on your way. Stane has summoned an army of wraiths."

"What do you mean summoned?" he shouted.

"I was just saying it's horrible. Go home and help defend your family and your Tenarie friend. The Seer can bring the sword."

"The Seer is dead. He died in the landslip."

She said nothing.

"Did you hear that? The Seer is dead!" he said louder. "But I have his sword, and I can still bring it to you."

After his shouting came her small whisper: "Did you say the Seer is dead?"

"Yes, he died in the landslip."

"I hope I didn't hear you right."

Her silence was a depth to drown in. We could barely breathe.

"Oh, no," she said. "He's here."

"Wait, don't go. Where are you?" Locke tensed up, as if a trap might be sprung at any moment. "I'm coming for you!"

I let go with a gasp. If she answered, we didn't hear it.

The mighty winds pulled, filling the atmosphere with noise. On the edge of that noise was a howl, high in pitch and piercing. Locke looked at the horizon as if he might see it. "Picke, I lied to her. I'm not coming. I don't know where she is. How can I help her?" He put a hand on his head, as if that might somehow keep things together. All of a sudden he turned and looked south, toward home. "Maybe this is the end."

I looked at him, but his image was blurred by the wind and the distance between us. I couldn't read him like I used to. "What do you mean?"

"With the water Honke gave me, I have just enough to get home. Maybe I can warn them before the Tenarie attack—and this army of wraiths."

"Home? Are you serious?"

"Of course I am."

"What about the Goddess? And the sword?"

"I promised to help Nicke, and I intend to. He and my dad are about to be invaded by Honke and a bunch of wraiths. They'll die."

"*Everyone* is going to die if we can't break the curse."

"Picke— I—" Twice he started to speak, but his thoughts were a storm. "Where do I start? I don't know where she is, so I can't go after her. With my hand like this, I stand no chance if the wolves find me again—or even a wraith for that matter. I'm hopeless. I have nothing."

"You still have water."

"And so?"

"You still have something."

"Alright, I have water. That's good. Fine."

"And you've escaped the wolves before. Maybe you can again."

"But maybe not, Picke. This evil is so big. He split the earth in half! I can't fight that."

I didn't reply, and he shook his head in frustration.

"You want me to die of thirst wandering in circles. I can't do that while my home in is danger. Someone has to warn them. I have to get Nicke out before he gets caught in the middle. I made a promise." After saying all that, his look said even more—that he was stretched too thin, that he probably couldn't go on even if he wanted to.

"What about Shilohe?" I asked.

"You act like I don't want to help her. I want nothing more. But *I don't know what to do.*"

"You can't just leave her."

"If I stay here and do nothing, it will be the same. A still wind dies."

I didn't look at him, so far away. Instead I frowned, hurt and afraid. I stared, not at my mother sky, but at the solid, unmoving ground. If Locke were to leave now, it would be cowardice. It would mean he wasn't the hero I wanted him to be—*needed* him to be—so that I could become heroic alongside him.

Indecision clawed at him. So did the horrifying distance between us. With a question on his face, he read my countenance in the wind. "And what about the banshee wolves?" He waited for an answer.

"I don't know," I finally said. "I can't see into the future. All I know is right now."

"And right now we're not supposed to go home," he said, finishing my thought.

"Yes."

I added nothing about my secret—about how we were supposed to die in place of the Seer, or in place of the Goddess. *How could I?* He hated death more than anything.

"Alright," he said with a reluctant breath. "Where do we go?"

Shilohe hadn't told us. The Seer couldn't tell us. We'd lost the living water, but it had never really worked.

Wait.

A sudden thought came to me, one that had almost completely vanished from our mind. But in that unlikely moment I glimpsed it again: "The map."

"What?"

"The Seer's map. Get it out."

He nodded and took off his pack. He held the map with just one hand and let it hang sideways, tilting his head to look, expecting me to point to something.

But I didn't have to.

Which was good, because I was having trouble getting that close.

He noticed it suddenly. Something familiar he'd forgotten, a dark brown smudge made with his own blood, a mark dried into a stain. "Mount Death. Why there?"

"I don't remember," I said.

Night may have been falling. If so, it marked the end of the seventeenth day.

Locke looked up with his elfe eyes. The Burning Mountain loomed not far in the distance, just across a stretch of wilderness. Its heights reached all the way to the darkening clouds and then vanished beyond. And we saw wings flapping around its slopes—so big we could see them even from this distance.

"Maybe that's where she's being held," I said.

He nodded, but without enthusiasm of any kind. Still, he trusted me, trusted my insight. With a frown he started walking.

And a sad wind dripped down on me.

54.

The Wraiths

LOCKE MOVED ONWARD.
The wind pulled his hair forward and high into the air. But he still walked toward that stain on the map.

To me, the burn on his hand had gone numb. He was so distant I couldn't sense his despair or tell what he was thinking. I'd never felt such a rift, such an unclosable gap. An elfe would probably feel a similar sensation if a sword split his shoulder from his neck. Only I kept living.

"Picke." Before telling me his thoughts, Locke paused to read my expression, and what he saw surprised him. "What? What's the matter?"

I swirled as I spoke, more unsteady than ever, and reached toward him as he moved continually away. "Locke, I'm losing my grip."

"What do you mean?"

"Remember when you dropped your grandma's hope chest and grandpa got so angry? The way your fingers wanted to hold fast and your arms were shaking? You held on at first, but sweat and strain were against you, and the chest shattered on the stairs. That's happening to me. I don't *want* to let go, but I'm losing my grip."

"Your grip on Numa?"

I looked down.

"On me?" he asked.

"I don't know. On both. Or on life. I don't know what's happening."

The clouds strung black overhead. Dying leaves whipped across the ground, pushed by the rising wind. He felt it too, whatever was happening to us. "We just have to keep going."

We descended a slope at the edge of the Astral Fields. Our view opened to a valley of scattered white trees—the Rueful Wilderness. The songbirds bickered in the distance ahead. The Burning Mountain loomed beyond, reaching up and through the clouds. In its foothills on the far side, a gleam caught our attention and then vanished. A large gray mass seemed to have assembled there. Another flash of light came—the glint of armor. *An army.* Maybe the Chief Captain had discovered the source and the villain. Maybe there *was* hope.

I sensed a flicker of breath. Something in the wind. Not a sound, but a movement.

Something behind us.

I turned. A flight of sparrows flittered out of the grass and into the dark sky, fleeing in the same direction we were moving. Locke slowed and glanced back, squinting, but we couldn't see over the hill behind us. A few moments later, a mob of deer skirted through the tall, dry grasses, fleeing toward us.

"Picke, do you think—"

A lone figure appeared over the ridge.

A shadowy silhouette, moving very quickly. Very quickly toward *us.* Cold fear pricked at Locke's heart. "I hate wraiths."

It was just one though. Locke had defeated three at once before. He looked at the green bandage on his burned hand. For a moment he considered pulling out his dagger, which he could wield with his weaker hand, but he opted for the longer weapon. He took the Shining Sword from his back and checked to make sure it was securely clipped into the sheath. He scowled for a closer look.

This wraith was different.

It was full grown like the ones we'd encountered earlier, with teeth and vacant eye sockets and coated in the downward-pulling black flame. But the darkness flowed around clothing and the things it carried: a sword and heavy armor—gauntlets on its hands, greaves on its feet, the skin of an animal caped over its shoulders, and a lordly helm over its eyeless head—a helm that was unmistakably familiar. A row of spikes ran down the center of the crown. Two horns jutted from the sides—one of which was broken.

It was the helmet of the dead warrior we'd taken the scroll from.

Locke turned and ran.

"Since when do wraiths care about clothing?" I said, struggling to keep up.

"What did the princess say about summoning wraiths?"

"Just that, I guess... I don't know."

"So he summoned one of the Hundred back from the dead?" asked Locke.

"No," I said. "I doubt it. Look at the face. That's no elfe's body."

But Locke didn't turn around. He ran.

"Maybe an elfe soul in a wraith's body?" I said.

"Maybe a deal with the Lord of Darkness…" said Locke, puffing.

"You don't believe in Saede."

"So *now* you want to argue my side?"

"Keep running," I said.

Though Locke moved fast, the creature moved faster. Its boots slammed into the grass, one after another, louder, closer.

"Face him, Locke!"

He turned, holding the glowing handle toward the attacker—wraiths hated light. But it didn't change course. It was on us, swooping down, swinging its heavy blade, overcoming us with stinging cold.

As the blow crashed, Locke gripped the scabbard with even his burned hand. He caught the attacking blade with the crossguard and shoved it and the wraith to the side, screaming through gritted teeth.

The monster continued down the hill.

Locke's whole frame trembled, but I could only imagine the pain.

I stared after the creature as it made its way quickly toward the Rueful Wilderness. "Where is it going?"

Before I got an answer, three more wraiths appeared on the crest. Each was dressed in armor and carrying heavy weaponry. A fourth emerged carrying the red banner of the Hundred, which flapped in the wind. Without eyes, they stared with dark, gaping voids and smiles meant to tear skin.

"What's going on?" said Locke.

"They're back," I said. "The Unstoppable Hundred." I didn't speak the worst part—that without the sun, no venom and no mutiny would stop them.

"This *is* the end of time."

"Run!" I shouted.

But he couldn't outrun fate. Their heavy steps thundered, and soon the storm was all around—not four but forty, or more, many more, coming down all around us.

Locke tried to retreat to the side of the charge. As he did, dust thickened the violent, freezing air. He squinted against it, barely breathing. His clothes and hair flapped in all directions. Two wraiths took swings at him as they galloped by. Sparks flew as he caught their attacks in the cross of the hilt. He cried out as he gripped the sheath. The blows brought Locke to his knees.

Dozens more stormed down from the hilltop.

"Picke—?" Locke called for help through gritted teeth.

I didn't answer. I was too small and too distant to help him. *Too insignificant.*

A flood of boots and steel crashed, filling our mind. Locke pushed the hilt against his attackers, fending off one blade and then another, screaming. The wraiths didn't stop to finish him off though. Instead they rushed on to some greater and more horrible purpose.

A heavy boot caught him in the ribs. He rolled backward, tumbling down the hill across bumpy ground, over, and over, and over. The grass cut at his face and fingers.

He looked up just in time to see a pointed spear rushing toward him. He squirmed like a snake to dodge the attack. The blow cracked against his backpack and bones. The attacker continued on, and warm liquid oozed from Locke's back—warm, like blood.

"Picke—!"

It ended suddenly.

Locke closed his eyes to slow the spinning. The sound withdrew from all sides but one, focusing in a single direction. The motion outside our mind stilled. I moved near my elfe—as near as I could get—still horribly far. Dust coated his clothing and exposed skin. His lips were pale and cracked. Blood streaked in a line across his face. He opened his eyes.

The Unstoppable Wraiths rushed onward, in a course toward the Burning Mountain, toward the unsuspecting army in the distance.

Locke reached to touch the liquid at his back and discovered it was thin. Not blood. It was water, gushing.

He took off his pack and saw a hole torn through the sides. He reached in and pulled out his pinkalue, soaked in water. In a panic, he drew out the leaking flasks and started sucking up as much of the vanishing water as he could. He licked it off his fingers as it dripped into the grass.

And something inside his mind snapped.

He was stranded and on the verge of death once again. All because he'd listened to me instead of heading homeward. His open eyes looked toward me in the distance. A glossy sheen covered their usual life. He looked, but he no longer saw.

He picked up the pinkalue.

I remembered him breathing music into it. Remembered how the melodies had taunted us. How they filled life with hints of something very big. Notes that gave clues leading to the Land of Song. Flecks of color in ribbons of wanderlust. Sparks of longing for the Goddess before we'd even met her. It had been all of these and perhaps more. All inside that one tiny, beautiful instrument.

But here on the edge of the Rueful Wilderness, it held no such music. Colorless dischord had replaced its song—had tainted everything. Now we found the opposite. Clues hinting at death. Trails winding toward the Necris. Paths leading lost souls in anguish.

Staring, he held the pinkalue like it was an ordinary stick.

55.

Dissonance

PERSUADE, FOLLOW, OR suffocate.
I had those three options.

If I couldn't persuade him, I'd have to follow along. And maybe become as hollow as the sylfe who followed his father—who never spoke to anyone, who simply lingered because he had to, having long since given up any aspirations for greatness.

Or I could suffocate.

Winds blew in the east, stirring up mists.

Locke grimaced as he again secured the bandage around his hand.

The unraveled threads of his bag failed to cross the gap left by the spearhead. Fortunately, the hole wasn't big enough to be much trouble. The jagged spear had thrust at just the right angle—if its course had been different by a finger's length, it might have torn through his torso instead of the bag.

"Lucky," I whispered.

I don't beweave in wuck.

Locke's fingers felt the moist leather of the flask. He tilted it above his open mouth, and a bit of water trickled onto his tongue as if to taunt him. He put his lips on the leather and sucked, drawing out the moisture, then repeated the process with each item from the pack.

As he lifted the phanos lamp and began to lick the drops from its surface, he noticed small cracks in the glass. He pressed his finger into one, and the split revealed its full length, running all the way through the bowl. The lamp was barely holding together—it must have cracked in the tumble. He set it on the ground. He skipped the vial of poison, not wanting to touch it with his tongue. He paused when he pulled out the Seer's leather map again. The bloody stain had nearly vanished in the moisture—the mark that had pointed us illogically to the Burning Mountain.

"I know we're supposed to go there," I said.

"Picke!" Locke shook his head as if my words had dumbfounded him. "The only time the Hundred ever lost a battle was when they turned against themselves. And now they're…" He shook his head and peered at the army in the distance—the battle would be over soon. "And if I somehow escaped them, I'll still die of thirst."

"You'll die of thirst if you head homeward too," I said.

"Maybe I'll get lucky." He gathered his things back into the pack and stood.

"Locke…" I began. "Don't you want to find out why the map pointed us there?"

"No, Picke. I can't. I can't do it. That's all I have. I can't hold fast anymore. I wasn't cut out to be the hero. You saw what we're up against. It's the Night of the Wolfe. The end of time. The end of everything. Not even the Seer could stop it. What makes you think I can?"

I stared across the great distance between us. I still couldn't feel the pain in his hand.

"I'm going to try to save Nicke and my dad." He started walking toward the southeast.

"What about the Goddess?"

He shook his head again and looked at the ground. "I *wish* I could help her, but I can't." He didn't stop walking.

I looked at his blurring form—worried it might be for the last time. "Our quest isn't over," I pleaded.

"I can't, Picke. I'm not ready to die."

The heaviness crushed down on me—the danger of what I was about to do. "I believe in it strong enough to stay," I said, "even if you go." As soon as I said it, I felt sick.

"I'm not enough. I never was."

"You are and always have been. The Seer knew it."

"Picke, you're not always right. He said he *didn't* want it to be me. He said he didn't know how it *could* be me. And it won't." He kept walking.

He was everything, and he was about to be gone. "Wait, Locke, please."

"Sorry, Picke. You chose the wrong day to draw a line in the sand."

But I had to. This was our chance. Our last chance. "Locke, I need you to go on, to be a hero, so I can be a hero's sylfe. If you don't become someone substantial, how can I?"

He frowned, still moving away. "I can't do this for you. That's not enough. It's too small and too selfish."

"There's something I have to tell you, something I should have told you a long time ago."

He actually took a step to the side, away from me, as if I were about to ambush him.

"I never should have kept it a secret," I said.

"Picke, what did you do?"

The haunting feeling from my living nightmares closed in, gripping me by the throat, holding me apart from my elfe. "I'm sorry. I was afraid of what you'd think."

"What is it?" asked Locke.

"When the Seer was dying, his sylfe whispered to me."

"And?"

"He told me the third part of the curse: the source, the sword, and the *sacrifice*. The curse can only be broken by giving a life to it. The Seer planned on giving his—that's what he meant when he said he didn't want it to be you. The burden fell to you, even though he didn't want it to."

"What?"

"You'll have to die to break the curse."

I'd said it. *Finally.* I'd told him the secret, words that couldn't be recalled.

He stopped, reaching his good hand to the ground as his knees touched down. He curled his wounded hand toward his heart and stared toward nothing—like a corpse crawling with anxious fire ants.

"My life?" Death's icy fingers stroked his neck. The hereafter wafted away as quickly and completely as a dream. The faerie stories he loved were nothing but crumbling pages. All he had was a few fleeting moments in front of him.

"Yes, our life," I said. "The princess went to sacrifice herself. The Seer wanted you to stop her, to get there first."

He touched the amulet at his neck. "Princess." It was barely a whisper.

He'd heard the call. To answer meant facing the path unknown, facing thirst, facing an army of sickening wraiths, facing a villain who could split the earth, and facing death himself.

Locke breathed audibly, his chest filling and collapsing in panic. But the breath didn't flow into me—we were too far apart, painfully apart. It was like that for a long time—desperate breathing that did nothing. Once the despair had penetrated everything, Locke glanced up from the gray ground. Not looking at me, but looking toward the Enchanted Wood—toward the last place that he might feel safe.

"Picke, remember that thing we always wanted? The mystery we longed for in the stars? The melodies and the adventures? The *wanting* we wanted?"

"I remember."

He nodded his head in pain, but he still didn't look at me. Misery was written all over his face. "It's home."

With that, he put his back to me and began to walk.

56.

Abyss

A CHILL RAN THROUGH me.

If I followed my elfe, my actions would contradict everything I'd said. Locke, I supposed, was willing to have me along. He hadn't banished me. He might have even been eager for company. But the monk's words rung loud, and I saw that final stare he gave me as he spoke them: "You have a role to play—one larger than you think."

I needed Locke to listen to me, to become the hero I was meant to accompany, and this was the loudest I could scream. So I didn't drift after him as I'd always done. He continued to move, walking away from me, and I held still.

It didn't take long. The loneliness pressed in almost immediately. So thick I couldn't tell which direction was up. My vision began to fade and blur—I couldn't see without my elfe. I couldn't see my elfe. But I could still hear his footsteps. Right then I almost darted after him. I certainly wanted to follow, as I always had. But maybe one more moment would be enough to convince him.

It wasn't.

I hadn't realized, but I'd nearly crossed a threshold, my chance to choose nearly gone.

"Locke," I said again, not moving, reaching out with my breath. "Please don't go…"

But I sensed he couldn't hear me anymore.

The further he got, the more sluggish my movement became. The wind rushed past, but I wasn't moving with it. It blew away from him and pushed against me, as if to increase the already impossible distance.

Okay, it didn't matter if I contradicted myself. *I needed to be with my elfe.*

I tried to fly after him, but I spiraled into stillness, above me, around me, and through me, with no farther side. Terror tightened its grip, overwhelmingly solid. It pressed on me, ramming downward, a current dragging into my gut, vacating my lungs, making me uncontrollably still. A stillness so strong it bit into me. Too tight for a sylfe to survive, much less move. Like my nightmare the morning this all began.

I needed Locke, needed to follow him, but I couldn't move.

I sensed Lonae in that moment. She could feel my distress, and she called out to me, a scream of sympathy—"Picke!"

I wanted to shout her name, to tell her I needed help, but I couldn't. My breath was gone. So was my melody—shoved more and more into stillness and wild discord. She tumbled away from me, further and further. Finally, it broke.

The consonance was gone.

Loneliness drove at me from every direction, confining me more and more, till the music of the whole earth faded. The abyss around me smiled, spiking teeth lined around a clenching jaw and hollow skull. I couldn't move. I couldn't breathe. I couldn't see. I couldn't live. I couldn't live. Exile smashed into my face, pushing me into oblivion.

Though I couldn't speak, words came to our mind—no, not *our* mind anymore. I was desperately alone. It was simply *my* mind.

Words formulated in my solitary mind. But they had nowhere to go— trapped in the claustrophobia of my unmoving prison, unable to escape:

Help. Please. I was wrong. I tried to do this my way, and I was wrong. If you can hear me, please, please give me another chance to become significant. I don't want it to end like this. I'd do anything.

The earth pressed down on me from above.

I tried to fly—I needed to stand on air, where I could breath. But it was too late; I couldn't get through the ground. It was too thick and too massive, looming above me. I struggled against it, but it wouldn't budge, and neither could I, no matter how hard I tried. And I couldn't breathe.

I couldn't breathe.

The fuzzy shape of Locke walked across the surface of the tilted world—his feet in the air and the ground leaning above him.

He went on as if he couldn't tell everything had been tipped askew.

57.

Nocturne

WITHOUT ME, DARKNESS came.
The winds fell silent. Fog dropped from the clouds like a predator, obscuring the already dark land.

Locke walked amid its swirls, looking back, as if expecting someone to catch up to him at any moment, but he found himself continually alone. He began to mumble. "I'm going to die. We all are. I want to die at home."

His thirst pressed into his throat and veins. Nothing mattered if he couldn't make it to water. His flasks were torn and empty. But he still planned to cross the Rueful Wilderness and the Majestic Sea, then follow the Great River through the Wisting Mountains. *So far. Much too far without water.* But what else could he do but try to go home? To what might mean a few more days of life and safety.

He gave another hopeful glance behind him. When he looked forward, gray had surrounded him. The fog crept across the ground, prowling on all sides, taking new territory on behalf of the skies. As he stepped into it, a cobweb stretched across his face. He brushed it off his nose, then off his ear, then tried his nose again. It wouldn't seem to go away.

The handle of his glowing sword shone over his shoulder, whitening the clouds around him. He stumbled on, and the fog stayed just out of reach, backing away, afraid of being touched, but never moving far. It closed in behind him too, keeping him imprisoned in blindness.

When he came to a tree, he gripped the deathly white bark, like a swimmer adrift in an ocean. He tried to brush another cobweb off his face. He clapped his palm against a creeping sensation on his leg, but nothing was there. After a moment, he plunged on, holding his breath out of worry. He veered toward another tree and clung to it, looking back to see whether he'd been walking straight. All landmarks behind were invisible. As he pressed on, he corrected his path wrongward. He second-guessed that and went more to the right. Then he stopped.

As he looked at the surrounding walls of mist, *nowhere* faced him in every direction.

He lowered slowly to his knees. He was lost. *Lost and alone.* And home was out of reach.

For some reason, it wasn't his sylfe or Nicke or even the Goddess that popped into his mind. It was the Nymfe, Tryse, the one he'd let slip through his fingers. That beautiful girl he'd missed because of cowardice. He'd deliberated too long, until it was too late. At least now she wouldn't miss him when he didn't come home—wouldn't be bothered by news of his agonizing death. His injuries throbbed, his hand in particular, accompanied by the bruises from the beating of the Unstoppable Wraiths and his other hardships. His sinews cried out for water, and the fog enveloped him. As with the Nymfe, his efforts had all turned to failure.

No, he just had to be still. And patient. After all, fog didn't last forever. Of course, he'd thought that about dark clouds. The thirst gnawed the tissue of his throat, making it painful to breathe. How long could he last if he had to wait it out? Not long. Not long at all.

"But what was I supposed to do? My Picke went crazy. He wanted me to stay and die."

The sword on his back barely illuminated the unknown. He wanted to draw the blade and cut the fog away, but this enemy was immune to aggression and the edge of a sword.

A sound, a ticking rattle, climbed through the silence.

He jerked the sword from his pack, gripping the scabbard with one weak hand. He clenched his teeth, searching into the fog, and his thoughts circled with the mists.

"Picke?" he called into the empty night. "Picke, is that you?"

What had made the sound? Or had he imagined it? He turned one way and then another, hearing his fears but nothing else, attacked by every invisible possibility and every impossibility too—leaving him to face all enemies at once.

He looked down, pleading to the earth. "Help, Picke. Or someone. Demigods. I *need* you when it's *dark*." He looked up, where he vaguely hoped some great good might be hiding. But it was gray too, and no answer came. In spite of how badly he wanted it.

"What were you expecting?" he whispered to himself. "You don't believe in them, do you? No, I don't."

He shook his head.

Talking to the demigods. Talking to himself.

Even if they were real, they wouldn't answer with help. They were just teachers. *Like Picke.* The one who'd taught him about miracles in the darkness of the cave. "Numa could whisper to me," Picke had said, "and I to you, and if you acted on it, a miracle could happen." If there was such a thing as divine help, it would come through a sylfe. Like the one he'd left behind.

Just when he was certain he would get no answer, he heard a voice.

But not the calm voice of his sylfe.

Not something that could ride the wind—it was too dark and heavy for that.

This voice spoke with the mouths of all his fears combined into one: the undying wraiths, the relentless wolves, the villain who wanted to murder an entire land, and even the power that ripped his mother away. The voice was all of these. A voice that spoke not a word. Instead it gave a victorious laugh. A laugh so deep and vile that it soaked up all hope. A laugh that echoed across the stillness. A laugh that appeared so unspeakably close it tickled the skin of his right ear.

He shrugged, swiped at his ear, and spun, afraid he might actually find the source.

"No, no, no," he said. "I *am* losing it."

In answer, the voice appeared again, sharp as a lance and weighty as lead, forcing its way into his solitary mind, echoing inside and out:

If there is a god, it is me, and I am death.

The words hit him like a spear, knocking him onto the ground. He scrambled back to his feet, looking around frantically, expecting the author of the voice to appear at his elbow while he wasn't looking. He grabbed his head with the palm of his good hand and with the back of his injured one, as if that might somehow protect him.

"Help me," he whispered into the loneliness. In that moment a sudden realization came. His chest bounced as he gasped against a surge of tears. "The one thing worse than facing death is facing death *alone.*"

His own words echoed in memory: *I can't, Picke. I'm not ready to die.*

"Picke, now I'm ready," he whispered, looking around to see if the voice had heard him. "I'm ready," he repeated, as if his willingness might somehow overturn this whole nightmare. "Ready to die. I'd rather do that than be this alone. Where are you?"

He'd left Picke somewhere not too far back. *If that way really was back.* He took a few uncertain steps. With each he worried he might run into the massive jaws of a voice that would swallow him infinitely. Something flickered at the corner of his eye. He turned his face away in a squint, expecting to be consumed. But when he looked, he saw nothing. Everything was emptiness.

"Picke? Please…" he whispered again.

But it was futile. He couldn't escape the shifting prison.

This spurred the strongest emotion yet—a desperate need to find his friend. It formulated into a deep, primitive cry, like a tiny child, and its sound scraped at the back of his lungs:

"PICKE!!!"

That solitary word echoed, spreading in an expanding circle into the night.

Locke's chest pumped in and out. He wanted to hear the mild voice of his friend.

Instead he was answered by a scream.

58.

Still

THE SOUND SCRAPED through the air, chilling like a ghost.
It pierced the clouds to the moon, a wail of death, stabbing through his ribs. A loud, screeching howl.

A banshe wolfe.

Locke turned, stared into the gray, and waited. This sound had haunted his footsteps ever since he touched the cursed scroll. If the wolfe caught him here, with nowhere to hide, he'd be torn to bloody pieces. Suddenly he wondered if Nicke was alright.

A second scream sounded, closer, from somewhere behind. *No, not two. Not both.* Had they surrounded him?

With a gasp, Locke broke into a run, perpendicular to the two sounds, dodging the trees that sprung out of the mist. A scream appeared in front of him, even closer this time. He smelled the odor too, one of death and decay mixed with a hint of sweet smoke.

He skidded to a stop. Had his path curved? Or were they on the move? Or maybe there were three now.

The light from the sword fell over his shoulder and onto the swirling mists, like a beacon. As he considered dropping it, he saw Shilohe's face in the fog. Another howl came, and his wounded hand began shaking. He breathed deep and let it out as slow as he whispered, "Picke would know what to do."

Then it hit: *Picke would tell him a wind only dies when it stops.*

But every direction looked the same—swirling mists, threatening his life, blinding him with unknowns. A vast mountain hid beyond his sight, not more than a few hour's march. Picke was somewhere closer. *But which way?* The howl of a pack echoed all around.

A foolish idea came to him—foolishness was all he had left.

He closed his eyes.

As blackness overcame him, he spun around like a kohkoo nut tumbling in water, two and half times, maybe three or even four. As the world turned, the wolves howled, louder and louder, nearer and nearer.

Still spinning, he whispered, "Whichever way I run is forward," too quiet for anything but himself to hear. "And stop talking to yourself."

He opened his eyes.

New shapes swirled in the walls of mist. If he had an inkling of direction before, even that had vanished. He only knew he was surrounded by wolves.

He began walking straight ahead, into the unknown. As Picke would do.

The movement brought a glimmer of hope, and he quickened to a jog. His small space in the midst of the clouds moved with him, limiting his vision to a few feet in every direction. Branches and trees jumped from the fog. He leaped and dodged, running to... *somewhere*. Or *nowhere*. But it gave him power, so he ran harder, faster, so fast the fog barely had time to twist away before he touched it.

The screams moved to his back. Terror nipped at his heels, teeth and all. He ran faster, with more strength than he knew he had.

Then something grabbed him.

59.

Grave

IT HOOKED HIS ankle and pulled.

He crashed to the ground and twisted to see what'd grabbed him, jerking his foot away. In the darkness, as his heart beat wildly against his bones, he saw a mangled form, clawing at his leg and crackling like dried leaves.

The branches looked like long fingers on a drawn-out hand.

Beneath the hand, practically in its clutches, was a pinkalue, one that looked almost like his own. He picked it up. No, it *was* his own. He held it lightly with his shield hand and felt the dips and patterns carved into its wooden sides. It must have slipped through the hole in his bag just as he tripped. Odd that it slipped out—the spear hole was midway up the pack. But somehow it did, and if he hadn't tripped he might have lost it forever.

The scream of the banshe wolves came again, unrelenting and close.

Even the plant life had been dragged under death's spell. Dead vines surrounded him along with roots the color of bone. The fog swirled in a graceful dance; the light of the sword glowed on its curves. He breathed quietly and listened carefully. For a moment, he heard no screams. Turning, he looked forward, in the direction he'd been running.

He'd nearly hit his head on a tombstone.

He eyed it, making sure to breathe. The fog whirled, converging on the grave in an uncanny way, as if pointing. It was beautiful and terrible. Was there some cavern below sucking the mists into it? If not, something else was affecting the fog—

A chill crawled up his spine.

As he was about to push himself back to his feet, he stopped.

The cobwebs and vines covered the stone, hiding some sort of writing. He scratched them away with a stick, his eyes shining more and more as he read:

Here lies Martigane, King of Elfland, Giver of Mercy, Slayer of Amaranthe, Chief of Swordsmen, Last of Minstrels, Friend of Cree. May they rest in peace.

He stared, eyes wide in unbelief.

"It's a faerie story," he whispered.

The tombstone didn't seem to care what Locke thought. It stood before him anyway.

"Wait, could this be…?" Branches reached down through the fog overhead. A giant stood above him whose trunk vanished upward. The bark was unusual, but he didn't know the species of the Rueful Wilderness. *Could this have been the actual place where Martigane faced off against death?* "… the actual Great Oak?"

As the realization came, he heard the hint of a song.

It was the difference between remembering a dream and living a dream— he glimpsed only the shadow of something much larger. But a little was enough.

The fear in his heart began to flee, replaced with… that feeling so hard to describe. The feeling Picke, who practically *was* words, couldn't even pin down. They'd started out looking for it, that elusive feeling, he and Picke had.

He breathed in as if inhaling a symphony. His shoulders dropped.

The memory of his mother was a piece of the music. So was Martigane's death. And Shilohe's charm; he touched the amulet hanging over his heart. Even this haunting place was part of it. That was also why Picke kept asking him to play the pinkalue—its songs were a part of it too.

He took the amulet in his fingers and brought it close, really looking at it for the first time. Four protrusions came off the corners of a silver circle, as if to represent radiating light. A sword crossed vertically up through the center of the circle, and the point fastened to the chain. Three words were etched down the blade:

MORE THAN LIFE.

"Oh," he whispered.

Martigane had only found the Melody of Echoes because he wanted it more than life. Shilohe said her father read her the story many times, and he loved the phrase too. Maybe he'd also died for some thing he wanted more than life.

Locke stared at the tombstone, nodding. "Okay, I'll do it. I'll do it for her. She's worth more than life."

As the music filled his soul, he wanted to stand up, raise his sword to the sky, and roar!

But as he was about to, he looked at the fog crawling across the ground, thicker now, and deeper. It pressed in close, creeping with a certain, strange, unbound claustrophobia. It didn't want him to forget his fear—the voices of wolves, of wraiths, and of death most of all.

He looked at the pinkalue in his hand and pressed his thumb into one of the wind hollows. He hadn't played it in so long. "Picke, where are you? I'm ready now."

Another foolish idea came to him.

Maybe it was his own idea. But maybe Numa had whispered through the atmosphere, speaking so subtle it was indistinguishable from thought. He scooted his back against the tombstone and pulled up his knees in front of him. He felt the indentations of the inscription on the stone. It would protect him from at least one direction.

The wolves had not found him yet. For some reason their sense of smell didn't compare to that of a regular wolfe. Maybe because they didn't have blood. Or maybe their own haunting odor interfered—he smelled it fearfully close. But surely they could hear just fine, or why would they call to each other?

Slowly undid the green bandage around his hand, revealing a messy wound. He cringed as he jerked it free and threw it aside.

His swallow scraped against his dry throat. He licked the insides of his lips and held the pinkalue to his mouth. The first tune that came to mind was the Angel's song—Picke would like that one. He positioned his fingers to play the first painful note. He took a breath, looking toward his unseen enemies. But the reluctance sank into his throat, and he didn't play, not for a long time. The mists floated around him.

He whispered, very quietly, "This has got to be the worst idea you've ever had."

His words hung in the air for a moment.

As if in answer, the wolves screamed—a sound like the dead were trying to shriek but couldn't open their mouths.

He'd spoken in his darkest hour—said he'd rather face death with Picke than feel such crushing loneliness. Now he had the chance to prove those words, the chance to call his friend and death at the same time.

He put the pinkalue to his lips. His tender fingertips burned as he pressed them into the wind hollows—

—and he played one solitary note.

As quiet as it was, it spread loud into the darkness, calling all fears toward it.

He glanced over each of his shoulders and saw nothing but fog. He waited, curled up, beneath that giant, lifeless tree, on top of a dead hero. His heart beat rapidly for many moments.

The answer chilled his blood.

Not a scream this time, but a growl. Somewhere nearby—maybe already in the graveyard.

Yet the thought returned, stronger now than before—to play the Angel's song. His heart thumped, accelerating its rhythm and his breath.

With his head bowed, he spoke toward his chest, almost silent: "I'm going to die. I'll die here, or of thirst in a few days, or if by some miracle, at the villain's fortress. I'll die no matter what. And if I'm going to die, I'd rather die with Picke."

He brought the instrument back to his mouth.

The notes flowed like a river, cutting into the silence.

60.

Windswept

FIRST I HEARD a melody.
It soared across the sky, whistling a warm tone, up and down like a summertide breeze, a zephyr gently lulling, a shining metallic sound, bright and warm. The song drew me toward it and lifted me skyward.

I breathed in the song.

The melody played on, bold as light, a spirit quickening in pace. It echoed all around, as if bouncing off the fog itself, coming from all directions at once. Metal tinkled against metal, somewhere very close, small keys jingling on a chain. A smiling young, angelic voice said everything would be alright. The notes came gently, ringing against the silence, reaching out to wolves and injuries, dawning at full rhythm.

Fear grew in equal crescendo: I jumped when something snarled right next to me.

A creature crept, cloaked in shadow, searching for the source of the echoing song. A musk of death accompanied it, repulsive and scraping.

But the song flowed around the terror. I began to hum along—receiving the music's power and giving it my own.

The music stopped.

Once again I was alone.

Air sculpted in the shape of a swirling whisper came drifting by, a voice like the soft fur of a bear cub: "Picke?"

But I couldn't answer. I didn't have enough breath.

Not until the music began boldly again.

It echoed off stones and trees and swirling mists.

I hummed along till the music enveloped me. I spun, lifting into the air, finally again in flight. I sensed phantoms looming in the fog.

"Picke!" It was a shouted whisper, yet the sound still had its distinct color—soft and warm mixed with the green of rain.

Oh, I loved the color of that voice. "Locke!"

A laugh came through a closed mouth, too true to be restrained.

Breath hadn't come to me fully, and I struggled for each word. "Where... are... you?" I needed to be closer to my elfe.

"I'm here," he whispered. "Picke, right here."

"Keep talking... I hear you..."

"I can't: *they'll* hear me."

"I'm almost there."

"Hurry!"

As he said it, he appeared before me, a corporeal ghost, slowly tangible. He sat curled with his back to a gravestone, holding the pinkalue in his good hand, the hero I'd followed for so long, my elfe.

My best friend.

With windswept hair, a scratch across his face, and the grin of a child.

I felt his urge to embrace me, a mortal urge, which I shared—a longing which couldn't be fulfilled. Instead, he breathed in deep, remembering my smell and the sound of my voice. And although we didn't know it, the sun was on the rise behind the fog and the clouds.

"I'm glad you're back," he whispered, not drifting away from me. Our mind had become one again, whole and healed, a single mind, just like when we were kid and sylfide.

"I'm glad I'm back too." We smiled.

A deep growl reached us through the mists. And that ghastly smell of imminent death.

Locke leaped to his feet. He clutched the pinkalue, and with that hand he waved for me to follow—something that had always been assumed before. He weaved around one tombstone and then another till finally he came to a wall. But he didn't hesitate. He tucked the instrument securely in his bag, ran back a few steps, jumped to the top of a small headstone then onto a taller one, and leaped for the wall. His weight forced him to use his burned hand, and he gave a cry of pain as he clung to the top.

A snarl came from the fog—it had heard us.

Locke pulled himself up, leaped off the far side, and rolled. With tears of pain streaking from his eyes, he bounded into a sprint, plunging into a mass of swirling gray.

A tree appeared too quickly.

Locke sidestepped, and his shoulder touched the bark as, with the grace of a dance, he twisted his body in a complete revolution and continued running. I flew slightly ahead, lashing with my might against the fog and forming a tunnel through it, to give Locke time to dodge obstacles. The beat of heavy paws crashed behind us.

"These don't look like climbing trees," I warned—we couldn't escape into the sky quick enough.

The steps grew louder. A banshe wolfe apparated through the mists.

For a moment even the fog stood still, while Locke's shining eyes stared into those dark, black, lifeless voids. An arrow protruded from from the beast's shoulder: it was the wilder one.

This monster, full of teeth, pounced with blind ferocity.

Locke dove to the side like leaping into water.

The jaws just missed him.

With a tuck and roll, he was back on his feet and running again into the clouds. The scaled pattern of the white hilt shone behind him.

The wolfe heaved in heavy breaths, and its paws beat like a rapid drum, right behind us.

I gathered the mists with all I could muster, pushing them thick behind Locke to hide his escape.

The wolfe scrambled into my cloak of fog, and he stared right at me, but my elfe had vanished.

I caught up quicker than the wolfe. Locke ran, weaving between bone-colored bark. The heavy breathing chased after us, and paws slammed into dirt and sticks. I frantically pushed more fog over our trail till our winding gained the advantage. Beat after beat, we put distance between us and the predator. Eventually we heard it howling its loss far behind.

Locke slowed, gasping, and giving me a thankful smile. He moved on, and the night fell silent, with only the slight sound of his moccasins to fill the night, footsteps crushing lightly into dead leaves.

He began to breathe easier.

Strangely though, the deathly odor didn't diminish. In fact, it seemed to be growing the farther we went.

Locke looked warily behind him.

A branch snapped beneath his feet, making a loud crack.

Paws beat again, rapidly. *Very close.*

Had the silver-patched wolfe circled ahead?

The steps padded toward us.

Locke changed course, wanting to be far from that broken stick when the wolfe arrived. He sprinted in full, crushing leaves, with the sound of the beast's heavy footsteps covering his own.

The paws stopped.

"Wait, shhhh!" I whispered, motioning for him to halt.

He did, as quickly as he could, and the Rueful Wilderness fell silent again, leaving only the quiet dance of the fog. In our mind we could see the clever predator waiting, just through that fog right there, and listening.

Locke hardly breathed, afraid even that sound might be too much. The odor was as strong as it had ever been, so close, and it seemed Locke must soon cough or faint or breathe and then be torn to shreds. With a small movement, Locke's chainmail gave a hushed clink beneath his tunic.

The wolfe took a step, just one—too close. It took another—it was headed right for us. Yet if Locke moved at all, it would reveal his position.

I knew what to do.

I moved as far from Locke as I could. The distance caused a shortness of breath and added to the fogginess around and between us. It reminded me of the suffocating abyss, but I fought through it. When I got as far as I could stand, I raced into the air and then shot toward the ground, pushing as hard as I could. The force kicked up leaves and sent a crackling rustle through the air.

The wolfe's footsteps leaped toward me.

Locke ran the opposite direction, and I sped to catch up.

We heard it take several more steps then pause.

Locke paused too, waiting in the overpowering silence.

The wolfe scampered—a few beats, followed by another pause. Perhaps looking around. Perhaps listening.

It moved, and Locke took a few steps, stopping before the creature paused.

Slowly, silently, we stole farther and farther away till we heard a howling duet far in the distance.

61.

Consonance

A T FIRST, ALL I could do was smile.
"Picke, I'm glad you're back."
I moved close, now that I could. He barely had to breathe for me to hear his words. The poignant odor of the wolves had faded.

"I'm glad you played the music," I said. "Even with your burned hand."

"I didn't even feel the pain. All I felt was music."

"I'm glad you dared. I was trapped. Couldn't move."

"Now you're so vivid. And what you did to the wolves…!"

"You're welcome," I said, and we laughed.

"I need you now more than ever," said Locke. "My throat feels like lyzard skin. I'm not sure I could even swallow water if I had any. But I can't tell which direction to go." He frowned into the fog.

"I can feel the easter winds," I said. "So north is that direction, and home is that way."

"We're not going home."

"What?"

"I'm ready now." He swallowed dryly.

"You said the feeling we'd been searching for was home."

"It *is* home, Picke. But it's more too. It's also the Goddess, and music, and finishing what you started out to do."

When he said that, for some reason I saw Shilohe's face—she gazed sincerely beneath her perfectly concerned eyebrows. I raised my hands to form my question: "So we're going to rescue her?"

"We're going to try."

"And what about home?"

He glanced wistfully in the direction I'd indicated before. "I guess I can't have it all."

"But what about dying? Aren't you afraid?"

"Of course I'm afraid! But I'd rather die chasing that unnameable song than live without it. Or live without you."

I smiled. Surprised, and yet... *not surprised*. He was acting like the elfe I'd seen in him all along, the kind whose soul was a mighty gale.

"On to Mount Death," he said.

I smiled again.

We set out with me guiding Locke through mists, farther from the wolves.

The crows cawed, the temperature rose, and the fog began to clear. We proceeded southwest, into the morning of the eighteenth day, and found ourselves in the middle of a dense wilderness. Through gaps in the branches, we caught glimpses of the Burning Mountain looming above, stretching so high it disappeared into gray clouds. Eventually we moved beyond the trees and other life to a wide expanse of gnarled black rock. There Locke stopped to cut another strip of the cowl as a bandage for his hand.

"Can I talk to the princess?" he asked.

I shook my head.

He gave me a painfully worried look.

"I'm sorry. I don't have the consonance anymore. It broke when we..."

"Oh," he said, and the sadness pushed his tone to the strongest mildness. "I wanted to tell her I'm still coming. She'll know it's broken, right?"

"Yes, Lonae will tell her."

"She's going to think I abandoned her. I did abandon her. Oh, what have I done? I was so scared, Picke." He stared across the thin remnants of fog. "I still am."

"Yet you're going on anyway." I smiled, but he didn't seem to notice.

"She's probably scared, now more than ever. She thinks I've left her."

"But you haven't."

"I did though."

"It doesn't matter. Let's hurry."

So we did, in spite of his weariness.

Moss still grew further out, the last bit of life. But as we drew closer to death's gaping mouth, even the moss turned back in fear. A dark crevice lay ahead, beckoning us. It was in the lower regions, but still quite a climb.

Locke asked for my story, but for me, there had been nothing. When he left, I'd fallen into perfect stillness—exiled into Pandemonium, Saede's domain, the realm of darkness. It wasn't a world of substance, so I kept no memories of it, but the fear of returning to it lingered. I asked Locke about his story, and he whispered it to me till we shared the whole memory. He told it like one of his bad dreams, moment by moment, explaining what it was like to be alone.

"And I may have heard the voice of Saede," he said.

"What!"

"I know."

"But you don't believe in him."

"I know. But I don't know how else to explain it. Either I lost my wits in there, or Saede or death spoke to me. Something very strange happened because you weren't there."

"I'm sorry," I said.

"No *I'm* sorry. I lost sight of the quest. I forgot the music."

"You remembered when it mattered though."

"Because I found Martigane's grave."

"What!"

He spoke quietly in spite of my outbursts, worried that the Hundred might be somewhere nearby. "Yeah, that grave, where you found me—it was Martigane's." A child's laugh skated out past his teeth. "He's real."

"Why didn't you tell me?"

"Because my heroic gift is running like crazy." He laughed aloud.

"That was really his grave?"

"It had his name inscribed, and it was under a giant, chalky oak, just like the story said."

"Wow. And that's when you wanted to—you know—do what the Seer asked?"

A lone nightjar sat on an outcrop calling, *"Wippur, wippur, wippur, wippur,"* as if trying to warn us of some imminent danger. Perhaps when his companions had deserted, he'd stayed behind for just this reason, because as soon as he delivered the message he rushed away.

"Actually, I still *want* to go home, back to where I feel safe. I just can't give up on our longing—even if it's always barely out of reach. I have to keep chasing, and hopefully that will do some good for the rest—for the princess at least. But even if it doesn't, it won't matter because I'll have been after the right thing, following the music, no matter the cost." He looked skyward, as if to ask the curtain of clouds: "You hear that?"

"You're praying now?"

"I don't know."

"You don't know?"

"I don't know." When he looked back down, a whirl of dizziness hit him, and he stumbled, putting his hands on the ground to regain control of his balance.

"You okay?"

"I need water."

"Your lifeblood is nearly gone."

"And if I don't get some, I'm going to die"—a weak smile sneaked across his face—"before I'm supposed to."

I gave him a sad smile.

A turbulent layer of rocks surrounded the mountain, as if some demigod had smashed the surface to pieces. Locke picked up a chunk, and found it was light, like a balse wood, like it wasn't real rock, so frail it sometimes gave way when Locke stepped, crumbling like sand, but still rough enough to cut viciously. I also didn't sense gnymes in the rock. Either they were quieter than usual, or these rocks were dead.

Several smooth channels cut outward through these uneven parts, glassy highways of stone, shaped like liquid, as if a Pyromancer had built them with a spell. We followed one, and it led us straight to the base, the place where they said fire was born, where Phose created the first salamindes.

As we ascended the forbidden slopes, smoke trailed into the sky with the wind, drawing our attention far below. It was the ruins of war. A few propped up banners waved to us gently. From this high, we saw a clear overview of the aftermath, and the death toll had been high. The distant bodies lay strewn across the ground, unmoving. *Elfe bodies.* Wraith bodies wouldn't have rested still.

"You remember the story about Phose adopting the wrecches?" asked Locke.

"Yes. They lost their sylves, and Phose took pity on them. But I don't remem—" I stopped short with a gasp, looking around wildly.

"What is it?" asked Locke.

"Someone is watching us," I said.

62.

The Face

L OCKE PULLED THE Shining Sword from his back.
"Banshe wolves?"
"No… It's a spirit." I swooped around Locke, searching the whole face of the mountain.

"A *spirit?* An elemental?" He glanced around but then watched me, waiting for me to see.

"I don't know. I can't see it, but it's here." I spread my fingers, trying so hard to… "I can almost see it, only… it's holding too still. It's blending in with the rock."

"Like a dead sylfe?" Locke took a cautious step forward. "Maybe we can sneak by and it'll leave us alone."

"I don't think it's going to leave us alone."

"Why not?"

"I can feel its eyes on us."

The crown of my head tilted back as I looked higher and higher up the mountain. The dim light made the shadows between rocks and crevices—the parts we couldn't see—all the more frightening.

"HOOOOOOOOOOOO!!!"

Locke dropped his weapon and shoved one hand and one forearm over his ears. But the ground shook so badly he dropped a hand to the ground, forced to bear the sound.

The boom surrounded us—not the loudest noise I'd ever heard, but it *was* the deepest, like the voice of the earth. And I couldn't see it either, strangely, almost like it wasn't a sound at all but more of a physical touch. I tried to fly away, but I couldn't tell which way was away. It was all around.

Then it was gone.

The mountain fell quiet, except for the small rocks tapping their way down the cliff and crevices as they looked for new places to be still.

"What was that?" Locke inspected the ground warily as he slowly picked up his sword.

"I think it was…" and I pointed.

Above us hung the familiar outcropping of a nose, two sunken holes for eyes, and a straight crevice cutting across beneath them as if it were a mouth. The mockery of daylight cast the shadows of a terrible grimace. But on closer inspection, it was just regular mountainside—not a sculpture at all, nothing more than a rough semblance.

"Did it speak?" asked Locke.

"I… I think… so."

Locke centered his attention on the stone above us, watching, afraid that crevice mouth might move while he wasn't looking.

"WHOOOO GOOOES THEEEERE?" Though this second phrase boomed more calmly than the first, still the ground shook, and more pebbles plunked down from above.

Locke breathed heavily, clutching the scabbard against the ground. "I… uh… I'm Locke of the Enchanted Wood."

"A KYRIE?" The mountain shook again, and Locke's head rung.

"Yes. And I'm so sorry to ask—I don't mean any disrespect—but can you please speak a little softer?"

"HAAA HAAA HAAA!" The immense voice laughed in tones so low they nearly broke me. The ground swayed, and this time a large rock tumbled down.

"Look out!" I darted in front of Locke and zoomed to the wrong side.

He followed my movement, jumping aside as a boulder crashed across the platform and rolled out of sight off the next ledge. Locke tried not to scowl as he looked up at the face again.

"Oh dear," said the voice, now in a very loud whisper, in overpowering muted tones. "I am sorry." This time the ground buzzed beneath us, but the fury of the previous rumbles had gone. Strangely, the face did not move as he spoke—he was still as any rock. Yet he somehow gave the impression of an expressive countenance. "I forget how fragile you are. When I talk this quiet, I can hardly hear myself. But I suppose you'll hear me just fine."

"Yes, I can hear you," said Locke.

"I will speak quieter," roared the whisper, "if you promise to speak up."

"I will!" said Locke, raising his small, bear-cub voice to a shout.

"I haven't had a Kyrie scale my walls for at least a generation. One of your generations, of course. There *were* no Kyrie in the last of my generations. No elves at all. And very few kynde for that matter."

"Are you a gnyme?"

"I am half gnyme, just as you are half sylfe."

Locke cocked an eyebrow. It was an unusual way for him to describe us, but we certainly were two halves of a whole—though I didn't know what you'd have called us while we were apart. A broken soul, I guess.

"Why don't all stones speak like you do?" asked Locke.

"That is a long story," said the face.

As Locke began putting together a polite way to say *never mind*, the face went on:

"In the beginning, when all the earth was united into one great whole, Gaie imbued the whole with wisdom undivided, to root all living things. He called it the Great Gnyme. But when Saede abandoned the light, he sowed chaos deep inside the earth. Awakened by the seeds of unrest, great giants of creation rose in anger toward each other. Mountains hurled rocks, peaks clawed down ridges, and fields rolled like seas. Before Gaie could calm them down, the smooth places had become scarred with hills and canyons. Straight ways had been made crooked. The Great Gnyme himself had been broken, split into many, many pieces. I myself am one of those pieces, hewn from the source. And to answer your question, the bigger the stone, the wiser the gnyme, for he embodies more of Gaie's gift. Pebbles are such small fragments of intelligence you can hardly recognize them. And at the center of the earth, the rest of the Great Gnyme still resides. One day Gaie will heal him by uniting us all once again."

Locke nodded reverently at the story.

"It is quite wondrous, is it not, little elfe?" The whisper came as loud as roaring wind. "We children of Gaie are given something like immortality, which we receive in exchange for our reach. But you children of Numa are given the opposite, a short life and a reach that extends nearly to the empyrean, though most of you squander it."

I wanted to rush at him for that—see if I could make him flinch—but I felt sure I'd only come away embarrassed.

"Now, my gentle friend," whispered the face, "why are you here?"

Locke lifted his chin, gazing up. "The living water led us here."

"You have been to the Well at the World's End?"

"Yes."

"It is the same water Nara used to create the ondines," said the voice. "And the first animals, just before the Lost Ages. The pool was vaster then. But its light grew dim as ondines retreated beneath the waters. Now so many have been kidnapped. Because the sylves sunk into darkness and gave their power to Saede."

"We didn't give our power to Saede!" I blurted.

"The sylves have each given some power to Saede," said the face, and he seemed to be frowning, "whether intentionally or not. Including you."

I thought he was looking at me, so I glared back.

"Yes, I am talking to you, sylfe. WHAT IS YOUR NAME?"

The rocks trembled under his thundering voice, and Locke put a hand to the ground to keep from falling over.

My whisper-sized voice puffed against the wall: "I am Picke!"

"Picke?" He settled his voice to a rushing whisper again. "I once knew a trickster with your name. He was shrewd and a knave."

But he was telling another lie. Elves named their children after people or things, like Locke, but Numa always gave her children unique names. Still I wasn't feeling like arguing as much anymore. "I'm neither, I promise."

"Is that true, Locke of the Enchanted Wood?"

"I guess so," said Locke. "He's good at making choices—better than me—and he gets more honest every day."

"HAA HAA!" The ground jolted Locke to attention. When it settled, the stone said, "Sorry..."

Locke stood back up straight.

"If you have been to the Well at the World's End," said the mountainside, "then where is your light now?"

"It went out... or was taken from us."

"If it was taken from you, you never really had it."

I wanted to bite his rocky nose off.

"I tried to keep it," said Locke.

"Why have you not gone back for it?"

"We uh... We would have, but we ran out of time. Luckily, we'd already marked our path on a map, which led us to you. We're not really sure why though."

"Why had you gone for the living water in the first place?"

"I'm trying to bring back the light of the sun to fight off the wraiths."

"Oh. This is serious then." A shadow seemed to have fallen over him, or *more* shadow.

"Why do you say that?"

"My plants are dying."

"Your plants?"

"Gaie is the caretaker of plants across the face of the earth. I am a fragment of his son, and these regions below are under my care; each green life is one of my children."

Locke turned and looked over the valley of white chalky trees where the Burning Mountain would've cast its evening shadow. It was odd to think of the Rueful Wilderness as a place worth saving, but it was the resting place of Martigane. Maybe that was enough.

The face rumbled on: "The pawn who created this curse pushed light and water beyond the earth and sky, spelling the end of life, including every last one of my children. When the lifeforces aren't woven together, Saede reigns with decay and death."

"I don't like the sound of that."

"I want you to bring back the warmth of Phose and the tears of Nara. Reunite the lifeforces and save my children."

"I'll try. But I still don't know what I'm supposed to do."

"Your map did not lead you to me. You are headed further up," and although the stone face never actually moved, we got the feeling that he looked toward the cliffs above. "But before you ascend my mountain, I must discover if you are worthy. WHO IS YOUR GOD?"

I gestured my surprise with all of my limbs.

"I don't have a god," said Locke.

"Oh, my. Only the authority of certain gods can grant access to the passage above, whether I want to allow it or not. Very old covenants are at play. You cannot rise as a mortal alone." He could have easily stopped us too. He'd only have to shout—we wouldn't last long.

"Then I don't know what to do," said Locke.

"Who is your god?" the face repeated.

"I don't have one."

"Then you cannot pass. To do so is not within the power of mortals."

"But I have a princess to save," said Locke. "I have to do something."

"WHO IS YOUR GOD?"

"I really don't know." Locke paused, thinking. "If *truth* were a person, that would be my god."

"SHE IS A PERSON!" The everlasting mountains shook with the words. Locke's shout was quiet by comparison: "She is?"

"Yes. And on her authority, you may pass into this realm."

"Th-thank you," stuttered Locke.

"ON ONE CONDITION…" thundered the face, shaking everything. Locke retreated once again to the ground.

"You must swear, with the mountains as a witness, to be faithful to this god, though she might ask you to sacrifice your own mind, your own will, or your own soul."

Locke nodded—*she already had.*

"I swear this oath," he said, bowing.

63.

Salaminde

A CREVICE SPLIT THE gray walls of the mountain.
Red light shone from within, steadier and brighter than we'd seen in many days, and it fell on Locke's face as he hesitated on the threshold.

"We may find the villain here," I said.

"But I don't know how to use the sword yet." He gripped the sheath in his hand.

"Time for a daring leap."

On that word, we left the open world and its roof of darkness and entered the earth itself.

Because of the thick, unmoving walls, the claustrophobia beat down on me, even in these bigger caves. I focused on Locke—as long as he breathed, I'd be okay. Only breathing wasn't easy for him either. Each time he drew in, his temperature seemed to rise, and each footstep sunk us deeper into the heavy, sweaty air.

"I need water," he said.

"We may find some soon. The clairvoyance guided us here."

The floor was made of fire that had once bubbled and flowed, then had dried into solid, hardened lava, maintaining the shape of hot liquid, but gray, like ash. This surface had shattered, leaving great canyons and jagged edges running everywhere. In these cracks flowed rivers of lava, pushing heat up toward us. The angriest parts of these streams shone white hot, then faded into yellow, and then a bright fiery red as they bore against the crevice walls. The farther the lava strayed from the source, the more its surface became gray and flakey, already transforming from fire into earth. But beneath these cooling shells, the red still lurked.

Locke pulled a gnawed stick from the ground and threw it down onto the stream. It landed lightly on the ashen crust, not heavy enough to sink. Flames appeared out of nowhere, as if magically, all around it. Soon the stick burned amid high flames, turning to black ash as it shifted downstream with the lava.

"Why does the face guard this place?" Locke stepped over a small stream of lava, and his burned hand twitched inside its green bandage as he peered down. "Who would wander in here?"

"Us," I said.

"He's been stationed there forever, just to make sure we didn't sneak in." Locke backed up, took a run, and leaped over a larger crevice. He landed and looked back with a sigh of relief. "It's strange a realm of fire is guarded by a gnyme in the first place."

"Remember what he said about the lifeforces uniting? Maybe the Kyrose work together more than I thought."

"I'm *not* jumping over *that*," said Locke. In our mind, we heard a scream as if he'd missed a ledge and tumbled into the blaze.

"Why don't you try going that way?" I pointed to the wrong side and down toward a thin ledge.

Locke looked at his bandaged hand and couldn't help but feel fire covering his whole body. "Good idea. I'm feeling a little afraid of heights right now."

After climbing and leaping our way upwards, we came to a chamber designed by nature's master architect. We stood at the bottom of what appeared to be a rough-edged staircase. Various lava falls poured down from one platform to the next and then spread like fingers across the flat ground until they found a place to drop to the river of fire below. Several tall mounds, like pillars that didn't reach the ceiling, dominated the highest level. These poked up from the surface and spewed white ooze from their mouths. Above them heavy plumes of smoke rose, as if to complete the pillars, widening and merging and then escaping through the cracks in the ceiling.

I drew back with a gasp.

Something hovered above us, approaching eerily. It shone visibly.

A salaminde.

It looked like—no, *he* looked like a group of stars moving rapidly, tiny particles, hot and glowing, burning orange and yellow and white—each bursting into existence, zipping this way or that, and then disappearing. This chaotic pattern remained within certain boundaries, giving the creature a specific size and dimension. He edged toward us, silent, and the air behind and around him shimmered, though strangely he gave off no smoke. He was at least four times my height, and he created mesmerizing light.

"Locke," I whispered.

Locke glanced at me and then looked up. A sickening feeling poured through his stomach. "I see it." He knew the vulnerability of his situation—this salaminde could sow fire as easily as I could sow wind. The twins had told us gruesome stories of elves who'd been burned alive. Back then it seemed fascinating.

The salaminde paused almost directly above us, an ideal position for attack.

"Hello," said Locke.

The salaminde didn't answer.

Stane had used some strange sort of salaminde in the torch Shilohe had stolen. That was how she'd exposed herself to capture. Did this one serve him too?

"We come seeking water," said Locke.

The salaminde stared with ember eyes, still with no response.

I searched for hostility but could detect no expression. Maybe he expected me to talk, one elemental to another, rather than through my kynde. "My elfe needs water."

The salaminde didn't reply. Was he deciding whether to burn Locke alive? Finally he spoke, in a voice jagged and rough and heavy like a furnace: "To what end have you come?" The sound was a hot iron inscribing painful words onto the surface of our mind.

"The clairvoyance guided us here," I said.

The salaminde stared deeper. "You have no living water."

"No, we don't," I said. "But before we lost it, we mapped our course here."

The salaminde gave another moment's pause. "To what end have you come?"

I cringed, not sure what to say. If our words incited him, how could Locke defend himself? No water, no shield, no way to repel its wrath...

But something had happened to Locke in that fog. Something I didn't yet understand. Something that made him suddenly breathe the truth, without reserve, not counting the cost: "We're here to break the sky and free the tears of Numa, to restore life to our homeland, the Enchanted Wood."

The salaminde glared.

Locke took up his courage like a sword, speaking bold as Martigane: "And we're here to rescue the lands of our brothers the Tenarie too. And rescue a princess, a Goddess, from the hands of her captors. Even if that's you."

I gasped.

The salaminde smoldered, ready to devour, maybe about to unleash a firestorm. "You must answer this riddle," he suddenly said with his burning voice etching more deeply.

"Or else what?" I whispered.

Then came the riddle, with the heat of a furnace:

"One amulet bleeds hard as rock,
Another, soft as snow.
A third is light as air; a fourth
Is heavy; next is gold.

"The hero gives his own away
When blinded by a flame.
The amulet is broken and
His self becomes a shade."

The salaminde fell silent.

I expected Locke to give me a don't-give-it-away sort of look, so he could have time without me blurting the answer. Instead, his look was of panic. The answer, apparently, was not apparent. His eyebrows dropped as he focused.

The amulet was something golden. Or soft. Or hard. Something that bleeds. The clues seemed to contradict themselves. But they centered around the lifeforces: rock, snow, air, flame. I didn't like that blinded-by-a-flame part. Did that mean we *were* about to get cooked?

"Well?" asked the salaminde.

"Can you say it again?" asked Locke.

The salaminde obliged.

Locke bowed his head, staring at the rocky surface beneath his feet. The repeated words echoed in our mind as we awaited the unleashing of the firestorm.

"Well?" I asked.

Locke thought and stared, but the answer didn't come. "Gah, I don't know it," he whispered. "Do you?"

"No."

"Maybe he'll give us a hint," whispered Locke, "since cleverness isn't our heroic gift."

Oh—the heroic gift! "I know what it is."

Now he got the look in his eye. It said I shouldn't tell him, a sort of jealous look. I couldn't blame him for wanting to be the clever one. But knowing I knew was the opposite of helpful, and his thoughts raced everywhere but toward the answer.

"Well?" asked the salaminde, ready to burn us alive.

"*You* gave me the answer," I whispered to Locke. "Give up?"

"I guess. What is it?"

"You sure?"

"Tell me."

"A heart," I whispered. "Like your heart of gold."

"Oh." He thought about it, putting my answer into the rhyme. "Oh." He looked up at the salaminde. "In the riddle, the hero gave away his heart."

The reply burned without expression:

"Come with me."

64.

The Realm of Fire

WE FOLLOWED WARILY, climbing the architect's steps toward the white-hot bubbling pillars, then passing into another chamber where the temperature dropped slightly, to our relief. We found ourselves in a room that appeared to have been sculpted out of burning rock, with explosive curves leading to a charred ceiling.

Before I could fully take in the room, I heard Locke whisper, "*Demigods.*"

"I'm not sure you should—"

Then I saw what had caused him to curse.

A large creature rested his claws and wings on the floor, a featherless type of bird demon, much bigger than the one grandpa had on his wall. This was a dragon, *in real life!*

As terrifying as the beast was, his food gave us a more horrible feeling: the mangled, bloody corpse of an elfe, with golden hair stained dark red. The meaty, faceless body called out for help. Or warned us back.

The dragon turned and gave a threatening glare, pulling back his lips, revealing a smiling mouth covered in blood. Bright colors and dark stripes flecked the scales of his red lyzard body. He looked both lean and powerful. His four paws rested on the ground, claws pink with bloodstains.

Locke squeezed his sword-club tight, even knowing it would do no good.

We felt awe mixed with the terror too though. When we were younger, we'd pretended to be a bird demon—Locke was the body and I was the wings. Legends from the Lost Ages told how they mastered flying, and of elves who'd befriended them to gain access to the skies. Though my hovering was tethered to Locke, the memory of true flight lingered with me—something from a previous or future existence. Together we imagined it would be the greatest of all mortal experiences, and we longed for it, just as we longed for the Land of Song.

Maybe we'd find them both soon, after we confronted death's gate.

Locke's grandfather had tried to rein in our imagination. The legends, if true, were long past. Now bird demons, he'd taught us, were vicious predators. Just over a hundred years ago, during the Roshikoes War, the Kyrie and Tenarie agreed to suspend the fighting so they could face the bird demons—the beasts had killed more soldiers than the battles themselves. Massive sections of fields and forests had been burned too. Locke's grandfather also told us how he slew a gryphine terrorizing his grove. They sometimes came to the outskirts of the Enchanted Wood to hunt. We'd seen them in the sky on occasion, once close enough that we ran. And people said when Mr. Colrye's son went missing it was because a dragon ate him. But that hide on grandpa's wall was the closest we'd actually been to one.

At least till now.

The dragon on the floor in front of us spread his leathery wings, flapping them but not in flight—warning us to stay away from his kill, or maybe threatening us that we were next. His wingspan stretched toward forty feet, seemingly too big for his body, and making the room seem much smaller. A gray scar cut across his neck, which he lifted as he peered at us with his darting, snake-like eyes. But he didn't stand, and since we hadn't bothered the feast, he continued, clenching his teeth around the elfe's shoulder. We looked away, but the sound of cracking bones and tearing sinews still hit us, and, combined with the heat and thirst, Locke nearly collapsed on the floor.

After a moment of careful breathing, we looked up again. Our salaminde guide directed our gaze away from the monster toward a throne at the top of the room. Upon it sat another salaminde. *A strange sight.* No sylfe ever sat on a throne in the Enchanted Wood.

A wide crevice separated the ground where we stood from the rest of the room. For a flying creature, it would have been an easy leap. But Locke could only cross over a rickety bridge that seemed to have fallen mostly out of use. Strands of decaying rope hung down from it, pointing at the river of lava. A group of salamindes waited on the far side, watching to see what might happen next. Interestingly, none of them seemed to have kynde with them. *What good was a guide without some creature to lead?*

"Come!" said a voice, beckoning us across—it was the salaminde on the throne. His voice, like the other, communicated words by burning them into us.

Locke gripped the rope railing, fighting a tremble. He'd demonstrated his courage at heights before, but somehow the threat of burning alive seemed worse than breaking bones. The dragon watched, maybe curious if his next meal would be fresh or roasted. The board beneath Locke's foot creaked, as did the poles to which the ropes were fastened behind us. He kept his chin up, moving step by step, with the bridge swinging gently as he went. He jumped quickly onto the farther side and let out a quiet sigh, now within breathing distance of the giant dragon.

Everything near the King Salaminde seemed to shimmer back and forth, distorted by his presence. "What happened to you?" His voice burned hot and rough, so different from the smooth songs of a sylfe.

Locke frowned. It took him a moment to realize the salaminde referred to the toll our adventures had taken. His hand was burned. The Tenarie had beaten him. The Unstoppable Wraiths had beaten him too. Not to mention the miles, the thirst, and the wolves. His green tunic was tattered and torn. He looked more ragged than the forest folk from the tales.

"Prinkipae, darling, see to this boy's injuries," said the King Salaminde.

As soon as he said it, a crowd of the salaminde forms descended. Locke's eyes got wide as they drew in close. Their proximity made me anxious, so I squeezed in next to his heart and felt it beating rapidly.

"Relax. Please, relax," said the King Salaminde.

"What's going on?" Locke held his muscles tense and still. The heat from the troop of salamindes sunk into him and seemed to touch his soul rather than his skin. He breathed quicker as the sparks reached through muscle and bone. I felt all this through him, but I felt it myself as well, a different sensation than the physical warmth that permeated the caves.

"Your body possesses the power to heal itself," said the King Salaminde, "the spirit of life and rejuvenation, its lifeforce. These kind servants are simply speeding up that process, nothing more. You can relax."

Locke breathed methodically, while the sparks of the salaminde forms tingled as deep as his marrow. One enveloped his burned hand in particular, and gave him the sensation of a thousand needles tapping the skin. Another hovered at his shoulder, another at the scratches on his face.

"If you hadn't been dressed like you were, you might not be alive." The King Salaminde leaned forward into what might have been a wicked grin. "We don't let people approach the grave of Martigane casually. Now, what's your name?"

Locke looked at the sparks near his eyebrows. Then he refocused on the King Salaminde in front of him. "I'm Locke of the Enchanted Wood."

"Tell me why you are here."

"We came to break the curse on the skies." The salamindes continued to burn all around him.

"And?" asked the salaminde, appearing genuinely confused. His countenance was more easy to read, and I sensed no belligerence toward us.

"We want to restore peace to the land."

"What does that have to do with my realm?"

"We're looking for the source of the curse."

"It is not here."

"Then why are we here?"

"I am trying to ask you the same thing."

"We thought… A map led us here. And if the source is not here, then I don't know why we came. Is the Goddess here?"

"Which Goddess?"

"Is Princess Shilohe here?"

"No. Do you know where you are?"

"Mount Death."

"You are at the birthplace of the salamindes, where life first began, a place that has become a refuge for all types of bird demons." He motioned toward the monster sitting on the ground in front of him.

"I see." Locke watched as the salamindes surrounding him floated off, leaving in unison without having spoken a word, rising in a symmetric dance toward the ceiling. He pulled the soiled bandage off his hand. The scar looked as if it had been healing for weeks. He worked his fingers rapidly like playing a pinkalue. "It feels great!"

"You can thank the power of Phose which glows inside you. But still I am wondering why you are here."

"What we really need, I guess, is the living water. It's supposed to show us where to go. Only last time it led us here, which was the wrong place apparently, so I'm not sure it even works. Besides, I think it's too far, and we're out of water."

"We have water. Pantirae! Bring this boy food and drink! What do you mean it is too far?"

"It's inside the Well at the World's end, past the Majestic Sea and across the Khalune. It will take us at least three more days just to get there. By the time we return, the princess might be dead. And the Tenarie will certainly have attacked and burned my village. There's also an army of wraiths, and who knows how much damage they'll do in that time. The destruction is worse by the hour."

"I know why you are here."

"Why?"

"We salamindes are not connected quite so solidly to our kynde as you elves are to your sylves. But we *are* connected."

"I see…" said Locke with a confused tone; he actually didn't understand how this related.

"We are allies with the bird demons. With my help, you could be too."

"Oh." An image flashed across our mind of riding on a creature's back across the sky.

"They can travel twenty times your speed. Some of them can go days without landing, as long as migrating birds."

"You'd do that for me?" said Locke.

"Don't be too excited. It is risky." And when he said it, the King Salaminde nodded toward the dragon chewing on the corpse.

Locke swallowed.

"I can help you, but that doesn't guarantee you'll be successful."

The giant dragon suddenly stood, and Locke jumped—it was on the move. The beast left his meal and lazily walked behind Locke, who fought the urge to run up the throne's stairs. Soon the massive form had moved out of sight behind half-pillars of bubbling fire. But the dragon reappeared soon, holding something in his mouth—something like a thick, charcoal-colored stick. He walked straight toward us, and Locke's heart thumped. As the beast got closer, Locke stepped back, fighting to look dignified, but his fear overran his thoughts.

"They sense your fear. You're creating the relationship between the creature and yourself. Fear makes you the prey, which in turn makes him the predator. Calm your mind and you can change the relationship."

Locke almost spoke, but his throat felt tight, and a quiver seemed to have gripped his whole body.

The beast came closer. He stood tall as a banshe wolfe and much longer, with lips stained in blood. He gave off a distinct smell too, of sweaty, dry skin. He dropped his head and put the charcoal stick on the ground at Locke's feet.

"Thank you, Gantas," said the salaminde to the dragon. Then to Locke he added, "You're lucky he has just eaten. Of course, if I weren't here, he'd have probably killed you and saved you for later. Don't let fear make you the prey."

"I'm sorry. I don't know what you mean." Locke took a deep breath. The beast breathed calmly through black nostrils, then went back to gnawing on the corpse.

"Bird demons are sensitive. The way you regard them shapes the way they regard you."

"You mean…" But Locke trailed off, unsure what to say.

"Have you ever been afraid of your sylfe?"

"No. I don't think so. Not like facing one of these."

"Of course you haven't. Because you don't consider him a predator. But you feared my dragon."

"Because he could do *that* to me." Locke nodded toward the shredded elfe on the ground.

"Yes, but he hadn't and didn't, so your fear was worthless. Except that it made him think more seriously about eating you."

"But I…"

"You can't let a negative, imaginary future have so much control."

Locke nodded, looking down. His fear *hadn't* come true. "Okay."

A second bird demon appeared from an adjacent tunnel. She was much smaller, a baby by comparison, and was the same type that hung on grandpa's wall—a gryphine. Her body was covered in short, soft fur, and her wings were made of elegant white feathers. With her feline snout, she delicately carried a piece of browned meat in the tips of her teeth, which she dropped at Locke's feet next to the stick.

"They don't usually cook meat," said the salaminde.

"Thank you," said Locke.

The gryphine didn't leave after dropping the meat, as if expecting a reaction. Maybe Locke was supposed to eat it now. He reached down and picked it up off the stone floor, wondering what type it was, and trying to remember which side the creature had bitten. Locke took a bite—of lava grilled something—and the gryphine watched. The flavor and tenderness surprised him. Suddenly his hesitations disappeared, and he began to wolfe it down gratefully. The gryphine walked away, hopefully to get water, though I wasn't sure how she'd carry it.

"You know I don't care much for your Seer?" said the King Salaminde. "Or his predecessors. Bad blood. Why are you helping him anyway?"

"He's dead. I'm just trying to save the princess."

"I see. That I can understand."

"Why are *you* helping *me?*" asked Locke.

"For justice."

"Against whoever caused the curse?"

"Not *whoever.* An elfe who deserves a thousand deaths."

"I've seen him."

"Then you know he is evil."

"Yes."

"It is not the first time he has ravaged a land."

"Did he come to your realm?"

The King Salaminde looked at us, hesitating.

Locke opened his mouth to decline, and the King Salaminde began to speak:

"A band of his raiders kidnapped some of our cubs playing in the wilderness. We hunted them down and rescued all except the two they had murdered. We killed most of the raiders, but a few escaped. That's when we realized one of our cub's salamindes was missing. I suspect she is now being used for works of darkness—forced to heal an elfe unworthy of life, forced to mediate a covenant between the worst of gods and the worst of kynde. Forced to curse us all…"

I thought of the salaminde torch Shilohe had carried. And the Seer said a salaminde had written the covenant scroll. Was this the same creature?

The King Salaminde's countenance had fallen greatly, as if he'd experienced not a memory but the actual event. "While our salaminde is gone, her bird demon suffers on alone. Some have suggested we kill the bird demon and end the suffering. But I have hope we may yet find our lost salaminde. Now my hope rests on you." His voice smoldered as he finished, still painful in a way, though it had become more soothingly warm as we acclimatized to it.

Locke didn't know what to say. He bowed his head in reverence, and the sympathy was well expressed on his face.

"Pantirae will get you water on your way out," said the King Salaminde, his tone now shrouded in sadness. "Take the wand back to the open sky, where the mountain's shadow would fall in the evening sunlight." Locke bent and picked it up. "There's a large open meadow. Put the wand in the ground then set fire to it. That will call down the help you need. And remember, don't make yourself the prey."

"Thank you," said Locke.

"One more thing. The villain has power over elements and elementals. He can stop a bird demon's power to fly. That was why we couldn't defend our wilderness against him. He's dangerously powerful. Be cautious."

"I will. Thank you." Locke looked at the ground and then at the blazing king. "How can I repay you?"

"Don't thank me too soon," replied the salaminde.

Locke smiled at the ominous words.

"But bring back the sun's fire, and we will be more than repaid. Bring back our lost salaminde, and we will be in your debt."

65.

Bird Demons

I SMILED WHEN WE returned to the open air.
Not only had the King Salaminde given Locke water to drink, he'd also given him new water flasks, though I couldn't fathom why salamindes would have flasks on hand. Unless they belonged to the chewed-up elfe.

We found a meadow amid the Rueful Wilderness, due east of the mountain. There Locke wedged the wand into the crevice of a rock so it pointed skyward like a small tree.

"I'm not so sure about this salaminde magic," I said.

"You worried they'll outdo you?" Locke wiggled his healed fingers like a spider.

"That could never happen."

He built a small fire, and with that he lit the top of the black stick. At first, just a small wisp of smoke came out, gray like the Seer's voice, and not bigger than a sylfe. After a short pause, it coughed up red smoke. First just a little, then more and more, till it floated up in a heavy stream, widening and reaching toward the sky, a bloody trail to heaven. The smoke drifted gently to the west.

For a long time, nothing responded but the wind. Waiting, even under the dark sky, felt peaceful, especially after the King Salaminde's healing generosity. The sky thundered, interrupting the quiet. It grew louder too, like a child demanding to be heard.

Locke grabbed his scarred hand and pressed his thumb into the strange grooves in his skin—the shapes of scales. He picked up a grainy lava rock and rolled it across his palm. He felt no pain.

Soon we saw specks against gray sky. At first they hardly seemed to be moving. But they grew in size as they got closer, till we could see white, flapping wings and even tails. *Gryphines.*

"I'm starting to have second thoughts," said Locke.

Suddenly, they were life-sized, directly over us, wings blocking the sky like clouds. A great wind rushed upward, and Locke's hair flew back and forth. The first gryphine pounded into the ground, hitting hard right next to us. I wondered whether he'd lost control till the second hit with the same force, trembling the ground in a wave, again within breathing distance.

Our immediate impulse was to back away. Even me. Or to run. But the urge was outweighed—by paralyzing fear mixed with a small bit of courage. Both told us to stay.

The rest of the pride came down like thunder, one after another slamming into the cracking ground. Soon we were surrounded by a dozen gryphines. One of them sat down on the outskirts and watched timidly. Or sadly. The rest trampled around us in a circle. None of them had a salaminde nearby, which still seemed strange. Elementals were supposed to accompany all life, except the unwhole like banshe wolves and wrecches. And apparently bird demons.

Gryphines were cousins to dragons. Their wing feathers were a white falcon color. These had shorter snouts than the dragon, less sinister and more feline. Instead of dry scales, they had short fur, which varied from gray to gold, some sprinkled with dark splotches or streaks, but all of them shining like silk.

As Locke looked at them, he remembered the King Salaminde's council— they were sensitive enough to read his aspect and how he regarded them. He just needed to think of them as friendly, and not worry about them eating him. And not think about the popping sound the elfe's corpse had made as the dragon tore off its shoulder.

Oh no.

A white gryphine, his fur flecked with red and blue, circled. He seemed to be the biggest. His shoulder blades tilted his back one way and then the other with each step. When he caught Locke's eye, he let out a roar like a wildercat.

Then he sprinted in a dead rush at us.

Terror rushed through Locke, but he stood his ground, clenching his fists. The animal was coming. His paws tore through the dying grass.

Without moving his feet, Locke began to shrink back, and he held up his sword hand in a feeble gesture to stop.

The gryphine skidded, scrambling to undo his momentum, kicking up dust, nearly grazing us with a wing. Then he stood calmly a moment before turning and gesturing with his chin up and down in a sort of a *yes* gesture.

Locke still held out his scarred hand, as if that feeble wall might protect him.

The beast lifted his head, sniffing with wet, black nostrils, lips close enough to take a bite. His whiskers brushed Locke's skin. Then, instead of clamping his teeth down on Locke's fingers, the beast reached out his tongue and licked Locke's palm and the gaps between his fingers. The tongue dipped into the grooves of the scar left by the sword handle. When the licking stopped, Locke moved his hand onto the beast's nose and stroked the face gently, scales on fur.

The trampling around us stopped, and the gryphines stared. The leader walked casually away from us and sat down lazily, licking his paws. Another followed his example, and then another, till they rested on the ground in a circle around us, and the aggression blew away with the last bit of the red smoke.

Locke breathed in deep and long and let it out in a quick sigh.

These gryphines seemed smaller and youthful—a pack of cubs. When Locke noticed this, he smiled. They weren't his enemies, but he'd realized this almost too late.

One of them remained standing. When everything was calm, she darted one way, and then turned sharply, scrambling on sliding feet. She ran up to us, head bouncing back and forth, and put her muzzle right in Locke's face, ready to lick him, or smile his face off. Her breath was sharp. She pressed closer, wagging her tail, till Locke nearly fell back onto the ground.

He pointed and commanded, "Back! Back!"

She dropped her head in shame, but the shame only lasted a half a moment before she darted back amongst the crowd, knocking a rock with the tip of her nose and then chasing after it. When she caught up to it, she leaped over it back and forth.

I wanted to bite her nose and shout at her to calm down. "I hope that doesn't mean she chose us," I whispered.

The others mostly ignored us now, cleaning themselves or napping. Except for one, the one that had first sat down. Her fur was a beautiful bright gold, nearly the same color as Locke's hair. She watched us with one eye, her head bowed, almost as if in shame. When Locke looked at her, she looked away.

"She's sad," said Locke.

"Maybe she's humble," I suggested. "Or unsure."

Locke kept his gaze in that direction, and when the gryphine looked back, Locke smiled. Her head dipped, but her black lips pulled wide, exposing her fangs, like a brief grin.

Locke took one step and watched for a response. The bird demons paid no attention. He dragged his feet on the next step. A couple of them glanced casually at him, but that was all. The boisterous one, dancing her head up and down, came toward him, as if eager to continue some game. But Locke waved a palm toward her, and said, "No! No!" She seemed to get the message, going off to play while the others watched.

The melancholy one shrunk further into the ground the closer we got. While many of the others stretched their wings out, this one tucked them in close. She had black marks above each eye, like teardrops falling upwards. Where actual teardrops would form, she had black lines streaking toward the end of her nose in a beautiful pattern that made her look both wild and forlorn.

Locke edged forward.

The anxious beast stood, as if to run, but she didn't. She didn't turn toward us either. She simply stood, looking with those sad eyes and bobbing her head, breathing heavily, and shifting her weight. She was standing on only three feet. Her wrong front paw hung in the air, as if for protection, maybe broken or injured. I couldn't help but wonder—what conflict had she been in and why hadn't the salamindes healed her?

Locke reached out and petted the creature. Her fur was soft like the finest pillow; it grew slightly longer on top of her head and down her neck in a subtle mane. She held rigid at first, but slowly she softened, and the breathing of her ribcage slowed. Finally she turned her head and began to lick Locke's hand, and the warm spit and the rough tongue tingled. When the beast stopped her licking, Locke stroked the fur of her head and the skin behind her ears.

"Can I..." began Locke.

The gryphine looked at him as he spoke.

"Can I climb on your back?"

She looked forward again, perhaps a little frightened. Locke was too. Still, he grabbed her soft mane and held tight, which she didn't seem to mind.

He leaped, pulling his leg over the creature's spine. With her paws spread powerfully over the ground, the beast held him even with an injured leg.

A sudden breeze picked up around us, strengthening into a gale, moving with greater and greater ferocity in the direction she was pointed, as if she magically controlled Numa's power. The wind pulled Locke's hair toward her, whipping it back and forth, and then his green hood popped up and covered his head.

The gryphine twisted her powerful neck, showing us her regal profile. She looked at Locke with a solemn mouth but a smile in her eyes. Locke pushed his hood behind his head and smiled back. She showed her approval by flipping her tail, and the dark tassel at the end whipped back and forth. She was our friend from that moment on.

The gryphine spread her white wings beneath us in a fantastic array.

The others, still sitting, watched carefully. With their silent approval, our gryphine began to run with the wind, dipping down on every fourth beat to protect her injured leg. Her speed surprised us.

Locke gripped her mane with both hands, squeezing his legs around her sides. At a distance, she'd seemed massive and threatening. Beneath Locke's knees, she felt thinner—powerful but lean. Her shoulder blades spiked and dropped with her steps, and her skin shifted over the cycling landscape of her tight muscles. She picked up speed, and the ground flew in a blur beneath us.

The wind pushed even harder, swooping upward, and the creature's spine lifted. As it did, all stability vanished.

We broke free of the ground's grip.

And rode on the shoulders of the wind.

Scroll Four

66.

A Triad in Flight

W E ACCELERATED TOWARD the dark sky.
The wind pushed into Locke's face and nose. "Oh, gah…" he began. As the ground sunk, so did his stomach. The white trees of the Rueful Wilderness shrunk to a mass of brownish gray far below. Locke gripped the bird demon's mane till his fingers turned white.

"Breathe, Locke."

The magic of breath flowed back through him, and his whole mortal frame relaxed, including his knuckled grip. For a small moment, the flight matched the beauty of his dreams. He felt safe, as if the air had embraced him securely—something it could never do.

"That's a good girl," shouted Locke, patting the creature with his shield hand.

The ground looked strangely different now that we were above it instead of on it. It was a detailed map, too small and strange to be our world itself.

The gryphine dropped.

Locke lifted off the creature's spine. As he did, he hooked his heels underneath her wings, to keep from flying off altogether. The sickening feeling now came back up, and he crushed the fur of her mane in his fists. The wind rushed so hard that breathing required extra focus. His hair swirled wildly. Together we plummeted straight for the ground, me soaring behind, trying to stay within breathing range.

Locke was at the mercy of the bird demon—he didn't know how to control her. Suddenly he started what sounded like a prayer: "Oh, demigods, oh please, oh please, oh please…"

The creature fell and the ground rushed up, for too far and too long. The trees were becoming huge. Locke wondered again and again whether it was too late for her to pull up.

Then she did.

The weight of his shoulders and arms pulled down, under the grip of a gnyme, and Locke gritted his teeth, his muscles tensing as he braced himself against the ground's power, fighting to breathe. The beast turned skyward, blasting higher with a rush of wind beneath.

When the upward curve ended, Locke's weight decreased to its normal size. He relaxed and started breathing. But, worrying it wouldn't last, he fought to keep his voice steady as he shouted, "Hey, I don't know how well you understand, but can you take it easy on those, uh, those drops?"

The bird demon banked wrongward, and during the turn she twisted her neck enough to look at Locke. Had she understood?

She dove again, and Locke's teeth snapped together, and a *guh* came from his throat. This time, the downs and ups were smaller, like riding the waves of the sea.

"I'm not sure the princess would like this," shouted Locke.

I shouted back through the rushing wind: "You're the one causing all this strain. You're holding on too tight. Wind doesn't cower to brute force, so stop fighting it. With some finesse, you can move with it and let it move you when it needs to."

He nodded and made an effort to relax over the next few bumps. He breathed, his grip loosened, his legs fell slack, and he smiled under the frowning sky. He noticed the beauty of the ground below and the air rushing past. The speed itself might've been the best part—so much faster than we'd ever moved. *Such freedom.*

As if to apologize for squeezing so tightly, he let go with one hand and patted the soft fur of her side: "Okay, okay. Good girl. I trust you now."

When the bird demon started into a long curve, Locke's hand snapped back to its grip on her mane. But he recognized the tension this time and loosened up. The creature's spine leaned to the right, and so did Locke. The curve pulled his weight in the opposite direction, deeper into the saddle, securing him sideways in the same way we were usually secured to the ground. He didn't really even need to hold on.

The gryphine held her head nobly, gazing with feline eyes over the landscape while her white wings pointed across the breadth of the sky, claiming it all as her domain.

"Ha ha!" laughed Locke aloud—the kind of breath more valuable than all others. With this feeling, he stopped being afraid. It didn't matter that he was hanging in the air—he was free—he was alive.

As for me, I felt like I was finally home.

67.

Temple Reprise

OUR BIRD DEMON owned the skies.

If claustrophobia meant falling as low as a soul could go, she brought us to the height at the opposite end—to an unbound freedom.

After Locke had gotten a feel for riding, he pointed toward the horizon in the direction of the World's End, and shouted, "That way!" She glanced back, seemed to understand, and turned our course immediately. It still seemed surreal, particularly for Locke, as he rested on her back. She'd become our own little earth, and beyond her was nothing but empty air and clouds.

"What will we call you?" said Locke.

She didn't reply.

Inside the Burning Mountain, the King Salaminde had commanded the bird demons, maybe through a power beyond voice. They'd responded to him but never with words.

"Something to do with her mastery of sky," I suggested.

"Valkalyse," said Locke in a whisper drowned by the sough of the wind.

It was the right name. *And so beautiful.* She was indeed like the daughters of Thaese, guiding the noble deceased to a fitting reward in the hereafter. In fact, it wasn't too far from what she was about to do for us. Her pointed ears could almost be her winged helmet. I smiled.

"Valkalyse it is then." Locke patted her back.

She purred then peeked back with those black-tear eyes and gave what looked like a grin, having left her melancholy back on the ground.

Locke made up a game where he'd steer by tapping her sides with his toes or by stroking up or down. Next he had me take the lead to steer her, and she went along—very intelligent. I went a little overboard with my newfound freedom, but Locke managed to stay in the saddle. We three made quite the team.

After the acrobatics were over, we sailed on in earnest for our goal, driving eastward across the vast sky road with the speed of the wind. We felt eager to see the monk again, expecting his wisdom to fill the void left by our Seer.

The Majestic Sea spread far below, and, *wow*, from this high, it did look like the wing of a bird demon. The sun might have been setting behind us, but the clouds maintained their gloom—no water dared fall and no light dared break. Life remained hidden behind the rolling blackness far above. From here we could see our homeland in the distance, and we thought of Nicke and Shaye. At least we saw light in their futures… so long as we could break the curse before the Tenarie attacked and the wraiths overran the whole land.

"I wish the princess could be here," said Locke. "I think she would like flying after all. I wish I could at least talk to her and explain. It's like the Isles of Time—we're living her story."

Locke tried to get Valkalyse to land for a break, but she seemed to insist on persevering. She sailed on the wings of the wind through the night, while Locke dozed. After many hours, the temple of the Well appeared in our view.

When we landed, the wind aided us again, rushing up as we came down. Valkalyse pounded heavily into the stone, and Locke dismounted. The beast's sweat had soaked the insides of his pants. Fortunately, Shilohe and Shaye were not around.

Across the terrace, the plants grew lush and beautiful, but now they were surrounded by gore—shocking gore. Pieces of the bodies of full-grown wraiths lay all around, black hands lying here, eyeless heads lying there, and severed spines in between. Black blood was spilled into pools and streams all over the stone. Their cold still haunted the air. To our surprise these wraiths had not been staked down, but they didn't need to be: Not one moved. They were dead without being scorched by sunlight.

"When I lopped off one's head, even that wasn't enough to stop its life…" I just shrugged.

Valkalyse panted, exhausted from enduring so long. She almost immediately flopped down and took the weight off her leg.

Locke looked her in the eyes and said, "We need you to stay, okay?" As he said this, he pointed to the ground. She looked carefully at him, but didn't acknowledge in any way.

"Too bad she doesn't have an elemental we could talk to." When I said this, Valkalyse turned, pointed her snout straight at me and stared, as if she had something to say. But after a moment of staring, she blinked and put her chin on the ground, looking up at us with drooping eyes.

"That's good. Good girl. You wait. We'll be back soon."

As we approached the doors of the temple, Locke stepped carefully among the carnage. Boot prints, made in blood, marked the footwork of a mighty warrior as he danced and poured out his wrath on these fallen enemies.

Then we saw him. The warrior who had done this.

The blind monk.

Never again would I hear the sparkling sands of his rough voice.

He leaned with his back against one of the temple's double doors. His head was bowed with his chin resting against his chest, showing us his dark-skinned skull. His eyes were now closed, hiding their murky grey color. The black pools that covered the terrace reached their hellish tentacles toward his still dripping boots. Blood marked the monk's white cloak with deep crimson. His shoulder was shredded. He had vicious teeth marks in his neck. Yet in one hand he still held his sword, a magnificent silver blade with an intricately designed hilt. In the other, he held the stem of a small blue flower, pinched between two fingers that rested above his knee, as if he were offering it.

We wondered how a man without sight had fought off such a vast army of these relentless monsters—a blind hero against a blind horde. He'd kept them out of the temple, it seemed. And then the valkalysae had carried him home.

A tear rolled down Locke's cheek as he crouched and accepted the gift. His skin brushed the dead hyuman's fingernails. Locke rolled the flower carefully into the leather map for protection and put it away.

Our entire land was up against the same foe. Each day the curse wore on, more people would die. More *good* people, like this venerable monk.

His sylfe must have still been here, waiting in dead silence to hear the song of his name. I expected the monk would return as soon as he could—he seemed like that sort of kynde. When I looked at his calm expression, a pang of sadness hit me, and I wished I could cry. His words had helped me—his encouragement in saying I had a role to play. Words I would yet hang on to.

Locke gritted his teeth and wanted to hit something. "How much longer till this happens to everyone?"

68.

Ascension

THE GIANT DOORS clanked as they closed behind us.

The room was much darker than when we'd left. Light no longer shone from the floor, walls, and balustrades—the pool itself was the single source. But amid those vast walls, we again heard and felt the white song, pure and full, ringing with holiness.

We walked down the platform toward the pool of living water. Blue light flickered on the floor. This time I noticed the etching representing the lifeforces merging into one—flesh, blood, breath, and light. Next the statues drew my attention: four Kyrose standing on pedestals in a circle around the pool, high above, with black scorch marks on them and vines growing at their feet, flickering with blue.

Of these four statues, Phose stood highest, his arms stretched evenly forward and outward. His face tilted down to gaze directly into the eyes of anyone who dared approach the gift he'd given to Nara. His fingers reached gently outward, as if casting light, or maybe inviting the onlooker into an embrace. Although no light came from the stone, his stance seemed to glow, as if fire honored him even when it was absent.

Nara sat childishly upon a stone wave like a chair, her knees touching, with one foot hiding coyly behind her other leg. Her shoulders tilted with the motion of her arms, one finger pointing down into the depths of the living water where she gazed, and her other arm floating gracefully above her head, her fingers pouring down like rain. This temple had been built for her.

Gaie rested on one knee, with his hands and one foot planted firm on the ground. His arching back and the sinews of his neck reflected the posture of a mountain. His eyes shone with power, ready to leap like a carnivore in the blink of an eye.

Numa floated next to him, most majestic of all, her right knee bent and her wrong leg flowing gracefully behind her, toe pointed, a sculpture so beautiful it seemed to lift skyward. Her arms flowed back, and her spine curved forward. Her fingers rested on a breeze, and her magnificent wings reached up, commanding the winds and all breath to follow. Her image stirred something in me, that strange longing we could never quite capture with words. The feeling flowed deep in me, like a song ready to burst into light.

I wished these four statues had the powers of the wrecches, that they would break forth out of their stone shells and appear before us animated in glory. We could surely use their help. But they remained still, silent as the skies.

Beneath the forms of these four divinities, we approached the pool of living water a second time, and I suddenly recalled the statue of Saede, the fifth Kyrose, lurking in the pit below.

I gazed at the statues as Locke and I spoke the words with one voice: "Dyn meis, Thaese, dyn meis, all to enoma siou doesi ta daksa."

The feeling came again, a sense that something had changed, though initially it was only something we felt. Suddenly the basin spilled over, and instantly the floors and walls ignited again, ribbons of blue running in strips, up and down and side to side, covering every dimension of the majestic temple.

As the blue light fell on his skin and green tunic, Locke stepped up to the pool with determination on his face, leaning forward so he could see his own reflection. The flames reached up around him, pressing azure toward his temples. First he saw our home, the cove. Black, eyeless shapes wandered through it, breaking and tearing, and yellow flames roared all around. He saw blood too, red and spreading. What he saw next was more horrible still: the tortured form of Shilohe, the Goddess, now bound in flames, screaming in pain with her arms stretched to the sides as she hung in agony.

"We've got to hurry!" Locke pulled the phanos lamp from his pack. He held the handle and dipped it into the roiling flames. The substance flowed into the glass bowl. But when he lifted the lamp, the blue light dripped from the cracks, out of the glass, and merged back with the body of blue. "It's leaking."

"Try again."

He did, this time pressing the bowl with two hands to seal the cracks tight. But after he scooped it into pool and lifted it up, the light flowed out of the lamp again. "She's in trouble, Picke. I think he's killing her! We have to do something!"

I looked at him in desperation, not knowing what to say.

"I have to get the clairvoyance," said Locke. "We're so close. She's going to die!"

He began testing ways to carry the watery light. He dipped his hair, the pommel of the white sword, and even her amulet into the pool. But the water wouldn't stick to any of these. He reached his naked hand out, inching toward the flames—his shield hand, just in case. The heat rose to touch his skin, waves of shimmering blue vapor. When the burning reached the edge of what he could bear, he darted his hand down and pinched at the ephemeral substance, trying to hold it.

"Aaaah!" he shouted, falling back. His thumb and finger smarted, and a gentle pain stabbed at him with every pulse of his heart. "Not again," he said, panting. "I don't know what to do." He bowed his head and squeezed his freshly burned fingers, pressing them to his lips. "I guess I wasn't meant to carry the living water."

"You can't quit now. We're so close."

"I have no lamp, and without the water…" Locke's vision blurred as he stared at the flames jumping up and down. Maybe he was right. Maybe this was as far as we were meant to go. "I can only hope some worthier hero is fighting his way to the villain—some unknown hope. Maybe one of the Chief Captain's men survived." He shook his head, doubting, and backed down away from the pedestal, away from the horrible story it reflected.

For some reason, that comment reminded me of Martigane and how he approached his end with fire. More importantly, it reminded me what his heroic sylfe did, just before they died. Martigane wasn't just a myth—we knew that now. I looked at the statues above and around us, at Numa's beautiful figure ascending into the sky. Nara, sitting on her wave, caught my attention. She was pointing at the pool.

An invitation.

"Locke, did you…"

He snapped out of his trance. "What?"

I started to feel it again, holy winds pulling on me, drawing me to the pool. The fear arrived too, and I worried I might see as fully as I had before—that rush of terrifying joy. I didn't exactly want to, but its pull was too strong.

I moved above the rippling flames.

Just as before, I saw my splitting reflection and an ocean of revelation, all in an instant.

I saw the futility of trying to hold on to Locke tighter than his choices or tighter than death. I saw my imposter obsession with the moment—with instance and presence and urgence—and how I'd never taken the ultimate dare. I saw my shallow intentions to *get* charisma and influence, to *receive* honor and respect, and how these fell infinitely short of heroically *giving* them. These truths pounded into me with great force, all at once, messages simple and profound.

Then I heard a voice.

A voice I'd longed to hear since the day I was named. The voice of my mother, Numa, Demigoddess of Air. Her breath caressed like wind and reached wide as the sky: *I want to give you eternity,* she said. *But you must give up your brief life in exchange.*

She fell silent once again—a hushed statue flying over flames. Her words echoed deep within me, relentlessly, while her sister pointed continually into the blue flames.

Trade my life for eternity.

I suddenly remembered my desperate prayer in the abyss after I'd drawn what I thought was my last breath. I'd been alone, abandoned, and falling into stillness. I hadn't even spoken the words. I'd only thought them in a last plea for help, a plea for another chance to become significant. I'd said I would do anything.

Anything.

At first the memory surprised me, coming at this of all moments. But then I realized I'd been given just that—the very thing I'd asked for. Another chance. I'd wanted charisma and influence, wanted to be substantial. Now was my test, to take the ultimate dare, to see if I was one in seven, to see if I was actually willing to *give*.

"I'm going to see if I have the gift, Locke."

His head jerked up in surprise. "What?" He looked carefully, perceiving my meaning with a worrisome stare. And he saw Dagonae wandering madly, drooling, eager to bite. "But how do you know you're one of the ones?"

"I don't."

"If you're not, you'll die. You'll be crushed, just like Tyne." He was right.

I'd be smashed between the fluctuating layers that divided the domains, shattered into incoherent, messy pieces.

"And *you'll* go mad," I said. Driven out of his mind, left to die alone, or killed by other elves—dying without a purpose and without rescuing anyone.

"Are you ready to die?" he asked.

"We're both going to die, whether we're ready or not and whether this works or not."

"But not now. I can't do it alone. I can't go on without you."

He was right. We might lose *now*. We might lose everything, everything short of legend. But I had to try. Just like Cree before he and Martigane died. "Then let's hope it works."

Locke nodded. He understood. I had to do this for him. And for me. And for the Goddess. And for Nicke and Honke and Shaye and everyone else, even Tryse. I had to do this so Locke could do what he had to do—for them. But the hesitation lingered in his eyes.

"I've feared this my whole life," I said. "Even mentioning it makes me sick. I couldn't bear being separated from you again, especially not before we've fulfilled our purpose."

"I know, Picke. So why are you doing this? Why now?"

Hovering above the living water, I looked at him. "This is the moment, my destiny maybe—fate's offering now. Time to leave a mark and show fear it's not in control." *Or have the world leave its mark on me.* "After all," I said, repeating words from Shilohe's speech, "what good is a life not given to others?"

That made him smile—a smile that broke through the fear—even knowing I was about to leap off a cliff.

And on that breath, I descended toward the pool.

As I went, I remembered the countenance of the Seer's sylfe as he was ripped away from this world. His haunting expression, his desperation, his need for the breath that death had stolen. I'd been on the verge of that same place. Now I stood at the threshold again.

I looked down, and my reflection—a being made of many possible futures and pasts—stabbed up at me. Its lances plunged deep into my soul. *You will die.* But I held my resolve, still descending, till I was just above the surface. I felt, or thought I felt, the heat rising up from the flames toward me—my body. *You will die.* Locke was standing away, so it couldn't have been the heat reaching him; *I* was feeling it myself. I dropped so I was lying with my face close to the basin and my feet above, a breath away from the living water. *You will die.* I spread my hands across its surface and tried to feel the rise and fall of the waves—like flames.

Then I bowed my face into the tremulous substance and inhaled.

YOU WILL DIE!

Mountains of sensation hit me all at once. It was not peaceful.

First of all, I didn't drink it—I couldn't—not like I'd felt Locke do with fresh springwater a thousand times. I breathed it in, deep, and I felt the heat flow into me, burning. Then I zoomed in the direction opposite of dizziness, toward too much unwanted stillness, just like in the abyss. The world and my head became too stable and too slow. Too little motion. Jarring. Clamping down. Making me sick.

Then falling. I was falling. And Locke was falling too, along with the temple. They were falling up while I was falling down.

"Locke, no! Stay close! Please!"

"PICKE!"

My thoughts were ringing.

I'd always doubted whether anything could truly stand still. Yet suddenly stillness was overtaking me. So still I felt sick. Trapped in a small, finite space. Pressing me too tightly from every direction, leaving no room to breathe.

I gasped.

And things started to change.

The world thinned around me. Sensation began to steady.

I felt my physical location. I was in the pool. Breathing. Rising out of living water.

"Picke?"

I turned and looked at my elfe. "What?"

"You're blue," he said.

I looked at the span of my wings, my hair floating upward, and my hands. *What happened?* Nobody, not even ondines, had such small hands.

"Picke?"

I was supposed to be bigger than this. I *was* bigger than this. "How could I even fit inside this... this... *form?*"

"You've always been that size."

"No, look at me. My wings…" I didn't know what to say. Maybe I *had* always been this size, only that size felt much smaller than it used to. *So small.*

"You're blue!" Locke laughed.

"I've always been blue."

"No you haven't."

"How would you know?" But I did feel like I was a little bluer than normal, or a more substantial blue, and I felt strange, blue tears in my eyes.

"I can see you with my actual eyes now, Picke, and your color is blue. Kind of a glowy blue, maybe azure. Not like you've ever looked before."

"Does it look funny?"

"It's… a lot different."

I turned my head, sizing up my wings and all the rest. "I touched it."

"And you didn't shatter." He smiled at me. The separate me. The one-in-seven, heroic me. The me he was glad to still have around.

With his joy, I broke free of the chains around my essence, soaring fast above the water, turning in circles.

And the glow of living water trailed behind me.

69.

Clairvoyance

A FLAME SHINED FROM me.
Light that touched the world, illuminating everything, changing our vision, giving us that strange feeling of being familiar with our future.

Memories had disappeared when Stane's dark sylfe put out the flame. Now they returned. Locke had put a bloody mark on the map, leading us to the salamindes and Valkalyse. It had led us to Shilohe too, shining in our desperate need.

Now that same light shined *from* me, *for* Locke. I was his lamp, and he was my see-er. He was the hero, and I was the herald, drawing enemies and calling allies, a causer and ender of wars, as our blind monk had said. But the monk lay dead among wraiths, leaving my questions without answers. Could a sylfe extinguish the fire inside me? And would that extinguish me as well? I had no idea what I'd become.

I glowed like a salaminde, which meant I'd gained some of the lifeforce of light.

I reached my hands to the sides to sense their capability. Fire and air weren't substantive, but water and earth were. And if I'd inhaled light, then I'd inhaled water too—lifeblood. I felt its corporeal weight hanging on my shoulders, running through my arms and wings. I darted and felt myself moving thickly—not simply *as* air but *through* air, a form, *my* form, made of frighteningly cohesive particles.

As an elemental, I'd embodied one lifeforce. But I didn't have four now, like a kynde. I only had three, like the unwhole: The banshes were bloodless; the wrecches were breathless; the wraiths were soulless. And the specters, which elves became when they died, were like me, formless, ghosts without body or bone.

And there was no undoing what had been done.

"Let's go outside and make sure it works." Locke started toward the exit, and I followed.

He was right—I was no phanos lamp. I carried the living water inside me. *Or something.* But I wasn't doing it in the same way—I could tell at least that much—and maybe to a smaller degree as well.

We burst back through the doors and onto the temple's porch. Across the terrace, the black blood shined amid chunks of carnage. On our right the sheer cliffs of the World's End fell forever toward the Sea of Mist. On our wrong side stood the Burning Mountain, far in the distance. Beyond the dead wraiths, Val's chin rested sadly on the terrace tiles, with her drooping, teardrop face. When she saw us, she scrambled to her feet and wagged her dark-tasseled tail fiercely, apparently refreshed and ready for more.

Locke nodded his farewell to the monk. We crossed the butchered wraiths toward the pilgrim's path.

Something needled at me.

"Locke!"

He stopped and looked with wide eyes.

"I can feel the stabbing pain in her injured leg."

"What?"

"I can feel Val's pain. Like I always feel your pain—I can feel a tingle in your newly burned fingers. But now I'm feeling the gryphine's pain too."

"You mean…"

"Her limp. It's painful—it's in her ankle."

Locke looked at me with his mouth open, as if to deduce the attributes of his new sylfe. "What have you gotten yourself into?"

I shook my head.

Locke chuckled.

"What?" I asked.

"It's odd that you of all people would feel others' pain." He grinned.

"Shut up." *Had I been cursed with empathy?* All this from answering Nara's one, small invitation.

"Don't take this wrong, Picke, but I want you to try something."

"What?"

"Just fly away from me. Maintain eye contact, but see how far you can go."

Even hearing him suggest it, I constricted, fighting for breath. But curiosity needled at me too. So I did it, breathing through the fear.

I took off, flying straight up, and blue followed in a trail behind me. At first slowly, maybe fifteen feet, which was pushing it. My breathing became labored, but I went on. And on. And I soon realized the shortness of breath came from panic, not from the distance. Soon I was far away, fifty feet, maybe a hundred, and still going. Locke stood far below, smaller than a sylfe, a speck on the black-bloody terrace. Even the cliff started to look small, as if the whole earth was mostly the Sea of Mist. I'd nearly reached the black canopy of clouds, yet I was still breathing.

No more teather. No more link between me and Locke. Just freedom. This scared me. It meant I could limp along on three lifeforces, alone. But I didn't want to be a specter, didn't want to be alone. I wanted to be an elemental. I wanted to be Locke's elemental. Then I realized: I hadn't *lost* one part. I'd *found* two. And maybe that mattered. Maybe it meant I could stay with Locke, could be his elemental by my own choice now, accompanying him to the end.

I looked eastward and saw the lightness of the sun behind clouds: the morning of the nineteenth day. To the west, five giant dust demons swirled across the surface of the Khalune Desert which lay flat and gray before the pale Wisting Mountains.

Then I noticed something else. "Hey, Locke, you see that?"

But at this distance, he couldn't hear me.

I rushed in a streak of light back to his immediate presence—*so soothing to be near him.*

"That was amazing," said Locke.

I smiled, landing on his shoulder and pointing. "You see that?"

At first he thought I was pointing to the long, thin dust demons, which stretched nearly from the ground to the blanket of clouds.

"Try closing your eyes."

He did, and our mind reached out to feel all present sensation. The sough of the wind trickling gently across the bridge of his nose, through his hair, and past his ears. The soft thump of his own heart beneath his ribcage, which filled and dropped, breath after breath. The metal scent that wafted through the air from my dip in the living water. Feeling all these, we had no mind left for memories or conjectures of the future.

And the path became clear as day.

Like waving a torch in a dark cave, the light lingered in a trail, an image burned so deep it shined through closed eyelids, accompanied by a ringing note, a perfectly mild sound that penetrated our soul. We saw the memory of our path into the future, a seam of bright blue. It didn't lead across the ground like before. It led through the air, a skyway soaring back to the Burning Mountain. But not to the base, to the top, where the rock vanished as it ascended above the clouds.

Locke opened his eyes and stared at me. "Picke, I feel more connected to you now, not less. If you were to stop breathing, I think I would too. And if you left me, I think *I* would die this time, *I* would fall into stillness."

At that thought, he glanced homeward, wishing he didn't have to die. And he remembered the vision the pool had shown: fire in the Enchanted Wood. Locke gasped as his fears showed Tenarie warriors and their adopted Honke marching south in the name of the Demigod of Fire. The Unstoppable Wraiths from the Burning Mountain and the Kyrie warriors would be there too—three mighty armies colliding on our home, slicing and gutting, leaving a trail of corpses and ash. They would bash down the gate of our cove and leave no survivors.

Rage built inside him like a fire. He was tempted to fly home. To try to save Nicke, and Shaye, and his father and brothers. And maybe Honke too.

I flew a trail from Locke pointing to Val's back. "Come on! If we break the sky, it will release the rains and sunlight, like the face said. Maybe if we hurry we can save them."

Locke nodded and strode toward his bird demon.

I looked at him with admiration. "I have to tell you, Locke. I tried to tell you before, but your heroic gift isn't your swimming. It's your compassion."

He gave me an embarrassed look.

"The way you treated Nicke and Honke. And even Valkalyse."

"Why are you bringing this up?"

"I just want to say it while I still can."

"Say what?"

"A sylfe could ask for no greater kynde. I'm honored to accompany you, no matter what we find down our path unknown."

He nodded but didn't smile.

As he closed his eyes, the clairvoyance rung clear—a seam of blue, through the sky to the top of the Burning Mountain. There we hoped to find the villain, free Shilohe, and give our life to save our home and the whole Land of Many Waters. Though we didn't know exactly how it would happen, our doom and our glory awaited at the end of this trail.

"We'll keep the light of the Goddess burning," I said. "She'll become the new Seer, and who knows how many other people she may inspire."

The Shining Sword angled across Locke's back as he climbed on Valkalyse. I felt like I was seeing them both for the first time: a pair as majestic as the heroes of legend.

I floated in blue above him. "Let's go meet our destiny."

Locke gazed ahead toward the clouds. "For the Goddess," he said with a stern grin.

Amid a huge gust of wind, Valkalyse leaped into the sky.

70.

Approach

I wish I could tell the princess we're almost there," said Locke.
The Burning Mountain brooded in the distance, a rock so tall it pierced the sky.

"And I'm sorry, again, for abandoning you." Even with a hint of sadness, Locke's heroic eyes shined.

"I forgive you a thousand times," I said.

Val pressed on like she was made of steel, with a will stronger than any mortal frailty. She took us across the desert and the wilderness without stopping, pulled along in the powerful stream of the wind.

Locke managed to drop off to sleep, slumped forward onto Val's neck. That made me laugh—he could sleep even on his way to die. Her fur was smooth and warm and increasingly sweaty. When he came to, we'd nearly reached the mountain. The crevices and angles and fallen ledges grew in size and foreboding. Though we felt fondness for the King Salaminde and his hospitality, these upper reaches reminded us of the mountain's nickname, Mount Death. Though they said life had begun here, we knew it would end here too.

"They say no creature without wings has ever scaled the slopes," I said.

"I'll bet Val could do it."

"Val has wings!"

"Yeah," said Locke, "but I think she could climb it without wings. Have you seen her claws?"

"But even if she didn't use her wings, it still falls within the parameters of the saying."

"Picke, we're flying to our death, and you're arguing with me over words."

"We're not flying to our death. We're flying to our greatest triumph." But even as I said it, I felt the torrents raging inside. I was afraid—the thought of something worse than death had begun to haunt me: Now that

I'd become—whatever I was—would I even die if Locke gave his life? Or would I live to tell the tale? The thought of going on without him nearly crushed me.

"At least I'll be fulfilling a purpose," he said. "Maybe that's why I never found a profession or a wife."

I wanted to cry. "You're fulfilling the greatest purpose, Locke—becoming a hero."

"Well, we're not there yet. Not till we play the final chord."

Valkalyse carried on, further and further up, closer and closer to the peak.

When I thought she couldn't go any higher, she took us higher still, till clouds began to whisk past Locke's ears. We labored to breathe, as if the air had drawn thin—I didn't like that. When Val couldn't go any higher, she made her way toward the face, found an outcropping, and settled her big clawed feet on it. Leaning against the wall, she lifted her injured ankle.

Locke's leg touched the stone, and Val's ribcage pushed out against it again and again. He leaned toward the wall—the instability of the thin space somehow seemed more frightening than being suspended in the air by wings. The ledge hung far above the mouth of the salaminde cave and further still from the face who shepherded the plants.

The ceiling of clouds weighed down directly above us. The lower clouds blew clear of our view, revealing nearly all points of our journey. The body of the sea demon lay sprawled in the middle of the Majestic Sea. Far to the west sat the Khalune Desert, keeping the Well far out of reach. Southward, between the peaks of the Wisting Mountains, the green valley of our home called.

Locke wished we were there now. Or at least that it was somewhere in our future. But it wasn't. He'd seen his family for the last time. And he'd lied to Nicke—he wasn't coming back. Locke swallowed against the emotion that welled up, blinking away the tears. He wanted to whisper goodbye. Maybe he would send Shilohe with his final words.

After a long break, Val shrugged her shoulders as a warning. Locke grabbed her golden mane, and she leaped clear of the rocks.

She swooped then curved upward, aided by a brief but strong gust of wind, flapping her white wings. As she drove higher, she fought for every few feet. As she entered the clouds, the atmosphere fought back, as if some evil magic had taken away the power of the wind. With Gaie pulling and the clouds pushing, she made little progress. Val swooped back toward the cliff face. When she found no ledge to land on, she latched her claws onto the rocks, panting.

Locke leaned forward and wrapped one arm around her neck. Some other creature's claw marks scarred the cliff face above us. He closed his eyes, hoping to see a faint blue trail leading upward, but it wasn't there. "The Burning Mountain broke the sky's impassible barrier."

Her wings were no use, so Valkalyse slammed her claws into cracks and ledges and pulled step by step up the rock face. As we slowly entered the clouds, our world became darker, like when we were imprisoned in the fog. The sky groaned a deep rumble, and lightning cast its pale flicker. It illuminated the blurry mass of charcoal gray all around us. We almost welcomed these jabs of light after such long darkness, even with their threatening ferocity. Soon the clouds thinned, and we punched through the black blanket that had covered our lives for so many days.

The sky opened wide.

Shining blue curved over clouds of ruffled gray and white, going upward for leagues. We were nothing but a tiny dark speck against color so full. The mountain continued on higher, but this time not out of sight. More clouds floated above, lighter gray, disconnected and sporadic, like the skies from our memory, clouds that lacked the sinister presence we'd just surmounted.

The evening sun on the rim of the horizon shown overpoweringly bright. It pushed our final day toward twilight, a day of legend. Locke squinted as the rays peeked brightly through, reaching in lengthy beams.

We'd gotten to see the sun one last time.

So we smiled, we three, a triad in harmony.

71.

Upon the Darkness

VALKALYSE CLIMBED TILL she found a suitable aerie.
She crawled up onto a wide platform of stone and panted as she circled it twice to carefully find the ideal spot; then she sat down and rested her chin on the rock. She lifted her eyes, checking if we needed more, but her attitude seemed to say she'd finished her part.

Locke walked to the edge and looked at the blanket of darkness from above. This was a strange and eerie place.

To our eyes, it appeared to be clouds, yet this unnaturally solid substance blocked Numa's breath more than any cloud should. It formed a vast landscape, a foamy new earth, a chaotic surface with great peaks that rolled into each other and deep gullies that fanned out in bizarre, unpredictable ways. Most of all, it was dark. A streak of light flashed beneath the surface, appearing and vanishing all at once. It was followed by an angry BOOM! Moments later another flash came, and multiple bolts of light cut across the surface simultaneously, all pulsing toward the same source—like the spokes of a wheel.

I suddenly realized we hadn't been guided to the peak.

Away from the Burning Mountain, in the distance of this cloud-top world, sat a dark building, the hub of the lightning wheel, pinning the whole structure in place. A building on top of cloud—*it shouldn't be*. And yet there it was. A winged creature, tiny in the distance, flapped above and then landed on top of the circular building. This was the source, the last piece of the puzzle—on his back hung the white hilt of the sword, and he himself would be the sacrifice.

"This is where it ends," said Locke.

I gave him the best smile I could.

"What do you think that flying creature was?" he asked.

"I don't know."

Locke patted Valkalyse on the head, while pointing at the building. "Come on, girl."

She just looked at him, chin still on the ground. I couldn't blame her either—I felt every bit of her exhaustion. Her black stripes looked like tears down her face, and I sensed her fear, fear of that building, or the flying creature above it, or maybe the magic that could take away her power of flight.

"Locke," I said.

"What?"

"Close your eyes."

Together we breathed as a great silence crossed the sky, followed by a rumbling boom that tickled the surface of Locke's skin, particularly on his lips. It took a long time before we started to feel calm. Then came a note with a solitary pitch.

The blue seam was very faint, but we could see it.

Locke opened his eyes and frowned.

"We climb down to there," I said, pointing, "and then… walk across."

"I can't walk on cloud."

"You can't tame a bird demon," I said. "You can't find a hyuman north of the rim. You can't—"

"Okay, okay."

He rubbed the baby-soft skin behind Val's ears. "I guess you're about the only person we'll get to say goodbye to. Thanks for the ride. Your flying was amazing, Valkalyse." When he said her name, he choked up, and the edges of his eyelids began to shine.

Val lifted her head and scooted forward to lick Locke's dragon hand.

"Sorry, I have to go," he said. "But keep an eye out. When I wave to you from that building, you have to come pick up the princess and take her to safety." She gave him no acknowledgement, but she hadn't before either, even though she seemed to understand most of what he said. He patted her soft fur one last time.

We left her there on her perch and followed the blue, traversing the mountain cliffs toward an outcrop that reached over the cloud surface. As we approached, I heard a growing hiss, steady and lingering. Locke walked out to the end of the outcrop and looked down.

"That's farther than it looks," I warned, and my own blue light shifted over his face and eyelashes.

Locke took a long blink, taking careful note. "But that's where the light goes. She's in that building, and I have to go one way or another."

"What's that noise?" I asked.

"What noise?"

"That *dying* noise."

He shrugged, still not understanding.

"I don't know," I said. "Like some immortal is struggling for breath, never relieved."

Without replying, and without giving himself time to reconsider, Locke put a hand on the ground and threw himself over the edge, just like Gante.

He gasped in that first moment, then held his breath as he fell.

The strange surface caught him, as if he'd jumped into spongy moss. His feet sunk deep. And continued sinking.

"Climb, Locke!"

He pressed face, knees, elbows, and feet into the substance, clawing and scrambling. As it fell beneath him, he climbed harder, slowly making his way back to the top. With great effort, he pushed enough of it below him that he got to his knees and then to his feet. He was on top of some strange, magical vapor. "What is it?"

"An unnatural land," I said. "All of it. The surface, and the stone on top, the bolts of light, the booming, and that horrible dying noise."

"So you don't know?" he asked.

"No."

Ice was water given the properties of earth—changed so you could stand on it but not drink it or swim in it. These clouds had undergone a similar transformation, but into something weaker than ice. The substance stretched to the point of breaking with each step, which ruined Locke's plan for a slow and cautious approach. He climbed through it, moving with great effort. "Maybe I'm on top of the souls of a thousand ondines."

I cringed, remembering the blood of bugs and mice and flying squirrels from our journey. Stane had murdered them, maybe with the help of the wraiths. And maybe those bleeding souls did constitute this surface.

A bright, jagged light zipped through the dark beneath us, like a winding road.

BOOM!

A rumble shook us to the bone, as deep as the voice of the face.

Locke fell backward, dropping his hands and rolling over, but they sunk so fast that by the time he got to his knees, his chin was touching. A moment more and he might sink right through and fall. Clawing, he got to his feet. As he bent his knees but before he could jump, another flash cut through the ground.

BOOM!

Locke's feet fell beneath him again into sinking blackness. The sound reverberated through his nerves. He scraped at the clouds, trying to regain his feet. He finally reached the surface again, panting.

"Look to the sky, huh?" I said.

He didn't have time to smile.

When the lightning flashed again, he timed his leap to be airborne during the BOOM! This kept him from sinking as far when the sound struck. He went on like this, running, leaping, and climbing across volumes of rising and falling darkness.

Between the thunderclaps, the hiss of that dying immortal filled the silence. I hated that noise.

Locke clawed his way up one final mass of cloud and leaped, sliding down the far side. The building loomed ahead, becoming clearer through the mists as we drew closer. He ran for it.

A giant circular base formed the foundation, an outer circle that covered a massive distance. From there, round steps rose inward and upward in rings. On the highest ring, a set of oddly shaped pillars stood in a circle, like massive planks of wood with odd bulges here and there, rudely cut as if by primitive masons. Across the tops of these pillars, more stones rested, bridging the gaps between, making an expansive circle high above. The cylinder of bulging pillars left the center open to the air, as if designed to channel magic. In the midst of the structure, a bright light shone from a cavity below and inside the highest ring.

If I hadn't known this was the source of the curse, I might have guessed it was a temple of Numa, raised above the clouds by sylves to praise their creator. But this wasn't a holy place. Atop the structure, two wicked creatures gripped the edge and stared down at us like gargoyles. They had great wings on their backs. The bluish gray skin of their elfe-like faces looked like stone, and they held as still as rock. If the twins had taught us right, these were wrecches, the breathless, an abomination created by Saede himself. They had no elementals, and they embodied only three lifeforces: flesh, blood, and spirit. They lacked breath, the element that was mostly me. That made them the worst of the unwhole, and I hated them and their condition. I didn't know exactly how they were created, but if a gnyme drank the living water, it would make something like a wrecche. Or if you ripped the breath out of an elfe.

Locke rushed to the base of the structure, to the outermost and lowest stair. He watched the wretched gargoyles carefully but didn't have time to draw his club-sword—the ground kept sinking too fast. Luckily the gargoyles still didn't move.

When Locke stepped onto the stairs, the solidness surprised him. For a moment he rested, panting after fighting so hard for every step. He kept his neck twisted so he could watch the wrecches. They glared at him, with painful scowls, still as stone.

Bands of light—the chains of lightning the Seer had read about on the covenant scroll—ran in jagged lines from the tops of the pillars down and toward the center, like ropes holding something up. But they reached below the rim of the highest stair and out of sight. These lights held their forms generally, so as to resemble chains, but on the small scale they twitched back and forth like struggling prisoners, flashing and avoiding any specific form.

The cloudy floor behind us flashed, and bolts of light raced from every direction toward us. The surge of energy disappeared beneath the circle stairs, passed up the insides of the pillars, and zoomed down the chains toward the center of it all. It seemed the sky was held together by a knot inside this building. Such majestic power, for such a murderous purpose.

"Shilohe told us about this paradox." Locke took his eyes off the gargoyles just long enough to look at the circular stairs beneath him.

I gave him a questioning glance.

"Volant stone."

72.

The Villain

L OCKE PULLED THE Shining Sword from his back.
He tapped his hand against the handle. *Still hot.* My blueness
hadn't changed that. When he closed his eyes and looked around, he saw
nothing but the visual echo of the blaze ahead. Maybe it was so bright it
was overpowering the blue light. Maybe the clairvoyance had decided our
need wasn't dire. Or maybe the gargoyles had left our mind too disquieted.

I noticed something else though: A lone torch hung from one of the
pillars, though the blaze inside was far too bright for its light to do any
good. "Probably the salaminde torch."

Holding the sword like a club, Locke ascended the wide, concentric stairs.
The wrecches crawled along the circular shelf above the pillars, tracking
us with their sunken eyes. Between movements, they'd stop, still as stone.
I saw suffering on their faces, but I sensed no pain in them, just a horrible
absence. I wished they'd turn to stone for good.

From the rim, the steps descended again in smaller and smaller circles,
like a volcano inviting an adventurer down into its fiery mouth. At the
bottom, the stone ended, leaving empty air at the center and an open pit
of clouds and darkness.

Above that hung a sphere of swirling, blinding light, too white for us to
see much of.

The lightning converged into the knot. Chains of energy jolted and jerked
back and forth in a continuous sporadic movement. The lowest steps were
within reach of the blaze, if a person could bear to stand that close. Locke
squinted against the brightness till it pushed his gaze away, and then he
realized he got a better impression by not looking directly at it. As he turned
aside, we suddenly saw a person, chained to the wall on the distant side of
the circular structure, beside and beyond the scintillating light.

Shilohe!

As she entered our vision, I began to feel her pain. Metal chains pulled her arms to the sides, perpendicular to her torso. Her entire body was weak, worn thin and desperate for release. Her hair was tangled and ratted and hung down over her face. Her brow was smeared in lines of sweat and blood that dripped like some demonic crown. Dried blood also streaked her neck, arms, hands, and fingernails. Her pain taxed my consciousness.

Locke began to run toward her. "Princess!"

I felt another pain, slightly to our right—

"You're not who I expected."

The words echoed behind us over the sound of the swirling blaze.

The gargoyles dropped from the pillars and landed on the steps, blocking our route. Their appearance, more hideous the closer they got, caused a visceral reaction in Locke, a rotting in his gut. They looked like elves twisted into a horrible new shape. They stood taller than hyumans, and because they didn't breathe, they held perfectly still, which gave me a nightmare feeling. Their skin appeared cold as stone. Dragon wings sprouted from their shoulder blades.

From behind a pillar to our right a man stepped out. I felt the sharp pain in his knee as he meandered toward us, as if he were *my* elfe. I hated it. It was the crumbling dark form we'd seen in the Rueful Wilderness.

The man who called himself Stane.

His pinched face had the expression of a hateful corpse, more loathsome than the wrecches he stood next to, maybe because he actually *was* the twisted form of an elfe. Blood streaked like lightning through his eyes. I felt pain in his teeth and gums. Blood was splattered on his face and fingers. His wispy white Tenarie hair fluttered. His elfe ears were too long and too low. Lines of purple and green showed through the thin, pale flesh of his hands and wrists. He walked a living death.

I hate the Tenarie.

The dying noise crashed into me, the sound of suffering. It wasn't physical, so Locke hadn't heard it. It was lifebreath, or what was left of it. Somewhere the dark sylfe was nearby, hidden, waiting, unbreathing.

One gargoyle glanced at its master. I saw no deference or respect, only contempt—clear as wind. This surprised me. Were they under a contract to serve him unwillingly? What leverage did he have over them? *Maybe he was keeping them from turning to stone.* Whatever the reason, they regarded him hatefully. This really was a friendless man. I couldn't imagine a more horrible exile.

"Not an army," said Stane. "Not a warrior. Not even a man. Just you."

His voice was dark, rough as a cast-iron pot boiling with hate. As he and his reluctant minions approached, Locke backed down the stairs and out of sight of Shilohe. Little did he realize what a favor he'd done me—once her pain was out of sight, I could fully breathe.

"I'm sorry to let you down," said Locke. "More will come if I fail." But he only hoped that was true.

"You will," said Stane. "But time is running out for any others."

He stopped at the highest ring between two massive pillars, positioning himself between us and the center, as if to block us from passing the stone rim.

Locke casually walked along a lower step, as if innocently pacing. Stane walked too, limping, keeping himself between us and the center, and his right kneecap stabbed with each step. His creatures moved with him, further back, and his sylfe remained hidden somewhere, which worried me. I didn't want to get attacked by surprise because this time *I* was the blue flame.

"Let me go to her," said Locke.

"What have you done to your sylfe?" asked Stane.

Locke glared but didn't answer.

"Another insolent Kyrie. Above kindness and reproof. Never guilty."

"*I'm* guilty," said Locke readily.

"You admit it?"

"I'm a coward, for one. I turned my back on someone who needed my help."

"Then this curse has punished you too."

"But *good* people are suffering."

Stane smirked. "They deserve it."

"Not my friend Nicke, or the lost hyuman Honke, or the girl you're holding prisoner—"

"You Kyrie deserve it most of all. But all creation goes on living in the face of injustice. This," he said, gesturing with both hands to the building and sky around it, "is for the help that wasn't given, the strength that kept to itself, the abundance that fled from those who needed it."

"Not her, and you know it. She's good. And she's a Kyrie."

Stane didn't respond. And he didn't deny it.

As Locke stepped up another stair, a dark needle, shaped like hatred, wiggled its way toward his heart. I fought against it and so did he, but it was powerful. Still, he retained a shred of sympathy for this broken creature who'd done so much harm. "I feel sorry for you."

"How dare you!" came the snake's whisper.

"I feel sorry for our people too."

"*Your* people."

"*Our* people. I have Tenarie friends."

"I don't," said Stane, and the wind tousled his thin, white hair.

Locke frowned with sympathetic disgust. He cocked his head as I whispered in his ear. Ignoring my better judgement, he said, "What about you, Stane? Who will punish you?"

"No one."

"And who will forgive you?"

"No one!" The anger in Stane's voice rose. He stared down at the blackness that his fortress was founded on then repeated the words as if to himself: "No one."

"Let me help you," said Locke.

"I don't want help. I want justice!"

"We need to end this, and I'm willing to pay the price."

"You haven't the slightest clue what you're doing, do you?"

Locke knew he had to die, but he didn't know how, and he didn't know what to say either.

"Then I'll tell you, boy. The first step is to get past me."

73.

Endgame

Locke looked at the villain, deciding what to do.

He could strike the frail old man with the sword—it wouldn't be difficult—but that might bring the wrath of the gargoyles. He could offer the blade to Stane, hoping it might burn him, but maybe Stane knew the secret to wielding it. Locke had his sling and two stones in his bag, and he was a dead shot—a hit to the forehead could kill the old man, so long as he could get the shot off in time.

As Locke hesitated, Stane stepped carefully down one stair, holding his neck still, which forced his body into an awkward, jerking movement. The pain shot into his knee as he landed. His physical strength was not great, but his magic—wherever it came from—remained a frightening mystery. If he had power to darken the skies, to break the earth, and to command banshee wolves, what could he do in a one-on-one fight?

"Aren't you going to draw your precious blade?" asked Stane.

Locke looked up, glaring. He wanted to believe he'd somehow become worthy to wield it, but he could still feel the heat on his back. "What's the second step?" he asked, in a low, embarrassed voice.

Stane shook his head and swiped the comment away with a mangled hand. The thunder beneath us growled. "You're stalling."

"*You're* stalling."

"Why not cut me down?"

"I don't want to kill you."

"Then you're a fool. The curse will survive as long as I do."

Locke nodded, remembering how Shilohe had pointed this out at the Seer's house.

"Take up your sword!"

Locke hated hearing the villain's taunting voice, but he also hated to be obedient to him. Besides, he couldn't hold the sword.

"I have taken your princess," said Stane. "I hate her and I hate you."

The comment hit the center of the target. Although Shilohe was out of sight, we saw her bloody face and the way she was chained. Locke's resistance weakened.

But I'd already passed resisting. I wanted to injure Stane, to give him all he deserved and more. My rage pounded so strong that I didn't feel the dark approach from beneath. Not till it was too late. While I faced the villain, his lifeless sylfe swept at my back, lancing toward me. Just like he'd done in the Rueful Wilderness. Only this time his target wasn't a lamp.

This time it was me.

Locke flinched, even though *I* was in danger, not him.

I turned to see the dark sylfe creeping. He was right there, a breathless, dark streak, about to stab at me. I backed away, frantic to escape but not knowing where to run. Backing wildly, drawing a blue path through the air.

A cold grip closed over me.

It happened in a flash, quick as a wildercat. Stane's wrinkled old hands clapped in front of me. No, around me. And I didn't whisk, like I always had. I stayed, trapped in his grip. He slowly squeezed his hands together into my form—my cohesive particles of lifeblood.

As he did, Locke grabbed his own chest, falling onto the stone and gasping.

An unforgiving magic clamped down on us. *How?* The power of earth could've never harmed me before, but even now I still only had three parts of life. I should have been as slippery as water, or a specter.

The villain squeezed his hands together.

Locke choked.

A hard and brutal force was wringing out our lives, both at once, crushing us like bone.

With power over elementals, Stane had kidnapped a salaminde and forced her to write a contract with the vile god. He'd captured and commanded a thousand ondines to bind up the skies. He'd chipped apart a massive gnyme causing its rock to collapse into a riverbed. Now he was throttling me, a spectral sylfe.

The grip squeezed.

"Locke... he's... killing... mmm..."

The villain laughed. "You are pathetic."

He shifted his grip, placing me in one hand instead of two—his wrong hand, in fact. As he did, he let up for a moment. I gasped, so surprised by the reprieve that I didn't sprint to get free till it was too late. Locke, even in such a small instance, leaped to fight. But Stane squeezed again, and shards of blackness shot into the corners of the world.

Locke fell down.

With a spiteful chuckle, Stane hobbled down the steps, with pain cutting through his knee and into me. He grabbed Locke by the collar and dragged him.

Locke didn't even fight back. He grabbed at his chest, wanting air, and stared with bleeding eyes, in the throes of a nightmare.

Stane looked at the cloudy floor beyond the building. He could easily drop my helpless elfe into clouds and oblivion. Instead he dropped him onto the stairs. As he did, his thumb spiked into me.

I felt the flutter of wings above. The gargoyles were withdrawing, eager to be relieved from service. Their master had gained more than a simple upper hand; he'd defeated us with the snatch of a hand.

The villain pulled the pack from Locke's back.

He took the Shining Sword and set it higher on the steps, never touching the metal. He dumped the contents of the backpack onto the stairs: the salaminde flasks, the broken phanos lamp, the flint, Nicke's vial of poison, and all the rest.

The pinkalue bounced, chiming a single note as it hit the stair, and then it rolled, singing again as it fell on the next and the next.

Locke, still struggling for life, did not jump to save it. But he wanted to.

I watched through a gap between Stane's fingers. The instrument teetered precariously on the final edge. I felt relief when fate stopped it from falling.

Then it tumbled and vanished into the cloud floor.

I cringed.

Stane squeezed. "Seems you were prepared for quite the adventure."

His eyes were deep caverns of hate.

"I hope you like how it ends."

74.

Hatred

HIS FACE PRESSED into the stairs.

Locke groaned, trying but failing just to get to his knees.

Stane pressed me tighter. I felt pain in his gnarled fingers, in the joints of his hand and in the bones, pain from some lingering wound. "Your people deserve this, her father the King most of all."

Locke, shaking, wasted breath on a few precious words: "Huhh... not... her... father."

Stane gave Locke a questioning look, then shook his head, ignoring the comment. He scooped up the phanos lamp and held the glass close to his eyes. "I served the King with humility as his closest friend, and I was rewarded with misery. He's a betrayer, like all Kyrie. Yet fate rewarded his arrogance with wealth and power and—" and on this last word he gasped, and his rotting teeth hung open as if they couldn't quite bite through the word... "—and *happiness*."

He grimaced.

"I tried to kill him on the Day of Redress, but he escaped, thanks to that miserable Seer."

Stane picked up the vial of venom, a large enough dose to kill a dozen of the Unstoppable Hundred. The fingers of his other hand curled around it like a claw, and he stared. "Where did you get this?" He looked skyward, as if he had a horrible question that needed to be answered.

Locke grunted, trying to say something.

Stane didn't let up on either of us. "I want you to understand that this isn't about me. This had to be done. For justice. To repay the wrongs the Kyrose continually let slide." He peered at me in his other fist. He then closed his eyes, and his next words were drawn out and labored: "*And I don't care about the cost.*"

Locke stared at him hatefully, struggling to breathe, unable to speak, yet somehow they communicated—they were both thinking of Shilohe. A flood of guilt crossed the old man's face. *Yes, guilt.* He held some shred of sympathy for her—we saw it in his expression. Something only he and she would know. She'd been the captive, but she'd gotten to him somehow. *Just like she'd gotten to us.*

"She tried to convince me to forgive him," admitted Stane, speaking lower and with much less confidence. "She said that was the only way for me to be free of the conflict in my *heart.*" The last word squeaked from his lips as if he were on the verge of tears.

And while thinking of her, the villain did something he probably didn't even notice. He let up on me—just a little sympathy for her and his grip relaxed, under her power, a reprieve for the smallest of moments.

But a creature my size only needed the smallest of moments.

The chains of lighting sizzled in the background as Stane spoke. "But it could never work for me. OUCH!"

I bit him on the finger then wriggled through and was free.

His dark sylfe buzzed around me in attack position, but nothing happened—apparently he couldn't extinguish my light after all. Fear alone had backed me into their trap.

The gargoyles turned their horrid faces and flapped their curious wings from the farthest side of the great building. In a moment they were airborne.

Locke took no notice—he was too busy gasping and scrambling to his feet. He leaped for the Shining Sword.

Stane ran, squeezing the black vial like it was a lifeline.

Locke was on him, striking a blow to the side. The crosspiece rammed deep into the old man's ribs, like a bolt of lightning through my eyes. "You bastard!" shouted Locke, raising the weapon and letting it fall a second time. "What did you do to her!"

I screamed: "Locke, don't! Don't! DON'T!"

The hilt struck again, cracking into Stane's old bones—and shooting through me.

"STOOOOOP!!!"

I screamed with all my might.

The word and the horror echoed in the air around us.

Locke stopped, panting, sweating, and a little afraid—he realized my scream had been the reaction to his deeds, a horrible scream.

The gargoyles hovered in circles overhead. It seemed they'd halted their attack because Locke had halted his. Maybe his show of mercy had saved his life.

But Locke was too busy looking at his hateful hands to care. His white knuckles clenched the scabbard, trembling.

Stane looked up at Locke's face with wonder and fear.

I gazed at my elfe too, wondering what damage he'd done to himself. "Locke, if you kill him, I think it will kill me."

He looked at me. Finally he said, "I have to kill him. Or everyone dies. The whole land."

Stane didn't disagree. He didn't say anything. But the look on his face was one of submission, of resignation—as if he *had* been defeated. I felt it all, thanks to Numa's gift of overwhelming empathy.

"Please don't," I said. "Kill *us* first if you have to, but don't kill *him*."

Locke stood there, wading in the deepest conflict. Thinking of Shilohe and the pain she'd suffered. Thinking of Nicke and his irreparable misery. Thinking of the wraiths and the loss of his own mother. Thinking of all the injustices life had served. He wanted to take them all out on this vile old man, but my words had struck, and he didn't know what to do. He'd come to his wit's end.

"He's an underdog," I said.

"What?" asked Locke.

"Your heroic gift."

"*He's* no underdog."

Stane switched the vial of venom from one hand to his other. He lay back on the stone stair and closed his eyes. The trauma was setting in—of the wounds Locke had inflicted. *So painful.*

"Look at the vial," I said.

Locke did. Stane was holding it in his wrong hand.

"He's suffered from the curse," I said. "Maybe more than anyone."

Locke gazed into memory, remembering our conversation about his heroic gift. "How can I have sympathy for—for someone so evil?"

"I don't know."

Locke looked away, as if the open sky might hold the answer. The gargoyles soared overhead, still holding their attack in reserve.

Stane rolled to his side, lifting his head to glare at Locke in pain.

"But I believe you can," I added.

The Shining Sword clinked onto the steps.

Locke had dropped his weapon. The rage and sympathy still battled in his heart. He fell to his knees and blinked as he whispered, "Numa, please help me. Arm me with your power. Help me care for so miserable a creature."

White light spread throughout the entire cloud and vanished.

And something snapped into place.

Locke didn't see a villain. He saw a man who used to be a boy. A boy with wild white hair, a bit like Nicke. A boy who'd suffered bad things over many, many years, things that tortured him into this shape—a boy who really had suffered more than anyone else.

An image flashed across our mind: Honke, slumped on his knees, his palms touching the earth, his fingers spread wide: "A shign of humble. Tenarie shign."

A single teardrop fell past the brown mark at the corner of Locke's right eye. He knelt on the ground, put his hands on the cold stone steps, and bowed his head onto the stair, facing Stane. He spread his fingers and imagined his bones breaking. Worse was the thought of losing his power to play wild music. Yet he spoke anyway: "Tenarie sign. I submit. To you and to fate. I'm truly sorry for your suffering, and I'm begging you, please, let her go. Let us all go."

The gesture didn't untangle the villain's heart. Instead Locke was about to experience its full symbolism. Stane slowly rose. "You'll regret that, Kyrie."

Locke already regretted a little.

Stane towered over us. Pain jabbed at the cracked ribs in his side. He leaned onto one leg, lifting the other. "Your humility is mockery if you cringe."

Locke maintained the pose.

And Stane slammed his boot into Locke's shield hand.

The bones crunched and split.

Locke's scream came through his nose, as he pursed his lips, containing the rest of the shriek deep in his chest. His face flushed red, and I drooped nearly to the ground, slipping for a moment toward the edge of consciousness. Locke remained firm, holding the position as if he were an oak. His broken fingers spiked us both with pain. His arm began to quiver.

"Maybe now you'll never wield a sword again." Stane growled through

clenched teeth, as if he'd inflicted the injury on himself, but he'd misspo-
ken, not knowing Locke was wrong handed. Stane raised his boot again.

Locke held firm, gritting his teeth and shaking—he hadn't lost his sword
hand. Not yet.

Stane's boot jerked down a second time.

I flinched, unprepared to bear more.

The boot smacked the stone next to Locke's sword hand—a juke, and
I'd fallen for it.

Locke hadn't budged. True to his word, he'd submitted to the full punishment. He'd proved his sincerity.

The villain's eyes closed. A whimper stole from his insides. His corpse
seemed to convulse as his sour face turned downward. He fell to his knees
as if melting and faced Locke. He rested his forehead on the stone and
reached his arms out. In his wrong hand he still clutched the vial in painfully
mangled fingers. He spread the fingers of his right hand, and they were
twisted outward, jagged too. For a long time, he just whimpered while his
body jerked. Finally, with his head still on the stair, he whispered, "How?
After all I've done to you?"

And then his sylfe gasped for air.

If a corpse had been prepared for burial, dead for over a day, ready to
be interred, and then it had gasped for air—it wouldn't have been more
shocking than this. Breath had returned to the thing that was dead, that
had been mortified. Stane's lifeless, blackened sylfe had gasped.

The horrible dying noise began to fade, and something dark spewed out
of Stane, an evil presence, something rotted and foul, perhaps a piece of
Saede himself. The shadow crawled away, and Stane lay there, moaning
in pathetic misery.

"He did this to me," said Stane, in a crying whisper, tapping the maimed
fingers of his right hand on the stone. "When I pleaded for mercy, when
I begged him to spare me from prison and ruin, the King gave me this as
a reminder. I'm sorry."

Locke sat up, leaning back and gritting his teeth. His shield hand was
already swelling. The skin was torn and bleeding. The pain made it hard
to think. He tucked the hand under his armpit. Fortunately, my blue light
seemed to salve the wound, but only slightly.

"Saede taught this to me," said Stane. "He appeared as an angel. Told me he was betrayed by his siblings, just like I had been. He fueled my hatred. Made me think I could set things right. Blinded me with what I wanted to hear. He taught me how to draw power from elementals. I knew it was wrong deep down, but I couldn't stop. So I avoided the truth until I believed the lies. Till I did this to us... and to her. I was deceived. He *is* the betrayer."

With his knees and hands on the stone, he wept.

"I hate the King. But I want it to end. I want to feel peace... like she promised."

In the silence that followed, Locke quietly asked, "What do we have to do?"

For a moment, Stane did not reply, and the clouds held their breath, waiting for an answer. "You have to kill me." Stane looked down at the steps. "*Someone* has to kill me. That is first."

Locke clenched his jaw and shook his head. "Isn't that enough?"

"If I could undo it, I would," said Stane. "But Saede controls this curse, not me. Don't you see? He tricked me, and it's already done. I murdered myself to create it. And I murdered the hero worthy to break it too. We were slain when it began."

Locke looked into Stane's eyes and nodded, knowing what this meant.

"I'm so sorry," said Stane.

Without another moment of misery, he, in a quick movement, leaned back on his knees, tore the lid from the vial, put the black thing to his lips. "She promised." He tipped back the vial.

It was fire.

The hatred of Saede poured down our throat, into our bloodstream, burning all the way to our fingertips.

Burning and burning.

Tears streaked from the corners of Stane's closed eyes, and he tilted his head back, mouth open. He spread his shaking arms and faced the sky as if calling to someone who wasn't there. The burning tore through our nerves and the roots of our teeth. His fingers curled in on themselves and his whole body convulsed.

"LOCKE!!!" I screamed.

Stane, drawing in one last breath, cried, "SAVE ME!!!"

His sylfe screamed too, one last time before falling deathly still.

The old man's skull thunked back onto the stone steps, the bones in his knees cracked, and his mouth hung open.

They were gone.

I gasped, struggling for air.

The breath soothed, etching at the very edges of the jagged pain, beginning to wear it down in miniscule strokes. Horror crept in to fill the void.

Already Stane's form looked like it had rotted for weeks, the skin too thin and too dry. His eyes stared skyward, forever. Dark emotion still covered his face, as if he weren't yet released from his hateful suffering.

Locke's eyebrows pulled upwards in horror. "Why did he ask to be saved?"

"I don't know," I said, barely audible, still staring at the shriveled corpse.

75.

Scintillating Light

L OCKE LOOKED TOWARD the rising stairs.
The blaze hidden inside the building's mouth reflected in his eyes. Above us wings flapped, dark and bat-like. The gargoyles abandoned their fallen master, flying high into the distance. It seemed Stane's death had released them from servitude.

With the Shining Sword still lying on the ground where he'd dropped it, Locke got to his feet and ascended the stairs till the fiery knot came into view. Beyond it was Shilohe, chained in misery, hanging with her arms stretched to the sides. Her anguish beat against the pain in Locke's broken hand, pushing away my consciousness, but my blue light fought back, trying to ease their suffering with its presence.

"Princess!" shouted Locke.

With his throbbing hand tucked beneath his armpit, he ran down the steps, cutting across the inner part of the circle. As he passed near the center, the heat from the blaze rushed in a wave at him, so hard he fell, touching a hand on the hot stone. He backed away till the heat became bearable. It seemed to emit the same sort of glory as the Shining Sword.

The light of the blaze pushed up into Shilohe. On her shoulder rested Lonae, blurry and faded but still breathing. Shilohe lifted her head and looked at us. She was alive. The purple bandana she'd worn so regally now hung around her neck like a choker. Her royal yellow top was stained with blood. A nasty yellowish bruise tainted the skin of her perfect face. I braced myself against her pain as we got nearer. She whispered something, too quiet for us to hear.

"What?" Sweat trickled down Locke's forehead. He squinted through the pain and did his best to smile at her.

"You don't have the sword?" she asked again, her face filled with concern, and for a moment her hope failed. *A Goddess almost.*

"I do. I have it. It's back there."

She gave a weak smile as if she were nearly asleep. "Good."

"Where's the key to your chains?"

"I think it's on the wall over there." She nodded her head toward the lonely torch, the one she'd carried through the woods. Locke grabbed the key and the torch and came back. When the first metal cuff released, she swung, collapsing toward the other chain and the ground.

Lonae fell off her shoulder and took flight, drifting dizzily.

"I'm sorry." As Locke took Shilohe by the waist and lifted her back up, he bumped his broken hand, which brought enough pain he nearly collapsed. With great effort, he freed her other wrist.

"Thank you." She smiled.

He helped her gently to the ground and cringed as his hand brushed her side.

Shilohe put her back to the wall, pulled her knees up, and wrapped her forearms around her gray moccasins, curled up like an infant, and aching nearly everywhere. She still wore the black fingerless glove. Locke sat next to her, his jaw tightened against the pain in his hand. For a while, they just stared together into the blinding white light that bound the skies till Shilohe spoke, barely aloud: "I knew you'd come."

Locke swallowed, remembering his journey into the fog and fear.

"What happened to Picke?" she asked.

"He drank the living water."

"He drank it?"

"Yeah, sort of. He's an ascendant one now."

She nodded and gave a tired smile.

"We don't really know how it happened," he added.

Shilohe gazed at me with such awe that I almost forgot the pain. "Ascendancy isn't a permanent thing. It happens in a moment by the grace of the Kyrose. Picke used his moment to drink the living water."

Locke nodded, too tired for questions.

"I admit, I did worry I might die here alone. But somehow you always gave me hope, even when I couldn't talk to you. That's what I meant about trusting you. I knew you wouldn't give up while someone still needed help."

He felt guilty and considered telling her the whole story. Instead, he reached over and put his good hand on her arm. "It's okay now. I'll send you home on the gryphine."

"You tamed a bird demon?" Her eyes gleamed with tired wonder.

"I guess so."

"You know I hate heights?" She cracked a grin. "I accidentally dropped my dagger down there. It's so far."

"It's the only safe way down. And you'll be flying, just like in your story."

She shook her head slightly as if to say *no*. Her head drooped, and her hair hung forward over her cheekbones. The exhaustion had nearly broken her. She reached forward and weakly grabbed the salaminde torch.

"I met the King Salaminde," said Locke. "He told me to release this one."

"It's high time," she said. "I'll do it." She held the torch near her mouth, and Lonae perked up, flying from her shoulder. Shilohe spoke three words which we didn't recognize followed by, "I release you." She and Lonae blew on the flame together. Sparks flew out of the torch, small orange lights zipping away. Only they didn't disappear like usual sparks. Instead they slowed and stayed, till more and more gathered into a recognizable shape.

The flame still flickered back and forth, but now a salaminde floated next to it, and she bowed to us.

"I'm sorry I couldn't have done this days ago," said Shilohe as Lonae moved back to rest on her shoulder. "You know I meant to, if I hadn't been outsmarted. Thank you again for not burning me or stealing my lifelight when we were strangers to each other."

The salaminde gave a subtler nod, and without saying a word, she vanished.

Locke and I stared in awe then looked at Shilohe.

She answered the question we hadn't asked: "A salaminde can move from one place to another faster than a sylfe's whisper. They just need a marker, which means from anywhere to home is easy."

Locke looked at her, waiting for more.

"Stane valued the torch. He used it to spy on the King and the Seer. He planned to use it on himself for more healing. So when I threatened to put it out, he came after me. That was my plan to find the source of the curse. The wrecches overpowered me though, and I never got to see if my father's dagger would've worked."

The evening fell quiet except for the hum of the massive blaze in front of us. Locke needed to know what to do after she left—how to become the sacrifice—but he didn't want to bring it up, hoping she might never leave.

"I'm glad you had compassion on him," said Shilohe.

"What?"

"On Stane. I heard your conversation."

"I didn't... I'm not sure I..." He gave up trying to explain.

"He was so miserable, so alone," she said. "He would talk to his dead brother instead of his sylfe. I know he was evil, but... I think you did the right thing."

Locke rubbed his hand across his face, not wanting to talk about the only thing on his mind.

"You remember where I hid my diary?" asked Shilohe.

"Green book with gold letters. But there's something I have to tell you, something the Seer told me before he died."

"Locke, I know. I read the scroll."

"No, not in the scroll. He told me *I* was supposed to be the sacrifice. So whatever's in your diary, you should just tell me right now."

She inhaled, about to speak, but then she just shook her head. "Remember what I said about my father? He's who you remind me of—King Benne. He was murdered... by the man who is now king. I know he did it, and I've nearly collected enough evidence to prove it. But I've hated him the whole time..." Tears trickled down her cheeks. "I've hated him so much... it's killing me. And I've hated my mother for marrying him too."

Locke looked, hardly believing it could be true.

"I've been trying to forgive, but not everyone is as strong as you."

"I'm not..." began Locke, but again he found himself at a loss for words.

"Locke, it's not supposed to be you."

The Seer's final words echoed in his mind. "It *is*. He said it was supposed to be me, even though he wished it didn't have to be."

When she closed her eyes, tears ran down her bruised face.

"But I don't care who it's *supposed* to be," he added. "I'm going to go through with it as soon as I get you away." *As soon as she told him how.*

She took his wrong hand resting on her arm and turned it over, exposing his scale-scarred palm. She felt the dragon grooves with her index finger and then rested her tattooed hand next to it, as if for comparison. His thumb touched her wrist, and he stroked her skin. These same two hands would've received the marriage tattoo, his wrong and her right, locked together as a pair.

"Locke..." She paused, overwhelmed with emotion.

He caressed the skin of her arm with his thumb. "It's going to be okay," he promised, in spite of himself.

Soon she stopped her crying. "To be honest," she said in a soft and whimpering voice, "something told me you were a hero the moment I saw you, when you held the scroll in your wrong hand—just like my dad. Not that I think that of every wrong-handed boy. But somehow, this time I just knew. I knew you were what it meant when it said I should look for someone like him."

"What *what* meant?"

"The Seer gave me a prophecy about my life. He told me about a hero I was supposed to look for." She took his hand and held it, squeezing and releasing as if drawing strength by simply being alive. The dried blood on her body and clothing stood out in contrast. "Locke, the sword won't let you hold it."

"I know: I already tried. But I don't care if it burns me this time. It will only last a moment."

"You don't understand. You *can't* carry it. It won't let you. Certainly not enough to strike a blow. That's part of its magic, what makes it so special."

"And you can?"

"Yes. My tattoo, the Blue Rose, that's what it means."

"Then I'll go get one of those tattoos and come back."

"It's not just the tattoo. It's the covenant and process that came before. It takes time, years."

"Then we'll go home together and take the time. Or get someone else to do it."

"Who, Locke? Who should I tell their life is worth less than mine?"

"I don't know. The King?"

"Don't do this. He's not worthy to break the curse either. Even if he were, I can't go back down that road. I have to forgive him."

Locke shook his head emphatically. "But I just... I don't..."

"Don't you see? Stane was tricked. Even if our people delivered up the dead king, Stane didn't have the power to end it. It's in Saede's hands. And *mine*."

"No! There must be a way *I* can do it."

"There's not, not quick enough. A war is raging, and the wraiths are coming."

"They've already come. I've seen it. But we'll endure them."

She smiled for a fleeting moment. "Every day more people die."

I thought of the monk sitting amid pools of black blood.

"Tomorrow it could be your friend Nicke. Or my little sister. If I spare my life now, I'll be trading mine for theirs."

"Shilohe…" He paused on the smooth sound of her name. It was the first time he'd called her this. He still admired her, so high above and out of reach, but now she seemed like a friend too, right next to him, holding his hand. Her skin and muscles were warm and full of life. "Shilohe… the Seer wanted it to be me. He foresaw it, my quest, because he wanted you to take his place, to become the next Seer."

"What?"

"He said so before he died."

"He said I was supposed to be the next Seer?"

"Yes."

Shilohe shook her head and looked more pained than ever, as if that knowledge filled her with immense regret. "It's not possible anymore, not without letting more people die."

"I came to save you," said Locke. "Now you don't have to die—I will. Somehow."

"Your quest isn't to die, Locke, but to choose to let me."

The possibility that he might live and she might not was the weight of an ocean. His shoulders slumped, and he rested his head against the wall, shaking his head. "What kind of a quest is that?"

"One more difficult than you probably ever imagined."

He nodded his head, tears formed in his eyes, and the emotions caught hold of his throat so he couldn't respond.

"More than life, Locke. My sister. And your friend Nicke. And the well-being of all our people. More than life. Besides, if I just walk away like a coward, if I *don't* do this, you won't think much of me."

"If you *do*, I'll never be able to *stop* thinking of you." His hand throbbed, and the heat made it worse, distracting his mind. "If our story ends this way, it's a tragedy."

She smiled a sad smile. "Even if this were the end of the story, Locke, I'd be happy to give my life. What good is a life that's not given to others?"

"But this means darkness wins. Saede wins. If he takes you—he'll take the best thing this world has."

"Maybe if this were the end…" she said. "But it isn't, Locke. Our story doesn't end here."

"You can't know that. No one has ever returned from death."

"Some day someone will."

"What?"

"Someone will go there and back."

"Who?"

"You know the Warrior's Song."

"That's a faerie story. It's not real. We're talking about your death, right here, right now!"

"I believe in a power that can undo all wrong, even death, especially death. I couldn't do this without it."

"But I…" His broken shield hand throbbed, swelling like it might burst.

"Our loved ones are dying," she said, "and we can save them."

He squeezed her hand and looked up, desperate to find another solution somewhere, anywhere. The teardrop stain on his face seemed like a fresh wound. When he looked at me, it came to him: He closed his eyes, searching the darkness for the seam of blue leading into the future. All he saw was the residual blaze, yellow shapes edged with pink and purple inside a dark mind. He breathed deliberately, tasted blood in his mouth, smelled the scent of her skin. But he saw no blue light. The choice was left to him alone. To do what she wanted, or to selfishly keep her.

"Locke, you've done so much," said Shilohe. "But the quest isn't finished, not yet. If you care about me, *let me do this for you.* And for everyone I love." Then she added in a barely audible whisper, *"And everyone I don't."*

This was too much. He was almost convinced, convinced to let her give her life. I couldn't let that happen. "Locke, you know her resolve," I warned. "If you give her the sword, you'll be sacrificing her."

She nodded, having heard me clear enough. "I have to do this, Locke. To cure my hate. It's the only way."

"What?"

"I don't expect you to understand."

He peered into her shining blue eyes. "What do you mean *cure your hate?* It's okay to hate. No one is that perfect."

She breathed and each breath pressed her painfully. "It's not okay. *I'm* not okay. It's killing me. I have to do this. You'll understand more when you've read my journal."

Locke looked up, his eyes red with tears. An overwhelming urge came on him to hold her and never let go. And maybe to kiss her, even though he was unworthy.

She threw her arms around his neck and began to sob.

He pulled her close. They were like that for a long time—as if their embrace could stop time itself, as if holding on to each other could hold that moment forever. Eventually the horror was replaced by a tentative calm. And they didn't let go.

Shilohe whispered, and the sound of the blaze muffled her voice: "Will you bring the Shining Sword?"

"I'm not—"

"No, Locke, don't." Her candle-flame voice flickered. "Do you know how hard this is? I have to do this. Just let me do it. Don't drag it out."

Locke nodded, realizing he was willing to submit even if it shattered his heart to pieces. He let go of her, stood, and walked out of sight over the crest of the stairs.

But I stayed. I wouldn't help him retrieve a sword to sacrifice her. And I couldn't bear to lose a moment of her fleeting presence.

Shilohe stretched out her Goddess fingertips and made a platform of her tattooed palm. When I stood on it, she smiled, and I felt her energy. In that desperate, fleeting moment, I was as near to being the Goddess's sylfe as I would ever get.

She looked at me and my blue reflected in her perfect eyes.

Lonae moved next to me. She looked steadily into me and began to hum, pouring her music into the air, a pure and unique melody, peaceful as a breeze. I played mine alongside her familiar and soothing song, matching her rhythm, till I could see and feel and move with her again.

We danced together on Shilohe's palm, till the consonance had been remade.

Locke returned and his throbbing hand reappeared in my thoughts. He'd strapped his bag again to his back, and he gripped the scabbard of the Shining Sword with his good hand. He tried to brace himself for the impact of seeing her again, but the blow was too powerful, and tears filled his eyes. He wasn't ready to hand her the sword, and he thought he never would be.

Shilohe looked straight at me. I saw suffering in her eyes, the suffering of Kyrie and Tenarie alike, and I felt it through her injured body. But she could fix it, or at least start to. Instead of taking like the rest of us, she was going to give.

She was going to give herself.

Amid swirling pain, and spiking fear, and weakening logic, I knew it had to be done. Shilohe had to give her life, and the sooner the better. I was convinced. But the choice belonged to Locke. He needed help. He needed me. So in spite of the injuries whirling around and through me—through all of us—I took my turn to whisper. I moved toward Locke's ear, rested near his shoulder, and spoke: "For Wokeezae and the injured Tenarie. For your father and the fifthers. For Val. For Honke. And for Nicke."

"By my bones," whispered Locke, staring firmly at me.

"By my blood," he said, and I said it with him. "By my breath," we continued, louder, "and by the empyrean, I will do whatever I can to heal his wounds."

With that, he looked up with a firm chin. Light and resolve shone in his eyes.

He squinted, turning toward the blaze. The heat bit at his lips and the tip of his nose. He felt the sword burning at his skin through the thick leather. He held the handle toward her. She grabbed ahold, and with it he lifted her to her feet. Once she stood, he pulled the sword away in surprise.

She held out her unscathed hand as proof—it had not burned her. She *was* worthy.

He knelt, both knees on the stone. In his garb of the forest folk, now torn and ragged, he bowed his head and offered her the sword.

She accepted the gift with a nod and a gentle smile.

When he looked up, her eyes burned brightly as she gazed back over the sword and into his soul. With a hand at his elbow, she bid him rise, and then she grabbed him in one final embrace, holding the burning blade against his shoulder. She spoke gently in his ear: "Locke, thank you for coming. I knew you were a hero. I knew all along."

A hairline crack broke through his heart. As tears trickled down his face, all he could think to say was, "You're about to find out what happens when we die."

"I already know," whispered Shilohe.

Her confidence, her certainty, was irresistible. It drew him in to eternal sadness. He held fast, willing to never let go.

"If I see your mother, I will tell her you miss her." She kissed him on the cheek as she let go.

Locke nodded his thanks through blurry eyes. He wanted to hold her again, but she drew the blade, dropping the scabbard on the stairs. The Shining Sword empowered her, renewing her vitality and shedding the heat and pain like scales. She held the sword lightly in her hand. "Locke?" She looked at him, in a sad and lovely way, with those shining, perfect eyes. "If there's a way, I want you to come find me."

"A way? What do you mean?"

"I don't know." She shook her head. "I don't know. But if there is, I want *you* to come for me."

He nodded. He would go to the ends of the earth for her. He would give his life for her if he could. "But what if there isn't a way?"

"I'm still doing this." In spite of her bloodied face, she looked as regal as ever, the paradigm of a heroine.

A Goddess.

"Locke, go now," she commanded. "Please, go to your bird demon."

He couldn't bear to leave her, yet he wanted to obey, and it nearly killed him. The sadness, like death, strangled, so he couldn't even get out one final goodbye. He just smiled as best he could. He walked toward Stane's fallen body, and this time I went with him. With each step, the weight of death increased, till his breath was barely flowing. He stepped out of sight behind one of the rugged pillars, and there he stayed, with his back to it, unable to obey further. He waited, listening, still hoping for some miracle other than the one that would take her away. When he heard nothing, he looked around the edge of the stone pillar but could barely see through the tears in his eyes.

Shilohe brought the handle to her heart, gripping the Shining Sword with both hands, pointing the blade toward her feet. She closed her eyes, and her bottom lip quivered along with her resolve. "Thaese." Her voice floated across the air as soft as a whisper. "If there's any other way, please show it to me."

One glinting tear dropped down her cheek and off her lip. She opened her eyes, lined in red, and looked to the sky as if waiting for an answer. Perhaps she heard one because she looked down with her resolve back in her power.

More softly still, she said, "But if this is the future you've chosen, I go willing."

Pain cut through Locke's throat and into his stomach. His heart was now enduring a weight heavier than it could bear. This choice, her final choice, had made her all the more precious, and he wondered whether he should follow, diving into the blaze after her. He blinked till he could see her face in profile. He wanted so much to keep her, and looking was the only way he knew how. He took in her features, desperate to record them in memory's fable before the book closed for the last time.

He didn't see me fly in front of him, but I passed gently under his arm, reaching one leg back to counter my hand stretching forward. I let music, the full spectrum, flow from me into him, and it surrounded his heart, forming a fortress to keep it from bursting.

The brightness pulsed at the center of the unholy structure, bathing the Goddess—from her face and hands to her feet—in brilliance. She stepped down the stairs toward the blaze, and I felt the heat rising till it almost overpowered us.

She took the sword in one hand and stretched it behind her, hefting it as if it were light as wood, pointing it back with the elegance of a dance. The blade itself shone like a bolt of lightning that never vanished, a calm just before the storm.

Gritting her teeth, she stepped quickly down the stairs and leaped.

She lifted one knee and stretched her other leg behind her, in nearly the same pose as the statue of Numa. As she flew, a burst of wind rushed beneath her, lifting her higher. Her hair and skirt flared to the sides. For a moment she seemed suspended in that heroic pose. Soaring, she pulled the sword into a two-handed grip above her shoulder, and the blade pointed in a trail behind her, with her elbow aimed forward to match her fearsome gaze. She breathed like a summer breeze, transforming the moment of action into a moment that stilled even time.

As she neared the chains of lightning, I expected the immensity to overpower her. But instead she smashed the sword into the blaze with booming force.

In that time-bound moment, her true nature was revealed from deep within her feeble body. When she touched the lightning, she became the lightning. But not some pulsing brilliance. Like the sword, she was a steady, unbroken glory, taking hold of the power, becoming the power.

Her stroke cut through the swirling mass of light, exploding into a cacophony of sound.

The magic enveloped her, body and soul. As light and heat swallowed everything, her pain dissipated into the air.

Locke squeezed his eyes closed defensively.

And still he saw white.

76.

The Fall

THE BLINDING FLASH engulfed time itself.

It was white. Pure white, all around us. Nothing but white.

She'd become the light, and it poured over everything. We stood frozen while it swallowed all darkness. The moment stretched for leagues, till it reached the stars, and till it dove below the dying earth into bedrock, caverns, and molten lava. It stretched in all directions and dimensions and illuminated everything—the minds of sylves most of all.

"Wait, Shilohe!" screamed Locke. "Please!" He fell on his hand and knees. *Not death.* His body was trembling—down to his fingers pressed into the stone. *Not you.* He gasped for air and clenched his jaw, trying to hold on while the light pushed against us.

The magnificence faded, restoring color around us, leaving only the memory glowing in our heart. We found ourselves still in a building atop the dark sky.

But only for a moment.

The stones beneath us rumbled, like the yawning of Hell. The diminishing blaze at the center began releasing its chains, one by one. As they broke, the tension snapped into great bolts that shot across the sky, loosed in snaking whips of fire.

When the ball of flame disappeared completely, the platform around the hole crumbled and dropped into the dark sky. Shards turned silently as they fell into the storm.

"Run!" I shouted.

The structure fell from the center outward, racing after Locke as he sprinted down the stairs toward the outer edge. Each stone dropped into the void at the very moment his feet leapt off of it. Stane's body disappeared into the black morass. Locke ran toward a dead end amid an open sky—when he reached it, if he reached it, he would have nowhere else to go.

He still ran, fighting the inevitable.

The stones fell. His heart pounded. And Val appeared in our peripheral. Her great, white wings stretched to the sides as she aimed in a daring curve around the collapsing pillars, risking her own life to come for us. If only we could reach her before—

A turbulent jolt threw pieces of stone in every direction. Rock chips stung Locke's cheek as he squinted. Pillars fell with larger stones on top of them. And Val disappeared underneath.

The crumbling stairs caught up to Locke. His footing sunk beneath him in the darkening void.

He screamed.

Swinging his arms to maintain his upward position, he twisted on the rising winds, and I sped after him. His hair and hood whipped violently in the air above him, and air blew into his face so hard he could barely breathe. The fragments of stairs twisted silently all around, faintly illuminated by my blue glow. The blackness raced upward, blowing spindrift violently into his face.

It was moisture.

He was falling through moisture. It soaked into his clothes and bit at his nose and ears as he turned in the roaring tempest. Droplets of rain stood nearly still all around, as if time had slowed while the clouds fell upward. Dispersed among them were the gushing bodies of ondines, also falling to the earth, now seeping from bondage into the freedom of death, floating in ghastly beauty. The chaotic cocoon was short lived.

Locke shot through the black into open air. Trees coated the tiny mountains on the distant, dark world. The surprise of suddenly visualizing his death fall attacked him, and he let out a second scream.

It was answered by a roar.

The roar of a bird demon.

Valkalyse pressed her wings against her sides, shooting like an arrow after us.

Locke spread his arms and legs, clawing with his good fingers, as if the wind were a giant sheet he could hold on to.

Val made her way beneath Locke, then spread her wings ever so slightly, rising up and elegantly catching Locke on her back.

"Oh," said Locke with a shudder in his voice, and his jaw clenched against the jarring torrents. "Thank you, Val. Thank you!"

Valkalyse spread her wings in full. The descent slowed, and the rain stretched into long streaks. Lightning flashed behind us, igniting each tiny drop—a thousand slices of white.

But we didn't slow quickly enough.

"Val, are you okay?"

The bird demon gave a pitiable cry.

"It's right there," I shouted, pointing—I could feel the pain of her injury. "Her wrong wing must have been struck by the collapsing rocks. It might be broken."

The earth multiplied in size, growing like a nightmare.

"Come on, girl. I know it hurts, but hold on… please!"

The dark ground smashed into us.

The impact threw large globs of mud into the air and onto Locke's face. He flopped off the bird demon's back and splashed to the ground. At first all we sensed was confusion and ringing.

A stench hit me, the smell of rotting death, clamping its jaws so tight I could barely move. The rain streaked down immensely, the heavy tears of Nara falling for her dead children. The noise of so many droplets filled the air, even more than the water or the stench, a cataclysm of sound, flooding the world.

Giant stones smashed down around us, flinging mud, and shaking Locke's body with one impact after another.

"Valkalyse?" Locke put a hand on her back.

The bird demon was lying still, though her eyes were open.

"Look out!" I shouted.

Locke glanced at the sky just in time to see another falling stone. He leaned forward, pressing his weight into the beast's side, but barely moving her a foot.

The slab's weight dug deep into the soggy soil, right at Locke's heels. It threw sharp chunks of earth into Val and him as it landed and shook the ground. He leaned against the giant stone, which slanted toward him and overhead. Being next to it seemed as good a protection as anywhere. Stone after stone hit, booming the drumbeat of monsters, like the demigods were building a primeval graveyard.

Very suddenly, the terror was over. The sound of stones ended, leaving only the steady noise of falling rain.

Locke bowed his head. His shoulders shook as he wept with the sky, letting go of emotions he'd guarded so carefully. Pain of a lost mother, and Nicke's unbearable tragedy, and a Goddess taken from the world… His emotions came gushing. The raindrops played high notes as they dripped into newly forming pools—and drenched the whole world.

They hit like hail all around me. I wove between them, trying to stay nearby. One hit me right on the head, pushing me nearly into the the pools. When the second one hit, Locke almost laughed. He sniffled and smiled, his eyes red, and scooped me from the air, putting me gently into the pocket on his belt—it was the first time I'd ever needed to do this.

We'd fallen somewhere on the Majestic Sea, not far from Wiks Pike. Already the water was filling in the shattered cracks. Puddles connected with each other, covering the dead fish and rot and hordes of insects scattered on the ground. It wouldn't be long till the giant stones would be covered too.

"Val, are you okay?" Locke put a hand on the gryphine.

Her eyes drooped, and she shook her head, attempting to look more alert.

"It hurts," I said. "Her head is ringing. She's re-injured her leg. And the wing is badly damaged. The pain is awful."

"I see it in her eyes," said Locke.

Lightning flashed in a blinding burst. The thunder boomed and lingered, eager for its hearers to cower. The festering stench remained, of rot and death. Locke looked around warily. In the midst of this pandemonium, one dark shape on the ground stood out to us, smaller than the massive stones all around. A crumpled body lay in the mud, dark clothes and whispy white hair.

The impact had half buried Stane's corpse already. Locke walked toward it. One arm was crushed beneath a large stone. A pang of sorrow hit Locke in the face. The world had mistreated this man; the King had mistreated him—an evil that festered and spread, leaving pieces of injustice lying scattered everywhere.

An evil that had taken the Goddess.

Locke glanced around for another body, possibly lying somewhere amongst the rubble. But she wasn't to be found—I'd seen her vanish into light. She would never fall.

As tears fell with rain, Locke clenched his good fist. He imagined a better world than the one he found himself living in. His soul longed for it, from his heart to his bite, even though he didn't know how to get there, and he hoped that if he ever found it, he would find the Goddess waiting.

"Locke, look over there," I said, pointing to another shape beneath the falling rain. The shape of a cross—a sword stabbed into the ground, the pommel aimed at the broken clouds.

"The Shining Sword?" asked Locke.

The blade was bright but not glowing.

Scales covered the handle leading to the open mouth of a dragon. It gave off steam as the rain touched it. The hilt itself was the color of cool metal. He tapped it and felt no warmth. He gripped the handle with his wrong hand while his right, still throbbing from Stane's crushing boot, hung gingerly at his side. Stane had meant to crush his sword hand—he'd said as much. But Locke had found fortune's favor. He drew the sword from the ground, the first time he'd really held it. The scales in relief fitted into the scarred grooves in his skin, a perfect match. He pointed the mighty tip toward the broken skies.

Banshe wolves screamed behind him.

Maybe his own departure from this world was not so far off.

They howled again, very close—somewhere among the fallen stones—a shriek that overcame the sound of pouring rain. Unlike the gargoyles, these hadn't abandoned their posts at the death of Stane. Maybe Saede himself, the creator of the curse, drove them on.

Nicke's words rung in our mind: "They say that once a banshe wolfe is on your trail, either you or it must die." Now they had abundant water too, giving them no more cause for retreat.

Locke scanned the dark landscape and dead stones, looking for a place to run. Then he realized that even if he could find one he wouldn't go. Valkalyse was lying there injured. We remembered how the wolfe tore apart the Seer's corpse to taunt us. Locke couldn't risk them doing it to her.

No, there was nothing for it. He had to face them.

He had to protect Valkalyse.

Or die trying.

77.

Martigane's Theme

HE GRIPPED THE dim two-handed sword with his good hand. The shoulders of the banshe wolves appeared above the fallen stones, lumbering back and forth. The rain plastered down their fur. The noses and fangs appeared, then their black eyes, glaring beneath sheets of rain.

Although they were within our sight, I sensed none of their energy or pain—nothing but the scent of death.

Locke stepped directly between our bird demon and the predators. His hand throbbed, and my blue light seemed to do nothing to ease the pain.

He blinked his eyes closed. Then he squeezed them closed for a little longer, as long as he dared. *Still nothing.* But our need *was* dire. Why were the demigods abandoning us now?

A strong auster wind pushed the rain northward, in long, slanting streaks.

Locke glanced around the stone graveyard, hoping it might lend him some advantage. One of the massive pillars had landed vertically, stabbing deep into the muddy ground then tipping partially till the muddy foundation stopped it at a steep angle. It leaned like a slanted roof, pointing toward us. Maybe he could run up it and strike from above, like Gante had done.

A low growl vibrated through the air, coming from the nearer wolfe—this was the mindless brute with the arrow in its back. It seemed eager to charge. The other wolfe had a silver patch on its nose and a deep slice under its eye—Gante's final blow against evil before evil had taken his life. It nipped at its companion, as if warning it to slow down.

The wild wolfe charged.

Locke didn't have time to climb to high ground. In fact, he barely had time to step forward, hoping to draw the action further away from our wounded Valkalyse.

In the midst of death's odor and the patter of rain, we heard a voice. A meager voice. A child voice filled with rage:

"Kheeaaaa!"

It came from a small boy with bone-colored skin, darkness under his eyes, but courage in his frown. He was running from quite a distance away, charging with his dagger through the pooling sea, and limping as he went.

"Nicke?"

Locke looked with open mouth. *So unexpected, so surreal.* How, and why, and why now?

For a moment, our mind stood perfectly still, not looking forward or back, but simply breathing in the bizarre scene and every sensation it created. A million droplets of rain stabbed down. A pure note rang high above the tumult, a calming sound, reaching out and touching everything. And then I saw it, even though Locke didn't—a premonition, a memory of our immediate future. I saw the wolfe charging in ghostly blue—ahead of where the actual creature ran. It crashed into my Locke, pounding a claw into his eye, then clamping open jaws deep into the flesh of his tiny throat.

I was back in the moment.

Rain slashed in torrents.

Nicke was just finishing his warcry, which for a moment had even distracted the wolfe. But only a moment. Because the wolves weren't after Nicke. They were after us.

"Follow my lead," I whispered, slipping out of Locke's pocket and into the air.

The wolfe labored through the mud, which splashed into its wet fur as it gained momentum, coming faster and faster. It bounded, kicking mud, and leaped off powerful hind legs.

"Duck!" I shouted, swooping in front of Locke's face, leading him down and to the wrong side. He tucked and rolled, just dodging the first set of claws. "And back!" He followed my blue slash again, pushing off from a squat into a backward somersault with perfection that should've been impossible. Rainwater flicked in a trail behind him.

Locke had escaped the leap of the first wolfe.

Almost.

The wolfe tried to change its course, and that second swing caught Locke's moccasin. This tumbled his backward somersault wildly out of control. He went sprawling through mud.

The wolfe slid to a stop and turned to face him, putting its back to

Valkalyse. As it rose to snap its steel jaws around Locke's hind leg, I darted between raindrops, flying at the wolfe's eye with all the physical force I could muster.

And this time I actually hit.

The wolfe yelped. It looked at me with terror, hating my hot blue light near its cold dark soul. I attacked again, this time biting the sensitive skin of its nose. The wolfe barked and actually backed up, snapping at me in the air.

I dodged and charged again, biting its ear.

The wolfe gave a frustrated snarl.

While I was engaged, the silver wolfe pranced carefully forward, not foolish enough to come barrelling past its target.

"Locke, look out!" I screamed.

It marched toward him, getting lower the nearer it got, ready to do what it had done to Gante—to smash and tear the life out of him all at once. Its thin black lips pulled back, showing white fangs.

Locke held his sword in a high guard with one hand. He would add one good slash to this monster's face before he joined Gante in death.

Then we heard the warcry—"KHEEAAAA!"

Nicke had run up the ramping pillar and was airborne. The dagger's blade jutted down from the bottom of his fist in a reverse grip. Nicke jammed the blade into the beast's neck, clinging to his weapon and fur.

The wolfe turned toward Nicke, flinching against the sting in its neck. Then it flung its head in the opposite direction, twisting from one shoulder to the other.

Nicke went flying.

And Locke's sword cut deep into the wolfe's exposed throat.

Though the metal no longer glowed, the edge remained razor sharp. It made a sucking sound as it pierced flesh and lung. The wolfe yelped a high pitch, spitting mucus through the bloodless wound. Locke dragged the blade out and swung it again, landing it deep behind the monster's ear.

It wheezed another growl, stepping deliriously forward, but it was no longer looking at anything.

Locke scrambled out of the way.

The wolfe crashed into the mud, exhaling for the last time.

Meanwhile, I'd been trying to drive the wild wolfe backward. It had been working until two raindrops patted me down in rapid succession.

That wasn't nearly enough to stop me, but it slowed me, and so I failed to dodge the raging wolfe.

Its massive paw slammed into me, scooping me downward, and pounding my deep blue into mud. I was surrounded by water and earth with no way to breathe.

Immediately the wolfe turned and lunged at my elfe.

Locke had just barely escaped the final collapse of the other wolfe, and he didn't see this attack coming from behind. Panic hit me like a thunderclap.

The beast was midair, its back legs stretched out in a forceful leap, its front legs reaching out to crush.

Val's swift jaws appeared from behind.

She caught the hind paw in a snarling grip. The wolfe and her jaw slammed into the ground, throwing mud.

Locke spun and jammed the point of the sword downward into the wolfe's spine, at the base of the large skull. But with only one hand to make the thrust, the stroke faltered.

The beast squealed.

The sword had sunk deep, but not deep enough.

The wolfe pushed its ravenous jaws forward, knocking Locke off his feet.

Locke kicked at the wolfe's face with his heel.

The creature squinted but didn't slow its crawling rampage.

The blade stood erect in the wolfe's neck, but still the creature lunged, growling as foam flowed out through its teeth.

Locke kicked, and the force smashed against his heel.

The brute caught Locke's ankle between sharp teeth, and I felt pinching pain stabbing through flesh toward bone.

Valkalyse, spreading even her broken wing wide, jerked at the wolfe's leg with all her might, twisting her body and tail. Though I was buried in mud and water, her move shot pain through us both. But her power jerked the wolfe back through the mud, and its jaws dragged Locke along.

With his ankle still caught in the teeth, Locke planted his free foot in the mud, and the momentum pulled him back to standing—within reach of the sword protruding from the wolfe's neck. He gripped the hilt with one hand and rested the wrist of his injured hand on the crossguard, leaning his weight down till he heard crunching sinew.

I cringed.

The beast gave one last bark and then was still.

Locke fell onto his back. The teeth of the dead wolfe still clamped tight around his ankle. Gritting his own teeth, Locke leaned forward, grabbed the wolfe's upper lip with his good hand and pushed down on the bottom jaw with his free foot. The clamp opened, and he pulled his bleeding mocassin free.

This was not the Night of the Wolfe.

The corpse stared at Locke, lifeless but not bleeding.

I braced myself against the pain, both Locke's and Val's. I fought through the mud and took flight, skimming across the ground toward Locke.

The feeling haunted us again, the ghost of death swirling past, clawing, but unable to get a grip. As it floated away, it took with it the ghastly scent, leaving nothing but two carcasses of what once were wolves.

Locke prodded gently at his new wound, testing the damage as blood leaked through the leather. The long teeth had broken the flesh, rubbing raw a large patch of skin. The muscle throbbed, and his mocassin felt tight.

"Nicke?" shouted Locke, looking around.

"I'm okay," said a voice through the rain.

Nicke limped toward us, having to correct his course as he stumbled, dazed, to the side.

Locke rolled back into the mud, till his wheat-colored hair was soaked. He breathed, just lying there for a long time with his mud-splattered face toward the sky. With open mouth, he caught rain on his tongue and the back of his throat.

The tiny drops were soothing and warm.

78.

Brothers

THAT'S A BIRD demon," said Nicke.

I watched him closely. His voice looked the same as when we first met him, the same red string, soft and thin, only the string had gotten thicker, stronger.

The leg of Nicke's pants was still shredded and stained dark red. Underneath a bandage wrapped his calf muscle. He retrieved his dagger from the wolfe's side, the same weapon he'd claimed from the Hundred after conquering them. As he approached us, he stared at Valkalyse with his big, dark eyes, and she returned his gaze, still with a hint of melancholy. Nicke sat next to Locke in the mud and groaned. "I left my crutch back there. My leg is killing me."

Locke lay on the ground, squinting toward the rain and the night sky beyond. "What are you doing out here?"

"Is he friendly?" asked Nicke.

"Yeah, *she* is. Her name's Valkalyse. She's a gryphine."

"What happened to your sylfe?" asked Nicke. "Wow!"

"Uh, he touched some water."

"It turned him blue?"

"Yeah, basically. Have you heard of the ascendant ones?"

"No."

"What are you doing out here?" asked Locke.

"You said you'd be back in a few days," said Nicke.

"Yeah, it's been a few days."

"It's been way more than a few. More like several."

Locke chuckled. "I guess you're right. I'm sorry I took so long. So you decided to come after me?"

"I told you I would. Besides, Ashe started speaking a few days ago, and he said we should leave."

"Because of the war?"

"Yeah. And I didn't want to cause trouble for your father. I was starting to like him."

"You were?"

"Yeah. Can I touch the bird demon?"

"Sure. Put that dagger away though."

Nicke scooted closer, through the mud.

Valkalyse, strangely, didn't even look at Nicke. With her chin resting in a rising puddle, she looked away as if distracted by something important in the other direction.

"She seems kinda shy," said Nicke.

"Did you see the Tenarie warriors attack the village?"

Nicke touched her soft, wet fur with his fingertips. His sylfe was looking at the gryphine too, much more animated than we'd ever seen him. For a moment, I considered what it would be like to form the consonance with them.

"Did you leave before the attack?" asked Locke.

"We ran into the Tenarie war party as we were leaving. I thought they were going to kill me, but they just smacked me around and sent me home—I didn't tell them I don't have a home. I headed north, and they..." His attention was again drawn to the bird demon. "That's strange how she's turning away. Why's she doing that?"

"I don't know."

"What's her name again?"

"We named her Valkalyse."

"Hey, Valkalyse, hey, girl," said Nicke in a soft, false-pitched voice, trying to get her to turn and look at him. The falling rain plastered his wild white hair against his skull. "I'm not gonna hurt you. I liked how you attacked those wolves! I hate those guys." He stroked his finger across her forearm. His tone lowered: "I always wanted to get this close to a bird demon. But I always imagined it would be hunting them."

Val's neck whipped around, and Nicke jumped back. Her black nostrils nearly touched his chin, and he held his hands in the air to surrender. Valkalyse stared, as if hoping to discover a joke.

"I'm sorry," said Nicke, eying her whiskers. "She understands Kyriglae? I'm sorry, Valkalyse. That's what all the stories are about."

Val's head dropped, and she pushed against Nicke's belly, scooting him away from her. She laid her chin back in the mud.

"I think she's starting to like me," said Nicke, and he scooted back over to pet her. "How'd you make friends with her?"

"It's a long story. I'll tell you on the way."

"On the way where?"

"Back home."

Nicke didn't answer—as if he weren't sure about going back.

"At the very least," said Locke, "we need to get off this mud before it becomes a sea again." He said this, but he didn't move, didn't even attempt to move. He just put a hand behind his head and lay back. The rain poured thick and gentle while thunder boomed in the distance. "If I can walk, I'm going to go find your crutch. And if Val can walk, we're going to keep going south. Where were you planning to go anyway?"

"I don't know. I was just wandering, kind of like how you found my village. For some reason I didn't feel afraid either. I just thought it would be okay. I can't explain. Hey, guess what I found."

"What?" asked Locke.

"Right before it started to rain, I was crossing the dry sea on foot. I was walking into the wind when I heard strange natural-sounding notes on the air." Nicke rummaged through his bag. "But the notes weren't my sylfe. They were something in the actual sky. I looked up, and this fell on the ground in front of me." He held up the pinkalue.

Locke and I laughed aloud, and for a moment he forgot about his pain and the Goddess and the corpse of the villain.

"Here you go," said Nicke.

Locke took it and smiled.

"Hey, what happened to your hand?" asked Nicke.

"I burned it."

"Those are dragon scales."

"Yeah. I touched the handle of this sword when it was really hot."

"You've heard about the Hero of Soule?"

"I don't think so."

"He had a hand just like yours. It's long—I could tell it to you on the way home."

Locke laughed weakly again. So Nicke had agreed.

"And your other hand?" asked Nicke, looking at Locke's swollen and mangled fingers.

"Have you heard of the Tenarie sign of humility?" His hand throbbed something extra when we thought about it.

"Yes. And I would never do it." Nicke stroked Val's neck, but his stare was somewhere leagues away, seemingly on some horrible memory.

"Did you see the stones falling from the clouds?" asked Locke.

"Yeah. It started to rain right after I found your pinkalue. And rocks came pounding down right in front of me. It was scary, but I stuck around because I thought you must be somewhere nearby."

"We were in that fall," said Locke.

"How? And where'd the rocks come from?"

Locke explained about Stane's volant stone and his temple in the sky. "I can't believe you attacked a banshe wolfe!"

Nicke grinned sheepishly' and looked at the giant corpses. "I can't either."

"You were so afraid of them."

"I know."

"It's a good thing you did, or I wouldn't ever be going home."

Nicke smiled, but then he gave an uncomfortable expression.

"What's the matter?" asked Locke.

"I'm still not sure I should go back," said Nicke.

"The war's over. The water's returned."

"I'm not sure I belong there."

"Yes you do. You're one of us—one of my family now."

"Just because it rained doesn't mean the war is over."

"There's no reason for them to fight anymore."

"The old reasons."

"I don't think they will. They'll be too happy to want to fight."

"Maybe."

"Besides, if you come home with us, you'll get to ride Valkalyse."

Nicke looked at the bird demon and then at Locke.

"Not right now—she's injured. But once she heals." Locke rolled forward so he was sitting up. The rain poured down his face and dripped from the tips of his hair.

"Okay, I'll come." A grin pushed against the darkness of Nicke's soul, a grin he couldn't quite hold back. But Locke didn't seem to share his excitement. "Why are *you* so sad?"

At the thought of her, the darkness stabbed at Locke, the same gaping void that appeared every time he thought of his mother. "Someone very important to me gave her life to break the spell." Nara's rain dripped across his face like tears.

"The princess?" asked Nicke.

"*The Goddess,*" I whispered.

"Yes," said Locke. "You talked to her, huh?"

"Yeah, across the river west of the cove. I was trying to be alone but I couldn't climb with my leg, and then she came bursting in my fort. Caught me off guard. But I didn't hurt her. She had a weird torch."

"What did she say?" Locke wanted the answer more desperately than he'd wanted water the past few days—a few more pieces of her memory.

"I don't remember exactly. But she was different than other elves. She was kind to me. And her sylfe was happy. She said my Ashe had been cursed by the villain in the whispering thorns. Then her sylfe said something to him. I'm not sure what, but I think maybe she commanded him to start talking. So he did. He's been feeling better ever since. Almost like magic. I keep thinking about her."

Us too.

Locke nodded at the bittersweet taste. These small recollections meant everything, yet they expanded the void in his heart.

"I felt… I don't know… like she didn't care if I was a Tenarie, or a murderer, or anything. She was just okay with me. And even though she didn't know me, she was willing to help me. Just like you. Seemed like that sort of person. The good kind. And when I told her you were my only family, she said she'd be my family too. That was the only time I've ever had a sister."

"She gave her life for you," said Locke, and pride lingered on his tongue.

Nicke nodded, and his soaking hair dripped all down his face. "For some reason, every time I think about her, I feel like I can forgive them for what they did."

"What?" I whispered—more in awe than really asking.

Locke looked at Nicke with my question on his face.

"The Hundred, I mean," said Nicke. "Most of the time I wish I could kill them all again. Except when I think about her. She lets me put all that weight down and just feel okay."

While Nara cried her heavy tears, I smiled.

Nicke smiled too, but just a little.

And Locke almost smiled.

79.

Rescue

WE HAD WATER now.
The sound fell all around us, but we only saw rain where it fell in front of shadows. The mighty chorus rose in crescendo, ebbed toward silence, then grew again—so many beats as one. The wind rushed through, creating waves of rain that we could see and giving shape to the roaring mass. It pooled up around Locke's legs and continued to rise, slow enough I could hardly see it, but each time I noticed, it seemed deeper. Small waves shimmered across the warm surface with the wind.

Locke bound his ankle tight with strips of green cowl. He could walk on it but not easily and probably not for long.

The bird demon was in worse shape. Her injured wing throbbed, and her wrong front leg, which never seemed could carry her long distances, had been re-injured in the fall. She was too big for us to carry, but she could limp along on three feet, at the risk of doing more damage to her remaining front leg.

"You could pray." It was what I thought Lonae might have said.

Nicke watched Locke curiously.

"I don't think I can." That was all he said.

Ashe and I hovered behind as the three of them limped along, each hating to walk but unable to do otherwise. We had to try to make it home. Their steps stabbed into me.

Raindrops fell, while golden rays broke through in the east, and the sun gently touched the grassy hills to the south. Its light would drive off the wraiths. The curse had been broken on the morning of the twentieth day. In the west, the dark sky still hid the peaks of the Burning Mountain. Against the shining gray, I saw small flecks in the sky.

"Locke, the bird demons are coming!" I shouted.

"Uh oh," said Nicke.

"No, it's okay." Though they hadn't walked far, Locke sat down without another step. I was glad he got his weight off his bleeding ankle. The other two followed his lead. "I think they'll help us. Mostly I hope they can help Valkalyse. Carry her home, somehow."

"Or heal her," I said, "if they can." The distant creatures flew on, growing in size against the horizon. We watched, not patiently but exhausted.

Mighty gusts of wind preceded their arrival, which threw the rain in all directions. A flutter of white feathers and scaled wings enveloped us. They splashed into the mud, roaring and purring, greeting Valkalyse and showing her sympathy. The rain dripped on their shiny, furry backs. Many of the same young gryphines were here, along with others with faded fur and great scars, and several dragons.

Locke rolled to his knees, picked up the Seer's blade, and then stood, leaning on the weapon to keep his weight off the injured ankle.

The wind rushed upward with more fury as the giant red dragon touched down. His wingspan reached farther and his shoulder higher than any of the others in the pride. He didn't greet Valkalyse; instead he moved directly toward Locke, pointing his long neck at us in a menacing way. His jaw hung unclosed in a strange grin too.

Locke fought the urge to back up or lift the sword defensively. He breathed, trying to regard the creature as his friend.

The dragon came close enough to tear Locke's face off. He opened his mouth in a wide yawn, like he was sizing my elfe for a single bite. From inside the jaws emerged the King Salaminde, burning without smoke in regal glory. As if that weren't surprise enough, a second salaminde came from the red beast's mouth. They hissed as they came in contact with the rain. Other salamindes appeared from the mouths of their bird demons too.

"Locke of the Enchanted Wood," said the King Salaminde, in his smoldering, dark voice. "My friend, you did it."

"I'm worried about Valkalyse," said Locke, truly concerned but also eager to duck the accolades.

"Who?"

"The gryphine who helped us. She's injured."

"So are you, it appears. Well, I know what to do. I want you to meet Vesanezatae. Her kynde is the bird demon you named Valkalyse." The

King Salaminde stretched a fiery, ethereal arm toward the salaminde next to him—we recognized her as the one Shilohe had freed from the torch.

"Hello, again," said Locke. "Can you help her?"

Vesanezatae did not speak but simply nodded the form of her head.

The King Salaminde spoke again: "We salamindes can heal most any kynde, with one particular exception: We cannot heal without the permission and help of a kynde's own elemental. So while Vesanezatae was kidnapped, her bird demon, your Valkalyse, could not accept our help. Now that they are reunited, healing can begin."

The King Salaminde turned to the others and commanded them to help. The glowing elementals responded immediately, surrounding Locke and Nicke and Valkalyse in three distinct whorls of fire, unfazed by the sizzling raindrops striking down in long lines.

They finished healing Nicke first, and when they backed away he said, "Whoa! Thanks."

Like before, the heat burned into Locke's wounds in a calming blaze. He gritted against the pain, his muscles tense at first. Slowly he relaxed, and his breathing steadied. The burning transformed into the warmth of life. He put pressure back on his wounded ankle, splashing it fully into the water. It supported him without grief. They healed the fingers he'd burned in the pool of living water, but his broken hand still throbbed.

The flurry of sparks retreated away from us, and the King Salaminde approached. "If the healing process takes the wrong course, it can meet a dead end and the injury will remain indefinitely. This happened to your bird demon's leg—because we were unable to help her when it mattered most. We cannot entirely correct the course the wound has taken, and what we can do will take a long time. Her wing, though, is doing much better. The same is true for you. We have done what we can with your ankle, and it is much improved. But we cannot heal the bones in your broken hand until they have first been set in their proper place. You need a healer from your own land, or the mending is certain to take the wrong course."

"I understand." Locke felt better, but not fully rejuvenated. The aching wound weighed him down, and his aching heart did all the more.

"Hurry then. Our sister is eager to carry you." He motioned toward Valkalyse, who was standing again and limping toward us. Locke smiled and Val seemed to as well, baring her teeth and breathing gently. The King

Salaminde and Vesanezatae moved back into the mouth of the giant red dragon.

"So she's not going to stay with Valkalyse?" asked Locke.

"That is not the salaminde way—it would not be proper. We are not tethered to our kynde as your sylves are to you, so it is the bird demon's prerogative to follow her elemental, or, as in this case, to leave and go her own way. Please keep her safe from your tribe, and bring her home when you can."

"I will," promised Locke.

The winds suddenly rushed against the rain, fighting upward. As the two collided, water splashed wildly. One by one the bird demons followed the red dragon into the sky, flapping their wet wings and soaring into the distance overhead.

"Thanks for staying, Val," said Locke with half a smile.

She nuzzled Locke's dragon hand till he patted her on the head.

He looked at Nicke and said, "Let's go home."

80.

Hopeward

NICKE HUGGED HIS arms tightly around Locke's chest.
When Valkalyse launched into the air, Nicke let out a deep, joyful laugh, stronger than the sound of rain.

Locke couldn't resist the onslaught, and in spite of what was lost, he laughed too. As we flew on, he tapped Val's sides with his feet—wrong and right and down then up. When Nicke let out a whooping battle cry, Locke laughed again.

From high above the Wisting Mountains, we looked back on the Majestic Sea. It was not yet majestic, but it was beginning to look like a sea again. We could no longer see the stones that had fallen from Stane's dark fortress—the water had buried them and their cursed master. The rain lightened and even stopped altogether in places, while the sun shone through in the east. Locke told our story, while I interrupted with comments and Nicke, with questions.

After an hour, Nicke's eyes closed and he slumped forward onto Locke's back, with his arms around his almost big brother.

Locke was exhausted, but he couldn't sleep. Not this time. The thunder purred far in the distance behind us. "I used to think that sound meant the end of time," he said into the rushing wings of the wind.

Nicke lifted his head and gave me a strange look through groggy eyes, but soon he put his head back down again.

"This is the beginning," I said.

Locke nodded, his expression solemn. "I wish we still had the consonance."

"Well, we..." I paused, unsure of what to say, unsure of the consequences.

"What, Picke?"

I tried to decide what he needed to hear.

"You said the consonance broke when we separated in that abyss," he said.

"It did. But when you left to get the sword, Lonae and I re-formed it."

"You did?"

"I shouldn't have brought it up. It was more of a final farewell, before they, before she..."

"I'm not sure she's..." said Locke.

"I know, but I just don't...." *I couldn't.* I didn't know the truth of the matter, so I left it unspoken.

"I want to try talking to her."

I looked at my elfe and wondered. The longing in his eyes was too much. Whether it was possible didn't really matter—he would long for her whether she was within reach or not. "Okay."

He scooped me out of the rushing wind and cupped me in his dragon palm. Holding me close, he inhaled. "Shilohe, are you there?"

As he spoke her beautiful name, I caught his words. They resonated through me and into the wind, traveling from us toward... I didn't know. Where had she gone? And where was her Lonae—frozen somewhere beneath the winds of exile? Or were they still together somehow?

The response was what I expected—*nothing.* "It's like before. I send the message, but I have no way of knowing whether she'll ever hear it."

I felt hope within Locke, a hope that didn't fade as moment after moment washed by. "You can feel when the consonance is broken, right? There's an emptiness."

"There's an emptiness now."

"So the consonance is broken?"

I hesitated, wanting only to speak exact truth. "I'm not sure."

"What do you mean?"

"It's not the same emptiness. It's different somehow, a different void. Maybe it's because of the blue light. Or maybe it's because our consonance stretches so much farther this time. It just seems different. I don't know."

"But you definitely had the connection before she...?"

"Yes."

"Then we just have to keep hoping."

He wanted me to look ahead, beyond now, toward some unseen thing in the future. I hated that. "I don't know, Locke. I've never heard of such a thing—a consonance with the deceased."

"You can't tame a bird demon," he said. "You can't find a hyuman north of the rim. You can't—"

"Alright, alright," I said.

"Just because we don't know about it, doesn't mean it doesn't exist."

81.

Home

THE WORLD CHANGED color in the rain.
The bark of trees turned a shade so dark the brown was almost black.
The reviving green became vibrant, purer and deeper. Red buds sprouted on
branches while droplets of rain dripped from their bottoms. The trees grew
full and lush, and the waterfalls roared. The Enchanted Wood had been
reborn. So had the Rueful Wilderness, I supposed, as the face had wanted.

We landed among the climbing trees, the place they said bird demons
destroyed so long ago. By proceeding on foot, we hoped to be seen by
fewer people.

It had been quiet in the darkness. Now mourning doves cooed, bugs
chirped, and the rivers spoke their soothing songs into the air. It looked
the way it was supposed to, aside from the bodies of wraiths strewn about,
staked down with large spikes, dissipating in the reinstated sun.

Many brightly colored doors faced the road, each nestled in the giant
roots of a blathae tree. As we headed up the final slope, the laughter of
kids reached us. They came dashing into sight, coming down the path in
our direction, but they slowed and then stopped. One kid turned and ran.
The rest stared. The whole scene fell quiet.

Locke's smile just barely appeared through his exhaustion. "Hey, guys.
Rede, Ponde, Slightly. I'm back."

No child moved closer, and a few moved back.

"It's a good bird demon!" Nicke petted Val on the neck. "Look, guys!
She's peaceful! See, Rede? She wouldn't hurt a boatsinker!"

"She's friendly, I promise," said Locke. "You can touch her if you want."

They looked suspiciously at Locke's bound-up hand and his torn and
bloody boot. His muddy, ragged clothes surely didn't help either. He turned
to Valkalyse and scratched the soft skin behind her ears. She squinted and
was noticeably pleased.

The kids giggled.

Rede approached. He got nearer and nearer, then dashed—making Val flinch—touched her leg, and darted back. The other children snickered.

When Slightly approached, Val turned her terrifying mouth down toward him, and he froze. The other kids held their breaths. They laughed when she licked his face over and over again. Slightly stepped back, eyes wide in surprise.

As Locke continued, one skinny little girl ran ahead of him with green eyes and crooked teeth, Mr. Lunke's youngest daughter—much cuter than his oldest. She tilted her head and pointed at me. "He's blue."

"Yeah, he... uh... he's like that now," said Locke.

"Blue is my favorite color," she said.

Locke smiled. "Mine too."

"Like your eyes," she said, blushing.

Locke blushed a little too.

The children followed us down the winding path. Slightly dared to ask for a ride. Locke couldn't lift with his broken hand, so Nicke grabbed the kid under the arms and heaved—though he was barely tall enough for the task. Then Nicke told the story of how Val defeated "two evil banshe wolves!" Soon kids were running to invite their friends, cousins, and parents to see the wonder. Even the cynical adults seemed to soften when they saw the children riding on our Val's back. Their sylves seemed a little brighter too, as if washed clean by the rain.

We passed between trees blackened from fire. A large portion of the village had been burned. Only the main braces remained of Mr. Colrye's former grand treehouse; the rest was ashes and charred branches. We gawked at the destruction. The path was lined with the scorched carcasses of wraiths and their leaking black blood. As we passed more treetop houses, people stared, at first with worry, then with wonder.

Soon we approached the cove and our own treehouse—the same stretch where we first ran from the wolves. Back then it had been a dark passageway. Now it was a garden corridor.

We entered through the main gate and saw Locke's father standing on the balcony, the same place he'd thrown the spear from. Pieces of the green door lay next to the roots beneath him. What was left of the green door hung lopsided, still pretending to keep things out. Locke's father watched us and the train of children with a smile on his face, unusual for the man we knew. We saw concern too, probably because of Locke's ragged appearance. Or because of the bird demon. When we got closer, he shouted, "Where have you two been?"

Was that an expression of concern for Nicke as well?

"It's a long story." Locke tried to smile as he walked weakly toward the treehouse. The newly fastened rope ladder reached so high into the tree that Locke felt like he might collapse on the ground right there. His tenacity had finally been spent. "I'm tired, dad. I need to rest. Maybe for a few days."

"Hi, Nicke," said Locke's father. As if that weren't shocking enough, he added, "Welcome back."

Nicke smiled and nodded.

Locke's father glanced a little warily at Val. I saw and felt a large gash that streaked across his forearm, and two of his fingers were throbbing. "You want me to pull you up?"

"Just give me a moment." Locke nearly chuckled. He put one hand on the ladder, gathering his strength for the final climb, which would be more difficult with only one hand. He turned toward Nicke, behind him: "You want to go first?"

"No, no. I insist," said Nicke with a grin.

"What happened to your hand?" asked Locke's father.

"It's a Tenarie sign… of…" Locke trailed off. "It's a long story. I'm going to need you to send for a healer."

"Maybe Shaye?"

Locke looked up with a questioning glance. *Why had he picked her?*

"She's come by a couple times," said Locke's father.

"Why?"

"Once to help Nicke. And I'm not sure why the other time. Aren't bird demons dangerous?"

"Not this one."

"What would your grandfather say?"

Locke shrugged.

"And what happened to your sylfe?"

Whoa. I couldn't remember the last time he'd acknowledged my existence. *If ever.*

Locke looked at me and chuckled. "He's blue." That was all the answer he could muster.

Locke's father didn't laugh, maybe too curious to find the humor. "And you've heard about the battle?"

"Not much."

"I knew this day was coming. I've been saying it. They passed right through here, a big old Tenarie war party, setting houses and trees on fire as they went. One arrow even hit near the stables, but I put it out."

"I'm so glad our cove was spared," said Locke softly, mostly to me.

"They arrived not more than an hour after we got news that the Chief Captain had fallen with his thousand. Their main attack was at the village. Our Fifth River didn't get hit half as bad. They came for our cisterns, setting everything on fire. It would've been a devastating battle, but it was interrupted by an attack from an army of wraiths. These weren't ordinary wraiths either. They wore armor, and some said they fought with the strength of the Hundred. They attacked Kyrie and Tenarie alike, till finally we joined forces against them."

Locke shook his head—it was baffling to imagine Kyrie and Tenarie fighting side by side.

"Of course we couldn't hardly do anything to stop them. We'd have been doomed if it weren't for the rain. The battle had just begun when it came. You wouldn't believe it: Quiet skies one moment and a flood the next. Just in time. Damn lucky."

Nicke folded his arms and nodded, with an expression of gratitude.

"At the last possible moment," said Locke's father. "Coming down so hard. The wraiths were smart. They knew the rain meant their time was up. They retreated, just like that, running to their caves. The water saved us all, I think. Hard to believe."

"It *is* hard to believe," said Locke. Shilohe had said that waiting would mean trading lives for hers. When she did what she did, she spared the whole village—the whole land even.

"At first people just stared at the sky. Some of the warriors dropped their weapons right on the ground. It put out the fires. And slowly the two sides just kind of fell back. Some of them even rejoiced together. Craziest thing I've ever seen. The Tenarie withdrew. I've known all along that bad times were coming; I just never knew they'd end so quickly. Five weeks to the day."

I whispered in Locke's ear, and he repeated my question to his father. "You mean four weeks, right?"

"Five weeks. Ask anyone."

I searched our mind, trying to figure out how we might have lost that many days. In the desert maybe, or in the cave, or when Locke passed out after his burn, or when he was prisoner, or the fog. I really wasn't sure. But to lose five whole days…

Locke's father bent to scratch his calf muscle, the whole time keeping an eye on our Valkalyse. "Oh, and a crazy hyuman was asking about you."

"Honke?" asked Locke.

"What?"

"That's his name: Honke."

"I don't know his name. When the fighting stopped, the Tenarie all left but he stayed behind. He kept saying he needed the boy with the white sword who was supposed to be called Locke. So they sent him here."

"And where is he now?"

"I sent him away. You don't have a white sword. That one's more of a light gray, isn't it?"

"So you don't know where he went?"

"No."

Locke didn't reply, looking down, too tired to hold up much longer.

"When the rain came, people got crazy," said Locke's father. "Standing out in the meadows where it was heaviest, just soaking it all in, getting drenched like they were out of their minds. It was a sight. So you going to tell me your story?"

"Let me climb up there first." He turned to Valkalyse. "I want you to fly to the top of our tree. You'll be safer. And it'll keep people away from you." She looked at him carefully, but didn't move. "I mean it. Go now." He pointed more firmly. "Go!"

She spread her wings, and the wind picked up, lifting leaves and sticks into the air with her as she flapped up to the higher reaches of our massive tree.

Once she was safe, Locke stared at the broken green door while he mustered the will to ascend the ladder. Moments later, we were inside the vine-covered treehouse, where Locke and Nicke scarfed down bread and milk. Locke told his story—though too softly for my taste, in a way you'd have to guess whether he was the hero. I didn't like that. Locke and Shilohe had saved the land—through her sacrifice and his courage.

We went back to our old room.

"You should take your bed back," said Nicke, "now that my leg's mostly better."

"No, no," said Locke with a grin, "I insist." He went out to the hammock on the balcony, where the sky was visible through a gap in the greenery, and closed his eyes before he was even lying down. He hung his broken hand over the side of the hammock. With his sword hand, he grabbed the silver amulet hanging around his neck.

Like that, he slipped into a dream.

82.

Octave

LOCKE?"
A soft, angel voice called his name.

"Locke, wake up."

He'd slept all morning, through the afternoon, and into the beginning of the night.

She took his good hand between hers and caressed it warmly—just as she'd done when they were children. She spoke his name once more, gentle as a song: "Locke."

He came awake with a hopeful gasp: "Shi—!"

But it was not the Goddess. It was the Angel sitting at his bedside.

His eagerness faded with a disappointed sigh, which he caught just a little too late. He tried to make up for it with a groggy smile. "Shaye, hi." When he noticed his hand in hers, he pulled it away skittishly and sat up, blinking and squinting with a puffy face. His heart beat faster too.

She pretended to take no notice and gave him a simpering smile, delicate and coy. Her tawny hair was wrapped thickly in intricate braids on top of her head, and each part of the weave shined in the torchlight. Her sylfe was a gem of equal beauty.

As the stars twinkled through a gap in the foliage, I slipped out of Locke's shirt to get a better look.

"Whoa," said Shaye. "What happened to Picke?"

I zipped behind Locke's shoulder, trying to get out of sight.

"Uh, he got wet," said Locke with a smile. "Couldn't get it off."

She smiled too, kindly not demanding a better answer, and gazing with that compassion in her eyebrows. "Reminds me of the time Tunke pushed you into the dyeing vat." She gave a delighted giggle.

"Except that was deep purple." Locke gave a mild but genuine chuckle.

Shaye waited while they both breathed in the laughter. "Nicke led me to your bird demon at the top of the tree."

"He did?"

"Yes. While there was still daylight. I wanted to see what I could do with her ankle. The injury is too long passed to do much, but I think I made her limp a little lighter, though it will become worse the older she gets."

"Thank you. You're daring."

"She seemed gentle."

Locke smiled at that. "Still climbing, huh?"

"Only when the adults aren't looking." Shaye wore a simple, flowing white windress, the nearly irresistible kind. It would've looked even more elegant catching the breeze and hovering just out of reach of the ground. White leggings underneath came down to her ankles. "I came to see *you* too."

"You didn't have to."

"My sylfe insisted. I've heard her more clearly since you… since the sky was broken."

"Me?"

"Yes. Nicke told me all about it."

"That kid's such a talker."

"I'm sorry if you wanted to keep it private. I won't tell anyone if you don't want me to."

"I don't mind if *you* know," he said.

Shaye looked at his hand, maybe wondering whether taking it would cause more or less comfort. She looked away at the whispering leaves overhead and then at the night sky. "They're beautiful." The starlight gleamed in her eyes—*she* was beautiful. More beautiful since she came back from the Sacred Falls. Even Locke couldn't help but think so. Under these stars, her flaw only added to her beauty. Or maybe Locke was seeing through me. "Each twinkle is like they're winking at us."

"I wonder what they mean by it," he said. "What secret they're trying to tell us…" *It wasn't a bad line—winking and secrets.*

She smiled. "I don't know. I'll bet they know a lot of secrets."

If I were to have guessed, I'd have said they were trying to get him to sit up and kiss her, but he didn't, even after I nudged him.

"So what happened to you up there?" she asked.

"It's a long story."

"Most people know that the Seer and the King's daughter were killed."

"She wasn't his actual daughter. Step daughter."

"Oh." She waited a moment, as if hoping he might say more. "Some even say they gave their lives to save us."

"They did. We owe it to them—her especially."

"Nicke made it sound like *you* played a role."

"Nicke thinks my sword hand is lucky."

"Maybe it is."

"What I did was nothing by comparison."

"You should write your story," she said. "People should know."

"Picke says so too. He wants to sing it."

"You should let him."

"I'm afraid they won't understand. They'll treat it too lightly—her death too lightly. Better that they don't know. Ignorance would be better."

Shaye nodded, agreeing, and perhaps understanding too.

Her sylfe, Naike, slowly made her way nearby, behind the bed and out of sight for both of our elves. She gave me a look that caught me off guard. She was inviting me to form the consonance, even after I'd abandoned it. *What forgiveness.* But I knew Locke wasn't ready to give up on the Goddess yet, so I pushed mischief aside and turned her down. Graciously, Naike's countenance didn't drop. She seemed to understand, just as her elfe had.

"I'm here to work on your hand," said Shaye.

Naike moved directly over Locke's swollen fingers. He jerked away.

"No, let her," said Shaye. "She's weighing the damage. Just relax."

"It hurts." But it was only his imagination. He laid his head back down and Naike continued.

"Here, drink this. The procedure will be painful, but I know you're up to it—so the healing can start in earnest, so you can play your pinkalue again."

He nodded and took the bottle from her, tipping back a few swallows of the red liquid.

"More," she said, and he did as he was told. She handed him a chunk of balse wood. "Put this between your teeth. Now close your eyes, and try to relax."

Evidently she'd learned a lot from the master healers, but Locke wasn't watching. She created an area of heat around the injury, and it began to tingle with a thousand tiny pricks, almost like the touch of a salaminde. Then she pulled at his hand, re-aligning the bones.

The pain shot through the sedative. Locke didn't scream, though his voice remained on the verge. Tears broke through the corners of his eyes squeezed shut, and his teeth left deep marks in the wood.

When she finished, she placed his hand on a curved piece of wood, as if it were relaxed around the end of an armrest, and bandaged the fingers tight. She wiped the sweat from his brow.

Locke closed his eyes, breathing heavily and letting the strain dissipate from his nerves.

Shaye stayed with him. After some quiet, she began to hum—the notes of the melody he'd imagined the Goddess singing, the song he'd played for me in my loneliest and darkest moment.

"Haa-la-la, haa-la-la, haa-la-le-liah."

As Shaye sang the notes, she brought a calmness as wide as the sky.

I felt Locke resisting, felt his fear that enjoying this simple pleasure might somehow wash away the one memory he grasped so tightly. He wavered between past and present. First a few notes would make him happy; then a few would make him sad.

She finished the melody, and all was quiet, except for the glistening sound of wind through the leaves and the distant whirring of a cricket.

Her proximity gave Locke comfort. And her breathing. He opened his eyes and smiled at her with gratitude and admiration: "Thank you."

"You're welcome," she said. "I appreciate that you kept from shouting. It will heal up in the next weeks and gain strength over the following months. Eventually you'll be playing your pinkalue as wildly as ever."

He smiled at her. "Thanks again. I mean it."

"I'm glad I could help."

After her act of kindness, she shone as plain and perfect as ever. She could have had a thousand flaws and they wouldn't have mattered.

Her grace overcame it all.

83.

Elegy

A DEEP BLUE GLOWED from below the lake's surface. The sun's final rays reached out to touch us. Soon the stars would appear across the face of the pure sky.

Valkalyse didn't hesitate over clothing or sharp rocks. She raced toward the water, leaped into a magical rush of wind, spread her feathery wings to be lifted higher, and pulled them in as she dove headlong. The splash started its way across the entire lake. When she surfaced, she had what seemed like a grin on her face. What an interesting creature—a child of Phose who commanded the air and loved the water.

Nicke charged after her, ripping off his shirt as he ran. Without a drop of hesitation, he plunged in the water, screaming his warcry: "Kheeaaaa!"

Locke stayed on the shore.

He found a comfortable spot, pulled a leather diary from his backpack, and began to read. The book had no title on the front, but we'd been calling it Shilohe's Song.

Without her charm or authority, we'd had to sneak into the Seer's house. It helped to have a hyuman, a Tenarie, and a gryphine as accomplices. The diary was just where she said it would be, behind a green book with golden letters. It was worth every pain to get it too.

She still hadn't answered Locke through the consonance, though he talked to her every day. But she spoke to us through the diary, confiding her deepest wishes and darkest secrets.

The sun turned oranger, then red, threatening to wink out entirely. Locke read on and on, though he'd read it all before, and his fractured heart became exposed once again. It took all I could do to keep the fragments next to each other. But the spaces—the scars in between the fragments—these couldn't be healed. Not by any method I knew of. Not in this life.

Nicke screamed with joy as Valkalyse launched him upward. He splashed down into the water.

Then again, maybe injuries like that could be healed. Not that Nicke was healed, but he seemed to be healing. The diary itself claimed all injuries could eventually be healed, though some wounds would take more than a lifetime.

Her words gave Locke a spark of hope.

And a spark was all I needed.

I took it, touched his heart, and poured the breath of life into him, mustering my power till it spread through his chest, his spine, his arms and hands, his legs and feet, and the crown of his head. And even with a broken heart, he was filled with light. In the dimming dusk, he took out his pinkalue and began to play.

Weeks had passed since the Angel had healed his hand. He could use it again, though it still ached. As he played the Angel's song, he felt the longing, mixed with some confusion—he wasn't sure whether the song was about Shaye or Shilohe. Maybe something else altogether.

Valkalyse spent days sleeping high in our tree. At night she'd go north to find food. Some of the neighbors gave us trouble, but nothing Locke's father couldn't handle.

Nicke had settled in nicely too, and his Ashe seemed livelier every day.

Locke found Honke and promised to take him to the rivers beyond the rim so he could travel back to his family. In the meantime, Honke stayed with us. Locke's father was excited to have extra help, but he soon realized Honke wasn't as hard a worker as his size suggested.

As for me, I began to hide when other elves were around. Being significant wasn't as great as I'd hoped, and I didn't like their pointing or staring. Once while hiding, I discovered that blood and fire were enough to mark a page. That knowledge gave my words power I'd never dreamed of, and with it I began to tell Locke's story the way it needed to be told.

"Picke." Locke dropped the pinkalue and gently pinched the amulet around his neck.

Nicke climbed up Val's neck and then dove off her snout into the water. She seemed to like the attention.

"What?" I asked.

"I started out wanting something, I'm not sure what. Truth maybe. Or feeling good. Or a spouse. I don't know—that song that can't be named. For a while I thought it might be the Goddess. Maybe it still is. She was all those things wrapped into one—an ideal, a feeling, and a person."

I just listened, sensing that was what he needed.

"She was everything. And then she vanished."

"Or became the light."

"Whatever it was, she's gone. Maybe the valkalysae carried her to some hereafter, some place where everything is music. Maybe she's encircled by generations gone before. Maybe she's spoken with my mom."

"I wouldn't doubt it."

"And yet here I am, still wanting—just like when we started."

"But it's good, right? It's better than not wanting."

"Maybe. But maybe I need to move on. Shaye offered us the consonance."

"She still likes you."

"Only I don't think I *can* move on."

"Then let's find her."

"Shilohe?"

"Yes," I said. "You have the Shining Sword. *I'm* more insightful than ever. Not to mention your pet gryphine. You're ready for another adventure."

"But what if she's unfindable? Remember how she said, *'If it's possible...'*? She believed in the hereafter, and yet *she* didn't even know if we could find her."

"I wouldn't let that stop you."

"So what do we do?"

"She had a little sister, and a mother who married the King."

The brief thought of the wicked King dampened the mood—the coward who let his step daughter die in his place, who had committed such horrible crimes. And yet she'd wanted to forgive him.

"And there's her mentor," I said. "What was his name?"

"Magister Crowe."

"He was a friend to the Seer. I'm sure he knows about the hereafter."

The green leaves took on a blue shade as night fell. The trees grew right at the water's edge and leaned out over the lake, with no liminal space of beach between forest and water. Locke closed his eyes and gazed around the darkness of our mind. *Nothing.* In fact, we hadn't seen the blue light since that fateful day, except for one small glimpse at Shaye's house.

He hung the amulet on a root, climbed out barefoot on the smooth bark of a trunk, and leaned into a dive. The water swallowed him in coolness, pulling away the heat and humidity of summertide. I hovered over the water, which mirrored my bright blue up and down its curling crests. The profundity below turned bluish black, far too deep to see bottom—even close to the shore in daylight. The far side of the lake seemed a league away, a magnitude of terrible power.

When Locke surfaced, he pushed a hand through the water, creating a miniature wave that crested and fell, and the counterforce twisted his body the opposite direction.

The world itself seemed nearly perfect—if it hadn't been missing such an important piece.

"Okay, Picke," said Locke. "I think I've got it."

"Got what?"

"The future is unclear. That's true. And I'm not sure if there's a hereafter. Even if there is, I'm not sure I can reach her."

"Okay."

"I can tell you a lot of stuff I don't know. But there's one thing I *do* know: *I still hope.* The hope won't seem to go away. I hope she's out there, somewhere, maybe up in the empyrean." He paddled his hands outward, apart, and then pulled them back together, treading above the water. He gave me a broken-hearted smile, and his eyes twinkled. "And if she is, I'm going to find her."

"But Locke, what if we *never* know? What if we wait your whole life and don't find her? What if we never have a consonance with anyone else?"

As he gazed at me, determination gleamed in his eyes. "Look to the sky."

I watched him for a long time, searching for some deeper affirmation. When I found it, I smiled, and my blue reflection bounded in the ripples, surrounded by pinpoints of starlight.

He smiled back, and together we looked up at the stars.

Pronunciation Guide

A misinformed cleaning crew, meaning to reduce the cluttered estate of the late Professor L. Clive Staples, built a large bonfire. The story presented in this book was rescued from those flames. The edges of the leather volume were blackened, but the manuscript, written in blue ink, remained intact. It began simply with this remark: "Translated by the Traveler into English from the original Kyriglae." *This line was omitted from the first published edition because of a controversy concerning the origins of it and other marginal comments written in black ink, allegedly by a different hand. The author of these black comments also created the following pronunciation guide, a loose leaf tucked in the middle of the manuscript. It is represented below with his epigraph included.*

Little is known about the true identity of the Traveler, including whether he was one person or two. Lingual clues suggest he had a propensity for Greek.

IN MY TIME there, I learned a few things about not only the reading but also the speaking of their language. The power of their world compels me to provide, as accurate as I can, a guide to a few basic principles of their language.

When I began translating, I was nudged toward using an *e* at the end of nouns to mimic the *al* rune used in the original script. In my earliest perception, I would have said this terminal *e* was a silent vowel. At the time, I was struggling to hear, much less emulate, the subtle nuances of their euphonic tongue. Now, though, having had a bit more experience, I would say they did in fact pronounce the terminal *e*, only it was swallowed up in the silence that followed the word, making it barely audible, leaving their mouths still open as if in song.

Having said that, I suppose it would not behoove an English speaker to mimic this without first being lingually submerged to a degree, as, when combined with ignorance, these pronunciations could easily sound silly, having an effect opposite of what they ought to.

a *a*bout
ă *a*sk
ā *a*pe
ä *a*wful

ĕ m*e*t
ē m*ee*t
er p*er*mit

ĭ f*i*t
ī f*i*ght

ō h*o*me

oo l*oo*k
u l*u*ck
ū l*u*ke

' *indicates stressed syllable*

Alphelose – ăl'·fĕl·ōs·(a)
Amaliyae – a·mäl'·ĭ·ya'
Ashe – ăsh·(a)
Banshe – băn'·sh·(a)
Benne – bĕn·(a)
Blathae – blăth'·a
Colrye – cōl'·rē·(a)
Crowe – crōw·(a)
Cree – crē·(a)
Dagonae – dă'·gä·na

Gaie – gäē·(a)
Gante – gănt·(a)
Gnyme – nĭm·(a)
Honke – hänk·(a)
Hyuman – hĭū'·man
Hyumanglae – hĭū'·man·gla
Kohkoo – kō'·kū
Kynde – käēnd·(a)
Kyrie – käē'·rē·(a)
Kyriglae – käē'·rē·gla
Kyrose – käē'·rōs·(a)
Lanse – lăns·(a)
Locke – läk·(a)
Lonae – lä'·na
Martigane – mär'·tĭ·gān·(a)
Naephe – nāf·(a)
Nara – nä'·ra
Naike – näīk·(a)
Nicke – nĭk·(a)
Numa – nū'·ma
Ondine – än'·dīn·(a)
Parathydume – pä·rä'·thĭ·dūm·(a)
Phose – fōs·(a)
Picke – pĭk·(a)
Pinkalue – pēnk'·a·lū·(a)
Robyne – rä'·bĭn·(a)
Saboan – să·bō'·an
Saboanglae – să·bō'·an·gla
Saede – sād·(a)
Salaminde – săl'·a·mīnd·(a)
Shaye – shā·(a)
Shilohe – shī'·lō·(a)
Stane – stān·(a)
Sylfe – sĭlf·(a)
Tenaglae – tĕn·ä'·gla
Tenarie – tĕn·ä'·rē·(a)

Thaese – thās·(a)
Tryse – trĭs·(a)
Tunke – tunk·(a)
Twiche – twĭch·(a)
Tyne – tĭn·(a)
Valkalyse – văl'·ka·lēs·(a)
Valkalysae – văl·ka·lēs'·a
Wokeezawokaiwokoomae – wō·kē'·za·wō·kāē'·wō·kū'·ma

Acknowledgements

Was J the only letter involved?

Nope. Not at all.

Many kind friends helped me write this book, and I'm indebted to them for their generosity.

To my alpha readers, who pulled the story from the blazing fire and folded it again and again, hammer and tongs, giving strength to the characters, plot, and setting: Ashley, Allison, Maurya, Abe, Zach, Dallin, Bentley, Christine, Nick, and Cherise.

To my beta readers, who pounded the manuscript into its final shape, paragraph by paragraph, grinding out the tip and edges and tempering it in ice-cold water: Shelley, Ginger, Matt, Dave, Bible, Joe, Hank, and Nancy.

And to my gamma readers, who polished the book free of misplaced commas and misspelled words till it shone like a mirror: Ashley, Zach, Stuart, Tunk, and Stephen.

This book became what it is thanks to you.

I'm also grateful to the hundreds of generous Kickstarter backers who supported this story when it was still mostly a dream. A few deserve to be mentioned by name: Daniel Houghton, Eric Mitchell, Jay and Lori Washburn, Jeff Edelstein, Jimmy Wayne Riley, John F., John Stuck, Lori Olsen, Mike K., Randy Merrill, Stephanie Robbins, Travis T., Trevor Rand, Carolanne L., Jon-Michael Dreher, Laci Wilson, Larry Daugherty, and Vincent Jouillat. Thank you for your support and your patience.

I'm glad to have the strength of a fellowship behind me.

If you'd like to see your name acknowledged in my next book, sign up for the chance to be a reader: http://betareader.jwashburn.com

About the Author

First, you're wondering about my name.

I knew it.

No, I'm not trying to copy J.R.R. Tolkien or J.K. Rowling. J really is my first name—my whole first name. Nope, not J-A-Y and not J with a period. (Abbreviating it makes it longer.) It starts and ends with J.

Just J.

Incidentally, if you throw a pen at a paper from at least five feet away, it nearly always spells my name.

"But what kind of a name is J?"—you're still asking. Well, I'll tell you. There was once a man named Melvin J. Ballard (whose middle name was Joseph, but he liked to abbreviate it). My grandpa was named J Ballard

Washburn in honor of this man. But he just got the J (without the period). I was named after my grandpa, and I just got his J.

Which is nice.

After all, brevity is the soul of wit.

Now, a few facts about me:

I was born in the middle of skinwalker territory, in Arizona, practically on the Navajo Reservation. Yeehaw.

I grew up with my siblings in suburban Idaho—in a neighborhood with a few good bike jumps, a makeshift hockey court, and even a safe-house for sneaking video games. To the south we had open fields, which, back then, looked surprisingly similar to the Land of Prydain, littered with streams and trees and wildlife. It was magic. Out there my siblings and I actually lived the adventures you've read in my books.

Then I accidentally grew up. On accident—I mean it.

But lucky for me, I still find adventure here and there—in places where it's easier for adults to see it, like Xi'an, Cuzco, and Stonehenge. Being a grownup also meant I had to become a productive member of society, so I decided that writing adventures would be the next best thing to living them. That's what I do.

I'm glad you could join me—we have some exciting things ahead of us.

FEEL FREE
TO EMAIL ME TOO!
ME@JWASHBURN.COM

What Is Ecksdot?

A grade-school hero fights the nightmares bleeding into his reality.

In ECKSDOT, you'll join Nate and Danny as they search for clues leading to a mysterious world of ghost robots, while the wall between dreams and reality begins to melt around them. You will laugh and maybe even cry as the two unlikely companions learn what it takes to be a hero and—more importantly—what it takes to be a friend.

ECKSDOT is also an artisan's story—written, illustrated, and typeset by the author—a masterpiece handcrafted from beginning to end.

A Brief Excerpt from ECKSDOT

I LIVED IN THREE WORLDS.

The first was the crappy real world, where I'd always look stupid in front of girls and never find any friends—and where I had to do homework and get beat up and picked on. I didn't like the real world that much—I could never make anything go my way.

The second world was my imagination. The world of rocketboots and excaliburs. Where heroes came blasting out of the sky to save the day. In that world, I actually did stuff that mattered. I liked it there. Only I couldn't hold on to it.

The third world—it was sometimes the greatest, where everything I imagined became real. And sometimes it was the worst, where I'd rather get beat up by Rudge any day than go back there. It was the world of dreams.

And nightmares.

My adventure began with a nightmare. Or a vision. I saw this figure, a robot man—an android from some other dimension, with wires for veins. He looked at me through pouring rain, but I couldn't see his face. And he spoke, but I didn't understand. All I could do was follow. He led me to a pair of doors chained shut, and pointed. And then the nightmare began, and I nearly drowned in a pit of mud.

When I woke up, I realized I knew the place. It was a barn owned by the Japanese witch lady at the end of my street. I was creeped out, but I was too curious to stay away. So I brought my slow friend Danny as backup.

I had no idea where the dream came from. Or how it got in my head.

And I never realized that a door lets you in...

But it also lets other things out.

What Readers Say about ECKSDOT

"A very original world with an ingenious set of rules." — KMK

"I was blown away with how Washburn nailed the mind of a sixth-grader. It was simply fantastic. Reading this book, you will be a kid again." — Sherry Torgent, author of *Like Ice*

"It made me laugh out loud and also brought tears to my eyes." — A.J.

"It was one of those I couldn't put down till it was done." — Jeff V.

"There were moments where I realized that I had stopped breathing. There were moments that I gasped, laughed, or commented out loud." — Ary

"This is compelling YA fiction that sets itself apart from other stories available today. It's unique, fresh, and appealing to both young women and young men. Kudos, J Washburn." — Strykera

"It is a fun mix of fantasy and growing pains, with ominous end-of-the-world consequences." — L. Sawyer

Get a Free Book

Every month, I write a letter to my readers. It's called The INFORMANT. If you subscribe, you'll never miss a book launch. (Including the two sequels to SONG OF LOCKE.) I'll also occasionally send free ebooks and deleted scenes. Oh and some interesting tidbits about my dating life.

Best of all, I'll send you SHILOHE'S SONG. For free.

Oh, you don't know what that is. The SONG OF LOCKE sequels tell of our hero's further adventures. But before they're released, I'm working on a novella about Shilohe, which follows her epic quest to save the Land of Many Waters. When I finish it, I'll send it to you for free. You just have to be on my mailing list when it comes out.

Subscribe to The INFORMANT: http://theinformant.jwashburn.com

You're the Hero

Dear Reader,

Stories have made my life better.

They're often entertaining, but they also give sympathy and insight.

That's why I wrote this book—because I hope to make people's lives better with it. That's also why I want to share it with as many readers as possible.

But this book wasn't pushed by a corporate machine and thousands of dollars. It's the work of one pair of hands and the encouragement of many fine friends. If it gets enjoyed by more people, it won't be because of money. It will be because of you, because you appreciated it and wanted to share. If you know someone who will love this book, you should tell them about it. You'll be doing them and me a huge favor.

If you want to do more than that, you can write a quick and honest review. They're important because they show a book's popularity and help new readers find it. (Incidentally, the more reviews this book gets, the more people will read it, and the sooner the sequel will become possible.) Posting a review is super easy. It only has to be 20 words long. A few moments of your day will literally rescue a guy from oblivion. Plus you'll be making some other reader's life a little better.

I'll finish with a quick story: A friend of mine made an amazing effort in critiquing this book. After an ambiguous comment, she said, "*I* don't know: it's *your* book." But I told her she was wrong: "It's at least a little *your* book too." And I meant it. That goes for everyone else as well—every reader like you. See, I can write all the words I want, but they sit dead on the page till you revive them in your own imagination.

So this isn't *my* book. It's either *our* book or *your* book. I'm just the author. And I couldn't do what I do without you.

Thanks a million.

—J

Hero's Quest Checklist

☐ **Receive Secret Messages**
Subscribe to The INFORMANT

☐ **Hoist the Gallant Flag**
Write an Amazon review

☐ **Recruit Daring Allies**
Tell a friend about this book